◆ THE CLIFFS OF LEAVENWORTH ◆

By

William James Hubler Jr.

TRAFFORD
PUBLISHING™

Note for Librarians: A cataloguing record for this book is available from Library and Archives Canada at www.collectionscanada.ca/amicus/index-e.html
ISBN 1-4120-7490-8

Printed in Victoria, BC, Canada. Printed on paper with minimum 30% recycled fibre. Trafford's print shop runs on "green energy" from solar, wind and other environmentally-friendly power sources.

TRAFFORD
PUBLISHING™

Offices in Canada, USA, Ireland and UK
This book was published *on-demand* in cooperation with Trafford Publishing. On-demand publishing is a unique process and service of making a book available for retail sale to the public taking advantage of on-demand manufacturing and Internet marketing. On-demand publishing includes promotions, retail sales, manufacturing, order fulfilment, accounting and collecting royalties on behalf of the author.

Book sales for North America and international:
Trafford Publishing, 6E–2333 Government St.,
Victoria, BC v8t 4p4 CANADA
phone 250 383 6864 (toll-free 1 888 232 4444)
fax 250 383 6804; email to orders@trafford.com
Book sales in Europe:
Trafford Publishing (uk) Limited, 9 Park End Street, 2nd Floor
Oxford, UK ox1 1hh UNITED KINGDOM
phone 44 (0)1865 722 113 (local rate 0845 230 9601)
facsimile 44 (0)1865 722 868; info.uk@trafford.com
Order online at:
trafford.com/05-2386

10 9 8 7 6 5 4

◆ THE CLIFFS OF LEAVENWORTH ◆

By
William James Hubler Jr.

A LARGE GROUP of well-armed Confederate soldiers cross the Ohio into Indiana to "buy" horses. Who can stop them? A group of citizen soldiers will try. They would have been labeled as unfit for military service by most standards. Yet, they answered the call in their country's time of need, gave it their all and stood tall.

◆ IN APPRECIATION, MY SPECIAL THANKS TO ◆

JANET HUBLER, my sister—without her encouragement, hard work and tireless efforts, this novel would never have been completed.

ALBERT CHISM, for his generous loan of reference books, and his help in searching through libraries.

SHIRLEY HUBLER, my wife, for her encouragement and understanding during the many hours that this project consumed.

FRAN ROLWING and the ladies at Excell Printing at Radcliff, Kentucky, for being very helpful.

LEAVENWORTH, INDIANA IS a very real and charming town. So are the other towns and places used in this novel. However, it must be remembered that this is a work of fiction. All the characters, incidents and dialogues in this novel are products of the author's imagination and are not to be construed as real. No disrespect to any place or any person, living or dead, is intended.

This book is dedicated to all those who answer their country's call in the time of need. Aside from our fulltime military forces, far too often we tend to forget our CITIZEN SOLDIERS. I refer to the dedicated members of our NATIONAL GUARD and RESERVE groups. Without them and their forerunners, the MILITIA and HOME GUARD, our country, as we know it, would very probably not exist.

Though *The Cliffs Of Leavenworth* is a Civil War novel, there are many parallels to modern day events. This is intended.

Though said many times before, I will say again, "Those that do not know their history are doomed to repeat it."

A nation's best defense is to BE PREPARED AND STAY PREPARED! Those who let their level of preparedness ebb and flow like the tides will always run the risk of being caught on low tide.

✦ CONTENTS ✦

◆ PREFACE ◆

WE HERE IN America are truly blessed. We have had no war or battles fought on our home soil since the American Civil War more than 140 years ago.

We have what we believe to be the world's best trained and best equipped military forces. More and more, the National Guard and Reserve units are being called on to help fight our country's battles. They most surely are doing their part.

What concerns me and others is the question that when too many of our National Guard and Reserve units are activated and sent far away, who takes their place in this country in the time of dire need? This is something worth thinking about most seriously.

Although the novel, *The Cliffs of Leavenworth*, is a work of fiction, it points out the practicality of having a reserve for the reserves, i.e., at least some sort of backup group to fill the gap in the time of need. Certainly this is true in today's world.

Another major point in the novel is that everyone does not necessarily need to be young or in top physical condition to be of service to their country. When willing people in the proper spirit band together, much can be accomplished.

—————————

ON THIS NIGHT in June 1863, Lt. Sam Buchanan had just woke up from his two-hour attempt at trying to rest. Though it's not generally known, resting just before an approaching battle is not easy. Sam made his way over to Capt. Herndon's position and said, "Captain, I'll take over now. It's time for you to try and get some rest."

"Okay, Sam, I am getting drowsy. I probably won't be able to sleep, but I'll try. Don't let me sleep past 4:00 AM if I do drift off. We must be on full alert and ready for whatever comes from then on. Lord, I haven't stayed up this late in years!"

So, at 2:00 AM on this night in June 1863, Capt. Elam Herndon wrapped a blanket around himself and his rifle. With his coat as a pillow, he leaned back against a mound of dirt to try to rest.

The men's small campfires were burning low and the conversations were getting lower as well. The night sounds were good and the air was fragrant with good smells of the wood smoke combined with the aroma of brewing coffee pots. The smells were also blended, of course, with the tobacco smoke from the soldiers' pipes, cigars and home-rolled cigarettes. All the good smells of a men's camp in the woods, but this was no ordinary camping trip.

Elam knew, only too well, that in just a few short hours these pleasant smells and sounds would be replaced by smells and sounds of battle, the unmistakable stench of gunpowder mixed with the sounds of men trying to send each other into the company of the devil.

Elam was very tired and soon he was starting to drift off. It all seemed like a vague, fast moving dream, but he knew that the recent events were real and far from a dream. As he teetered between the edge of full alertness and that of dreamland, he started recounting the past few weeks.

Years ago, Elam had resigned himself to the fact that he was a partially disabled army veteran and was no longer fit for military service. Even if he were not handicapped, his age would make him an unlikely candidate for anyone's army.

But the fact was that here he was, at 57 years old, with a leg that didn't work all that well, a shoulder that never let him forget the war in Mexico, and a group of men looking to him for leadership in a fast approaching battle.

Here in Southern Indiana, on a rock strewn cliff near the Ohio River, was where it would happen. Now, Capt. Elam Herndon of the Leavenworth Home Guard Reserve was trying to remember Leavenworth as it was. He was also still finding it hard to believe that his accepting command of a unit, basically formed for the purpose of babysitting a town in the absence of the regular Home Guard, could ever lead to this. Never in his wildest dreams would he have thought that his little unit of "citizen soldiers" would ever find themselves in a situation like this.

But yes, as Elam drifted off, he thought, "This is real. We are here and we will do what we have to do."

ONE

Life In Leavenworth
1863

IN THE SUMMER of 1863, Leavenworth, Indiana, was a small industrial town, humming with activity. Located on the beautiful Ohio River on the biggest bend of the river, it was a beautiful place. At the back of the town were very high, steep hills, densely covered with large trees. To the west of Leavenworth, about one quarter of a mile, were high cliffs of limestone, etc. Though not sheer cliffs, they were climbable but very steep. The view of the river was truly spectacular from the top of the cliffs. Near the river's bank, below the cliffs, was the river road which ran close to the base of the steep incline. The river road was the only practical land route to Leavenworth, coming from the west. At times, this road was well traveled. The most traffic going to or by Leavenworth was by way of the mighty Ohio River, the main link to the rest of the world. Leavenworth had a good steamboat landing as well as a large wharf boat for storing incoming and outgoing freight. It was a busy river port, usually bustling with activity.

The Civil War had been going on for a little over two years. Most of Leavenworth's young men had left to serve in the Union Army. A couple of these soldiers had died in battle and their remains shipped home. A few men had been wounded and either discharged or sent home to heal. As far as the war was concerned, no actual fighting had taken place in Leavenworth as yet. Of course, everyone hoped the battles would be fought elsewhere.

Leavenworth had come a long way in a few short years. Starting out as a small settlement of pioneers in small log cabins, the town now had a population of around 1500 people and boasted some fine homes and buildings.

Nothing ever seemed to change very much or very quickly in Leavenworth. In general, it was a community of honest hard-working people. Life was good in this place in the summer of 1863.

Elam Herndon was one of Leavenworth's leading citizens. He was a wounded veteran of the Mexican War and had been granted a small pension for his service to his country. He and his wife lived modestly in a small home near the base of the hill. Elam walked with a limp, but was able to work at very light labor and office work at the river port. Between his small pension and the part-time work, he was getting by. At age 57, this was his life.

At the outbreak of war in April, 1861, Elam Herndon had volunteered for the army, at any rank. He had been discharged from the army at the end of the Mexican War with the rank of captain. Elam was rejected from military service by reason of partial disability (from war wounds) and age. Elam's feelings were hurt further when the young recruiting officer had suggested that Elam, "Go home and play with his grandchildren." That young first lieutenant never realized how close he came to being disabled himself for making that insolent remark. Elam was known at times to have an explosive temper. However, he held his anger and limped homeward.

The territory around here was a hunting and fishing paradise.

Elam had a small collection of guns and liked to hunt and target shoot. Among his many friends, he could usually find someone to hunt or shoot with or go fishing. He and Jim Running Deer often were out in the woods together. His friend Moses Jefferson often took Elam fishing in his "Leavenworth Skiff". Of course, the hunting and fishing helped lower the grocery bill.

Another friend of Elam's was Capt. Eli Mattingly of the stern wheel boat the "Concordia Queen." The boat was due in Leavenworth any day now. Elam had known Capt. Mattingly for ages and they were close friends. They always had a few laughs and got current on new happenings when they got together.

The "Concordia Queen's" boat whistle had been tuned to make a distinctive sound, three tones from very low, to mid-range, to very high. There was no mistaking the "Concordia Queen's" whistle when it was blown. Elam had just heard that special sound coming from downriver. Elam started toward the boat dock with a smile on his face. There was always a certain amount of excitement when a boat came in. Naturally, it was good to see old friends. If Eli had time, perhaps they could tilt a few.

Yes, life was good in Leavenworth in 1863, except for the damned war!! Hopefully, it wouldn't last too much longer.

Leavenworth was a little unusual for such a small town. It had a diverse mix of people of different races, religions and cultural differences. For the most part, they got along together quite well. A couple of the town's well liked people were Moses Jefferson, age 55, and his good-natured wife, Tillie Mae, age 54. They had arrived in Leavenworth aboard the steamboat the "Concordia Queen" some ten years ago, back in 1853. They were both hard workers and had done well here. They took good care of their modest home near Cedar Hill and were solid citizens. Moses worked at the Dan Lyon's Boat Works and Tillie Mae was head cook at the Flag Hotel. Her skills in the kitchen were known far and wide.

One thing that made Moses and Tillie different was the fact that they were the town's only black people. Another was the fact that they were both escaped and runaway slaves. Thanks to their many friends, the slave catcher/bounty hunters had been forced to leave Leavenworth empty-handed. Some influential friends had filed legal papers at the Crawford County Court House that showed both the Jeffersons as having been born as free and natural born citizens of Crawford County, Indiana. Nowadays, the slave catchers didn't even try to question them. At long last, since the war, these slave chasers no longer came around.

Moses Jefferson had been born a slave. His father had been a slave of the plantation owner's father. Thus, Moses Jefferson had been inherited by the present owner along with the plantation and all that went with it. He had never had to endure the humiliation of being sold on the slave auction block. No chance, for Moses had been born as he was, a slave. Tillie Mae was the personal property of the plantation owner's wife, having been brought along as part of her marriage dowry.

When Moses and Tillie asked permission to get married, their master and mistress had given them permission. They were both given the standard pep talk, encouraging them to have as many children as possible "for the good of the plantation."

Now, in 1853, Moses was forty-four and Tillie was forty years old. They had only one child and it had been stillborn some years back. They were well aware that some owners got rid of non-childbearing slaves and that prospect worried them very much. They were very much in love and the thought of being apart was unthinkable.

Moses was a slave around the main mansion. Part of his duties was to watch after the master's son and daughter, sort of teach them practical skills, and help with their education. Tillie was main house help and also cared for the two children. They couldn't help it. They both became very fond of the children and, at times, felt like they were their very own.

The plantation produced large amounts of tobacco and tobacco products. There was also a rather large whisky distillery on the plantation. At least three times a year, the plantation took several wagon loads of whisky and tobacco, etc., up to Owensboro, Kentucky, to the auction and to dealers.

This trip, in October, 1853, the master's children asked to go along to see the city and scenery. Moses and Tillie were taken along to care for the eight year old girl and ten year old boy. The master and his wife would be busy with social and business activities, as they always were.

While at the riverfront wharf at Owensboro, the master became happily engaged in sampling different whiskies from other producers and partying in general. Some of these other distillers produced some great blends too!

In his joyous condition, the master paid no attention to his two trusted slaves. This was the opportunity that Moses and Tillie had been hoping for.

A large steamboat was ready to untie and pull away. No one noticed as Moses and Tillie slipped aboard. With only the clothes on their backs and a small bag that Tillie carried, they made their attempt to be free. They knew full well what happened to runaways that were brought back, but they had to try. They quickly found a place to hide in the box wagon bed of the Owensboro brand farm wagon that was part of the boat's cargo. They didn't know where the boat was bound for; they only hoped they were headed for freedom.

Little did they know that old Capt. Eli Mattingly had seen them slip aboard. They also didn't know that the old river captain hated slavery as much as they did. They had slipped aboard the sternwheeler, the "Concordia Queen" and Capt. Eli was its master and owner.

Later that night, the captain quietly went to the cargo deck with some food, water and blankets. He gave the armload to Moses and Tillie and told them to remain quiet. Eli had a plan. He said, "You two stay hid and out of sight. In the early morning hours when the passengers are asleep and we are upriver some distance, I will take you both up to the passenger deck. There is an empty stateroom at the stern of the boat. Promise me you'll be quiet and I'll help you."

"Oh, we surely will Captain. We surely will," they said.

"Now, I think I know of a place and some people that you will like. The place is upriver about three days. Stay quiet and out of sight and maybe you two will get lucky."

Three days later, Moses and Tillie came off the "Concordia Queen" at Leavenworth, Indiana. They were unobserved, hidden under a tarp in the box bed of an Owensboro wagon. The wagon had been ordered by a rich gentleman farmer, Mr. Buford Beasley. Capt. Mattingly had arranged for Elam Herndon and Sam Buchanan to have Mr. Beasley come to the wharf with a team and get his new farm wagon. The three took the new wagon and its secret cargo to Buford's farm.

Life then started anew for Moses and Tillie Mae and they would be ever grateful. That was all ten years ago and now they were very much a part of Leavenworth.

And still on the subject of life in Leavenworth and its wide variety of people, a few lines about another unique individual, Jacob Silverstein.

Jacob Silverstein had migrated to Leavenworth from Cincinnati, Ohio, back in 1860. He was a jeweler and clockmaker by trade. He figured that a growing town like this was bound to be a good place for him to locate. The town had no jeweler and he was to be the first. Jacob Silverstein was Jewish and this was also a first for Leavenworth. Jacob was well-liked and quickly accepted by the community.

Jacob was an optimist and thus was always looking for the brighter side. The jewelry/clock repair business did not turn out to be really enough to earn a good living in Leavenworth. However, Jacob's new friend, Elam Herndon, had the answer.

Elam said, "Jacob, you know that the actions and firing mechanisms on most rifles and pistols and such are much similar, in general, to the working parts of clocks and watches? Why don't you teach yourself to work on guns?"

"Elam, I think you may have a gem of an idea. Thank you, my friend."

Soon, Jacob had a thriving combination jewelry/watch and clock repair/gun repair business. In this time in history, it was very important to keep guns in good working order.

Leavenworth was good to Jacob Silverstein and Jacob would be good for Leavenworth.

Another in the community's wide mix of people was Jim Running Deer. Jim was a Shawnee Indian. He had been left for dead along the "Trail of Tears" in the harsh winter of 1838. The "Trail of Tears" was the forced march westward of thousands of Indians by order of the U.S. Congress. The U.S. Army under the command of Gen. Winfield Scott forced the march. This was a shameful and brutal page of our past.

A kindly old couple had nursed Jim Running Deer back to health from the brink of death. They sort of adopted Jim. They settled on forty acres and built a cabin, just east of Leavenworth. Jim repaid the kindness of Solomon and Grace Mills by staying with them and caring for them in their old age. Before they passed away, they had willed their place to Jim.

Jim mainly made his living by hunting and fishing and selling meat to people in town. Jim was widely known to be a good shot with any weapon handed to him. Jim was a good scout and possessed insight not commonly seen among white men. He had proved to others that he could hear a steamboat coming on the river for at least three minutes before it could be heard by the average white man.

He was also particularly adept at the art of "listening to the ground," Indian style. He could lie down, put an ear next to the ground and tell if horses, etc., were coming—from what direction and about how far away they were. Some even claimed he could tell about how many there were. Jim Running Deer made no such claim as he jokingly said, "I'm not good with numbers."

Jim Running Deer had many friends around and was well-liked. Elam Herndon and Sam Buchanan both counted him as a close friend. The three of them had hunted and fished together for many moons.

Still another improbable Leavenworth citizen was Hibachi Takaguchi, age 41. Hibachi was a native of Japan and was the only Oriental person for many miles around. He was born in Nagasaki, Japan to a fishing/pearl diving family. Hibachi had worked in the cultured pearl industry back in Japan. The Japanese had developed a method of inserting foreign material into a pearl oyster whereby a pearl would develop around this inserted material. The art of developing pearls in this manner had been in development for around seven hundred years.

In 1848, an uncle had bought ship's passage to California, U.S.A., for Hibachi. The idea was for him to try to start the cultured pearl industry there.

In 1849, Hibachi succumbed to "Gold Rush Fever." He forgot all about pearls and headed for the California gold fields.

He did not find much gold there, but he found a friend as good as gold. He was befriended by a gold seeker from Indiana named George Armstrong. George was around thirty-six years older than Hibachi and he sort of thought of the young man as the son he never had. They became prospector partners and got along well. George did his best to teach Hibachi to speak English and had some success. In turn, George was able to learn very little Japanese.

In 1851, the gold was becoming more scarce. They had made a modest sum for their efforts, but both could see it was time to leave.

Hibachi Takaguchi came to Leavenworth, Indiana, with old George Armstrong.

A new industry had recently been started in Leavenworth. It was a button factory that made buttons from the shells of mussels (a type of freshwater oyster). These buttons were in great demand and sold worldwide. They were both hired by the factory and were soon prospecting for paydays rather than gold. They both started out as button cutters, cutting button shapes out of mussel shells.

Occasionally, mussels had a pearl inside them, often a very high grade valuable pearl. This set Hibachi's wheels turning.

Soon after learning this, Hibachi was in charge of a project to try to cultivate pearls to further the industry, only now he was not diving in the Sea of Japan, but rather the Ohio River.

In 1863, George and Hibachi shared an old house on Nelson Street, Hibachi still trying to learn English and George trying to teach it.

And yes, there were others around Leavenworth who spoke different languages. One was young Albert LeCroix. The other was Helmer Schmitt.

Albert LeCroix was a descendant of some of the early French, flatboat river men, that had once been numerous in this area. There were still a few families left, most living in the northwest part of the county. Most could speak English, but among themselves, French was commonly spoken.

Albert was 17 years old and worked at the winery, "The Wine Works."

When Albert became excited or agitated, he would often forget and start speaking in French. As his friends said, "When this happened, very few knew what the hell he was saying."

Helmer Schmitt was of German descent. He was from Dubois County, Indiana, a little village called St. Meinrad. Like his friend Albert, he was raised speaking German more often than

English. At times, he too would drift back and forth between English and German.

Yes, for a small town in the Hoosier Hills in 1863, Leavenworth was a colorful mix of peoples and cultures. For the most part, they got along reasonably well with one another and were well known to give help when help was needed.

Nelson Street Leavenworth, Indiana retail business district
Nelson Street ran south from the Court House to the Wharfboat
Courtesy Stephenson General Store

⋄ Two ⋄

———

Leavenworth's Industries

BY 1863, LEAVENWORTH, Indiana had grown from a few pioneers' cabins to a thriving town. It now had a population of around 1500 people. Also, many of its people were skilled craftsmen. The businesses and industry provided jobs for many. In those days, if you were unemployed, it was because you wanted to be unemployed. For sure, this was true in Leavenworth.

The "Arena" newspaper was successful and widely read. It had several employees.

The Flag Hotel, owned by John Tadlock, was a thriving business, had a great dining room and employed several.

John Bahr, known as "The Hoop Pole King" had many people cutting hoop poles all around. These were used in barrel making and were in great demand. Hoop poles were stacked in great piles all around the town and in every vacant lot. The products were shipped from the Port of Leavenworth in great quantity.

The Sharp Wool Manufacturing Company, owned by Horatio Sharp, had many employees. They made a high quality yarn which was shipped far and near.

Leavenworth Furniture Mfg., owned by Squire Weathers, employed skilled craftsmen. They made fine quality oak furniture which was in great demand. They could rarely keep up with the orders coming in.

One business was known over much of the world. It was Dan Lyon's Boat Works owned by Dan Lyon and Norm Whitcomb.

They produced rowboats known as "Leavenworth Skiffs." These skiffs were very well made and graceful in design. They were very stable in the water. Large river boats often stopped to pick up shipments of these skiffs. Now that there was a war on, Dan Lyon's Boat Works had received a contract to build small square nosed floats called "pontoons" for the Union Army engineers. These were used to make quick "pontoon" foot bridges and were important to the war effort. The Boat Works was at full production.

Another important business was C. J. Paxton Builders of Boats, Barges and Wharf Boats. Many men worked here also. They had a contract with the government to build river barges, also important to the war effort.

Then, there was The Tannery owned by Mr. Cook. He normally employed ten men. The tanning of leather from rawhides was big business in 1863.

Volney Price was a wagon and carriage maker employing several skilled men.

Leavenworth Button Works was a booming business. The locals would dredge up mussel shells (similar to oysters) from the river bed. They would open the mussel shells, remove the meat, boil it and feed this part to their hogs. The mussel shells were then sold to the Button Works. The shells were then water soaked again (to take out some of the brittleness) and the form of a button was then punched out and finished. Skill was important here also. The buttons were in demand worldwide.

The Grist Mill, owned by Zeb and Seth Leavenworth, did a brisk business. Their mill was the first wood fired/steam powered mill for miles around. Their mill operated year 'round. The water powered mills were often stopped by the winter freezing of their streams.

There were many orchards in Crawford County producing bumper crops of apples, pears, peaches and plums. Much fruit

was shipped out by boat. However, these orchards produced the basis for more industries.

The Wine Works made great fruit wines and kept several people busy.

Best Brandy Distillery made many gallons of full-bodied apple and peach brandy for the enjoyment of all those so inclined. Tasty Brandy Distillers also made much brandy of various flavors which was shipped worldwide.

The Salt Works was a much needed business. The salt was made by boiling down water from several brine wells in the area. The wood fired boilers kept many men busy supplying wood for fuel. Many more people were always busy putting the finished salt product in wooden barrels for shipping. Salt was vital in curing/preserving meat. Salt was also needed to use in tanning hides, etc. The world always needs salt. This was shipped in all directions.

There were several lime kilns in the area. The process entailed crushing limestone and drying this powder in wood fired kilns. This hydrated (slaked or dried) is very necessary in pickling some foods, a must have ingredient in making of Portland cement, mortars, etc. Many worked; much lime was shipped.

The Brown Brickyard was located near a large clay pit and again the kilns were wood fired. The abundant supply of wood in the area was vital. Much of the brick produced here was used locally but, again, much was shipped away.

The rugged hilly terrain made the building of a railroad to Leavenworth impractical. In fact, one was never built to there. The vast Ohio River was Leavenworth's main link to the world. The river port was managed by John L. Smith. He had helpers too. It was a busy place.

Of course, there were some sawmills and much of their product was sold elsewhere. One of the main products was railroad cross-ties. As usual, they were shipped out by river to be used to

build railroads somewhere else.

Last, but not least, the town boasted four general stores, three restaurants, six taverns or saloons, and, yes, Jacob Silverstein's Jewelry Store, the bank and the court house.

In mid-1863, there was beginning to be a shortage of manpower in the area. Too many men had left to fight in the war.

There was a company of "Home Guards" (a militia type unit like the modern National Guard). Approximately 80 men belonged to Major Woodbury's Home Guard unit. Like their modern day counterparts, they worked their regular jobs. They trained and drilled in the evening or on weekends.

It was obvious that if the Home Guard unit was ever ordered to active duty to leave and fight, there would be a severe manpower shortage. If this ever happened, there would be a big slow down for most industries and some would probably just have to shut down, at least for the duration of the call-up.

The town fathers then started to wonder who would guard the home front if worse came to worse. In any case, at this particular time, business was booming in Leavenworth.

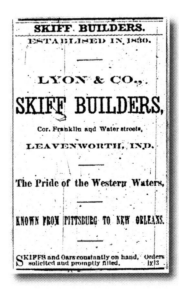

SKIFF BUILDERS.

ESTABLISHED IN 1830.

LYON & CO.,

SKIFF BUILDERS,

Cor. Franklin and Water streets,

LEAVENWORTH, IND.

The Pride of the Western Waters,

KNOWN FROM PITTSBURG TO NEW ORLEANS.

SKIFFS and Oars constantly on hand. Orders solicited and promptly filled. ly13

A barge loaded with D. Lyon's skiffs, ready to begin trip south
Picture courtesy of Stephenson General Store

D. Lyon Skiff Shop with crew at work building a Leavenworth Skiff
Founder Dan Lyon emigrated from Vermont to Leavenworth in 1820, and started
Skiff Shop in 1830. Picture courtesy of Stephenson General Store

A-4

_____

THREE

Volunteers Leave; Wounded Vets Return

AS A MATTER of respect, folks around town referred to Elam Herndon as "Captain Herndon." He was a captain when discharged at the end of the Mexican War. Though years before, he was still "captain". This was fairly customary in those days.

On this morning in May, 1863, Capt. Herndon was at the wharf at the Ohio River. Three more of Leavenworth's young men were also there waiting for a boat. The steamboat "Grey Eagle" was coming upriver. The "Grey Eagle" was a very large boat. Her usual route was Memphis, Tennessee to Cincinnati, Ohio and return. The three volunteers, soon to be soldiers, were going to board the "Grey Eagle," travel to New Albany, Indiana, then walk to Camp Noble to be inducted into the Union Army.

Capt. Herndon had just given the three some advice and a pep talk. He had said, "Now, men, I know you men are young and eager to serve your country. We are all proud of you and want to see you all return home unharmed. Here are some things to remember. Number 1: When your sergeants and officers talk, you listen and listen close. They are not just talking to hear their heads roar. They are trying to train you to be the best soldier you can be. Some of it may seem silly at first, but play the game. The best players are usually the winners. Winners come home; losers do not. When they bark, you jump. They are there trying to help you, not hurt you! They are on your side. Don't forget it! Good luck, soldiers. I know you'll do us proud." Capt. Herndon then shook hands with each of them.

When the "Grey Eagle" docked, Elam anxiously looked to see if anyone he knew was coming back. He recognized Cpl. Hiram Kinnaman, age 19. He had been wounded in the left arm. He was not officially discharged from the army, but was home on a sixty-day convalescent leave. Hiram stood tall in his army uniform, even with his left arm in a sling. Elam said, "Welcome home, Corporal. We heard that you were wounded. Glad to see it was not worse. Hold it, son. I'll carry your bag and your rifle for you."

Hiram replied, "Dammit, Capt. Herndon. You're stove up worse than I am. Thanks anyhow, Captain. If you can carry the carbine, I can carry the bag."

Thus, they left the boat. Hiram said, "Captain, getting back to my arm being in a sling, if that Reb officer had another round in his revolver like he thought he did, my ass would have been in a sling. Damn, Elam, I came close."

Elam chuckled, "Hiram, close only counts in horseshoes."

"Yes," said Hiram, "and a manure fight. Remember? You told me that years ago."

Cpl. Kinnaman was glad to be home. He was looking forward to a restful time. Leavenworth was beautiful to him. He soon noticed that there were not as many people out and about as before.

Elam said, "Hiram, as you can see, our population is way down. The war is taking its toll. There seems to be more women and children in town and few men. I know that some of your friends you want to visit with are gone. Come on. Let's stop at the Dexter Saloon and I'll buy you a welcome home drink of St. Theresa's apple brandy. As I remember, it was your favorite."

Hiram, replied, "Thanks, Captain. It is and I will."

On entering the saloon, they noticed Newt first. Elam said, "Newt, look who's back. Have a drink with us, on me."

Newt quickly accepted the generous offer. Normally, poor Newt would have to work at sweeping the saloon floor and stocking shelves for over an hour before getting a "free drink" for his efforts.

Newt Watson was a right decent guitar player. He had taught Hiram quite a lot on the guitar when Hiram was around twelve to thirteen years old. Newt said, "Hiram, that arm is sure gonna hurt your guitar playing."

"Yes, Newt," said Hiram, "and that arm wound also crimps my rifle shooting style. That was my skill that the army valued the most. Well, the corporal laughed, I guess I could still shoot a pistol if I had to."

The three finished their brandies and Capt. Herndon and Cpl. Kinnaman left. Newt was ever so grateful for that drink. Now, he would only have to work about an hour and he could have another drink.

"Damn," he thought to himself, "someday I'm gonna slack off of that stuff."

Talking as they walked toward Hiram's mother's house, Elam was filling Hiram in on the latest news. Elam said, "Corporal, we have another soldier home. He is on sick leave. He is Cpl. Milo Weathers. He had pneumonia twice and nearly died. The army is hoping that with some rest and good Indiana air, he will get well enough to return to active duty."

"Why, Captain," said Hiram, "Milo is just a kid. You said he was a corporal. How can that be?"

"He was barely fifteen years old," said Elam. "He really wanted to enlist and his dad signed for him. Milo turned out to be one real good soldier and was promoted to corporal at the Battle of Antietam. He came down with pneumonia late last winter. He recovered for a while and then caught it again. This time, it was worse. So, he is home on medical leave. Milo is now just over sixteen and a corporal."

Said Hiram, "Why, Captain, compared to me being 19 and Milo only being 16, I feel like an old soldier."

Elam laughed, "No, Hiram. I am the old soldier."

Cpl. Kinnaman's mother welcomed her son home with open arms.

Capt. Herndon limped up the street toward Sam Buchanan's house. He and Sam were close friends from way back. They had served together all through the Mexican War. Sam had been a first lieutenant under Elam back then. Lt. Buchanan had been wounded twice in his left arm which was of very little use to him these days. Sam Buchanan and wife Martha survived on the pitifully small government pension he had finally started receiving. It seemed the army and government were of short memory when it came to veterans.

Elam and Sam were much like brothers and, of course, always had much to talk about. "Old soldiers," it had been said, "never die. They just fade away." In any case, the two old soldiers hadn't faded away just yet. They both agreed though that they were both "fading."

Sam said, "Elam, have you got a count on how many local men have left because of this war?"

Elam replied, "Yes, Sam, and it is kind of scary. Some of the businesses are getting pretty shorthanded because of it. Now I hear that some of the wives and widows are working at different places, trying to take up some of the slack."

Sam said, "I know it's getting worse. My Martha is taking care of six kids while their mommas work. Elam, sometimes with all them young 'uns, it's as noisy as some of them Mexican battles. Ha, you know, Elam, sometimes I wish we were back younger and still being soldiers."

Elam shot back gently, "I know, Sam. Sometimes I'm that way too. It's all a distant dream, Sam. Our soldiering days are over. Hell man, we are damn lucky to be alive. You know it!"

"I know," Sam replied. "At least we are not totally crippled."

Elam said, "Getting back to our wounded vets, if I have it right, as of now, May of '63, we have twelve Crawford County men wounded or sick bad enough to be sent home and/or discharged. Of those twelve soldiers, six are from right here in Leavenworth, or close around."

"Yes, Elam," Sam began, "you and I helped carry some of those men off of the "Grey Eagle" and the "Concordia Queen." Remember the sedan chair we cobbled up, two hoop poles 'neath the bottom of a straight back chair with four men carrying."

Said Elam, "Yes, Sam, I hope we don't have to use that carry chair again, but we probably will. Anyway, it's some damn poor soldiers that can't carry their wounded home."

Elam started, "You know, I believe one of the most wounded men I've seen return from this war is old Pvt. Mike Baysinger. I mean, he wasn't physically wounded, but his pride was wounded something awful. You know, the colonel of the 66th Indiana Regiment discharged old Michael 'cause they said he was moving too slow. The papers said he was being sent home due to old age. Hell, he was 69 years old when he volunteered. Then, only one year later, at 70, he's too old."

Sam said, "The way I heard it, age or moving slow didn't hurt old Baysinger's aim none. He proved himself in the heat of things more than once. Oh well, the army does make mistakes, but in my mind this was a heller."

Elam started, "Sam, next week, let's go out to Mike Baysinger's place and visit. We could take along a couple of rifles and we could have a three way target shooting match."

"Okay," said Sam, "but I ain't gonna bet no more money when he calls his shots. I've learned my lesson."

Elam said, "You know, Sam, if there ever was a battle and old Mike was involved, I'd sure want him on my side, old or not!"

The next day, the steamboat "The Lady Pike" stopped to pick up and deliver mail, passengers and freight. The mailman was the bearer of bad news. He had the sad duty of delivering the news to Alice Bowman, now Dr. Ben Bowman's widow. Dr. Bowman had left his medical practice to volunteer in the Union Army as a major in the Medical Corps, only eight months ago. The army was in dire need of doctors. When the call was made he went without hesitation. Major Bowman had died in the Battle at Chancellorsville, Virginia, serving under Maj. General Joe Hooker.

Now Leavenworth was without a doctor. Actually, the town had been without a doctor for the past eight months since Dr. Bowman had left. Alice Bowman, the doctor's wife, had helped in their medical practice for many years. In her younger years, she had gone to the School of Nursing up in Louisville, but had lacked one year of completing the course.

Many people claimed that Alice Bowman knew about as much about doctoring as the good doctor did. After twenty years of assisting him, she knew much about the medical profession.

During the time that Dr. Bowman had been gone, Alice had carried on, though unofficially, trying her best to provide medical treatment for the townspeople. There were no other doctors. Her eighteen year old daughter, Susan, was now acting as her aide. Now, Tillie Jefferson, Moses' wife, was helping out and learning also. The lack of a doctor's diploma hanging on a wall doesn't mean much if the one trying to help you is the only medical help around.

FOUR

Elam's Military Past

ELAM HERNDON WAS a rather short man, but in many ways, he was as rugged as the Southern Indiana hill country where he was born. He was born in 1806 at Leavenworth, Crawford County, Indiana (then, Indiana Territory).

He had yearned to be a soldier for as long as he could remember. Elam knew early on that military life would be for him. When he was only about eight years old, he heard some of his first ever tales of wars and battles from some of the men around Leavenworth who had seen action in the War of 1812. When the men often sat on the porch of the general store and told tales, Elam took it all in. One veteran, Dan Lyon, had been with Gen. Andrew Jackson at New Orleans. Dan told a good tale and Elam Herndon never forgot one word.

Elam was a gun lover from the start, and would rather hunt and shoot than anything else he knew of at the time. He became a really good marksman early on. By age 12, he was doing quite well in the local shooting matches.

In 1824, when Elam was barely 18 years old, he joined the army. Years back, his dad had passed away and he figured he could help support his aged mother with his army pay.

Elam loved the army, army life, and all that went with it. By 1826 he had been promoted to regular sergeant after only two years of service. He was well-liked by his fellow soldiers and was known to be someone you could count on in a rough situation. He was stationed at various forts and camps, not being in war except for a few Indian skirmishes in the Southwest.

In 1831, Elam had risen to the coveted rank of first sergeant; he had only been a soldier for seven years. Elam was quite happy being first sergeant and would have been quite contented to serve 'til he reached retirement at that rank.

In 1846, Elam was 40 years old and had been in the regular army for 22 years. His plan was to retire from the army after 30 years of service.

Soon, the United States of America was at war with Mexico. In short order, Sgt. Elam Herndon was in battle, real honest to God battle, in several places in Mexico. As a first sergeant in an infantry company, he had plenty of chances to put his marksmanship skills to good use.

In April, 1846, Elam was pleasantly surprised when a new sergeant was transferred into his company. He was Sam Buchanan, a boyhood friend from back home in Leavenworth, Indiana.

Their top commander was Brig. Gen. Zachary Taylor and their first major battle was at Palo Alto, May 8, 1846, against the troops of Mexican General Pedro Ampudia. Gen. Taylor's men were victorious here as well as on May 9th at Resaca de La Palma.

Their next big battle was fought at Monterrey, Mexico, Nuevo Le'on Province. This was a fierce battle on September 21-23 and Monterrey finally fell on September 23, 1846.

In this battle, First Sgt. Herndon was wounded twice, but fought on. One bullet had grazed his left upper arm; another had wounded him slightly in the right hip. He refused to be taken out of action, had his wounds dressed and continued the fight.

Shortly after the battle at Monterrey, Mexico, Elam's company was part of the troops drawn (transferred) to the command of Gen. Winfield Scott.

Gen. Scott's plan was to take his forces by sea, through the Gulf of Mexico, land at the coastal town of Vera Cruz and capture it.

After this, he planned to march his forces inland to Mexico City. He knew that if he defeated Gen. Santa Anna's army at Mexico City, the war would be won.

First Sgt. Herndon and Sgt. Buchanan, along with many others, were in the thick of things at Cero Gordo. First Sgt. Herndon was knocked down by the concussion from a Mexican shell that killed three of his fellow soldiers. He didn't hear very well for a while, but he picked himself up and got back in the battle. After two days of hard fighting, April 17-18, 1847, they had defeated part of Gen. Santa Anna's army at Cerro Gordo, Mexico.

The infantry company that Elam was part of was gradually becoming a little smaller with each battle and action. They had been losing some men in every battle. This was fierce combat. The enemy was constantly suffering more casualties than the Americans were, but they had the luxury of being able to replace lost troops as they were in home territory. On the other hand, the Americans had no provision for replacements and thus their ranks were growing thinner.

Sgt. Herndon's company had already lost ten men by this time. One had been the second lieutenant which now left the company one officer short.

They moved on against light resistance until they came up against some of Santa Anna's best at Contreras on August 19, 1847. That was not an easy win. They lost four more men in the process.

On August 20, they were met by more crack Mexican troops at Churubusco, Mexico. There was a heated battle. The Americans lost three more men, but they were victorious.

On September 8th, 1847, they engaged the enemy at Molino del Rey. The Americans lost no men, though two were wounded. Again, this was a hard fight, but they came out on top.

The American soldiers were now starting to get close enough to Mexico City to know that some of the worst was yet to come.

On September 13th, they reached a place called "Chapultepec Hill." Gen. Scott had passed the word that this place was a key position for the Mexican's defense of Mexico City, the capital. Just past this obstacle, the causeways made travel easy from this point on. The enemy was likely to fight to the death for Chapultepec Hill.

Sgt. Herndon's unit had started out in this war with a maximum strength of 120 men. Now, the total strength of the company was 89 men and two officers, one first lieutenant and the company commander, a captain.

American artillery tried to soften up the resistance on Chapultepec Hill with a concentrated barrage of cannon fire. The company commander, Capt. Olsen, had his orders from above, "This hill had to be taken; this was a must!! Once taken, it must be held!!"

Regimental command considered Capt. Olsen's company as one of its best and it was ordered to take the center position. He ordered the only other remaining officer, First Lt. Johnson, to have the men start the assault on Chapultepec Hill as soon as the cannon fire stopped.

The nearly 30 minutes of sustained cannon fire was over. This should have made the enemies' resistance lighter, but it didn't help much. Their troops were better entrenched than thought and they had suffered fewer casualties.

Capt. Olsen gave the order to advance. He and Lt. Johnson bravely went at a point near the lead troops.

The fire from the Mexican troops was withering. Capt. Olsen's troops fell in sickening numbers. The men were fighting valiantly, but were greatly outnumbered.

Capt. Olsen was shot in the neck and died instantly. Very soon, Lt. Johnson was horribly wounded and died shortly after he fell.

The men were shouting above the deafening gunfire, asking whether to stop the advance or continue??

It was then that First Sgt. Elam Herndon realized that he was now in command! Though only a sergeant, he was the highest ranking man left in his now very small company of troops. He ordered a quick halt as the remnants of their company of infantry sought whatever cover they could find behind two small sand hills.

Sgt. Herndon ordered his men to do a quick ammo count and even up the ammunition among them. First Sgt. Herndon and Sgt. Sam Buchanan had the men "count off", to see how many men were left. The count was 50 men total, including Elam and Sam.

Much to the Mexican's surprise, the lull in the advance did not mean that the American troops had given up. On the contrary, the advance started again very quickly. The small group of soldiers made it through some hellish fire and was making the Mexicans pay very dearly for trying to hold Chapultepec Hill.

Of those that were able to move, the Mexican soldiers retreated.

First Sgt. Herndon and his 40 remaining men now held the main part of this important hill.

The American troops prepared as best they could for the counter attack which they knew was sure to come. The counter attack came in the form of some of the previously retreating Mexicans, supplemented with some fresh replacement troops and more ammunition.

First Sgt. Herndon had prepared his troops by having them gather up extra muskets from the fallen Mexicans and as well from their lost men. Most of the American soldiers now had at least two loaded weapons close by ready to pick up and fire, as well as their regular arms.

The Mexicans' counter attack was strong. They were, however, very surprised at the Americans being able to meet them head on with not one, but three volleys of fire in such quick order, thanks to the extra loaded weapons. Normally, after the first volley, the enemy would try to overrun his opponent during the reloading process.

Mexican soldiers dropped in large numbers.

Sgt. Buchanan was shot twice in his left arm, but refused to fall.

First Sgt. Herndon received a bad wound to his left leg, from a Mexican musket ball, followed by a wounded right shoulder from a Mexican captain's sword.

The Mexicans gave it up and moved back.

The Americans were now in control of Chapultepec Hill. The Mexicans tried one last time to retake the hill, but again were beaten back by its now very small group of 37 American soldiers. First Sgt. Elam Herndon and his men held the key hill for sixteen more hours, long enough to be relieved by fresh troops.

Gen. Winfield Scott ordered that the two heroic men be given battlefield promotions. First Sgt. Elam Herndon was promoted to the rank of captain and was given command of his infantry company.

Sgt. Sam Buchanan was also given a battlefield promotion and was made a first lieutenant.

After a brief trip to a U.S. Army Field Hospital tent, both Capt. Herndon and Lt. Buchanan were back with their men.

A horse had been provided for the captain to ride, due to his leg wound, and Lt. Buchanan would have his left arm in a sling for a while, but they were not about to get out of the game just yet.

American forces quickly advanced over the causeways to the western gates of Mexico City. After only a brief few hours of resistance, the once proud and now not so fierce army of General Santa Anna surrendered!! This happened on Sept. 14th, 1847, only one day after the stand at Chapultepec Hill.

Gen. Santa Anna escaped capture and very soon resigned.

Both Capt. Herndon and Lt. Buchanan's days were numbered

as combat soldiers. Their wounds were slow in healing and caused much pain. After a stay at an army hospital back in Texas, they were both released from the army as, "Physically Unfit for Military Duty" on January 28, 1848.

Capt. Elam Herndon and Lt. Sam Buchanan traveled home on steamboats via the Mississippi and Ohio Rivers to their beloved hometown of Leavenworth, Indiana.

A few months after coming home, Elam had tried to become a member of the local Home Guard. He loved the military and wanted to stay connected, at least to some extent. He was told, rather curtly, that he was no longer in physical condition to be of service to the military in any capacity.

After the Home Guard had rejected Elam, Sam Buchanan knew that he would also be rejected for the same reasons, so he did not even volunteer to join.

Even though Elam and Sam had many years ago been released from the military, they were still referred to as "captain" and "lieutenant" as a matter of respect.

Elam Herndon would just as soon have forgotten his military service, but his old wounds would not let him forget. Every time his left leg ached, he thought of the Mexican soldier who had put the musket ball there. As well, every time his right shoulder throbbed, he had vivid memories of that Mexican captain and his damned old sharp sword. Oh sure, one of Elam's men had put the finishing touch to the Mexican captain, but Elam's shoulder still reminded him of it all, in full color!

It was the same with friend Sam Buchanan; he had an almost useless left arm. Elam and Sam had much in common.

When the American Civil War had broken out in 1861, Elam and Sam had volunteered their services to the Union Army, being willing to serve at any rank or in any capacity, no matter how small or insignificant. This time, they had both been rejected for reasons of partial disability and also, to add insult to injury, they had been told that they were "too old!"

Now, in the summer of 1863, the Civil War was becoming more intense every day and all these two old soldiers could do about it was talk about it.

FIVE

Captain Mattingly, Elam's Friend

RIVERBOAT CAPT. ELI Mattingly was one of Elam Herndon's oldest and closest friends. Elam had worked for Capt. Mattingly for a few months back in 1850, but had to give up life on the river as his wife, Ruth, did not like for Elam to be gone so much.

Capt. Eli Mattingly was a familiar figure along the Ohio River. In 1863, Eli was in his seventieth year and a great part of these years had been spent on the river. He was the captain and owner of the stern wheel packet boat, the "Concordia Queen."

The "Concordia Queen" was officially listed as being from the home port of Concordia, Kentucky. On paper, Eli Mattingly lived at Concordia, but in truth, he lived most of the time on his boat. His wife, Liz, had grown very accustomed to living more like a widow than a wife. As she often said, "That old river rat thinks more of that boat than me!"

A packet boat was one that hauled passengers as well as freight. The "Concordia Queen" was 125 feet long and approximately 24 feet wide. She drew about three feet of water (meaning that she would float in water as shallow as three and a half to four feet deep when loaded.) The "Queen's" lower deck consisted of the engine room with the rest of that level of the boat for hauling cargos of general freight. She hauled everything from livestock, farm machinery, food products, produce, lumber and also much tobacco, whiskey, brandy and wine. You name it; the "Queen" can haul it.

The "Queen" was powered by two steam engines connected to a stern paddlewheel by chain and cog drive.

The upper deck was for passengers and crew. The "Concordia Queen" had a lounge/sitting room, a kitchen (galley) and small dining area. There were 12 small rooms for the passengers while the crew slept (when they slept) in a room fitted with four double deck bunk beds. The captain and first officer (when there was one) shared a small room located next to the stairway which led the way up to the third level of the boat to the pilot house. Yes, and lest we forget, the passenger deck also was blessed with a small bar/smoking room area with a card table, as was the custom in those days. Good Kentucky bourbon and various brandies were sold by the drink. Business was usually brisk in this section of the boat. Of course, there was often a card game in progress.

The "Concordia Queen" had been built by the Howard Boat Works at Jeffersonville, Indiana, back in 1848. Eli had worked as pilot on the new boat for the first two years. The owner had suddenly died and Eli had managed to buy the boat. Even now, in 1863, he still owed the Brandenburg Bank a fairly large sum of money which they wanted payment on monthly, promptly and in the full amount!

By 1863, many of the steamboats were fired by coal to heat their boilers, but some still burned wood. Coal produced more and quicker steam power, but was much more costly than wood. Capt. Mattingly did keep a bunker of coal on board for use in emergency situations, but mainly, he relied on the abundant low cost supply of wood along the Ohio River.

As was common along the rivers, some people made, or at least supplemented, their living by cutting wood to sell to the steamboat captains. Since the boats' schedules were nearly impossible to predict, the wood was sold on the "self-serve/honor system." The woodcutter would pile up wood at certain places along the river. The boat captain would stop, lower the gangplank and the crew would load the wood on board, i.e., self-service. Nowadays, since the war was causing a manpower shortage, old Capt. Mattingly at times had to help load the wood.

The boat captain would then count out the pre-agreed amount of money to pay for each cord of wood. The money would be left in a jar or box that the woodcutter provided, thus the honor system. The money was seldom ever stolen, for taking a woodcutter's hard earned money was right up next to horse stealing. No one wanted to risk being cut up by a sharp axe. The system worked.

Over the years, Capt. Mattingly had built up a nice business on the river. He ran mainly between Tobacco Landing, a small place real close to Laconia, Indiana, and Owensboro, Kentucky, a river distance of 140 miles. He loaded and unloaded at all stops in between these two points. This type of freighting was very labor intensive at times due to the fact that when near full loaded, freight that needed to be unloaded often had to be shuffled around freight that had just been picked up and vice versa. Again, the resulting manpower shortage due to the war also made life harder for everyone on board.

Running with less than a full crew, there were times when they would have to tie up at the bank so the crew could get some rest instead of steaming on. All these things added to the gypsy, no set schedule, type of business. This meant that, at times, the captain could only stop briefly at his home in Concordia, Kentucky. One time, wife Liz saw the "Concordia Queen" go on by without stopping. Needless to say, Eli's ears burned and the air was blue. Liz even implied that he was of doubtful ancestry. He did not want to risk her wrath again, if at all possible. If he did need to pass by home without stopping, he would do it in fog or cover of darkness.

Late last evening, the "Concordia Queen" had just happened

to arrive at her home port. There had been cargo to unload and also to take on. That night, the crew got some rest. There were only four passengers on this trip and they had no objection to a short layover in Concordia, Kentucky. That night, Liz and Eli slept together for the first time in two weeks. Eli loved his wife, home and family dearly, but river boating was demanding business and the bank wanted their payment monthly. Last night the captain had told his engineer, Josh Freedman, to keep the fires on low, but real early to start building up a head of steam. Before sunup, all lines were away and they steamed away and headed up river against a slow down current.

As Capt. Eli Mattingly stood at the helm of his boat, his memory went back to that night in Owensboro, Kentucky, when he first met Josh back in 1860. He had just finished speaking in the "speaking tube" to the engine room. He had told Josh to, "Lay on some wood; full speed ahead!"

Josh answered back promptly, "Yes sir, Captain. Full speed it is."

Josh had been working on the "Concordia Queen" now for three years. But back in '60, Josh was in different circumstances.

Capt. Eli Mattingly didn't have very many vices, but he had a few. He did smoke and chew, cuss occasionally, and he also drank his fair share of whiskey and brandy. He also liked to gamble a little, especially play poker, and was known to be either lucky or skilled, or both. After all, life itself was a gamble and he knew full well that life on the river was one big gamble.

He thought back to that night in April 1860. Capt. Mattingly had to stay the night in Owensboro to finish taking on some farm machinery the next morning. He went into his favorite saloon, "The First Chance Saloon," and had a taste or two of good Kentucky bourbon as he studied the room. The place was crowded that night, the smoke was thick, and the card tables were full of action.

He narrowed his attention to the table with the most money

and chips laying on it. Four men were at the table and were playing straight draw poker. One of the men appeared to be more well-to-do than the rest, dressed in the clothes of a gentleman, fine to the last thread. This "dude", obviously a big fish in his home pond, also wore three large diamond rings, had a fine gold watch and fob, as well as a striking stick pin, also blessed with diamonds, stuck in his immaculate neck tie.

At the end of the next hand, Eli said, "Gentlemen, would you mind if I sat in?"

At this, the prosperous one replied, "Why no, sir, we would be delighted to have you join us in a little game of chance! Wouldn't we fellows?"

The other three card players agreed.

The Southern gentleman said, as he extended his hand in a friendly handshake, "Sir, please allow me to introduce myself. I am Col. Lyle B. Jackson from Big Oak Plantation near Helena, Arkansas and late of the Arkansas Militia. Please do us the honor of a little friendly gaming with us."

"Thanks for your hospitality, sir. I'm Eli Mattingly. I believe I will sit in."

Eli couldn't help but notice the poorly clothed young black man standing a few feet away and said, "Is that black with one of you?"

Col. Lyle B. Jackson proudly answered, "Why yes, sir. He belongs to me. I bought him at the Memphis auction some years back. When any one at this table needs a drink or a cigar or such, he will fetch it. You hear that, Josh?"

Josh humbly replied, "Yes, sir, Marse Jackson!"

The poker playing resumed in earnest with the five players at the table.

Eli made a point of playing poorly on purpose for a few hands, calling when he knew he had a losing hand.

Now, it was time for Eli to start playing poker for real and said,

"Gentlemen, I suggest that we raise the ante from one dollar to ten dollars and also the betting raise limit from fifty dollars to one hundred dollars. Agreed? And Josh, here, take this gold piece and bring us another round of whiskies for the table on me!!"

"Yes, sir, Josh is on the way, sir!"

Capt. Eli made a pretense of being a little drunk, but he started winning in a big way. By now, he had the largest pile of chips and money in front of him. The other three poker players went broke and left the game.

The once jovial Col. Lyle Jackson realized that his healthy pile of chips and cash now looked anemic. In a desperate move to try and recoup his lost assets, he said, "Sir, I suggest we take off the bet limit and play 'The Sky's the Limit.' Do you agree?"

Capt. Eli Mattingly agreed. The only two players left were he and the colonel. "Deal, sir," said Eli.

Eli won the next pot with an ace high straight. The colonel looked disgruntled, but went for another hand. Maybe, his luck would change?

The pot was big and it was Eli's turn to raise, "Colonel, I'll see your bet and I raise you nine hundred dollars," as he pushed that amount to the center of the table.

Trying to maintain his composure, Col. Lyle Jackson said, "Sir, I find myself temporarily financially embarrassed. I have adequate funds, but unfortunately not at this card table at this moment. I assure you, sir, I am a man of honor. Would you accept my personal I.O.U. marker in lieu of cash?" He was sure he had a winning hand and his pot would make him whole again. He was sure of it!

Capt. Mattingly stated that, "Sir, I'm sure you are a gentleman as well as a man of honor, but your home plantation is so far from my home that, no offense, sir, I'd prefer to have something more tangible on the table. Sir, you own that slave, Josh, over there, don't you?"

The humiliated gentleman assured Eli that was certainly the case.

"Well, sir, why not draw up a quick 'bill of sale' on your property and place it on the table? If you win, he's still yours. If not, he belongs to me. He surely would be worth $900.00 on today's market, don't you think?"

"Sir, I assure you that that black is worth that amount and more, much more. Agreed. I'll wager him."

At the request of Eli, Josh went to the bar and returned with pen, ink and paper. A quick bill of sale for Josh was drawn up and duly witnessed by three reputable people. The paper was then placed on the bet pile at the middle of the table.

The confident colonel said, "Sir, I call you."

Capt. Mattingly showed a king high straight flush in diamonds against the colonel's queen high straight flush in hearts.

An angry Arkansas plantation owner stomped from the room. "Hell," he thought, "I came up here to buy farm equipment and play some cards! Now, I've lost a bundle as well as an expensive slave! Damn the luck!!"

On the other hand, a now sober appearing Capt. Mattingly, all smiles, was gathering up his winnings and cashing in his chips. He said, "Josh, you belong to me now. Where are your belongings?"

"Yes, Marse Eli, I've been sleeping in the hayloft at the livery stable next to the hotel where Massa stayed. I have a sack of stuff there."

"Okay, Josh. Let's go by there and get your things. We will be staying on my boat. Let's go."

The next morning, while the rest of the cargo was being loaded, Capt. Mattingly took Josh Jackson down to the engine room saying, "George, this is Josh, your new helper. Teach him all you can, quick as you can."

The "Concordia Queen" was soon underway headed upriver.

After a few stops for loading and unloading, they tied up at the wharf at Cannelton, Indiana. More to load; more to unload.

The following morning Capt. Mattingly said, "Josh, you come go with me." They headed for the Perry County Court House and went to the County Recorder's office. Josh thought, "Now what? Is this old river man going to sell me again?"

Capt. Mattingly said to the clerk in charge, "I want to file legal papers to make this slave a free man. I want it official and recorded right. Here is the bill-of-sale where I got him. Also, I want him to have papers to carry with him that proves he's a free man."

"Yes, sir. We will be happy to do that. Now, for the records, what is this man's name and what name do you want on the papers?"

"Well, his owner's last name was Jackson. Josh, do you like the last name of Jackson? Do you want to keep it?"

"No, sir. I don't want to keep nothing that reminds me of him or his place!"

"Well, Josh, now you are a 'freed man.' How would you like the last name of 'Freedman'?"

"Capt. Eli, I would love to have that name."

"Very well, clerk, he is now going to be 'Josh Freedman.' Let's get it done!"

They went back to the wharf and Eli said, "Now, Josh, you are your own man. You are free to come and go, when and where you please. Do you have any idea what you would like to do?"

"Yes, Capt. Mattingly, I'd like to learn to be a river man."

"Okay, Josh, I will hire you to work in the engine room. That's where I need help the worst. Now, remember. You ain't a slave no more. You will get paid just the same as the rest of the crew. Also, a bunk and your meals go with the job. You are hired, Josh Freedman. Let's get aboard. The "Concordia Queen" needs to be churning water."

Capt. Mattingly was suddenly jolted from his daydreaming recollections by a loud anxious voice on the speaking tube. "Captain, are you awake up there? Have you forgot about that sandbar at the bend below Alton? We are about to hit it!!" The captain snapped to in time to turn hard and miss the sandbar.

"Thanks, Josh. I must have drifted off for a spell, thinking about other days. Hell, Josh, I'm gonna have to start teaching you to pilot the 'Queen' so I can sleep now and then." He then hung up the speaking tube and tended to business.

The boat docked at Alton, Indiana, to unload some, load on some more. They continued on up river and put in at Wolf Creek, Kentucky. Here, they unloaded some farm wagons and plows from Owensboro and loaded some tobacco destined for Owensboro on the trip back down river.

Capt. Mattingly knew there would be some cargo to offload at Leavenworth, Indiana, and it being late in the day, the "Concordia Queen" would be tied up there for the night. He gave a long pull on the boat whistle to let all in Leavenworth know that the boat would be there shortly. They would know it was the "Concordia Queen" coming because of her distinctive three chime (note) steam whistle. No other boat whistle even came close to sounding the same. Old Jacob Silverstein, Leavenworth's jeweler/gunsmith/tinkerer, had adjusted the boat whistle years ago to give it its unique sound.

Capt. Mattingly was always glad to spend some time at Leavenworth. For one thing, he had several friends there and he usually had some news for them and vice versa. One of his good friends was Capt. Elam Herndon. Tonight, they would have some time to 'tilt a few' and swap stories. Another pair of special friends were Moses and Tillie Jefferson. He had grown very fond of them both over the years.

Elam Herndon, among others, was at the wharf to see the "Concordia Queen" come in. As Capt. Mattingly and Elam walked up toward the Dexter Saloon, they were catching up on the latest about the war, their mutual friends and so on.

After a sip of brandy, the river captain began, "Elam, I know you will want to hear about this one. I read about this in the Owensboro newspaper! Our old friend Capt. Nathan Collins, who now works for the Union Navy, just had one hell of a close call!!"

"Yes, Eli, I try to keep up on Nathan as best I can. The last I heard, He was captain of the Union Navy boat the "Harrison" down on the Lower Mississippi in the thick of things.

"You're right. He's on the "Harrison" and for sure, where the action is. The story in the paper said that he was asked personally by General Grant to volunteer to run past the Confederate gun batteries to try to get men from the 23rd Indiana Volunteers and food supplies past the big gun emplacements and on down to New Carthage, Mississippi, where the food and troops were badly needed. When the "Harrison" came under very heavy fire from the Confederate batteries, he saw that his boat was going to be shot to pieces. So knowing that the way the big guns were placed, they could not aim very well to targets too close to them, what do you think mild mannered old Capt. Collins done?"

"Mild mannered, hell, ain't no telling what Nathan Collins would do. Like as not he'd spit in the devil's face!"

"Well, Elam, he came close to doing just that. He steered the 'Harrison' real close to the bank and kept on moving. The shore guns didn't blow them plumb away, but they did play hell with the boat. The pilothouse was nearly shot away and three spokes were shot out of the pilot wheel. Not one man aboard the 'Harrison' was lost and Capt. Collins landed safely at New Carthage."

"Do you reckon General Grant appreciates the effort?"

"The account said that Grant was very grateful. I'm sure he was."

"If we had more men like Nathan, this war would have been

over by now."

"Eli, how many men do you have left in your crew on the 'Concordia Queen'?"

"Elam, we are running real shorthanded. If you would see or hear of a warm body that would work on my boat, please see if they would sign on. I need help. Right now, all that's left is me; Josh Freedman, my engineer; old Hargus Smith, trying to be my fireman; and the two men I have left as deck hands and freight wrestlers. Everyone is wore out.

"Elam, we have to tie up to a tree most nights 'cause of being short of help. We don't have a cook anymore; we all take turns cooking. You have to serve yourself, clean your own table and make your own bed. Sometimes, when we have passengers, I offer a deal to anyone who will help do most anything. I tell 'em that if they will help the crew, I'll knock off some on the price of passenger fare or even let 'em ride and eat for free."

"Capt. Mattingly, it's my turn to buy a round. Come on, Newt. Join us and have one on me."

A grateful Newt said, "Many thanks, Eli. I never turn down a good offer like that!"

"And, Eli," began Elam Herndon, "you ain't going to believe this. The local Home Guard major is trying to talk me into organizing a "Home Guard Reserve" group, just to be in reserve in case the Home Guard would ever be called for active duty away from here."

"Are you gonna do it?"

"I haven't really made up my mind yet. Like I told Major Woodbury, I don't think that things would ever come to be bad enough to need a back-up group like that. Also, I told him that the way it looks to me, there just are not enough people left around here to start a group like that. Eli, just look at the problems you are having with trying to get crewmen for your boat. Just look around town here, not as many men here as there was before this war started."

"Well, Elam, I think you ought to go for it. You know how much you like military things. And besides, that would give you more to keep your mind occupied. Besides that, a group like you're talking about could come in handy in a pinch."

"I haven't given Major Woodbury an answer yet. I'm thinking on it."

Picture courtesy of the S&D REFLECTOR

Boat similar to the CONCORDIA QUEEN

· Six ·

Organizing The Homeguard Reserve

ONLY THREE WEEKS ago, Horatio Woodbury, the local home guard major, had convinced Elam Herndon of the need for a Home Guard Reserve unit. Elam had reluctantly agreed to form and command such a unit. Major Woodbury, in due military form, had presented Capt. Herndon with a quite impressive military certificate authorizing the formation of the unit. This all being duly signed by Indiana Governor Oliver P. Morton and Major General John Love, Commanding Officer, Indiana Legion of State Militia. Elam was sworn in as captain and commanding officer. Major Woodbury was quick to explain that Elam was on his own as the regular Home Guard unit was very busy training and could possibly be called away on short notice. There was a real war going on.

When Capt. Herndon finally had a chance to read the fine print, he had to laugh. First off, he was only authorized a maximum of 100 men in his unit. "Hell," he thought, "I'll be lucky to raise ten men." Of course, he couldn't recruit members of the Home Guard; these 80 or so men were off limits. He quickly realized that the only men left were either very young or quite old. Many of both were disabled in one way or another.

The next thing he realized was that there were no provisions for arming or equipping the Home Guard Reserves. They would be on their own and expected to provide their own weapons and supplies. There were also no provisions for uniforms, etc.

There was a provision for army pay for the men of the unit when on active duty. "Yes, the whopping army pay!" Elam laughed to himself. "Now there's a reason to join!"

Capt. Herndon kept telling himself that once he had organized a reserve unit, they would probably never be needed as a fighting unit. Perhaps they would have minor duties as anti-looting, law enforcement and fire watch, should the regular Home Guard troop be called away, but actual combat duty? Very unlikely. In any case, on with the recruiting.

After three weeks of masterful recruiting efforts, Capt. Herndon had assembled a grand total of eighteen boys and men, not counting himself. Just yesterday, he had two more volunteers, but they could only promise temporary short term service as they were both on sick or convalescent leave from the army. They would have to return to active duty when well enough. They both figured no more than six weeks at most.

So now, the Leavenworth Home Guard Reserve unit had a "strength" of 21 men. Oh well, strength may not have been the best choice of words. Numbered twenty-one men would have been a more accurate term. Capt. Herndon was not known to be a quitter and decided to do the best he could with what he had. The men were an agreeable bunch, in general, and all seemed eager to serve. This for sure was a positive sign. In any case, Elam had picked through slim pickins to start with and had been blessed with these twenty men. One could not accurately describe them as twenty-one "able-bodied" men for this was not the case. There were no more men to recruit unless some appeared from out of nowhere. Capt. Herndon had picked the area clean.

The Leavenworth Home Guard Reserve now consisted of twenty-one people. They were white, black, red, yellow and all shades in 'tween. They ranged in age from 14 years old to 87. About one-half of the group had some previous military experience. Three of the twenty-one had never shot a gun. Six of the group had disabilities in one form or another. Three more men were definitely "senior citizens" but still game to try. For the most part, the group spoke English, well, sort of.

Following is the roster of all members, a few details about each of them, and their military experience, if any. They are also listed in the order that they volunteered:

1	Capt. Elam Herndon - age 57 - speaks English and some Spanish - partly disabled - slight limp in the left leg - wounds from the Mexican War
2	1st. Lt. Sam Buchanan - age 54 - speaks English and some Spanish - partially disabled - left arm - wounds from Mexican War
3	Pvt. Michael Baysinger - age 70 - combat veteran of current Civil War - mustered out reason: old age – able-bodied - speaks English - excellent marksman
4	1st. Sgt. Levi Wildman - age 66 - speaks English – able-bodied - professional soldier - retired from regular Army - Mexican War veteran
5	Pvt. Jacob Silverstein - age 57 - speaks English and German – able-bodied - no previous military experience - a jeweler by trade, also gunsmith
6	Pvt. Buford Beasley - age 87 - elderly, able-bodied, but moves slow - no previous military experience - gentleman farmer - hunting enthusiast - good with guns - speaks English slowly
7	Pvt. Moses Jefferson - age 55 - speaks English - a Negro, former slave – able-bodied - no previous military experience - boat carpenter
8	Pvt. George Armstrong - age 77 – able-bodied - speaks English and bits of Japanese - ex-gold prospector - no previous military experience - works at Button Factory
9	Pvt. Hibachi Takaguchi - age 41 - Japanese – able-bodied - speaks Japanese and bits of English - ex-gold prospector, pearl diver previous military experience - works at Button Factory
10	Pvt. Tad Martin - age 20 - crippled left foot - slight limp - speaks English - school teacher and works part-time at local newspaper - no previous military experience

11	Pvt. Lemuel Moore - age 19 - very slight mental impairment (had been kicked in head by cow as a child and was thus); otherwise able-bodied - speaks English - no previous military experience
12	Pvt. Jim Running Deer - age 60 - Shawnee Indian – able-bodied - speaks English, plus some French and several Indian dialects - no previous military experience - skilled woodsman and excellent marksman
13	Pvt. Dan Lyon - age 81 - elderly, able-bodied, but moves slow - speaks English - is a veteran of War of 1812; was with Gen. Jackson at New Orleans - retired owner of boat works - His son is a captain in the Leavenworth Home Guard - a willing volunteer - says he can still shoot
14	Sgt. Harley Bratton - age 64 – able-bodied - speaks English - hunter/woodsman very good with guns; had been member of regular Home Guard unit for 25 years - resigned back in 1860 because of remarks criticizing his age
15	Pvt. Newt Watson - age 51 – able-bodied but known to be a two fisted drinker - when drinking, he would often overdo - speaks English - no military experience - guitar player in local saloons - good natured and willing - promised Capt. Herndon that he would stay dry on duty
16	Pvt. James Corbin - age 14 (soon to be 15) – able-bodied - young and eager to join - speaks English - no previous military experience - farm boy
17	Pvt. Helmer Schmitt - age 16 – able-bodied - speaks English and German (more comfortable with German) - no previous military experience - apprentice furniture maker at local factory
18	Pvt. Chet Hatfield - age 15 – able-bodied - speaks English - young and willing - no previous military experience - worked at local blacksmith shop as apprentice
19	Pvt. Albert LeCroix - age 17 – able-bodied - speaks English and French (more French) - no previous military experience - worked at local winery
20	Cpl. Milo Weathers - age 16 - currently on sick leave from U.S. Army - decorated combat veteran - could only volunteer as temporary as he would be ordered back to his unit when well enough
21	Cpl. Hiram Kinnaman - age 19 - currently on convalescence leave (arm wound); combat veteran - temporary member - would return to army when well

Capt. Elam Herndon knew that he had assembled one of the, if not the, most diverse group of soldiers ever. That fact did not make the unit unable to function. With some leadership, drill and education, the captain had high hopes of molding this group of men into a well oiled military machine. At times in the past, Elam had been accused of being a dreamer. His philosophy was that sometimes you have to make a dream come true.

The next order of business was to organize the group, elect officers and noncommissioned officers. After that, he would drill some military discipline and organization into this very special little group of volunteers.

On June 1, 1863, Capt. Herndon called a meeting of the reserve members. They met at the docks at the Ohio River. They ended up using part of the wharf house for their meeting when it started to rain.

"Attention!" said Elam, "Men, the first order of business is to get organized, elect officers, sergeants and so on. I have been appointed Captain and Commanding Officer of this group. We have a total strength of twenty-one. We should have more members, but as you all know, this was all we could muster! We will just have to do the best we can with what we have!

"My army experience tells me that for a unit like ours, we will need one lieutenant, one first sergeant, one regular sergeant and two corporals. The rest will have the rank of private. I would like to nominate Sam Buchanan to be first lieutenant. Buchanan and I served together in Mexico. I can vouch that he is a good soldier, a brave man and a good leader. Also, he still suffers as a result of some of his Mexican wounds the same as I."

By a show of hands, Sam was elected as first lieutenant unanimously.

"Next," said Elam, "we need someone to be our first sergeant."

From the back, a deep voice spoke loud and clear. Everyone knew Buford Beasley. At age 87, he was the oldest member. He was a large farmer and also known to be one of the best marksmen in Crawford County, Indiana.

"I nominate Levi Wildman to be our first sergeant. We all know that he retired from the regular army as a first sergeant. He may be sixty-six years old, but he can still do the job."

Of course, Levi Wildman was elected first sergeant.

Moses Jefferson then spoke, "I nominate Mike Baysinger to be our regular sergeant."

Mike replied, "Thanks for the thought, Moses, but I don't want no rank or no responsibilities. If'n it comes to it, I need to give all my attention to my rifle and my shooting. I'd like to nominate Harley Bratton to be our regular sergeant. He's a tough old bird and damn close to being as good of a shot as I am."

Harley Bratton was elected regular sergeant.

Elam then said, "Now, men, we need two corporals. We already have two men with us that hold that rank. One is Milo Weathers and the other man is Hiram Kinnaman. They are both home on leave to heal and recover so they are only temporary members, but I think they should be our two corporals."

To a man, these two were elected to be corporals. This left fifteen men with the rank of private.

Capt. Herndon began, "Now, men, I will explain how the chain of command works in the army, at least in this unit. If we were to get into a battle, or a bad situation and I were to be killed or put out of commission, then Lt. Buchanan would be in charge. Then, if the same were to happen to the lieutenant, then First Sgt. Wildman would be in charge. Should the first sergeant become unable to command, then Sgt. Bratton would have to take over. If it came to only privates left, they are to choose those among them to lead. The main point is that just being without leaders is never a reason to give up a fight. You fight on! Now, men, Lt. Buchanan has something to say."

"Men, as you probably already know, this outfit is pretty much on its own. The government made no provisions for uniforms or much of anything else. The main purpose of uniforms in the military is to 'tell them from us.' Here is what we will do. Every man who has all or part of an army uniform will wear what he has. On top of this, every enlisted man will wear a bright red bandana around his neck. The two officers, Elam and I, will wear bright yellow bandanas. In this way, we will be able to tell them from us easier in dust, dim light or smoke of battle."

"The next item," said the captain, "is the matter of guns and ammunition. I want every man to make a list of all the guns, firearms of any type, that you own or have access to! Yes, even to borrow them if you must! If we need to be soldiers, we will need something to point besides our fingers!

Men we will meet here tomorrow at 5:00 PM. This will give those that still work at jobs a chance to do a full work day. As I said, bring a list of weapons you can acquire, or own, or better yet, just bring them with you."

The next day, all reservists reported as ordered. Capt. Herndon and Lt. Buchanan had a table set up to use as a desk. Lt. Buchanan had a ledger book and was to record all the information about guns the men had or could get. Of course, a few of the men could not read or write. These men had to verbally report the information to him.

The captain was observing the information given and from the very start was quite disappointed. He and the lieutenant could see from the start that most of the weapons listed were outdated and very obsolete. Some, they feared, would be downright useless in a real firefight and, possibly, dangerous to shoot.

It soon became apparent that some of the men did not own guns and had no access to any.

In the final list, most of the men did have weapons and some owned two or three or more. Some share or loan deals would, no doubt, have to be worked out.

Together, Elam and Sam tallied the available weapons, powder, lead, etc.

Capt. Herndon was beginning to dread the thought of ever having to engage a real enemy with his small group and their underpowered, outdated weapons. "Oh, hell," he thought, "it would probably never come to that anyhow."

He then said, "Men, don't forget that there is a real war going on! Things could get desperate very quickly. We all need to train and drill as much as possible, to be ready if needed.

"Men, this is what we need to do. Those of us who no longer have to work every day need to meet and train Monday through Friday from 10:00 AM to 6:00 PM. This will let those members that still work to spend at least an hour training with us in the evening. On Saturday and Sunday, we will all train and drill together. This is a must. If push comes to shove, we must be the best that we can be!! Men, that is our schedule. Those are my orders. Dismissed."

Elam's old wounds were aching again and he limped up the street toward the Leavenworth Saloon. Perhaps some of their excellent brandy would ease his pains and soothe his nerves.

"Damn," he thought, "If we had to fight, we would surely need God on our side. I hope He would side with us."

◆ SEVEN ◆

The Birth Of The Southern Storm

HIS NAME WAS Major Renfro Miles, C.S.A. He was twenty years old in 1863. Renfro had excelled in battle and had proven his leadership ability and daring in the heat of battle. He had risen from the rank of second lieutenant to that of major in only two years. He had been a cadet at the Virginia Military Institute (V.M.I.) at the outset of the war. The cadets had taken it upon themselves and had fought fiercely against the Yankee invaders.

Major Renfro Miles was from a fine South Kentucky family. His family's plantation was near Bowling Green, Kentucky. Renfro planned on returning there and resuming life as a gentleman should. Of course, this would have to wait until the South was victorious in this hateful war. "Ah, the beautiful thought of life at Meadowland Plantation." He loved the home place.

On this day in June 1863, he had taken leave of his troop of Confederate Cavalry to meet an old family friend at Regimental Headquarters. Major Miles had an appointment to see Gen. Braxton Bragg.

After an hour's ride, Major Miles was at Gen. Bragg's headquarters. He then told the general's aide that he was expected. Shortly, he was ushered in to Gen. Bragg's inner sanctum.

After returning the young major's salute, the general warmly greeted him. "Renfro, 'er, Major Miles, it is so good to see you. How are your mother and daddy? Well, I hope?"

"Thank you, General, for asking. All is as well as can be expected at Meadowland. Mother and Daddy speak of you fondly and often, sir. Of course, all will undoubtedly be better as soon as our Confederate forces win this war."

"I am in total agreement, Major. Never said better," replied Gen. Bragg. "Major, may I inquire if this visit is social or military in nature?"

"Of course, sir, I feel that what I have to say could be of the utmost importance to the Confederate cause."

"Very well, Major. Let's hear your thoughts."

"Gen. Bragg, I have devised a tactic and plan that I feel sure you would agree with. Sir, as we all know, the damnable Yankee forces have been invading our territory all too often. They are doing great damage, and demoralizing our citizens. I propose that, with your permission, sir, I could finish organizing a select group of volunteers to invade Union territory north of the Ohio River. The purpose would be to demoralize, disturb the Yankees, and to 'raise hell in general' plainly said, sir. To give them a taste of their own medicine, of course, at the same time we would be acquiring financial backing for our cause and also much needed remount horses for our gallant troops. Also, my plan has another phase."

The general said, "Major Miles, while I appreciate your fervor, we are not currently in a position to risk a great number of men. Also, as you must realize, once we invaded north of the Ohio River, we are not presently in a position to occupy and hold such territory."

"Yes, sir, I realize the truth of that, but my plan does not call for all that many men. We would have no thoughts of occupation and, as I said, my plan could well have another reward besides acquiring funds, remount horses and generally disrupting the Damn Yankees' tranquility."

"Very well, Major. Before we discuss this further, how many

of our troops would you envision for this action? If very many men were needed, it would be out of the question with no further discussion."

"Sir, please hear me out. I am confident I can do this mission with only 62 men besides myself. Also, General, I have already handpicked an elite group of volunteers from my command in the event that you were to approve and authorize this mission. Also, sir, if only four men were transferred from each of 15 other units, my old command would be at near full strength in my absence and the other 15 units would not be noticeably under-manned."

The general replied, "Very well, Major Miles, the 62 men could be arranged for, but I feel that this would still be too few men to accomplish much. Is there more to your plan?"

"Yes, sir, much more," said the major. "Gen. Bragg, the key element of my plan is to arm and equip my men so that they would have the firepower of a group many times their actual number. In addition to making 63 men equivalent to 400 to 500 Union troops armed in the standard manner, just think of the shock effect a super, well-armed unit such as ours would have on our enemy. Think how the word would spread!"

"Major," said Gen. Bragg, "As far as the Confederate Army is concerned, your troops are already quite well-armed. As you know, standard issue, per man, is one each .52 caliber, single shot, breech loading Sharps Carbine, one each .44 caliber six shot revolver type pistol and one standard cavalry saber."

"Sir, with all due respect, the standard arms you list are adequate for a standard battle. However, to accomplish my proposed mission, my men need to have the ultimate in weapons and firepower. We will most likely end up against far superior numbers of Union troops, thus we would need a high rate of fire to come through. Added to this, we need extreme firepower also for its 'shock value' and psychological effect."

"Well then," said Gen. Bragg, "what type of weapons do you have in mind, Major?"

"Sir, I propose that the standard cavalry saber be left behind. In its place, each trooper would be equipped with an extra .44 caliber Colt, six shot revolver, also one extra loaded cylinder for each revolver. This would make for much faster reloading, just change from an empty cylinder to a loaded one in a heated situation."

"What else would you need, Major?"

"Even further, I want to leave the single shot Sharps carbine behind and in its place equip each man with one of the latest and best repeating rifles available. The one with the least shot capacity is the 4 shot .56 caliber Colt revolving rifle, up to the one with the potential capacity of 16 shots, the .44 caliber Henry repeating rifle."

"Damn, Major, we don't have that many of the ultra modern arms available and, furthermore, I don't even know where to start looking for them. Do you have any ideas?"

"Well, sir," said the major, "I have been doing some work in the direction of procuring weapons. Five of my men already carry two Colt .44 caliber revolvers. This would mean that we would need 58 Colt .44 caliber revolvers, plus 126 extra cylinders to be carried loaded, for faster, easier reloading when needed. My sources tell me that these revolvers and cylinders are available at our Selma, Alabama arsenal. I have also learned that the Confederate arsenal at Macon, Georgia has 22 of the tube feed .52 caliber Spencer repeating carbines with 36 extra tube magazines. They also have a fairly large supply of the cartridges that this weapon uses. I am told that the Spencer carbines, etc., are captured weapons and still in same as new condition.

"Sir, would you be able to procure these weapons for my men, should you approve this mission?"

"Yes, Major. If these weapons are still among us, I can and will arrange for them to be issued to your unit."

"General, my Daddy, Col. Miles, is currently working to acquire some more very modern weapons through private channels and at our family's expense. Some of these weapons should be arriving at Meadowland Plantation soon, according to his most recent letter."

"Major, your daddy is a patriot and a true southern gentleman. He is also one of the finest old soldiers I have ever served with.

Major Miles, I am leaning toward approving your proposed mission. You did mention another possible reward coming from this mission?"

"Yes, sir, here is the rest of my plan. Besides our standard cavalry mounts, I will need one medium sized pack horse. This pack horse will be to carry the explosives for what possibly could be the most important part of our mission. Two of my men are explosive/demolition experts. The pack horse will be their responsibility.

In brief, the overall plan is this. We will ferry across the Ohio River from near Cloverport, Kentucky, to a landing near Tobinsport, Indiana. Then our raid starts. We will terrorize the former county seat at Rome, Indiana. while at the same time acquiring funds for the support of the Southern cause. Of course, along the way, we will destroy whatever facilities that we deem supportive to the Union war effort. We will repeat this course of action at every town and village along the way—Derby, Dexter, Rono, and Alton, Indiana, then on to Freedonia and up to Leavenworth, Indiana. Leavenworth has more wealth and industry. We plan to really change their way of life there. From Leavenworth on we would start 'liberating' all the good saddle horses we can find to bring back as Confederate Calvary mounts. When we reach a place known as Tobacco Landing, just upriver from Mauckport, Indiana, we plan to ferry back across the Ohio River.

Sir, what could be the best and most important part of the mission would start at Tobacco Landing. The two demolition men and the pack horse laden with explosives would separate from the main force there. They will only be a few miles from Jeffersonville, Indiana, their place of interest. At Jeffersonville is the Howard Boat Works. Howard is vital to the Union war effort as they make gunboats for the Union Navy. Their gunboats are playing hell with our forces on the Mississippi River. Although the Boat Works is well guarded, it can be blown.

I figure that by the time we cross back into Kentucky, there will be Federal troops in pursuit of us. Hopefully, the two men and three horses will not be noticed and/or followed. If the demolition men do a wide circle and come down to the Boat Works from the north, they would have a very good chance of being successful. What do you think of the plan, Gen. Bragg?"

"Major Miles, I like your plan and will approve it. I will see that the proper orders are cut as soon as possible. I will also have Headquarters Supply begin procuring the weapons you requested, plus more if they can be found.

Renfro, I have one simple request and this is it. If your men do make it to the Howard Boat Works and blow it, I insist that they leave a Confederate flag at the scene of destruction. Then, there will be no doubt that it was the work of our men."

"Yes, sir, I will see to that very important detail."

"Major Miles, I suggest that you return to your command and inform your men that they have my full support and blessing and that I wish them all good luck. The Confederacy wishes them the best.

"Then, Major, after informing your men, I'd like for you to take a few days leave and visit your family at Meadowland Plantation. Be sure and tell your daddy that I remember him as a very gracious host and a good soldier.

"It might be that Col. Miles has by now acquired those mentioned weapons for your men. On your return to duty report back to me and we will finalize the arrangements for your mission."

Major Miles thanked Gen. Bragg and was about to depart.

Gen. Bragg asked, "By the way, Major, have you thought of a good name for your unit yet?"

"No, sir, I have not."

"It seems to me that 'The Southern Storm' would be appropriate."

"The Southern Storm it will be, sir."

The Major thanked Gen. Bragg once more, saluted and left.

It would be good to be back at Meadowland, even if only for a few days.

• Eight •

Equipping And Training The Reserves

AT THE NEXT meeting of the Home Guard Reserves, the men assembled with whatever weapons they could come up with. Some came empty-handed. A few had two or three guns. Capt. Herndon had a small collection of guns, all in good condition. Buford Beasley had several rather nice guns as he was an avid hunter and gun fancier.

On inspecting two of the old Model 1816 .69 caliber smoothbore muskets, Lt. Buchanan remarked, "Damn, these two old guns could be more dangerous to the shooter than the shootee. Private Silverstein, would you see if you could help these?"

"Yes, sir," replied Jacob, "I'll save 'em if they can be saved." Jacob, the jeweler turned gunsmith, would give it his best.

The weapons, for the most part, were a mismatched collection of very obsolete weapons.

The tally of weapons was very mixed. The unit had a grand total of 36 long guns of various type and calibers, two old cavalry type single shot pistol carbines and, in all, 9 revolver pistols, various makes and calibers.

"Oh, great," thought the captain, "for 21 men, that would break down to two weapons per man plus five to spare. And, to boot, enough different calibers and types to make supply one big, big problem."

The inventory of weapons was as follows:

	MODEL	CALIBER	NAME	#
A.	Model 1816	69	Smoothbore Musket - Flintlock	7
B.	Model 1816	69	Smoothbore Musket - Percussion Cap Lock	11
C.	Model 1841	54	Mississippi Rifle - Percussion	6
D.	Model 1854	52	Sharps Breech Load Rifle - Percussion	2
E.	Model 1843	52	Hall Breech Load Carbine - Percussion	4
F.	Model 1854	52	Sharps Breech Load Carbine - Percussion	3
G.	Old	10 gauge	British -Double Barrel (34") Shot Gun	1
H.	Old	8 gauge	U.S. - Double Barrel (36") Shotgun	1
I.	Model 1855	58	Muzzle Ld. Single Shot Springfield Pistol Carbines	2
J.	Model 1851	44	Colt Walker - 6 Shot Revolvers	4
K.	Near New	44	Starr Army Revolver - 6 Shot	2
L.	Late Model	36	Whitney Navy Revolver - 6 Shot	2
M.		44	English-Kerr Revolver - 5 Shot	1
N.	Late Model	44	Colt Revolving Rifle - 6 Shot	1

These were the weapons they had and these were all they could acquire at the time. Capt. Herndon and Lt. Buchanan agreed that it was a nightmare of a mix and that the men would need to be cross-trained in the use of this variety of weapons.

Also, they saw that they were not overly supplied with ammunition. They would have to figure it out and do the best they could with what they had.

Capt. Herndon said, "Now, men, normally when a group of volunteers is organized, one of the first things to do is to drill and train in military customs. This includes the Manual of Arms, military courtesy, close order drill and marching. After that would come actual weapons training, followed by training on the rifle range and marksmanship skills. We will have to start our training differently!

"As I look over the information on our unit's enlistment roster, I can see that the first thing in our training should, and will, be intense training in the use of military hand signals, the army's version of 'sign language.' Even though we are only a group of 21 men, if there ever was an outfit that needed hand signals, this is it."

Elam continued, "We have three members who speak their own ethnic tongues better than English, one member who can barely speak English, two or more who could easily slip into other tongues when excited. There are several more who speak different dialects of English and all this is to say nothing of some of us who may not hear too well, due to reasons of age or whatever.

"We must all be able to understand one another one way or another. It could mean success or failure, or life or death. We will learn army hand signals. We will be sign talkers when needed. The first sergeant will start off by dividing us into groups, one in each group who knows hand signals well enough to train the others."

Lt. Buchanan said, "First Sergeant, be sure to keep Privates Armstrong and Takaguchi in the same group! It's for sure that George is the only one who can communicate with Hibachi at all in Japanese and I believe that is limited."

"Yes, sir, I'll see to it."

The captain then explained that at least an hour and half would be spent every day on hand signals training, 'til all were proficient at this needed skill.

Lt. Buchanan then said, "Men, the next order of business after the hand signal training will be training in marching as a unit, Manual of Arms, close order drill and so on. It is a fact that some of our group have disabilities. Those that are physically unable to march and drill will just have to sit on the sidelines, watch and observe and learn. There is no shame in this. We are still all one outfit, but just a little different kind of outfit."

He then read the following names, "Cpl. Weathers, Pvt. Martin—you two may just observe. I know Cpl. Weathers is still not at full strength after pneumonia; Pvt. Martin's foot slows him down. Also, Pvt. Beasley, I know you move a little slow. If you don't feel like marching, just observe. It's your call. It's up to you."

"Lieutenant, I believe I'll just sit with the other two, no need of me slowing down the rest."

The Leavenworth Home Guard Reserve proceeded to march and drill, two officers, 16 men and three men on the sidelines. It started to jell after a couple of drills. The unit was coming together.

Next came weapons training. Again, the men were divided into smaller groups, making sure that an experienced man was teaching those who were inexperienced. The variety of different weapons was a big problem. Cross-training was a 'must' as every man needed to know how to load and fire all the different weapons. Obviously, the need for these skills could likely come on short notice.

Capt. Herndon was proud of his men's grasp of new skills. They were eager to learn and were learning quickly.

At the next drill, First Sgt. Wildman made the following announcement, "Now, men, every man in our group has had some experience with firing guns, with three exceptions. Pvt. Tad Martin is a school teacher and has never fired a gun. Pvt. Hibachi Takaguchi also has never fired a gun. I guess pearl divers

don't shoot oysters. Also, Pvt. Lemuel Moore has never been per-
mitted to use a gun. This is going to change as of now. You three
men go with Sergeant Bratton and Pvt. Baysinger. They will take
you three and, in short order, will turn you into riflemen. Your
teachers are some of the best."

Sgt. Bratton, Pvt. Baysinger and the three beginner riflemen
were given arms and ammunition and they proceeded toward
the cliffs.

Sgt. Bratton placed some old bottles and tin cans at 50 ft.,
100 ft., and 150 ft. distance. The base of the cliffs would be their
shooting range backstop, being mostly dirt.

With old Private Baysinger demonstrating the art of 'squeez-
ing' the trigger instead of pulling or jerking it, the three soon
caught on.

Next, Baysinger showed them how to aim and hold your breath
at the trigger squeeze.

In sight of two hours, Sgt. Bratton and Pvt. Baysinger had the
three trainees shooting better than expected. They were learning
to shoot on the old Model 1816, .69 caliber, smoothbore cap lock
muskets. These old relics kick like a mule and they were man-
sized weapons.

Pvt. Hibachi was nearly knocked on his rear from the kick of
the recoil, but he soon learned to 'lean into it' when firing and
did better. He was a small man, but not weak. He was starting to
hit the targets quite well.

Pvt. Lemuel Moore turned out to be the best marksman in the
first shooting session. Sgt. Bratton remarked that, "Lemuel had
the makings of becoming a damn good shot."

Pvt. Tad Martin could see from the start that guns would never be the love of his life. However, he did hang in there and hit a
few targets. He could see that shooting was something he had to
learn. He did wonder though, how a man could ever come to like
anything that kicked him so brutally in the shoulder.

After the second session with the three beginners, Sgt. Bratton and Pvt. Baysinger agreed they were ready to shoot with the rest of the men.

That evening, the whole group went out to the base of the cliffs. With axes, hoes and shovels, they all worked at quickly building a makeshift rifle range.

Tomorrow, just after hand signal training and march and drill, they would all start training at the range.

By now, the Leavenworth Home Guard Reserve was starting to look and act like an honest to God military unit. They were learning the necessary skills fast. Capt. Herndon was quite proud of his men and he showed it.

The group made an impressive sight. Two men wearing partial Mexican War era uniforms, four men wearing current Union Army uniforms, one wearing his old Indiana Militia Cavalry style hat, while the rest wore their usual everyday garb. The one common thread was the bright red bandanas worn around each man's neck, with the captain and the lieutenant wearing bright yellow bandanas. By this means, you could at least tell that they were part of the same group.

Capt. Elam Herndon had just had a good laugh. He had just learned that one of the wags in the regular Home Guard had dubbed the Reserves as "Herndon's Hope." "Oh, hell," Elam chuckled, "We have to be called something."

That night, the two officers and the two sergeants held a meeting for the purpose of tallying the unit's store of ammunition. It was bad enough to be short on weapons, but to be short on ammunition for them was even worse.

After totaling up their store of powder, lead, etc., they quickly realized they were in shorter supply than first thought.

The captain then said, "Men, we just do not have enough ammo to have everyone firing at the rifle range. For one thing, the bullets and balls for the odd ball weapons, like the .36 caliber

Navy revolvers, the old .58 caliber pistol carbines, and some of the different revolvers made in England, take some very different ammo. Does anyone have any ideas?"

First Sgt. Wildman said, "Sir, why not do it this way? Out of the twenty-one of us, ten men are experienced riflemen. These ten are capable of firing all our different weapons and do it well. This would leave eleven men who do need target practice. I suggest we let these eleven men fire while the rest of us act as teachers and coaches, mostly one on one."

The captain said, "Good thought, Sergeant. If we waste too much powder and lead on training, we might be left defenseless if push ever came to shove. Oh, I know that we probably will never be much more than 'baby sitters for the town,' but I'd rather be prepared than look like a bunch of fools later."

"Captain, I have a thought or two?"

"Yes, Lt. Buchanan, go ahead. Let's hear it."

"Captain, it looks to me like we have more .69 caliber musket balls than any other lead. We are not as short on powder as we are on lead. I suggest that we let the eleven trainees practice and fire with the old Model 1816 .69 caliber smoothbore muskets. Then, we could have them fire just a few rounds through the other rifles and carbines, just enough to use them in a pinch. As for our mix of pistols and revolvers, we could just let them 'dry fire' these, as we cannot spare practice ammo for these."

Capt. Herndon agreed and said, "Do you sergeants agree with this plan?"

All agreed; they now had a plan.

"Yes, Sgt. Bratton, do you have something else?"

"Sir, I think I may know how we can come up with some more musket balls and bullets, but it ain't gonna be real easy. We might could go door to door and see if folks would donate their fishing tackle sinkers and also any doorstop weights. Lots of them are made of lead. This being a river town, there are lots of fishing sinkers and then sinkers are used on the drags they use to drag for mussel shells."

"Good thinking, Sergeant. I'll bet it will work. Tomorrow, after our day of training, let's all fan out and go door to door and just see how much lead we can collect?? But, you know, that's only half the battle. Then, we have to figure out a way to melt lead and mold balls and bullets."

"Here's a thought," replied the lieutenant, "Chet, er, I mean Pvt. Chet Hatfield is an apprentice blacksmith with Otis Callahan at his blacksmith shop. I know Otis is a Regular Home Guard member and for now is training all day every day, but Otis would probably let Chet unlock the shop and run the forge to melt lead for us. I'm sure we can find enough bullet molds around town to start production."

"Very good thinking Lt. Buchanan, and the rest of you too. It's amazing what some far out thinking can accomplish sometimes."

The next morning Pvt. Buford Beasley showed up with a nice team of big Belgian horses and a big box bed Owensboro farm wagon. He said, "Men, it's for us to use 'til we no longer need it. I figure that when we march out to the rifle range, some of us sort of stove up and not in too good of shape can ride instead of march."

"Good thinking, Buford, and very kind of you. Thanks a bunch," said Elam.

So eighteen men went marching and three men went riding, Pvt. Tad Martin, Cpl. Milo Weathers and Pvt. Buford Beasley, as driver.

At the rifle range, the captain explained to the men about their unit's ammo situation and about the plan on who would actually be firing at targets.

Before the men were paired up with their shooting coaches/ trainers, the captain said, "Is there anyone besides the ones I read off of the roster that feels they need to 'brush up a little' on their shooting?"

Pvt. Dan Lyon said, "Well, Captain, maybe I better practice shoot some. I can shoot, but it has been awhile."

With a broad smile, Capt. Herndon quipped, "Hell now, Dan, it ain't been all that long since the war of 1812 and he gave 81 year old Pvt. Lyon a nod. OK, Private, I know you are a good shot, maybe a little refresher will make your shooting even better."

Quick witted old Dan came back with, "And, Captain, something else. Them there Model 1816 Springfield muskets are 'state of the art' weapons to me, especially with the upgraded cap lock firing instead of the old flintlock."

Everyone got a laugh at that. Dan did have a sense of humor.

The noise of the muskets and rifles was amplified at least ten times by the sound bouncing off of the cliffs and the continuing echoes. The report from one gun sounded like much more, like claps of thunder.

The trainees tried hard and were learning fast. Pvt. Moore and Pvt. Takaguchi were becoming good marksmen.

Just after the noon chow from the bean pot, Lt. Buchanan pulled Pvt. Lyon off of the live firing line saying, "You're good enough, Dan. Hell, there ain't no use of you getting to be a better shot than me. Why don't you go be a coach for one of the new guys?"

Pvt. Dan Lyon had regained his feel for a gun and even though he was 81, he had restored his self-confidence. Now, he would spend time sharing some of his gun knowledge with one of the "kids." He spent the rest of the day coaching 14 year old James Corbin. James was young enough to have been a great-grandson of Dan, but for now, they were fellow soldiers and friends. By quitting time, Pvt. Corbin's shooting had improved for sure. Dan Lyon was not only a good boat builder and carpenter, but a good teacher as well.

After a long day of training, drilling and shooting, the members of the Leavenworth Home Guard Reserve set about going door to door trying to get donations of lead of any type. A few people even donated their tie up weights for their buggy horses. Some of these were made of lead and weighed upwards of fifteen pounds. Pvt. Beasley followed along, driving the team and wagon to haul the donated lead. It went well. Things were looking up.

Tomorrow night, they all planned on working at the blacksmith shop melting lead and molding musket balls, rifle and pistol bullets. Of course, they would also make some double OO (ought) buckshot and number four turkey shot. The shotguns needed to be fed also.

The next day, after hand signal training and drill, etc., the Reserves headed for the shooting range, same as the day before. The difference today would be that besides just target shooting, they were going to be taught some basic tactical combat skills, or at least they would be lectured on these skills.

Capt. Herndon began, "Now, men, I know that those of you who have seen the heat of battle have already heard all this before. Those of you that ain't been there before need to listen damn close! Then again, it won't hurt you veterans a damn bit to be refreshed. It all pays the same so pay attention. We'll have more time for fun things later, we hope. Now the first sergeant will share some military wisdom with you men.

"Okay, men, I know that a lot of the close order drill, marching and stuff may seem a little silly to you new soldiers. But, trust me; there are good reasons for all of it. For one thing, you get used to doing things on 'command' at the same time, exactly. One of the best examples is that of firing on command. You know, 'Ready, Aim, Fire!!' This is very important to learn to fire on command, not before, but 'on command!' One nervous trigger finger can mess up a plan. Now as a group, we will all dry fire our weapons 'til we get to the place that all squeeze the trigger at the same time, on command 'fire.' After we all get this worked out, we will practice this with loaded weapons, 'Ready, Aim, Fire—click!' over and over."

After dry fire practice, Sgt. Wildman ordered, "Now, men, load those pieces and sight on your target. Ready, Aim, Fire!!" The cliffs echoed like a thunderstorm.

"Not bad," said the sergeant, "Almost right, but just a little ragged. A couple of you fired just a split second late. Again, load and sight on your target. Ready, Aim, Fire!! Very good, you got it right. That volley sounded very much like one giant shot. Now you have the basic idea, 'on command!!' We can't afford to expend any more ammo on this, but you now know. Remember!"

The first sergeant then said, "Okay, boys, take a break."

At which 87 year old Buford jokingly replied, "Thanks, Sarge, I ain't been called a boy in years." Buford actually was feeling younger lately, since joining the reserves with his friends. It was a good feeling to be a part of something that was as full of life as this bunch. He intended to do his part.

After a short break, Capt. Herndon began, "Now, men, I want to tell you a few things. Some I've said before, but I'll say again. Number one, if we should get in battle and the officers get put out of action and the sergeants do too, and even if the corporals were lost, just keep on fighting. Keep on trying. Just because your leaders should be killed or wounded is no reason to give up. The fact of the matter is that the privates do most of the fighting anyway!! If Sam Buchanan and I had gave up on account of lost leaders, we both would still be in Mexico, taking a long dirt nap! What I'm saying is, keep on trying.

"The next thing is this, if one of your comrades should fall and he has a better weapon than you, take it and carry on. And one more—one of the oldest and truest rules in war is this, 'You only have to have a weapon good enough to get a better one! Now, men, Lt. Buchanan has his turn at the pulpit."

"Okay, men, now you are, for the most part, shooting well enough to pass for soldiers. Now we will have Sgt. Bratton and Pvt. Baysinger demonstrate proper shooting methods and also some pretty simple, but quite necessary, tricks about sighting your weapons and allowing for differences in elevation and windage."

The men trained and practiced on these new skills 'til they got the idea.

"Now, men," said the captain, "We have come up with a make-shift way to teach you the art of shooting at and hitting moving targets. As you see out there at the 100 yard mark, we have a two gallon jug with a long ½" rope tied to the handle. We then have Cpl. Kinnaman pulling the rope from one direction and Pvt. Bay singer pulling the rope to return it to the other position. Now, make damn sure you don't shoot them. They are two of our best men. You are trying to hit the jug, okay? This exercise will let you use and practice sighting your weapon for 'windage' or as some say 'leading on your target.' This simply means that you learn to aim not directly at a moving target, but aim a bit ahead of it so your shot gets at the target when it should. If you aim directly at a moving target, you'll likely miss 'because by the time your bullet arrives, the target will have moved. Different speeds, different leads. You will learn; it takes practice. When you get this down better, we will move the moving target farther back, and then you will have to allow for elevation (you can aim higher since your bullet or ball starts to drop at greater distances) as well as windage."

The men were learning fast and, considering their very few days of training so far, they had come a long way.

This evening, the Home Guard Reservists had another fun-filled time at Callahan's Blacksmith Shop, melting lead and molding musket balls, rifle bullets and shot.

After but very few hours of sleep, they were all back for morning formation.

Again, more drill, Manual of Arms, etc., which was followed by more Army Hand Signal Training. Some wisecracking observers remarked that during the hand signal practice, the group looked much like the kids on the playground at the Louisville School for the Deaf. No matter, they could now communicate in most any situation.

After the rifle range practice, Capt. Herndon announced, "Men, we are going to have to stop live fire shooting practice. We will live fire one more day. We must save what ammunition we have just in case we would get in combat. I know this isn't likely, but we can't take a chance. Now, we will drill, practice and get more classes and lectures. We have some old soldiers that have been and done. They are no strangers to battle and all that goes with it. Now, Lt. Buchanan has some words."

"Now, men, the Army Manual of Training says that somewhere around this point, we are supposed to train in the time-honored art of hand to hand combat. Capt. Herndon and I have talked this over and, considering the ages and physical condition of most of us, this just isn't going to happen. We feel it would be for the most part a waste of time. Instead, think like this, 'If we were in combat and you were to run out of ammunition, then just think of your rifle or musket as a big heavy club.' It's better than throwing rocks."

The next day, after more drill and hand signal training, the unit moved out to the rifle range. This would be their last day of live firing, due to the ammo situation.

The captain began, "Men, second best in most things isn't too bad, but second best in a gun fight isn't for crap. Now, simmer down; think it out; draw a fine bead. Shoot as if your life counted on it. It damn well could work out that way 'fore too long."

First Sgt. Wildman then took his turn. "Now, men, just remember, these targets ain't shooting back, but when and if it comes to the real thing, that won't apply. Now straighten up and try to shoot better! And, one more thing to think about. Getting shot at, hell, that ain't no big deal. But, getting shot—that really hurts. That is a big deal. Don't forget it!!"

The hills and cliffs echoed for several seconds after the last target practice shots were fired. It sounded a lot like a bad thunderstorm.

Pvt. Martin observed, "It makes one gun sound like three or four!"

NINE

The Southern Storm Equips And Trains

AT THIS TIME in 1863, this part of Kentucky was officially in the hands of the Union Army, but mostly this was only on paper. In reality, the Confederate sympathizers outnumbered those that supported the Union cause by a margin of about three to one.

For the most part, a Confederate soldier could move through this area at will, as long as he kept a low profile and did not directly confront the Yanks.

As Major Renfro Miles rode across the Warren County line, he knew he would soon be back at home at Meadowland Plantation. It was really a good feeling. He had not been home in more than three years.

He had been away from home for nearly a year as a cadet at Virginia Military Institute when the Yankees had invaded. Now, the war was in its second year.

As Renfro rode his horse up the long winding lane to the family mansion, he was truly at peace with the world. The large old Magnolia trees that lined the road were magnificent. He marveled at the sight of pastures full of fat cattle and beautiful horses. Yes, and the many large fields of tobacco were looking very good for this time of year. Now the family home, Meadowland Mansion, was in full view. Oh, the graceful architecture, the beautiful columns, and the verandas. Then, he caught the aroma of two of the plantations main products, the good smell of curing/drying tobacco hanging in the barns and the delightful fragrance of the family distillery. The excellent bourbon whiskey made here was of the highest quality and was much in demand far and wide.

Old James was waiting at the hitching rack to greet Renfro and take his tired mount. "Welcome home, Marse Renfro. It's so very good to see you."

"Yes, James, it is very good to see you as well."

"Marse Renfro, let me take your mount, sir. I'll see that it's attended to. Your family is expecting you on the south veranda," said James.

"Thank you, James. I'm headed that way."

Old James had been one of Renfro's family's slaves for longer than Renfro had been on this earth. James was a good man and was held in high regard by all at the plantation.

Officially, old James was no longer a slave and neither were any of the other blacks at Meadowland. They had been set free by U.S. government order. However, the hard truth of the matter was that even though they had been freed and the Union Army controlled this area, they were still much the same as slaves. They had no land, very few possessions, no money and no where to go. Life was not all that bad at Meadowland Plantation. At least, they had decent food and shelter as long as they stayed on and worked.

Most of the ex-slaves had stayed on. Very few had chosen to leave and exercise their newly gained freedom just yet. Most understood that these were troubled times and there was a harsh world out there!

Renfro's mother, father and sister were waiting for him by the fountains on the South Veranda, near the rose garden. Col. Rafe Miles, wife Melissa and Renfro's sister, Virginia, all gave Renfro a warm "welcome home." They were all so glad to see him back at home and apparently in good health as well. After much hugging and greetings all around, Mother Melissa Miles said, "Son, you probably want to go to your room and freshen up after your long ride. Everything is the same in that room except for the fact that my special son has not been there in more than three long years. Welcome home, Son. Dinner will be served at the usual hour."

Renfro was quite pleased, finding a glass of his favorite whisky with a sprig of mint ready and waiting for him on the reading table in his room. Old Mandy Mae, James' wife, was a house servant and had helped look after Renfro since the day he was born. Mandy Mae was a thoughtful woman.

After a bath and a change of uniform, Renfro went with his father for a short walking tour among the many buildings at Meadowland Plantation. It all looked so good.

Renfro was not surprised to see that the farm overseer was still Rufus Dowell. Rufus greeted Renfro warmly. They had known each other for many years. Col. Miles had always said that overseer Rufus could get more results from the slaves quicker than any other overseer he had ever known. At times, Rufus Dowell was not the most pleasant of men. After a short chat they moved on to the distillery building.

At the plantation's distillery, Mr. George Carter was still the "Head Distiller," he was totally in charge of this part of the plantation and was widely known and recognized for his skill and knowledge in whiskey making. George was genuinely glad to see Renfro and after a friendly handshake welcomed him home with a small glass of his best "Kentucky Sipping Bourbon." George Carter was a master of the distiller's art and was a valuable asset to Meadowland. George was a kindly man and knew how to get top production from the blacks at the distillery without resorting to cruelty. After all, when it came to taste testing the various distillations, George had to have a diversity of taste opinions.

Renfro complimented George on the high quality of the drink and thanked him.

Col. Miles said, "Son, we have time for a short tour of the cigar making operation, then we best be getting back to the main house if we are to have time for before dinner drinks."

During the social hour on the veranda, Col. Miles said, "Son, I have good news. The arms and ammunition we spoke of has arrived from the northeast. These armaments had to be purchased through clandestine channels and at an inflated price. The main thing is that they are now in the right hands, Confederate hands, to help the Southern cause.

"Daddy, what weapons were you able to get for us?"

"Renfro, your group will now be armed with at least some of the most modern firearms made, at least twenty of your men will. We now have in our possession twenty brand new .44 caliber tubular feed, lever action Henry repeating rifles. They have a fifteen bullet capacity in the tube magazine, one round can be chambered, then one more added to the tube, thus a sixteen shot capacity before needing to reload. They shoot a new type of metallic cartridge and I have purchased enough of these to last for quite some time. In the hands of a skilled, trained rifleman, the rate of fire is limited only by the shooter's ability to lever another round and take aim. Compared to a Yankee firing a single shot, muzzle loading rifle, a good Confederate soldier could fire sixteen shots while the Yank tried to get off three aimed shots. Major Miles, what do you think?"

"Damn, Father, that's great. What did they cost?"

"Son, the going price up north is forty dollars per rifle. These had to travel south, so they cost fifty dollars each. The ammunition cost another thousand dollars."

"Father, the army has provided me no funds to reimburse you."

"Think nothing of it, Major. It's for a great cause. A toast, 'Long live the Confederacy.' Mandy Mae says it's time for dinner. Let's dine."

After a sumptuous dinner in the dining room, everyone moved to the parlor. Mrs. Melissa Miles played the piano. Virginia played the violin and George Carter accompanied them on his guitar.

Rafe Miles, Renfro and the other male guests smoked excellent handmade Meadowland cigars while sipping ever so smooth Meadowland bourbon.

Except for the war, life here was nothing short of excellent.

After an all too short two day stay at Meadowland, Major Miles headed back to his regiment's camp. The next step would be to finalize plans for the mission of "The Southern Storm."

Coming along with the major was an Owensboro wagon, pulled by two of Col. Miles' best horses. On the wagon were two of the plantations' best men and they were well-armed. In the wagon were the newly acquired Henry rifles and the ammunition for them. Along with the arms, Col. Miles had thoughtfully sent along a gift for his old friend, Gen. Braxton Bragg. In a well-padded crate was a good supply of Meadowland bourbon along with some of Meadowland's finest cigars. It's well known that "War is Hell," but aids like this can lessen the discomfort.

After unloading their precious cargo, the men bade Major Miles, "good luck and farewell" and headed back to Meadowland with the team and the wagon.

After a short rest, Major Miles was back at Gen. Bragg's headquarters to finalize plans.

Renfro was ushered into the inner sanctum, and the gift from Meadowland was well-received.

"Ah, thank you, Major. Your daddy is such a considerate man."

Renfro began, "General, I am proud to report that I am back with twenty brand new Henry rifles and much ammunition for them, compliments of Meadowland Plantation."

"Very good, Major. I also have good news. We have arranged for the arms you requested and they are being shipped your way as we speak. The two shipments from the Selma, Alabama, Confederate arsenal and the Macon, Georgia, arsenal should be at your camp in two more days. We also have an added bonus. We have located 18 Colt revolving carbines and three Colt revolving rifles, along with extra cylinders and ammo. These were found at our San Antonio, Texas arsenal and should be here no later than four more days from now. A toast to our cause, Major Miles. Salute. Long live the Confederacy."

Renfro sat down his empty glass, saluted the general smartly and left. He was in extremely high spirits. His plan was coming together.

A few days later, the handpicked volunteers of the Southern Storm were being issued their new weapons. They were to start training with them that very day. They were told that the training would be intense and vigorous.

Major Miles how had sixty-two men, extremely well-armed and quite capable of producing a monstrous rate of fire. By his best estimates, armed so well, his sixty-two men had the approximate firepower capability of four hundred fifty to five hundred Union soldiers armed with single shot weapons. There was absolutely no doubt in his mind that in this place and time, he commanded the best armed group of soldiers in the world, bar none.

Upon receiving one of the new Henry rifles, Sgt. Duval had quipped, "Good Lord, this is the kind of rifle you can load on Sunday and shoot all week!!"

There was much laughter in the ranks, but in these times, a rifle capable of being fired up to sixteen times before needing to be reloaded was truly a wonder. Besides that, the rifles worked well and were quite accurate and hard hitting.

Next, the men of the Southern Storm practiced much on changing from an empty cylinder in the revolver type weapons, to an already loaded spare cylinder. They finally got it down to the point they could make the change out in the matter of a few seconds.

In the new Spencer repeating rifles, the cartridges were fed to the chamber by way of a seven shot tube magazine which was in the stock of the weapon (from the butt end). They had extra tubes kept loaded so they also improved their skills in replacing empty tubes with loaded ones.

Although each trooper had two Colt revolvers, for the most part it was not practical to use a revolver in each hand. Unless your horse was trained to turn by knee pressure from the rider, if moving, you were not in control of your mount. However, Major Miles' reasoning was partly that just the appearance of a man armed with not just one revolver, but two of them, added to the shock value and also made a greater show of force. Of course, in a fire fight, a man could change from one empty revolver to a loaded one a bit quicker than he could change cylinders. The process of reloading an empty percussion type revolver's cylinder was rather slow business.

Major Miles was then provided with several detailed maps of the area to be invaded. This would be the first incursion on the State of Indiana. He felt sure that the people of Indiana would not appreciate the Southern Storm coming through and would probably be inhospitable. Renfro chuckled at the thought. Frankly, he didn't give a damn!!

The unit was issued plenty of ammunition, but very little in the way of food rations. They would be foraging or living off the land.

A special courier arrived from headquarters with two sets of saddlebags and gave them to Major Miles. The bags were stuffed full of Confederate military script (C.S.A. Army money). Most of the script was in large denominations. Of course, it was an impressive looking piece of paper and was imprinted with the key statement, "Backed by the full faith and credit of the Confederate States of America."

There were orders in the bags of script that no one was to take anything from anyone in the course of this invasion without paying for anything taken with a fair value in this Confederate script. Gen. Bragg states in the order that, "In no way shall we be seen other than as honorable officers and men, and not plunderers. We will pay fair market value for all things furnished to us!!" (In Confederate script, of course.)

Major Miles then put Second Lt. Clay in charge of the paper money and designated Lt. Clay as his Finance Officer in charge of procurement activities.

The Southern Storm was nearly ready to head north as soon as they received the rest of the explosives needed for the Jeffersonville phase.

Word came that the Southern sympathizers near Cloverport, Kentucky, would be ready and prepared to ferry the Southern Storm across the Ohio River to near Tobinsport, Indiana. They had three old flatboats and figured it would take two trips per boat to complete the crossing.

Major Miles and all the group were eager to start and could hardly wait for the time of departure.

Shortly, the special demolition explosives arrived and were secured on the pack horse.

Major Miles had a meeting with his staff and ordered that anyone they met en route going through Kentucky would be told a cover story. They were to tell, if asked, that they were on a two fold mission, to search for Confederate soldiers who had deserted and also were just involved in maneuvers, nothing special.

The Southern Storm, although part of the Confederate Army of Tennessee, would be on their own after crossing into Kentucky.

Kentucky was a "divided state" in the war and alliances varied from area to area.

It was already well-known that the Confederacy was in the process of trying to set up part of Kentucky as the "Confederate

State of Kentucky." The plan was for Bowling Green to be the new state capital.

Col. Rafe Miles had confided in his son, back at Meadowland, that the new Governor of the new State might well be named Rafe Miles. It could well come true, for he did have friends in high places.

Major Miles turned his thoughts from home and back to the business at hand. Right now, he was trying to move his unit, quietly as possible through Kentucky without making waves or attracting much attention.

Moving a unit of Confederate soldiers through Kentucky at this time in history had its problems, but was not all that difficult. More than most people realized, Kentucky was a very divided state. Though not a widely publicized fact in the North, the Confederate Flag contained a star representing the "Confederate State of Kentucky." This was done even though Kentucky was never officially a Confederate state.

Southern troops escorting the "new government to be of the Confederate State of Kentucky" were on their way to Bowling Green, Kentucky, to set up the new government back in October 1862. They were met by the large force of retreating soldiers under Gen. Braxton Bragg's command who were retreating from their recent loss at the Battle of Perryville, Kentucky.

The entourage of "officials to be" was turned around. They went back south with Bragg's forces. Though their plans were put on hold for awhile, they really never gave up on the idea of a "Confederate State of Kentucky."

Even in May of 1863, with Nashville, Tennessee in Union control, there were still very large numbers of people in Kentucky supporting the Southern cause. Thus, it was not terribly hard for the Southern Storm to move through Kentucky and make few waves.

TEN

The Home Guard Must Leave; Reserves Stay!

AROUND 2:00 PM on this day, Leavenworth Home Guard Major Woodbury hurriedly made his way down to the river port wharf house where Elam Herndon was working. He had important news of recent developments.

"Elam, 'er Capt. Herndon, I just got word in the morning mail! The Leavenworth Home Guard is being ordered to active duty as of midnight today! We are ordered to be fully-equipped and combat ready at no later than tonight at midnight."

"What then, Major?"

"We are going to pull out at 5:00 AM tomorrow, all 80 of us and our horses and our six pound cannons."

"Where is your unit being sent to and for how long?"

"We are going to Jeffersonville, Indiana, by land. There has been an attempt to sabotage the Howard Boat Works, where they are making gunboats for the Union Navy. The Rebs weren't successful this time, but more security is needed there. Elam, I have no way of knowing how long we will be gone. It could be for quite awhile.

"Now, Capt. Herndon, I have also been ordered to order you and the men of the Leavenworth Home Guard Reserve to active duty for an indefinite period of time. As of midnight tonight, you and your unit will be responsible for the security and defense of Leavenworth, including its citizens, homes, businesses and industries. Capt. Herndon, you will be in charge here. You call it like you see it. I know that the town will be in good hands."

"Thanks for your confidence, Major. We will take care of the home front while you and your men are gone."

"Capt. Herndon, I know that your unit is still short on powder, lead and weapons. You have already scoured the area nearly clean of these things. I have put together a small amount of powder, lead and caps for you and your men. It's not much, but it's all we dare to part with. Come on. Let's go get it. It's at John Bahr's warehouse. Also, I am donating one of my personal weapons to your group. It's an 1841 Mississippi rifle, .58 cal., percussion, and it's a real straight shooter."

"Thanks very much, Major. We may need all the help we can get."

They proceeded to Bahr's warehouse and Elam shook hands with Major Woodbury and wished him well.

Elam then went to the blacksmith shop and the signal was given by a series of distinctive beats on the large anvil. Around 20 minutes later, most of the members of the Leavenworth Home Guard Reserve were assembled. Buford Beasley was there about 15 minutes after that and he reported that Jim Running Deer would be there shortly. Buford had seen Jim in a boat on the river and Jim had hollered that he was rowing straight for the Leavenworth dock. Within an hour from the time the alarm was sounded all twenty-one of the Home Guard Reserve were standing tall. It was now approximately 3:00 PM.

The citizen soldiers stood formation in two ranks, with one rank of ten men and one rank of nine men. Lt. Buchanan called the order, "Attention!" and reported, "Captain, the unit is complete and assembled as ordered. All men are present and accounted for!"

"Very well, Lieutenant. At ease men and give me all of your attention. I was just informed about an hour ago that the regular Home Guard unit has been ordered to active duty effective at midnight tonight. They will be pulling out at 5:00 AM for an unknown period of time. Their first deployment will be at Jeffersonville, Indiana. They have no idea how long they will be gone. As of midnight tonight, we of the Leavenworth Home Guard Reserve are being ordered to active duty and will remain on active duty until we are ordered otherwise. From tonight at midnight, we will be responsible for the safety of the town, all its citizens and their possessions, as well as all businesses and industries. At midnight, we will assemble with all our equipment at the wharf house. You men go and notify your families, employers, and all concerned of the situation. Report back here at midnight as ordered. Dismissed!"

At midnight, though some were only half awake, the Leavenworth Home Guard Reserve assembled as ordered. They were all armed, equipped, as best they were able, and anxious to hear what their duties would be.

Capt. Herndon began, "Men, there is no special crisis or matter of urgency as of right now. However, that could change very quickly. As I have said before, we need to be the best we can be and be as ready as we can be. This means that at least for a few days or weeks, we will train all day every day.

One of our first concerns is that of seeing to the security of the town. I am sure that the news of the Home Guard leaving will spread like wildfire. This, of course, is likely to attract thieves and looters if they think that our town is unguarded. Of course, we will have Sheriff Cummins, but he is laid up from getting throwed from his horse last month. He will be at the jail part of the time, but not able to do much. His two deputies are Home Guard members and will be leaving at 5:00 AM with the rest.

"Starting now, Sgt. Wildman will pick two man teams to start patrolling the riverfront and town in two hour shifts during night time hours. These men will be armed and are under my orders to shoot anyone attempting to loot or steal, no questions asked!! The Leavenworth Home Guard Reserve will from now on be referred to and known by its initials, that being the L.H.G.R. This will save time and ink and paper. Understand?"

"Yes, sir," was the answer in unison.

"Now, men, at 5:00 AM, the Home Guard will be pulling out and we will be standing in formation to give them a proper send-off. Go try to get a little rest and be back here by 4:30 AM. Dismissed."

At 4:30 AM, the L.H.G.R. reassembled as ordered. At 5:00 AM, the 80 man Home Guard unit was mounted and ready to pull out. Major Woodbury gave the order for his mounted troops to form a column of threes and prepare to move out.

Capt. Herndon called his men to attention and ordered them to "present arms," the traditional military salute given when men are under arms.

The 80 man unit made an impressive sight as they moved out of town in a large cloud of dust accompanied by the thundering sound of horses' hoofs and the rumbling and clanking of the two caissons and the two 6-pound cannons. In a few minutes, they were out of sight and hearing. A new deathly quiet settled in on Leavenworth.

But, this was not to be for very long. Capt. Herndon said, "Men, listen up. We have much to do so we will be starting shortly. Right now we are, more or less, just babysitting the town, but this could easily change and change very fast. So, we are going to get as prepared as possible for whatever might come our way. For openers, we are still not overly blessed with powder and lead."

Sgt. Bratton said, "Captain, maybe we should fan out across town and hereabouts knocking on doors and see if we can get some more donations of powder, lead and such. I know we went around asking before, but maybe we might find a little more."

"Good idea, Sergeant. See to it and detail the men for it."

After a four hour campaign of begging for supplies, the men of the L.H.G.R. had accumulated a fair amount of supplies of varying types and amounts. The owner of the stone quarry had donated a 20 pound drum of black powder. They also gave some scrap lead.

The team of horses and the wagon which Buford had loaned to the unit was coming in very handy in the collection of the needed supplies.

The elderly Widow Hartford donated two of her late husband's old guns, one being a double barrel 10 gauge shotgun and the other a model 1816 smoothbore musket. Jacob Silverstein had to work on both guns, but made them operable.

There were some more small amounts of powder, lead, caps and patches donated by a caring, generous community.

Otis Callahan, the blacksmith who had just left with the Home Guard unit had left a key to the blacksmith shop with Chet Hatfield. Very soon the shop was opened and the forge was being used to melt lead. Again, the L.H.G.R. members had a fun-filled evening of molding various types of bullets, musket balls and shotgun shot.

The next day, Dr. Bowman's widow, Alice Bowman, contacted Capt. Herndon. Though not really a doctor, she was unofficially acting as the town's doctor. She was actually a nurse who was officially one year shy of graduating nursing school. However, her many years of assisting her doctor husband had broadened her knowledge of medical skills.

Nurse Bowman volunteered her medical services to Capt. Herndon's unit and promised to respond if and when needed. Further, she had arranged for her daughter, Susan, to help as a nurse along with Tillie Jefferson, Moses' wife.

Capt. Herndon was grateful that Nurse Bowman had organized this small team of medical personnel. He understood quite well that more often than not in this time in history, a wounded soldier often had no other choice than to treat his own wounds, and then only if able to do so.

The men of the L.H.G.R., or "Herndon's Hope" as a local Home Guard wag had dubbed the unit, was training every day and coming together in a short period of time. Their drills were going quite well, near precision—much smoother and better than Elam and Sam had ever dared to hope.

The typical training day was: a little over an hour of training in military hand signals which the group was learning quite well. This was followed by training and practice in the Manual of Arms, lasting about an hour. This was usually followed by a period of close order drill and marching. They were now starting to look and act like real soldiers.

Most days, there was a lecture or two given on military tactics, usually given by one of the sergeants, which covered some of the finer points of war. These included overlapping fields of fire, firing at moving targets, firing at targets at greater distances and learning to detect and decide where the rifle was that had just been fired in your direction.

The usual routine was then for the unit to proceed over to the rifle range for live firing practice. The team of Belgian horses with Buford, Milo and Tad on the wagon followed the other eighteen men marching at right shoulder arms in a column of twos.

At the rifle range, things were going quite well. While some of the men had become pretty good at hitting what they aimed at, others would only be fair shots. But, remember, some had never shot a gun before and they had come far.

The target shooting at moving targets (the jugs pulled by ropes) was also progressing very well. In fact, jugs were starting to be in short supply. Many jugs had been wasted and there was now a large pile of broken pieces of jugs at the left side of the rifle range.

By now, jugs were not the only thing getting in short supply. Quite a lot of powder and lead had been used up in the live range firing. The captain and lieutenant decided to suspend live firing target practice.

Capt. Herndon said, "Men, you have all done well enough at marksmanship, some damn well. I'm proud of you all. For now, we need to conserve what ammunition we have left just in case we would need it for the real thing. Right now, we are more or less just babysitting the town, but if we have to do more, we damn well can. Men, we are about as ready as we can be for most anything that might come our way. The most important thing is that now we can function as a unit. I can see that you men take pride in your outfit and I just want to tell you all that I take pride in the fact that I'm part of it too!"

Life in Leavenworth was moving at a much slower pace now than it had before the war had started. Little by little—by ones, twos and small groups—men had left to serve their country. Some were to never return. Some, only their remains had returned. While others had returned maimed, crippled or disabled in one way or another. Now, with the 80 man Home Guard unit gone, the town seemed more or less lifeless. Even the twenty-one men of the L.H.G.R. were now not working at their normal occupations which added even more to the sense of emptiness of the town.

Life in Leavenworth goes on, but at a much slower pace—you could say "at a crawl."

Capt. Elam Herndon knew full well all that was expected of him and his men. He felt an awesome sense of responsibility and took it very seriously. The town was, for the most part, at this time, filled with relatively helpless people. These included children, mothers, elderly men and women. Some men were disabled by the current war and for other reasons. Besides this, there were all the possessions and means of livelihood that were precious to everyone.

Yes, the town did seem empty and more or less lifeless, but life did go on.

The hard reality of all this was that, for now, the only real security or protection that this community could count on to safeguard them from whatever might come was a pitifully small group of volunteers, with all their own problems. Added to this was the fact that they were poorly armed, for the most part, with antique weapons.

In any case, the men of the Leavenworth Home Guard Reserve were willing to try!

⋆ Eleven ⋆

The Southern Storm Crosses The Ohio

MAJOR MILES AND the Southern Storm had made it to a point near Cloverport, Kentucky, without coming in contact with any Union Army forces. They had purposely tried to keep a low profile by traveling on back roads and lesser traveled routes. Their aim was to not create havoc at any point in Kentucky, but rather to go for the shock effect of surprising the Yanks on the Indiana side of the Ohio River and carry out their mission of spreading terror, creating general confusion and obtaining good cavalry remount horses for the Confederacy. If they were able to acquire financial backing for their cause, so much the better!

At a prearranged point just above Cloverport, Kentucky, at the Ohio River, the Southern Storm met a group of Southern sympathizers as planned. There were three old flatboats tied at the bank. Each flat boat had a wooden loading ramp to load the horses on board and also to unload at the opposite shore. The boats were only large enough to carry ten or twelve men and horses per trip. It would take two round trips for each of the three flatboats to ferry the Confederates across the Ohio River. Each flatboat had several long oars and a few long poles to propel them across the river. There was also an eighteen foot skiff boat with three sets of oars and a rope for towing should it become necessary.

It was nearly dusk by the time the crossing was completed. The operation had not been seen by anyone to spread an alarm and had gone smoothly and quietly.

Major Miles thanked the flatboat men and they soon drifted downriver toward the Kentucky side.

The major and his men kept a low profile that night and camped quietly as possible along the Ohio River, just a few miles above Tobinsport, Indiana. No cooking fires were built so as not to give away their position. The tired men ate cold rations and rested from a hard day's ride.

Early tomorrow, they were going to strike unsuspecting Rome, Indiana.

Promptly at 7:00 AM, the Southern Storm broke camp, mounted up and formed a column of twos. With as much quiet as was possible with 63 men and 64 horses, they proceeded toward Rome.

Rome, Indiana, had been the county seat of Perry County, but just a few years before, in '59, the seat of government had been moved to a new location at Cannelton, Indiana. The former court house at Rome was now being used as a school, known as the Rome Academy. There were three stores in town, a Post Office, a small bank along with a hotel, blacksmith shop, two churches and a one room school. Of course, there was a wharf boat and river landing close by.

Rome did have a company of Home Guard troops, but the members were not expecting trouble and were scattered over a rather wide area, going about their usual civilian occupations. In short, the town was caught off guard.

According to plan, Major Miles gave a signal for the column of twos to separate just at the edge of the village, one column going left and the other going right. In very short order, they had formed a circle of heavily armed mounted troops around the main part of the small village of Rome.

Up to this point, none of the townspeople had really caught on to what was happening.

Major Miles signaled and all of his troops fired their weapons, as in a massive rifle salute. They all fired three rounds each as rapidly as possible, then ceased fire and held their weapons at the ready.

This thunderous round of fire was designed as their calling card, to announce their presence and to draw attention to the fact that each and every man of the Southern Storm was armed with a repeating rifle. The dramatic arrival and announcement of the Southern Storm worked quite well.

The streets were soon filled with terrified people and Major Miles announced, "Let me have your attention! We are part of the Confederate States of America's Army of Tennessee!! We are on a mission to raise support for the Southern cause and we feel sure that the clear thinking people of this community will surely want to help the Confederacy in every way they can and as much as possible. We will gladly accept any financial help from you private citizens, just see our Financial Affairs Officer there, Lt. Clay.

"Meanwhile, some of my men are checking with the bank, the stores and various other institutions to see what they would like to subscribe to our cause."

The mail boat, the Lady Pike, was at the wharf unloading U.S. mail. The captain and crew decided to do the right thing and their steamboat was spared. They were allowed to continue on down river, minus what had been in their safe.

Only a few of the local Home Guard members had weapons close by. They tried to put up a fight, but soon found that single shot muzzle loaded rifles were no match for repeating rifles. Four of the brave men paid with their lives. The sounds of gunfire were quickly over.

At the bank, there were some complications and one citizen was killed at the Rome Mercantile General Store.

In short order, the Southern Storm was leaving town with a rather large amount of U.S. currency as well as gold, silver and various other things of value.

On the other hand, the stunned townspeople and businessmen, including the banker, were holding some rather large amounts of Confederate money.

As the young major had pointed out, each denomination of paper money was imprinted with the all important phrase, "Backed by the Full Faith and Credit of the Confederate States of America."

The Rome Academy had been spared the burden of investing in the Southern cause. The Headmaster, Rev. William S. Hooper, had convinced the Confederate lieutenant that it would not be proper for an institution such as the Academy to support a war of any kind. The till in Rev. Hooper's office was nearly destitute in any case.

In a huge cloud of dust, the Southern Storm moved upriver toward the busy little town of Derby, Indiana!

Modern day picture of the old Perry County Court House
at Rome, Indiana. It was the Perry County Court House
until 1859. The old house seen in the background was once
used as law offices and also as a hotel. The present owners
of the historical old house are in the process of restoring it
to its former grandeur. Picture courtesy of Ex-Gov. of
Indiana Ed Whitcomb

Twelve

Captain Mattingly Spreads The Word

The "Concordia Queen" had just completed offloading cargo at the wharf boat at Stephensport, Kentucky, around 8:30 AM on June 17, 1863. The weather was fine and there was very little down current in the Ohio River. This had the makings of an ideal day for steam boating on the river.

Capt. Mattingly steered his big boat out of mid-stream. The next planned stop would be at Rome, Indiana, only about one mile away. Even above the noise of the boat's steam engines, he thought he heard the unmistakable sound of heavy gunfire. Now, he could see a large column of smoke rising from the Indiana shore, just down from Rome! A very large barn was burning and obviously would burn to the ground.

As Capt. Mattingly steered toward the Rome wharf boat, he could see that there was much confusion and many excited people in the streets. Someone tossed a mooring rope to the boat and Eli was very surprised to see that it was Jesse Esary who had thrown the rope. Something was very wrong, for Jesse was a captain in the local Home Guard, he worked at the Rome Bank, not the wharf.

Capt. Mattingly hollered above the noise, "What's wrong, Jesse. What's going on?"

"Eli, it's just good luck for you that you didn't get here fifteen minutes sooner than you did or your boat might be burning like that barn you just came by!! Our town has just been raided and robbed by an extremely well-armed troop of Confederate cavalry."

"Jesse, where are they now? Which way did they go?"

"They left here just a few minutes before you showed up. They are headed upriver and I can only guess, but I think they are probably going to stay close to the river for easier traveling."

"You said that they were extremely well-armed. What were they using for weapons?"

"Eli, I've never seen anything like it. Each and every man was carrying, not one, but two Colt revolvers and all seemed to have extra cylinders for them. Besides the handguns, they were all armed with the latest most modern repeating rifles, all of them!! They had lever action Henrys, Spencers and lots of them had Colt revolver carbines. I just couldn't believe what I saw!"

"Jesse, how many men do you think there were?"

"I didn't get an exact count; things were happening too fast. I'm pretty sure there are at least 60 of them, maybe 65, just around that many."

"How did they catch everyone off guard so badly?"

"Eli, no one had a clue that trouble was on the way 'til we heard the damnedest volley of small arms fire I have ever heard anywhere, any time. That's how they announced themselves, with about 30 seconds of sustained fire, not necessarily at anyone, just buildings and things. Then their leader, a young major, yelled that, 'The Southern Storm has arrived!!' "If we had even guessed that they were coming, we could have alarmed the Home Guard and maybe been ready for them, but it was a total surprise. A few of our men that had guns did try to fight at first; four of our men got killed for their efforts. Another citizen got shot and killed when they robbed the general store and the Rome Academy office. When they robbed the bank, the teller got a bad shoulder wound.

"Even if we'd had a warning and tried to stop them, we would have been slaughtered. They would have had us terribly out-gunned. I'd say that the way that those Rebs are armed, that even if there are only 60 or so of them, they have the firepower of at least 400 or more of our troops, armed with muskets."

"Jesse, did they just shoot and rob?"

"Oh no, Eli, they said that they were on a legitimate military mission for the Confederate States of America to raise funds for the Confederacy and that all that would 'invest' in the cause would be given Confederate Military script or money equal to the amount 'invested.' Their major explained that these pieces of paper were backed by 'The Full Faith and Credit of the Confederate States of America!!' The major referred to a young second lieutenant as his 'Finance Officer' and said he would handle the details of the financial transactions."

Eli then asked, "Well, Jesse, how were the people disposed of that were unwilling to 'invest' in the Southern cause?"

"The major simply pointed to the smoke and flames coming from the burning barn at the edge of town and said, "Now, that hardheaded man that owned that barn made a very unwise financial judgment!"

"Jesse, it seems to me that the people upriver need to be warned and it seems to me that the word can be spread quicker from this boat than any other way!!"

"You're right, Capt. Mattingly. For what little good it will do, they need to be warned. I know there would be but little military resistance, if any, at Derby, Indiana; none at Rono; and maybe some at Alton, Indiana. I heard the other day that the Leavenworth Home Guard had been called out to go up to Jeffersonville. If that's right Leavenworth will be defenseless."

"Jesse, how far upriver do you think those Rebs might go today?"

"I would estimate that they will make it up to around Dexter, Indiana, or Rono, somewhere around there. They haven't been gone from Rome very long. They're probably only a couple miles out of town as we speak."

Capt. Mattingly then said, "Look, lots of people are gonna get mad at me, but there is no time to mess with freight now. We are shoving off right now and we will try to spread the word as best we can!! We will be back when we get back and we will tend to the freight business then! All away, we're on our way!!"

As they started upriver, Josh yelled up from the engine room through the speaking tube, "Captain, let's don't forget that we are getting low on wood. We need to put in at the wood yard on Oil Creek near Derby."

Capt. Mattingly hollered back into the tube, "Josh, lay off of the damn wood!! It's time to lay the coal to it, Josh. What we need is power and speed, all we can muster!!"

"Yes, sir, Captain, me and Hargus are both laying the coal to it now. Things ought to pick up in a few more minutes!!"

"Thanks, Josh. I don't plan to make any stops so just try to keep up a full head of steam, up to where the pop off valve is about to blow!! We are gonna stay closer to the Indiana side. When we get close to a town or landing, I'll whistle ahead. Then, we'll swing in close and I'll holler through the bullhorn and try to explain and get folks braced for the Southern Storm. We ain't gonna stop unless we get stopped!!"

"Yes, Captain, me and Hargus understand."

"Josh, tell the rest of the crew to kind of stay out of sight. We may pass these Rebs and they are likely to shoot at us. We are running with a skeleton crew now. Can't afford to lose anyone."

The captain had just barely got off of the speaking tube when a huge cloud of dust caught his attention. There on the Indiana side, he could see the Southern Storm, galloping in all its glory. Just as Jesse Esary had figured, they were staying close to the river.

Instinctively, Eli turned the pilot wheel hard right and steered the "Concordia Queen" toward mid-river. He did this maneuver none too soon. Bullets were hitting the boat and some wood splinters were flying, but the boat was soon out of range.

Eli yelled into the speaking tube, "Did anyone get hurt?"

"No, Captain, no one hurt. These bullets made holes in the aft cargo bay. The only other damage I can see is that one barrel of molasses is leaking now and a case of bottles of whiskey got wasted, but that seems to be all the damage."

"Damn the luck," Eli replied, "Okay, Josh, try to plug the molasses leak. Lord, I hate to see good whiskey get wasted like that. Oh well, we are in a war."

About one mile below Derby, Indiana, Capt. Mattingly pulled three long blasts on the boat's whistle. As the Derby wharf came in sight, he could see several people standing, waiting for the boat to land.

The captain picked up his big old bull horn/megaphone and at the top of his voice yelled, "There's big trouble coming! Mounted Confederate cavalry headed this way. They are well-armed and spoiling for a fight. There are about 60 men. Be ready!!! We can't stop. We are going ahead upriver and spreading the word!! We will be back in a few days to deliver and pick up. Good luck!"

The "Concordia Queen" swung back out in the river, picked up speed and headed upriver. The stern paddle wheel churned up a frothy foam in the Ohio River as the two smokestacks gave forth much black smoke from the coal she was burning!!

Capt. Mattingly could see people at the landing at Flint Island, Kentucky. He yelled through the bullhorn, "Can't stop. Emergency. We'll be back later!"

The landing for the small village of Dexter, Indiana, was next in line. Again, the captain blew the boat whistle. When he swung close to shore, he gave the same warning he had given at Derby.

Although he was on the Indiana side of the river, he was now across from his home at Concordia, Kentucky. There just would be no time to stop. He had to spread the warning! He hoped that his loving wife, Liz, would not recognize the "Concordia Queen" in all the black smoke. Then he thought to himself, "Fat chance of that. She already probably heard the "Queen's" boat whistle. Oh well, I'll try to make peace with Liz later."

Capt. Mattingly steamed on to Rono, Indiana, swung close and gave the warning as before. He gave the warning at Galey's Landing, Alton and Freedonia, Indiana, and churned on upriver. Josh and old Hargus were still laying on the coal and the steam pressure was running at the top side of the "safe level."

About one mile below Leavenworth, Capt. Mattingly gave three long whistle blasts. He would stop at Leavenworth. He figured he had now warned most people for around forty miles along the Indiana side. As the "Concordia Queen" slowed down and docked, he saw Capt. Elam Herndon and Lt. Buchanan waiting. Eli figured that by Leavenworth being more people, businesses and industry, the Southern Storm would be likely to play rough here.

Capt. Herndon met Eli at the ramp and asked, "What's up? What's happening?"

Capt. Mattingly told Elam and Sam all about the Southern Storm/Rebel raiders as quick as he could, with all the details he knew. When he came to the part about the Confederates wanting "tribute" in the form of U.S.A. cash, gold or silver, Elam came "unglued" and damn near had a seizure. Capt. Herndon stated loudly, "Who the hell do they think they are? Damn 'em. We ain't got no gold and silver for 'em. I guess we will just have to pay them Rebs off in lead, in various denominations, of course!"

"You mean in different calibers don't you? Dammit now, Elam, don't do nothing stupid. You can't have much more than a token force here!"

"Yes, Eli, but this 'token force' may make a damn good accounting of themselves. We will see. You know it ain't really over 'til all the smoke clears!!

"Eli, how long do you estimate it will be before the Southern Storm blows into Leavenworth?"

"Capt. Herndon, this is just an educated guess from an uneducated old river rat, but I'm thinking that they will probably make it to around Dexter or Rono, somewhere around that tonight. Again, just guessing, I'd calculate that the next day, on the 18th, if they don't meet too much resistance, they will probably raid Rono, Galey's Landing, Alton and, probably, Freedonia, Indiana. I'd think they would be tuckered out by then and bivouac somewhere around Freedonia. I'd say you could expect them to be here early on the 19th. Of course, if they kept going at night, they could be at Leavenworth sooner."

"I'll bet you are close to being right, Eli. That will give us a little time to arrange for a proper reception for our self-invited guests. Maybe we can show our 'Hoosier Hospitality' by giving them a really warm welcome.

"Capt. Mattingly, we all owe you a bunch for letting us know about this and we thank you very much. We will have to postpone our social hour 'til another trip. We'll tilt a few then, old friend, and it will be on me. Maybe you had better think about getting the "Concordia Queen" away from here. You don't want her to be a prize of war, do you?"

"Hell no, Elam, I still owe the Brandenburg Bank thirty more payments!"

"We have got to start getting prepared, Eli. It ain't like I don't have anyone behind me. I have a right good bunch of soldiers.

I'm real proud of all of them. If those Rebs think they are gonna ride over us without seeing some muzzle flash, they had better think again."

"Elam, I hate to leave good company, but I'm gonna head back downriver and make sure I hang close to the Kentucky shore. I've done got a passel of customers peed off 'cause I didn't stop today. I've got to go back down to Rome and start unloading and picking up freight at each on the way back up here. With what little crew I've got left, I'd near work 'em to death shuffling freight and trying to move cargo three or four times to run my route any other way. I've got to get a move on or the Brandenburg Bank will own the "Concordia Queen" once again. Damn, I hope none of my customers try to pay me with Confederate money!"

"Be careful, Eli, and thanks again,"

"Good luck, Capt. Herndon. Keep your wits about you. Give 'em a warm welcome. I should be back up this way in two or three days or so. We will compare notes then. Salute!! All away. We're on our way. Lay the wood to it, Josh!"

"Capt. Eli, have you forgot, we are running low on wood?"

"Josh, it did slip my mind. We will stop over at that landing on Big Bend on the Kentucky side and fill up on wood. They always have lots of hickory and oak, makes a good fire."

"Yes, Captain, does make for a better, hotter fire."

"You know, Josh, if this boat goes by my house one more time without stopping, I'm in deep stuff. What about us stopping at Concordia for three or four hours. Liz will be tired of me by then."

"Capt. Eli, you're the man; run it the way you see it. I could use a nap myself."

Eli thought to himself, "I'm getting to where I'm starting to miss the 'comforts of home' more all the time. I think I'll have Liz find someone to watch the house and then I'll take her along next trip. I'll take the comforts of home with me."

• THIRTEEN •

Frantic Plans - Tight Spot

AS THE "CONCORDIA Queen" steamed away, Capt. Herndon said, "Sam, we have got to have a meeting with our two sergeants right now. We have to make some serious plans and we have to do it quick!!"

"Yes, Captain. I'm on my way to find the sergeants now!"

In a few minutes, the four men were down by the wharf house in serious discussion.

Elam and Sam filled Sgt. Wildman and Sgt. Bratton in on the details Capt. Mattingly had given them.

Sgt. Bratton said, "Damn, Captain, are we gonna bump heads with a troop as bad as them?"

"Sergeant, there ain't one bit of doubt about that! We must; it is our duty! There are too many helpless people here counting on us. If those Rebs think that we are gonna rollover and play dead, they've got another think coming! We will do what we have to do. The thing is that we got to decide exactly where we will make our stand and make the best plan of action we can! Has anyone got any good ideas?"

First Sgt. Wildman said, "Yes, Captain. I have a thought. I think that if we are gonna do it, and it looks like we are, for the sake of keeping our people and the town out of the shooting, I think we should set up our defenses about a mile down river on the river road where the trees are thick."

"Well, Sergeant, I thought of that, but wouldn't we do better at the cliffs, up in the rocks, just about a hundred feet above the road?"

"Yes, sir, of course. We would probably be better off up in the rocks, but look at the shape some of our men are in. It would be hard to get all of us and our equipment up there. I don't think that some of them could make it. Also, it would take some time. Captain, how much time do you think we have?"

"Well, men, here's the problem. We don't know for sure how much or how little time we have to get ready. If, as Eli Mattingly thinks, the Rebs bivouac tonight in the vicinity of Dexter or Rono, I'll bet he's probably right about that part. If they started out today where I think they did, both the men and their mounts would be in bad need of rest around Dexter or Rono. The next day is what I'm concerned about. What if, on the next day, they met very little resistance at say, Galey's Landing, Alton and Freedonia and still felt real good? Instead of bivouacking at Freedonia tomorrow night, they might get extra ambitious and try their stuff on Leavenworth tomorrow evening! That would mean that we would need to be in place and ready for action by then, tomorrow evening. Since we have no way of knowing for sure when they will be here, we will just have to pick our positions and stay there until the so called Southern Storm arrives."

"Okay, Captain," said the lieutenant. "Where are we gonna make our stand and when do you think we should start moving into position?"

"Yes, Lieutenant. I say we do our thing at the cliffs, just real close to our rifle range. Then it looks to me like we need to do a few things yet today. After we get our act together, we need to be getting in place to move our men and weapons up into their positions no later than 10:00 AM tomorrow morning.

Yes, First Sergeant. What is it?"

"Captain, I still don't see how some of our old and half crippled men are gonna make it up to the place we need to be. Do you have a plan?"

"Yes, I have a plan and it will work. It has to. It will take some time and it won't be easy, but we can and will make it up there, all of us! Sgt. Bratton!"

"Yes, sir."

"Sergeant, you go find Nurse Bowman and tell her we will be needing her and her two nurse helpers to be ready by tomorrow around noon. Tell her there might be a need for more bandages, tourniquets and such. Also, maybe some blankets if she can find them. After that, go find about six hoop poles from one of the piles by the Wharf. Then, get our pole carry sedan chair from its place in the wharf house. Put the poles and the pole carry chair in Buford Beasley's wagon!!"

"Yes, Captain. I'm on my way!"

"First Sergeant Wildman!"

"Yes, sir."

"Sergeant, get the men together and pick men for details. Detail men to find several good ropes at least 120 feet long. Also, some good tarps at least 6 foot by 8 foot. Also, we need to find enough bacon, beans and coffee to last 25 people for at least two days. Go to the stores or wherever you can find these supplies. We will settle for this stuff later. After those supplies are found, take them to Buford's wagon and cover it all with a tarp. After that, set some men to cutting patches for the old 1816 smoothbores and see that the powder that the Quarry donated to us is poured into as many powder flasks and powder horns that we can find. We may have to load some of our weapons the old fashioned way!"

"I'm on the way to get things moving, sir!"

"Thanks, Sgt. Wildman."

"Sam, let's you and me take a walk out to the cliffs and give the area a real close look. We have the start of a plan now. Let's see what we can build it into."

Elam and Sam walked out to the Leavenworth cliffs and studied them to find the best and easiest way to position men up there, about 100 feet above the river road. The place was not a sheer cliff, but it would be difficult to climb, especially for someone not in top physical condition. Unfortunately, this description applied to too many men of the L.H.G.R. or "Herndon's Hope" as the regular Home Guard wag had dubbed them.

Sam finally pointed out a sort of path that looked to be an easier route up to the height they wanted to be. At first, they had overlooked that way of going up because you would have to start the ascent around two hundred feet up river.

Elam said, "Good, Sam, that's the way. Now, do you see those two other winding ways facing the road? I think that would be the way to get down from there quicker. You couldn't actually walk, but a man could scoot and slide and get down to the road fairly quick."

"Yes, Elam, both those would be too hard to climb up, but you could come down that way fairly easy."

"Okay, Sam, let's go back to town and get the men together and fill 'em in on tomorrow."

Sgt. Bratton reported, "I notified the nurse. She said she would be ready. The rest of the stuff I got is in the wagon."

"Very good, Sgt. Bratton. Thanks. Good job."

First Sgt. Wildman reported that his work details were nearly completed. The four men filling powder horns and flasks would be done in about an hour.

"Thanks, Sgt. Wildman."

"Men, everyone be here ready for first formation at 7:00 AM tomorrow. Bring your weapons and I mean all of them. Anything that is capable of shooting a bullet out of the business end of the muzzle will be needed. Bring them all. Also, I know that it's summer, but it gets chilly at night up in the rocks. So, bring your coat and a blanket or something. We may very well have to camp out tomorrow night. Does anyone have anything else before we are dismissed?"

"Yes, Captain. Sgt. Wildman got the bacon, beans and coffee. I'll bake up a big batch of cornbread for us, enough for a couple of days."

"Thank you, Pvt. Beasley. You are truly a kind soul. Thanks much. Dismissed!"

At 7:00 AM, the L.H.G.R. stood at first formation. They were a colorful group with nineteen men wearing bright red neckerchiefs and their two officers sporting bright yellow ones. Capt. Herndon and Lt. Buchanan were wearing their army officer caps and coats left over from their Mexican War service. First Sgt. Wildman, Cpl. Weathers, and Cpl. Kinnaman were wearing the standard Union Army uniform of the time. Sgt. Bratton was wearing what he had left of his army uniform from his days in the Leavenworth Home Guard, basically 1855 style cavalry clothing and cavalry style broad brim hat. The rest of the company were dressed in their normal work clothes, some wearing bib overalls, some wearing jeans, no two of them the same. The one common thread which showed that they were of the same unit was their neckerchiefs.

"All men present and ready for duty, sir," Sgt. Wildman reported.

"Very good, Sergeant. Have the men put their spare weapons and their gear in the wagon with our other supplies. Pvt. Beasley will drive his team. Cpl. Weathers and Pvt. Martin will ride along. The rest of us will march in formation, double file, to the cliffs area."

"Attention!! Form a column of twos. Right face. Right shoulder arms. Forward march!" The L.H.G.R. marched out proudly to set up their defenses against the approaching Southern Storm!

After the march to the cliffs, all the extra weapons and supplies were unloaded from the wagon. The men quickly set about carrying out the orders given.

Lt. Buchanan took Sgt. Wildman and nine of the men over to the best winding trail leading up to where they planned to be. Each man was carrying his weapon and ammo. Besides this, five men were also carrying the long coils of 5/8" rope. After about twenty minutes of difficult struggle, they were on the tabletop or ledge where they wanted to be. The position was only around 12 feet front to back and continued for around 150 feet along the face of the incline. There were two very steep ways to come down by way of narrow rocky depressions in the earth and rock. For the most part, it was rock. By sliding and scooting you could come down, but it would have been very hard to go up.

After the eleven men were in place, the ends of two ropes were thrown down. The next part of the plan then began. The captain then had the rest of the men start bundling the extra weapons, three in each bundle and ammo in blankets. These were then rolled up in a canvas tarp with two hoop poles inside for stiffener to protect the contents from the rocks. These bundles were tied to the two ropes coming down, while two more ropes were tied on to be used by the men at the bottom to pull the bundles away from the jagged rocks, when necessary. The rest of the extra weapons and supplies were hauled up to the position this way and it worked quite well. Only once had they had to lower a bundle a few feet and start the upward pull again. After about an hour and a half of hard work, the food, water, extra guns and ammo were up into position. It was now midday and much more needed to be done.

"Now, men," said the captain, "there are ten of us still down here and nine of us need to get up there."

Helmer Schmitt blurted, "But, Captain, don't all ten of us that are left need to go up?"

"No, Private. Jim Running Deer will be staying down here. Jim has a special talent that none of the rest of us has. He will put this skill to good use. When the time is right, Pvt. Jim Running Deer will come on up there with the rest of us."

"Captain, it looks to me like some among us are going to have a damn rough time getting up that bluff," said George Armstrong.

"You're right, George. We are going to have to help those that need help. Now, Pvt. Martin's bad foot makes it near impossible to make it up there. Cpl. Weathers is still not strong enough after his two bouts with pneumonia to take the climb. Also, no offense to Pvt. Buford Beasley, but an 87 year old man might be too tuckered to aim a gun after a climb like that."

"So, just how will they get up there?" said Albert LeCroix.

"Albert, you and Hibachi go to the wagon and get the pole carry sedan chair, on the double."

In a short time, Albert and Hibachi were back with the carry chair.

"Now, men, three of our own are going to be taken up there in style. Pvt. Beasley, you get to go first. Get in the chair."

"Oh, Captain, this ain't fair to the rest. I can climb it!"

"Oh, I know you could, Buford, but you wouldn't be in very good shape if you did. Now, just get in the chair and you go first."

The six men got Buford up to the position in about 25 minutes by taking turns on carrying. Tad Martin was carried up next. Cpl. Weathers was the smallest man of the three and was taken up last.

It was now almost 2:00 PM and the men, weapons and supplies were at the high position.

Buford's team and wagon had been taken about one quarter mile up in a grove of trees, hopefully out of the way of the coming battle. Nurse Bowman and her two helpers, Susan and Tillie, were there with a horse and buggy containing what medical supplies they had been able to round up.

Capt. Herndon had told the nurses to stay there out of harm's way 'til the shooting was over and until they were called for. Like the men, the nurses were prepared to spend the night there waiting for whatever was to be.

The captain ordered a ten minute break, after which they would start finalizing the plan of action.

Pvt. George Armstrong said, "Capt. Herndon, I have a question. Why did we nearly bust ourselves bringing all them extra guns and stuff up here? We can only shoot one gun at a time!!"

"Well, Private, it's because we have a terrible mix of some rather poor weapons. We have just got to arrange it all so we can get the most good out of what we got. Besides that, we got to try to even up the odds a little bit."

"Captain, speaking of odds against us, do you have any idea how many Reb troopers we are going to have to fight or will we just find out when they get here?" asked Pvt. Watson.

"That's a fair question, Newt. You men have the right to know. According to Capt. Levi Mattingley's information, there are around 63-65 men in this here Southern Storm that's headed our way. If there are 63 of them, that makes the odds very lopsided in their favor, three of them against one of us, the way I figure it. Okay, break is over. We have got to finish getting ready in case our uninvited guests do arrive today!!"

Lt. Buchanan ordered, "Okay, men, here's the plan. We have a place here in this sort of a ledge or shelf of rock and dirt that is about 12 foot front to back and about 150 foot wide. This position is one of the best a soldier could ask for. There is nothing in our line of fire except for the river road down below. Besides that, we definitely have the high ground advantage, much better to shoot downward than up. The sergeants will show each of you men where to get in place, about seven feet from each other, and in a straight firing line so we don't accidentally shoot any of our own men."

First Sgt. Wildman and Sgt. Bratton placed the men as follows:

one combat experienced man would be in between two without combat experience in some positions. In some cases, there would be two green soldiers between the experienced vets.

Capt. Herndon also saw that Pvt. Jacob Silverstein would be at near the center in case he needed to work on a gun that needed attention.

"Okay, men, listen up!!" ordered the captain. "Now you know where your right position is to be. Hop to and help in unwrapping the extra weapons and ammunition. Lt. Buchanan will select who gets what."

In short order, the troops were in place. Then, Sgt. Wildman gave some instructions, "Now, men, remember where your spot is in case we have to stay here very long! Now, some of you wondered why we brought every weapon we had up here. Well, here's why. It's so we can lay out more fire faster. As you can see, eight of you men have been issued three muzzle loading weapons each. Now you men take note. Pvts. Armstrong, Takeguchi, Martin and Moore each have one Model 1841 Mississippi rifle. What I'm about to say does not apply to the Mississippi rifles. You four men, plus Pvts. Corbin, Schmitt, Hatfield and LeCroix all have Model 1816, .69 caliber smoothbore muskets, most with percussion lock but a few are flintlock. Now listen close. On the .69 caliber weapons, load them with a normal powder charge, but also add an extra quarter measure of gunpowder to that charge. This will increase the range and knockdown power a bunch."

"Sgt. Wildman," Albert LeCroix began, "will the breech hold with that much powder in one of these antiques?"

"Yes, Private, we done it a lot in Mexico. Them old U.S. made Springfields are good uns."

"But, Sergeant, it kicks like a damn mule now. What will it do with that much extra powder??"

"Well, Pvt. LeCroix, now it will kick like a team of mules. Not only will you notice the difference, but the one on the receiving end will feel it more too. Now, all you men load the old .69 caliber pieces like I just told you. Do not add extra powder to the Mississippi rifles. They don't need it. They reach out good and are real accurate just like they are."

Lt. Buchanan took his turn. "Now, men, you might as well know it. These Rebs that are coming have the best repeating weapons to be had. The only way we stand a chance is by total surprise and to pour as much lead into them as we can before they know what hit 'em!!"

"How are we to do that, Lieutenant?"

"Well, Pvt. Armstrong, this will answer your question as to why we brought all the stuff up here. The only way we can even come close to fast sustained fire is to fire one weapon and make that shot count, lay it down and pick up another loaded weapon and do the same. Lay it down, pick up another loaded weapon and fire!! Of course, this won't work for but a short time. Hopefully, it will work well enough. Every man among us has more than one weapon and our goal is to lay down as much fire as we can as quick as we can. Pvt. Beasley has the only repeating rifle among us, that Colt .44 caliber, six shot revolving rifle. He has two extra loaded cylinders for it and I know he will make his shots count. The rest, for the most part, have breech loading single shot weapons, but they can be reloaded much faster than the muzzle loaders. The plan is for me, with my crippled up left arm, and Cpl. Kinnaman, with his left arm in a sling, to fire a first round through the two old 1816's we have, by resting them on a rock then switching to firing revolvers."

Pvt. Moore said, "It looks to me like we need a cannon!"

Capt. Herndon quipped back, "We do, Private. We do. Pvt. Newt Watson has been designated the cannoneer of our outfit."

"Where's his cannon, Captain??"

"Those three shotguns he has by him are about as close to cannons as we could come up with on short notice. As you can see, they are all double barrels. Two of them are ten gauge and the other is one of Buford's prized possessions, a rather rare eight gauge with 36" barrels. When you add their report to the echoes around here, they will damn well think we do have a cannon or two! Newt is also going to load them all a little more generously than their makers intended."

"Okay, men, load everything you have. Get in your places and settle down. We may have visitors yet this afternoon. Now, remember how we trained about overlapping fields of fire and above all, don't forget and all of you shoot at the same targets. Let them all have their fair share throughout their troop. Okay? Spread it around!"

Tad Martin said, "Captain, what's Jim Running Deer doing? It looks like he's taking a nap down there. He's laying down on the road."

"Well, laughed the captain, "that ain't what it looks like. Jim is a very skilled 'ground listener.' He can put an ear to the ground and hear horses, cattle or whatever coming long before any of the rest of us would even have a clue that something was headed our way. If any of the rest of you men tried 'ground listening,' all you'd probably get out of it would be a real dirty ear. But, Jim Running Deer hears things and knows the situation."

Jim sat upright and hollered up the cliff, "Capt. Herndon, if anyone is coming, they wouldn't be here for at least another half hour. I don't hear any sign of large movements!!"

"Okay, Jim, stay with it. We will stay in place and be ready for action in the meantime." Everyone was tense and serious, but they all knew they had to make a stand and better to do it here than in a town with women, children and others getting hurt or being in harm's way.

Capt. Herndon, Lt. Buchanan and the sergeants shared their thoughts on the situation.

The captain said, "You know, men, it's getting late in the day. I say that if the Rebs don't show up here by an hour before sunset, they won't be here today. I'm certain that they would try to avoid moving in the darkness, especially in strange territory. After all, they can't see any better in the dark than we can. If Jim Running Deer doesn't hear them coming by around 7:30 PM, we can maybe relax a little. What do you men think?"

All agreed with Capt. Herndon's thoughts. They would stay as they were until dark at least.

Sgt. Bratton said, "Captain, do you think that the Rebs might send out an advance scout or two?"

"No, Sergeant, I'm pretty sure they won't. I think they already know that this whole territory is the same as defenseless. I'd bet my boots that they know all about the Leavenworth Home Guard being called away. I say that they don't even bother to send out scouts. They probably think they will be unopposed. If we don't pull this off right, they will be almost unopposed.

Men, listen up! Be damn careful with your guns. Let's not have any accidental gunfire. Just one shot from here could be heard for miles and could ruin our plan. We must have total surprise and total discipline. No nervous fingers when we fire our first volley. I want it to be like one giant shot. On our first volley, we fire on command, just like we trained. After that, lay down a wall of fire the best you can and as fast as you can. Does everyone understand!??"

The answer was, "Yes, Captain," to a man.

The Lieutenant asked, "Sgt. Wildman, did you think to place Armstrong and Takaguchi next to each other?"

"Yes, sir, I did."

"Good, because if something happens after dark, hand signals will be useless. At least they can understand one another."

It was very quiet now and tension was high. All the men were in position and very ready. There were many sweaty palms. It was starting to get dark and the approaching Southern Storm had not appeared. Deep down, they all knew that the threat was very real, but it was beginning to look like the storm would be tomorrow.

Pvt. Jim Running Deer just sat up after making one more "ground listen!" He hollered, "Captain, nothing coming that I can hear. I'd say they won't move after dark!"

"I agree with you, Jim. Why don't you swing by where the nurses are camped, check on them and let them know the situation. Then, come on up here for tonight!"

"Yes, Captain, I'm on my way." Jim picked up his breech loading Sharps rifle and quietly moved off in the approaching darkness.

An hour later, the order was given for men to be on 50 percent alert, meaning that at least half of the group must be awake at all times during the night. They would do this in two hour shifts. Everyone was hungry. It had been a long day, no time for noon rations. The captain okayed making two small cooking fires and soon the good smell of beans, bacon and cornbread being reheated made the whole cliff smell very pleasant. Two large pots of coffee were being brewed and the campfire storytelling began. If it were not for this damn war, this was a very nice place to go camping. The moon was bright tonight and it made a beautiful reflection in the wide Ohio River. The whip-poor-wills were singing their pleasant song and, higher up in the rocks, two hoot owls had a conversation going. From very far upriver, they could hear the very faint sound of a steamboat whistle. Yes, even at night, this place had a beauty all its own.

Jim Running Deer said, "Capt. Herndon, I went by to check on our three nurses. They are going to do alright. I done my best Indian stealth act and tried to see if they were on the alert. They were. Alice Bowman had her late husband's .36 Navy Colt out and Tillie Jefferson had an old single barrel 12 gauge shotgun at the ready. Susan Bowman said they heard me coming from 30 feet away. Hell, I guess I'm losing my Indian skills, gonna have to brush up on my stealth moves. Ha!"

"Did they have a place figured out to sleep tonight?"

"No problem, Captain. They had a canvas tarp tied over the box bed on the wagon and were going to sleep there. Buford's team of horses and Alice's buggy horse were hobbled and grazing. They had made a little fire and were cooking their supper when I got there. Susan said that they had seen these fires on the cliff, so they figured it was okay."

"What did you tell them about tomorrow morning, Jim?"

"I just told them that we were 99 percent certain that the Rebs wouldn't be here tonight, so rest easy. I told them I was coming up here for awhile tonight, but I'd be back down on the road with my ear to the ground before daylight and I would know the enemy was coming for quite a while before they get to the cliffs."

"Real good, Jim. Buford has the cups and pie pans over by that fire. I know you're bound to be hungry. Eat your fill and get some rest. There are blankets over there by that pile of rocks."

"Thanks, Captain. Oh, by the way, Moses Jefferson can you hear me from over there?"

"Yes, Jim, I hear you loud and clear."

"Moses, I have a message for you. Your wife Tillie Mae said, and this is a quote, 'Jim, tell my sweet Moses that I miss him bad and I hope we never have to spend a night apart ever again. Love and kisses!' So there, sweet Moses, I gave you her message."

The rest of the men got a good chuckle when they heard Tillie's love message.

Moses said, "Boys, this is the truth. I've loved that little woman since the first day I ever seen her. I miss her a big bunch too. This is the first time that we have ever spent a night apart. A real good woman is hard to find and she surely is a good woman. Thanks, Jim, for bringing me those words."

Lt. Buchanan said to the others, "I know how it is with Moses and Tillie, but take myself, Elam and Sgt. Wildman, for instance. Us three were all soldiers and gone so much for so many years that our wives didn't usually give it any notice when we left."

"That's right," said Elam. "Back years ago, I got transferred to an army post way out in the west part of Texas. I was gone for nearly eleven months. Coming home, I thought I'd surprise Ruth and not let her know I was headed home. Well, I slipped in the house and set my satchel down and said, 'Honey Babe, I'm home!' She looked up from her newspaper and said, 'You have been gone?' So, you can see some women tolerate absent husbands better than others."

Campfires and storytelling always seem to go well with one another and in combination they seem to calm taut nerves. So, the storytelling was in progress around the fires and the men were relaxing as best they could trying to block out thoughts of the coming morning and all that would come with it.

Meanwhile, about a quarter of a mile away, at the nurses' camp, the women engaged in serious talk as their small campfire was dying down.

Tillie said, "Oh, I do hate to be away from Moses. We are most always together. I love that old man so much I just don't think I could go on if anything was to happen to him."

Alice Bowman replied, "Yes, Tillie, I know exactly how you feel. I loved Dr. Bowman very much too. But, when he got killed in this hateful war, I just kept on going on, even without him. I must admit that I still feel hate for the Confederate Army because they took his life, but he had always told me that war was not personal. That it was, simply, those that believed in one cause fighting those that believed in another cause. He also often pointed out that no matter which side a wounded man was on, a doctor or nurse was supposed to try to help, when able. But, I still must admit that I have no love for the Confederates or their cause, none at all!"

"Mother," Susan began, "I just can't be as big a person as you are. I hate the Rebels and their damnable army. I can't forgive them for killing Daddy. Nurse or not, I don't think I could bring myself to try to help one of them!"

"Susan, I know how you feel, honey, but as nurses we have no choice in the matter. We must help those in need of help whenever possible, no matter their race, religion or what army they belong to. After all is said and done, they are still human beings."

Tillie said, "Well said, Alice. We know you are right, girl. It's just hard to see it that way sometimes."

"Girls," said Alice, "this is a very beautiful night, but it's bound to be followed by a very ugly tomorrow. Let's try to think of more pleasant things and try to get what sleep we can. When the fighting happens, we will just have to do the best we can. Now remember what Capt. Herndon said. We are not supposed to move from here 'til the noise of battle is over. He ordered us to stay here and out of harm's way 'til they tell us to do otherwise. Pleasant dreams."

Meanwhile, back at the cliff, the tales around the fires kept on keeping on.

Jim Running Deer began, "Here's another story boys; it's an old Indian tale."

Mike Baysinger shot back, "Jim, how come your stories are always 'old Indian tales'?"

Jim laughingly answered, "Dammit, Mike, I guess it's because I am an old Indian!"

"Okay, then get on with it."

"Well, this came from my old Grandpa who was the best hunter in our tribe. See, when you are hunting something like buffalo, an old Indian trick is to only shoot the ones at the back of the herd first. Most of the time, the ones in front don't even miss the fallen ones behind. So, by doing it that way, you have a better chance of dropping more without spooking the herd."

Dan Lyon said, "Okay, Jim, what's your point?"

"Okay, boys, the point is this—buffalo ain't the only thing that this will work on. A column of cavalry are sort of like a buffalo herd in a way."

Mike agreed that a strategy like that would probably work.

Someone said, "Dan, tell us a war story about the War of 1812 and General Jackson at New Orleans."

"Well now, that all happened a while back, but one little thing comes to mind. Men, I know you have all heard that old line, 'Don't shoot 'til you see the whites of their eyes!' Well, there is good solid reasoning behind that statement. It was said a lot during the Revolutionary War and it was also a favorite line of Old Hickory. It simply meant that those old smoothbore muskets were only accurate out to about 100 yards and that was about how far off a men with average eyesight could see the whites of the other soldier's eyes. So you see, if you used your shot at too great of a distance, you were more likely to miss. Then, the enemy might get you while you are trying to reload. It's worth thinking about. You know we are blessed with a bunch of them old smoothbores! With the added powder, they are better, but what I'm saying is—don't forget the extra powder."

Capt. Herndon said, "Dan, I'm glad that you told that one. It is worth remembering. Now, maybe we could get Hibachi to tell us a tale, maybe one about pearls and oysters."

"Capt. Herndon, how about I tell one about pearls and mussels, okay? Well, you see the place I'm from, Japan, people have been working for about 700 years to find the best way to make an oyster grow a pearl. This can be done by partly opening the oyster and placing just the right size piece of sand in just the right place and closing it back shut. Very lot to know, much skill, but done right you can grow real big pearls this way, valuable pearls. Now, in this land the same thing will work on the mussels that live in this big river. I do this thing for the button factory where I work and they pay me good. But, there is more. I, Hibachi Takaguchi, also have some mussels of my own and they are growing pearls for me. I only do these when not working at button factory. This is the land of opportunity and Hibachi see opportunity, okay? The place where I am growing these mussel pearls is big secret. I cannot tell place where is, but fellow soldiers, please do Hibachi a big favor and try not to shoot no stray bullets in river in front of us. No telling what they could hit. Okay?"

"Okay, men, you heard Hibachi, be careful where you shoot. He works hard for his living!" Then, the captain asked who else had a tale?

Cpl. Weathers said, "Men, I ain't breathing good enough yet to tell a big windy without getting winded, but there's a couple of stories going around town about Mike Baysinger. One is that he was the oldest combat soldier in the Indiana Volunteers. The other is that he was the best rifle shot of all of the Indiana troops. Mike, let's hear your version of these things."

"Okay, Milo. Now, about that age thing, now that is all true. When I joined the 66th Indiana, I was 69 years old. We were in some hard fights in a bunch of places and I usually hit what I aimed at. Late in '62, when I was 70 years old, one morning I moved a little too slow to suit the captain and in a short while our colonel had me mustered out of the army and sent home. The paper said, 'due to old age.' I thought that it was a damn ungrateful thing for them to do. It was like they'd forgot all about asking me to do 'sharp shooter duty' in an exposed position at the big battle in Richmond, Kentucky, last August. They knew damn well that I didn't waste many of their bullets. Most all of them went where it counted the most!!

"Now, as far as that story goes about me being the best rifle shot of all the Indiana troops in that competition, well, that just ain't so. The truth of it was that I was only the second best shot in that contest. I came close, but as Capt. Herndon always says, close don't mean much unless it's a bullet that just missed you!"

The men all laughed, but they all respected old Mike. Privately, every man agreed that they were glad to have the old soldier be one of their own. The colonel in the 66th Indiana had made a serious blunder discharging an excellent marksman such as old Mike. Conversely, no one had any doubt that it was anything but extreme good luck that Capt. Herndon had managed to recruit such a good soldier for the Leavenworth Home Guard Reserve. Great riflemen don't grow on trees. In fact, they are few and far between.

It was getting late and some of the men were starting to consider the possibility of taking a nap or, at least, trying to rest some. The captain had ordered fifty percent alert and everyone understood which fifty percent they were in. Some tried to make some makeshift beds or resting places. Most were soon to discover that only the very seasoned combat soldiers are ever able to rest much before approaching battle. Even they can't truly rest well, unless they are in a state of complete exhaustion. For the most part, those trying to rest did not fall asleep. The thought kept gnawing in most of their minds that there was a very real possibility that they might well end up in a very deep sleep of long duration, should the coming action not go as planned.

For the most part, they leaned back in silence and thought their private thoughts.

FOURTEEN

The Southern Storm Continues Upriver

MAJOR MILES' ORIGINAL plan was to only start acquiring horses after they passed Leavenworth, Indiana. He figured that his men could collect about all the horses they could easily herd and keep track of between Leavenworth and the place at Tobacco Landing, Indiana. Tobacco Landing was the planned crossing point to cross back over to the Kentucky side and head back south.

Just a short way out of Rome, Indiana, the horse population was great in numbers and many of them looked like they would make perfect cavalry remounts. The major changed from his original plan and started acquiring horses just upriver from Rome. Most of the farmers were cooperative and, for the most part, these acquisitions went reasonably smooth. After all, these farmers were getting paid for their animals. Well, sort of.

The horse transactions were slowing down the progress of the Southern Storm a bit, but Major Miles felt it was worth it.

So far, no one from Rome had come in pursuit of the Southerners, but if they did, they had no doubt that their superior firepower would change any pursuers' minds. Just a while back, that curious steamboat captain had come a little too close to shore, but a few shots had convinced him to move farther out in midriver.

Meanwhile, the town of Derby, Indiana, had been warned of the coming raiders. Capt. Mattingly had swung close, slowed down, given the warning and continued upriver, leaving a heavy trail of coal smoke.

There was a small Union Army prisoner of war camp at the top of the big hill at Derby, Indiana. The POW camp had become too crowded and just a few days ago about half of the local Home Guard unit had been given the job of moving about thirty of the Reb prisoners up to Indianapolis to Camp Morton, the big POW camp there. As a result, the Derby Home Guard was at about half strength with only approximately twenty men and a young inexperienced second lieutenant in command. They were poorly armed and most of them had old smoothbore weapons.

There was little time to plan; the raiders would be there very soon.

The frenzied signal was given by firing the anvil at the black-smith shop and ringing the bell at the school house. In just a few minutes, all of the remaining members of the Derby Home Guard unit had assembled on Main Street.

Nineteen year old Second Lt. Jason Harris was the only Home Guard officer left in the town of Derby, Indiana, at the time. He assumed command of the remaining 19 Home Guard troops.

Of the company of 19 men, Sgt. Yake, age 50, was the only one in the group with any previous combat experience. He had seen combat in the Mexican War, back in '46 and '47.

The brave remnants of the Home Guard had reported on the double. They all bore arms, such as they were. They had 12 Model 1816 smoothbore muskets, four Mississippi rifles, five Model 1855 cavalry carbines and two Colt revolvers. To say the least, they were not well-armed, but they did intend to stand their ground.

Lt. Harris knew that the time was short and the Rebs would likely be there soon. His first concern was for the women and children of the town. He had to decide many things in short order.

The lieutenant ordered two of his men to quickly call for the women and children of the small town to be assembled and marched in a group up the steep hill to the Catholic Church there. He figured they would be safer there than down in the main part of town.

Father Augustus Bessonies was the priest at St. Mary's Church and would do his best to protect those inside his church.

There was a small Union Army prisoner of war camp less than a quarter mile past St. Mary's Church. The POW camp was only garrisoned by fifteen Union soldiers with a first lieutenant in charge. They needed to be warned of the coming trouble. The camp had around 130 Confederate prisoners. If the Rebs learned of this camp and turned these prisoners loose, things could become worse in short order.

Lt. Harris knew at the outset that the POW camp garrison could spare no men for the defense of the town as they were already terribly undermanned. There were barely enough guards to keep order in the camp twenty-four hours a day, seven days a week.

The two men were soon back from taking the women and children up to the church.

As Lt. Harris had expected, the POW camp could spare no men and could only hope that the Reb raiders did not learn of the camp's existence.

There was some hurried talk of moving the contents of the Derby Bank's vault to another place, but time had just run out.

The Southern Storm had just announced their presence with a thunderous three shot salute, i.e., 189 shots.

Lt. Harris ordered his men to open fire and one Reb trooper was wounded.

Before the Home Guard had a chance to reload, the Southern Storm opened up on them with murderous fire.

In short order, the Home Guard lost four brave men and a fifth suffered a bad shoulder wound.

Lt. Harris quickly ordered his men to surrender. To resist these raiders was the same as committing suicide.

After the Home Guard was disarmed and things were quieter, Major Miles announced the purpose of their mission.

The townspeople now realized that their financial support of the Southern cause was important to the safety of their town.

Again, as at Rome, the Financial Affairs Officer, Lt. Clay, was exchanging paper Confederate money for United States currency. Being a fair-minded man, Lt. Clay was giving one and a half Confederate dollars for each U.S. dollar received.

Soon, the transactions were completed at the Derby Bank, three stores, the hotel and both taverns. Things went rather smoothly at every place except for the barrel factory and the sawmill.

Major Miles had one man with a slight shoulder wound which was quickly dressed. The man was still able to ride and use a gun. The Southern Storm were soon mounted and leaving town.

As they looked to the rear, they could see the smoke rising higher from the barrel factory and also from the sawmill. Major Miles remarked, "It is truly a shame that the owners of those two businesses could not have been more agreeable and supportive of our cause."

Major Miles called a halt so that their thirsty horses could drink from the Ohio River, just down from the small village of Dexter, Indiana.

During the break, Capt. Lewis said, "Major, you know we met some resistance back there at Derby. Do you think we are apt to meet more resistance in the next towns and places?"

"No, Captain, I don't think there is any cause for worry. It's plain to see that these Yanks don't have much backbone. If they do so much as lift a finger against us, they won't believe the firepower we have available. I think we can go most anywhere we want, most anytime we want. For their sake, they had better hope that they don't catch up with us."

"Okay, Major, I think that you are probably right, but don't you think the people at Rome and the mail boat captain and the people at Derby have sent for help by now?"

"Yes, Capt. Lewis, I'm sure that they have sent for troops to pursue us, but like I just said, if they do catch up with us, they will be in for a surprise. We may be only 63 men, but we will respond like ten times our number."

"Major," said Capt. Lewis, "these horses we are accumulating are starting to slow us down some."

"I know, Captain, but the remount horses are one of the main reasons for this raid. As you can see, we are acquiring some very nice horses and the Confederacy will be very glad to get them."

"Don't worry, Captain. If the Union troops do manage to head us off before we reach our planned crossing point at Tobacco Landing, I have a plan. We will simply wait at one of the steamboat landings until a big boat shows up. We would then commandeer the boat and use it to cross the river or escape."

"Yes, sir, sounds like a prime plan."

At the small village of Dexter, Indiana, there was no resistance as the place was nearly deserted.

Lt. Clay negotiated with a farmer and obtained two more fine saddle horses.

Major Miles gave the order to move out and the Southern Storm proceeded on toward the little river port town of Rono, Indiana.

There was no Home Guard unit at Rono, but Capt. Mattingly had warned the town of approaching danger. The townspeople had mustered eleven men with rifles. They were determined to make a stand. They were reasonably well-armed and had taken up positions that offered some cover, and were ready.

In a cloud of dust, the Confederates swooped into town, announcing their arrival with their special 63 rifle, three shot salute. Before Major Miles had a chance to make his opening remarks, the town's small group of defenders fired a volley, but hit nothing except one soldier's hat brim.

The Rebs returned a murderous wall of fire and now the town's defenders were only nine. They quickly surrendered and Major Miles' men went about the business of raising support for the Confederacy.

Rono was but a tiny village, but it had a good river port, two stores, a hotel, saloon and a Post Office.

Job Hatfield was the Postmaster and owner of one of the general stores. Besides the store and Post Office, Job Hatfield owned the wharf boat at the river terminal. In addition to that, he and the Hatfield family owned and operated a rather large commercial slaughterhouse, butchering and meatpacking operation just at the edge of town. The Hatfields had a contract to supply meat to the Union Army and the family fortunes would suffer greatly should any harm come to their family owned business.

Being quick to realize what they stood to lose, all people in town cooperated with the Rebs and invested in the Southern cause as much as possible.

During the transactions at Rono, Major Miles noticed one local man standing with his feet placed in a peculiar fashion. They established eye contact and Major Miles moved close to the man. When close to each other, the man said something in a low voice, one word, 'Nuohlac,' and quickly and discreetly handed the major an envelope folded into one fourth its normal size.

Major Miles, unnoticed by anyone else, slipped the small folded envelope in his coat pocket and gave the man a nod and a knowing wink then moved back to his men.

It was getting late in the day and horses and men were tired. When they learned of the Hatfield meatpacking business at the edge of Rono, it was selected as a very good place to bivouac for the night.

Knowing the wisdom of being gracious hosts, the Hatfields provided the men of the Southern Storm with some very high quality meats at no charge.

There was good grazing and water for the horses and excellent hams and steaks for the men. They were camped for the night on a hill overlooking the Ohio River just at the edge of Rono. It had been a very long day and the men were nearly exhausted. After a hearty evening meal, courtesy of the Hatfield Meat Company, much needed rest was the next order of business. Five men were picked for sentry duty for the first four hours and the rest prepared their bedrolls.

Meanwhile, Major Miles, Capt. Lewis, Lt. Clay and First Sgt. Calhoun were quietly having a staff meeting. Major Miles began, "Did any of you take notice of anything unusual happening in town in Rono this evening?"

All answered that they had noticed nothing unusual taking place.

"I didn't think so. Okay, very well. Now, a second question, have any of you ever heard of an organization called the Knights of the Golden Circle?"

Capt. Lewis and Lt. Clay both answered that they had heard of the organization, but knew very little about it.

"Well, men," said the major, "the Knights of the Golden Circle. also shortened to K.G.C., is a secret organization made up of Northern men who secretly support the Southern cause. They endeavor to help us by undercover means as much as possible, however they can. When the Confederate Army does finally invade the North, their plan is to surface and openly help us to the fullest."

Sgt. Calhoun said, "But, sir, that's all nice to know, but why are you telling us all about it now?"

"Well, men, here's why I'm explaining all this. We had some unexpected good luck today. There was a man standing in front of one of the stores in Rono. He had his feet placed in a peculiar position, which caught my attention. This was a secret clue to me that he was a K.G.C. member. We established eye to eye contact and I moved close to him. He then said one word in a low voice, 'Nuohlac.' Then, I knew for sure that he was one of us. He quickly handed me a small folded up envelope and no one else seemed to notice."

"Why all the secrecy and how did you know for sure that he was a K.G.C. member?" asked the lieutenant.

"Well, the main reason for all the secrecy is that this K.G.C. member has to remain undercover for now lest the others with strong Union loyalties dispose of him in one way or another. As for the one word he said to me, 'Nuohlac,' which is simply the name Calhoun spelled and pronounced backward is, I know for sure, to be one of their secret identification passwords. When he uttered that word, I knew him to be genuine.

"Now, for the most interesting part, the envelope that he slipped to me contains much valuable information."

"Will the information he gave you help us much on this particular mission?" asked the sergeant.

"Yes, this information should help us a great deal. For openers, he tells us that we will find some very nice horses shortly after we start out in the morning. A short distance from here, at a place called Galey's Landing, there is a family named Prather. They are a father and four sons. They are well-known to be interstate horse dealers, our informant says, and also that it is common knowledge that these horse dealers have little or no cash investment in these horses. The K.G.C. man further informs us that this family will claim, at first, that they have no horses at this time when the truth is, they keep the horses in a secret rock walled canyon called 'Penitentiary Rock' which is close by. Also our K.G.C. friend says that the Prathers always insist on being paid in gold. I guess Lt. Clay could perhaps negotiate around this 'gold only' policy of theirs, couldn't you Lieutenant?"

"Yes, sir, I'm sure we can work out some arrangement on this."

"Major, this sounds like great information so far. Is there more?" said Capt. Lewis.

"Yes, the information gets better and better. This friend of the South further tells us that the next three towns, Alton, Fredonia and Leavenworth, though all three have well-armed Home Guard units, will be easy to handle. The reason being that the Home Guards in all three places have been activated and sent up to Jeffersonville, Indiana. We should meet only very light resistance, if any."

"Major Miles, that is great news," said the lieutenant.

"Yes, men, if all goes as well as expected, we should do our fundraiser in Leavenworth tomorrow evening. I am also told that there is a good hotel in Leavenworth with a great dining room. Perhaps tomorrow night, we will have accommodations befitting Southern gentlemen. Men, let's get some rest. Tomorrow will be another busy day."

Soon, the men of the Southern Storm were drifting off to sleep, under the stars, on this warm Indiana night.

The men of the Southern Storm were up early and anxious for another thrill filled day of raiding, spreading terror and confusion and acquiring funds and fine horses for the noble Southern cause.

The major informed the men that, barring any unforeseen delays, they would more than likely be the guests of the people and town of Leavenworth, Indiana, by nightfall. Yes, this was the plan and he felt that the second day of this raid would probably be as successful as the first, perhaps even more so.

After a hearty breakfast, compliments of the local citizens and businesses, the Southern Storm moved out smartly. They made a striking appearance. All men were still dressed in the best Confederate cavalry uniforms that were to be had.

Gen. Braxton Bragg had ordered that the men of the Southern Storm would be a shining example of the best soldiers the South had to offer. Of course, this means good uniforms with all the braids and trimming as well as shined boots and polished brass. Though, by now, carrying some trail dust, the Southern Storm still had the looks of the "Pride of the South."

Major Miles had already told his officers and sergeants of the first planned stop of the day. They would stop at Galey's Landing, only a short distance away, and negotiate with a Mr. Prather to see if perhaps he would be willing to sell some of his better horses.

The unit stopped in the road in front of the Prather place and Major Miles called loudly, but in a friendly tone, "Mr. Prather, is anyone at home? We would like to have a word with you, sir!"

At first, Mr. Prather didn't want to come out of the house, but finally did. He came out on his front porch and was very uneasy when he saw this extremely heavily armed group of Confederate soldiers. He replied, "Yes, sir, what can I do for you?"

"Well, sir, we understand that you are a good judge of horse-flesh and are a dealer in high quality horses. We are looking to buy some good horses."

Old man Prather answered, "While I appreciate being thought of as a dealer in good horses, at the present time I'm plumb out of horses to sell. Ain't got none 'cept for what me and my boys ride. Sorry, Major."

Major Miles was ready for this and as prearranged, he signaled First Sgt. Calhoun who promptly left with five troopers at a fast trot. They went up the road a short distance, turned left up into the rocky hills. Sure enough, they finally came to the rock walled canyon that the Knights of the Golden Circle informant had told Major Miles about in the note slipped to him.

At first, Sgt. Calhoun and his men thought that the informant had been wrong about there being horses hidden at this place called Penitentiary Rock. Then, he noticed a faint trail that went farther and deeper into the canyon. After some diligent tracking, they found a small herd of twelve horses hidden in a thick grove of sassafras trees.

Even stranger, they were being guarded by Mr. Prather's four pistol packing sons. When Sgt. Calhoun and his men showed up, the startled Prather boys started to reach for their guns. However, they quickly changed their minds when they realized how badly they were outgunned and outnumbered.

Sgt. Calhoun said, "Good morning y'all. Your daddy and our people are fixing to do some horse dealing and he sent us up here to help you bring this bunch of horses back down to the main place."

The Prather boys did not believe it for a minute, but saw they had little choice. Half-heartedly, they began rounding up the horses and after another thirty minute delay, men and horses were back down to the house where the dealing would take place.

When the twelve horses were back, a surprised Mr. Prather awkwardly said, "Why, those must have been some I forgot about having. You know, sir, at times horse dealing is right confusing business."

The major quickly responded, "Yes, sir, I can well imagine that your type of dealing could be rather confusing. You know, some of those horses sound to me like they whinny with a Southern accent. Do you happen to remember where this bunch came from?"

"No, Major, I don't. Like I just said, sometimes business gets confusing."

Sgt. Calhoun said, "Major, I say that all twelve of these horses are up to our high standards and I think we should buy all twelve of them."

"Very well, Sgt. Calhoun."

"Mr. Prather, what would you say is a fair price for these horses?"

Prather answered, "Well now, I don't rightly know. Even though I forgot I had 'em, I didn't really want to sell them." However, when he started realizing that there were dozens and dozens of cocked guns being carelessly brandished about, he started thinking more clearly. He then said, "Well now, you know that good horses don't come cheap. I reckon that I'd have to have at least fifty dollars a head for horses of this quality."

It was common knowledge that these days, twenty-five dollars was a good fair price for a good horse. This old dealer was trying to gouge the Southerners. The truth of it was that these horses had cost him and his boys only time, ingenuity and travel.

Major Miles said, "Sir, just to show you that we are fair-minded people, we are going to pay you twice your asking price for these fine horses. We will pay you one hundred dollars per horse."

Prather quickly answered, "You do know that I much prefer to be paid in gold. I like gold much the best."

"Well, sir, you'll have to see Lt. Clay there to get your money. He is my Financial Affairs Officer."

Lt. Clay said, "Mr. Prather, I know that you prefer gold, but today you'll just have to take paper money." At which time, several more Confederate weapons were cocked. Lt. Clay proceeded to count out the agreed amount of paper money then he added, "Sir, those are very fine horses. Here is an extra hundred dollars as a bonus. Thank you, sir. It has been a pleasure doing business with you."

As the Southern Storm started up the road with their horse herd close behind, Mr. Prather was recounting the paper money when he realized that he had been paid, not with U.S. money, but rather with Confederate money.

Mr. Prather cursed loudly, "Dammit, they ain't nothing but a bunch of damn thieves!!"

The oldest Prather son said, "What did you say, Pa??"

All in all, Major Miles figured that this transaction had put his group at least forty-five minutes behind schedule. He felt that it was worth it to get those good horses, but he hoped there would be no more delays today. They proceeded on to their next planned place of business, the small thriving town of Alton, Indiana.

Just about three miles below Alton, the Southern Storm had another unexpected stroke of good luck. There, nosed up to the river bank, was a beautiful, nearly new packet boat, the "Tarascon." The boat was a side wheeler and some bolts had come loose on the paddles on the starboard side paddle wheel. The loose bolts were being retightened as the captain and crew anxiously watched. They had been warned of the possibility of coming trouble from the Southern raiders when they had stopped at Leavenworth. They were on the alert, but this was an unplanned stop for emergency repairs.

The repairs were nearly completed, no more than five minutes longer, and the "Tarascon" would be underway again. Suddenly, there was the deafening sound of the Southern Storm's calling card rifle salute. The surprised captain and crew now had fifteen heavily armed Rebel soldiers on board and quickly taking control.

There were about thirty passengers on board. After they heard Lt. Clay's solicitation for funds to support the Southern cause, they contributed very generously indeed. The captain and crew decided to contribute as well. Of course, the safe was found to be about one fourth full of other useful items.

The beautiful big side wheel packet boat was spared in view of their contributions and, thus, the "Tarascon" proceeded on downriver as the Southern Storm continued on toward Alton, Indiana. Again, the Storm had encountered another thirty minute delay, but it had been a profitable delay.

The K.G.C. informant's information was once more proved

to be correct. The Home Guard unit, the Hartford Guard, were gone, all sixty of them. However, the town had been warned of approaching danger and fifteen citizens, merchants and farmers had taken up arms and were very determined to make a stand. They had heard the gunfire from downriver and were as ready as they could be.

The men of the Southern Storm split into two columns at the edge of town in their usual manner, formed with the main part of town between them. They quickly announced their arrival with their distinctive rapid fire calling card.

The town's defenders answered back with a decent return fire, considering what they had for weapons. However, their resistance was puny in comparison to the Southern Storm's advanced weaponry. Two of the town's defenders fell and the rest, seeing the futility of it all, quickly did the wise thing and surrendered.

One Reb trooper had suffered a very minor graze wound to his right arm, while another had his beard singed by a very close passing bullet.

Some semblance of order returned. Major Miles announced to the assembled citizens the purpose of their fundraising mission and expressed the hope that the people would contribute or invest wisely and generously. He also added that schools, churches, clergymen and medical people were exempted from the fundraising activities.

Things went rather well at the Alton Bank, and also at the river port and the town's three general stores. Several private citizens even decided to help. Up to this point, the mission went well for the Rebs, but they had overlooked one thing that was going to result in a rather long delay.

The Southern Storm was preparing to leave the town of Alton and the major and captain took a brief look at their map of the area. Capt. Lewis said, "Major, the map shows that there is a bridge over a river that we have to cross at the edge of town. The map says that the bridge is real close to that big grist mill. The mill should have a sign saying Fullenwider's Mill." Indeed, they came to the edge of Little Blue River at Fullenwider's Mill, but there was a hitch. There was no bridge across the river.

Major Miles took a closer look at their map and saw the problem. The map was an old one, dated 1848. It merely showed the site of a proposed bridge to cross the river. As of this time in 1863, the bridge had not been built. Instead of a bridge, there was a small rope pulled ferry boat to cross the river at Fullenwider's Mill. The next problem was obvious. The small ferry boat was operated by a young man named James Riddell. James had heard the gunfire and shouting in town and had quickly thought of a way to interfere with the Rebel raiders' progress.

Just as the Southern Storm rode up to the edge of Little Blue River, James Riddell had pulled the ferry boat to the opposite side and was in the process of tying the boat to a large piling with some knots that would not be easily untied. James ignored the calls from the Mill landing ordering him to bring the ferry back across. He knew the area very well and quickly went up the bank and disappeared in the woods. As James made his escape, he was muttering to himself, "I'll see 'em in hell before I ferry that bunch of rabble across the river."

The river, though not huge, presented several problems for the Southern Storm. If they tried to swim across, their pack horse and its packs full of explosives destined for the Howard Boat Works at Jeffersonville would likely be ruined by getting wet. Also, the herd of remount horses would be difficult to herd across the river. Some horses like to swim; others don't. Another major problem was that the, by now large, collection of paper Yankee money would get wet. Water is not good for paper money.

One of Major Renfro Miles' biggest objections to a wet crossing of the Little Blue River was of a public relations nature. Up to this point, the Southern Storm had maintained its splendid appearance as a shining example of a well-dressed, well-equipped Confederate cavalry unit, just as Gen. Braxton Bragg had ordered. Even up to this point, they were standing tall, shined boots, brass and all. Major Miles knew full well that if they were to do a wet crossing, they would present a very bedraggled appearance.

He had no intention of letting his men look like drowned rats. This would not be good public relations!

Capt. Lewis sent two men upriver to try to find a rowboat or canoe so someone could cross Little Blue River, untie the ferry boat and pull it back across. In about twenty minutes, they were back down the river in an old Leavenworth skiff boat and were in the process of untying the ferry and returning it. The crossing finally went smooth enough, but it was a slow process. It took five trips to ferry all the men and horses across.

After this unexpected three hour delay, the Southern Storm continued upriver. It was becoming clear that they would probably not reach Leavenworth in time to do their fundraiser during daylight hours, though it was still too early to tell for sure.

Their next stop was a tiny village called Cape Sandy. There was only a general store and a few houses. Major Miles decided to dispense with the rapid fire calling card here, since there were too few people here to fully appreciate its significance. The homes and their residents were not asked for support as the area looked none too prosperous. The owner of the Cape Sandy general store did donate an adequate amount of ham, cheese and crackers for the raiders' mid-afternoon break. He also worked very hard at pumping water for the horse troughs as the thirsty horses drank. Since he was such a good sport about the matter, he was not asked for a cash contribution.

Three more horses were acquired, two at one farm and one at another. Their owners had been paid well above the going market price. Lt. Clay was careful to explain to all those he dealt with that if the seller had any concerns about the Confederate money being good at this time, all they had to do was hold on to it 'til the South had finished winning this war, then most surely there would be no problem. Surely these were words of consolation.

At approximately 5:00 PM, the Southern Storm arrived at the small town of Fredonia, Indiana.

As the Southern Storm had predicted, their reputation had preceded them. When the town fathers at Fredonia learned of the extremely well-armed Rebels heading their way, they realized that it would be an exercise in futility to resist. Fredonia had a very good Home Guard unit, but they had been called away. The town was the same as defenseless. There were too many valuable businesses and buildings to just let it all go up in smoke, so an alternate plan had been worked out at around noon.

An urgent meeting had been called by the town's leading citizens and business owners, including John McFall; William Conrad, a saloon owner; John Leggett, owner of the local hotel; Nancy Collison, lady saloon owner; Esau McFall, owner of the town's second hotel; Mr. Best, sawmill owner; and last but not least, Mr. Collingswood, owner of the local leather tannery.

Mr. William Conrad called the meeting to order and made these opening remarks, "Ladies and gentlemen of Fredonia, listen closely. We must come up with a plan and be quick about it!! We have been forewarned about the raiders headed our way. We are not well-armed enough to properly defend our people and possessions, to say nothing of our town's many thriving enterprises. We stand to lose much if we handle this the wrong way. Does anyone have a suggestion?"

John McFall suggested, "People, there's more than one way to skin a cat! As we all know, our forty man Home Guard company has been called away, so I say that we should kill these Rebs with kindness."

At which Nancy Collison said, "And, John, how would you suggest we go about killing 'em with kindness?"

"Well, I think we ought to quickly organize a phony town wide celebration of some sort, maybe pass it off as a 'Founders' Day Celebration.' You know, celebrating our town's sixty year anniversary or something of that sort. When the Rebs get here we welcome them as guests and do our best to try not to rub their fur the wrong way! Does anyone have any ideas?"

Bill Curry quickly came up with a brilliant idea. He said, "You all know that no celebration is ever complete without an adequate supply of liquid refreshments. I will donate two kegs of my best brandy from my saloon for the occasion. I'll bet that Nancy would volunteer to be on the refreshment committee as well."

Nancy Collison came back quickly with, "Count me in for more brandy, wine and some whiskey too. I have some 'Old Wildcat' Kentucky whiskey that I'll bet those soldiers would drool over."

The impromptu celebration was coming together quickly. It had to for the town's sake.

Mr. Collingswood suggested that they start a large fire in the middle of Main Street and start cooking up all the beef that they could find on short notice.

Esau McFall was against the beef idea and said, "Folks, if the Rebs see us cooking beef, they might get the idea that we are a prosperous bunch and expect more from us than we want to contribute. I say that we start cooking up a couple of huge pots of ham and beans and cornbread to go with it. If they see us with 'poor people's food,' they may be more apt to believe that we are poor people."

The menu was decided and people were rapidly delegated to their tasks of building cook fires, gathering food items, etc.

Mr. Best said, "People, listen to me. Don't dress in your best clothes. The idea is to look poor! I would also suggest that you try to hide most of your valuables, not all, but most."

John Leggett said, "We need to round up all the best horses we have, except for maybe a couple. If they want our oldest worn-out nags, I say let 'em have 'em!!"

Fredonia was soon a frenzy of activity. Three teenage boys soon had the best horses gathered up. They were under orders to drive the horses to a densely wooded area near Schooner Point along the Ohio River and lay low, keeping the horses safely out of sight until someone came and notified them that the Rebs had left.

Very soon, Fredonia had all the appearance of a town in celebration. Flags were flying, food tables were set up, and a long well-supplied refreshment area was set up 'neath the big oak tree by the village pump, close to the old court house.

The beans were not really cooked enough by the time the Southern Storm arrived, but they were getting there.

The towns' people saw the two columns of heavily armed Confederates coming and forming their circle around the center of activity, but did their best not to panic.

The Southern Storm once more announced their presence with their, by now, traditional attention getting 63 gun three shot salute!

When the major was sure he had the crowd's undivided attention, which was soon, he made his opening remarks. In his most official authoritative voice, the major began, "Ladies and gentlemen, please allow me to introduce myself. I am Major Renfro Miles, Army of Tennessee, Confederate States of America. My unit is known far and wide as the Southern Storm. We are on an official military mission on orders from Gen. Braxton Bragg, Army of Tennessee, C.S.A. Our mission is that of procuring good remount horses for our cavalry, as well as soliciting investments in support of the Confederate cause. So far, we have found the people in this part of Indiana to be quite supportive of our cause and hope the people of this town will prove to be no different! Please be assured that we are honorable men and nothing will be taken without proper payment. Lt. Clay is my Financial Affairs Officer and you need to see him at yonder table to make your investments and contributions."

The major had made his point quite clear and people were soon forming a line at Lt. Clay's table. The people were "investing" but it seemed in very much smaller amounts. Being a fair-minded man, Lt. Clay was exchanging one and one half Confederate dollars for every U.S. dollar invested.

Mr. John McFall approached Major Miles and said, "Major Miles, on behalf of our town, I'd like to welcome you and your men to Fredonia and invite you to be our guests in celebrating the sixtieth anniversary of our town. Though it is poor man's food, it is good and you are all invited to share in our food. As you can see, we also have plenty of liquid refreshments as well. Also, Major, please allow me to thank you and your men for the fireworks display. We had wanted to have some fireworks, but were short of funds. But, thanks to you, we had fireworks anyway.

"You are quite welcome, sir. Now, as for your invitation for food and drink, that is very kind of you and your people. I am quite sure my men are hungry as well as thirsty; we will accept your hospitality. There is one thing, sir. As a gentleman, I insist that some of you and yours partake of food and refreshment first. It would be rude of us to do otherwise."

Mr. McFall said, "Very well, Major, as you wish." He and some of his people began filling their plates and glasses.

Major Miles was a tad bit suspicious of these people. They were just almost too damn friendly and hospitable. He also remembered something from his military academy years about the old rule, "Never eat the enemy's food 'til he tries it first." Poisoning an enemy is not a new thing.

The townspeople were eating and drinking and everything smelled so good.

The officers and men of the Southern Storm first had a little happy hour at the beverage table. The brandy was very good. The major cautioned his men to not overdo, but, in some cases, his words of warning fell on deaf ears.

Lt. Clay negotiated for the only two horses in town that seemed up to the high standards of the cavalry of the C.S.A. It seemed that there were no other good horses around to be had. As for the town's cash contributions to the Southern cause, this was also on the weak side. On the positive side though, all agreed that these Yanks were gracious hosts and very friendly.

After approximately two hours of happy hour and filling up on ham, beans and cornbread, Major Miles and Capt. Lewis called an end to the business at hand. It was now past 7:00 PM.

John Leggett and Esau McFall, the two hotel owners offered to provide lodging for the Southern Storm for the night, but Major Miles politely declined the kind offer. He then thanked the townspeople for their hospitality and also for their support for the Southern cause.

It took a few minutes, but order was restored among the troops and they moved about one quarter mile from town to bivouac for the night. It was now too late to do Leavenworth tonight, much better to move in unfamiliar territory in daylight.

Capt. Lewis said, "Major Miles, do you think we might be wise to send a scouting party ahead to check things out?"

"No, Captain, no use in doing that. I'm quite sure that by now, they know we are coming, but I feel that there's very little they can do about it. I'm quite sure our reputation has preceded us."

"Captain, have Sgt. Calhoun put two of our best men on guard with Lt. Clay and the saddlebags of cash and other valuables tonight. Gen. Bragg will be very pleased when he sees the support we have raised for our cause. Also, Captain, make sure the new horses are watched closely tonight. I think we have about all the horses we need for this drive."

"Yes, sir, I'll see to the security details."

"And Capt. Lewis, one more thing, make very sure the explosives destined for the boat works at Jeffersonville are also secure.

We are getting closer to the point where that part of the mission will separate from the main group."

"Yes, Major, it will be done."

"You know, Captain, it went about like I figured. These Yanks don't seem to have much backbone. You saw how it went today?"

"Major, you were right about that part of it so far. I just hope there are more of their kind ahead of us."

"Nothing to worry about, Captain. We will whup up on Leavenworth tomorrow. After that, we will head for Tobacco Landing. The flatboats will be waiting there to ferry us across the Ohio. After that, we will head back in the direction of Dixie. The boats will be waiting for us the day after tomorrow if all goes as planned. Oh, how sweet it will be, on a back road headed back to Dixie."

"Capt. Lewis smiled broadly and said, "I'll say amen to that. It will be nice to head south."

STEAMBOATS. ETC.

Speed, Safety and Comfort.

Regular Leavenworth and Louisville Packet,
SANDY.

NAT. P. BALDWIN..................................MASTER
SOWLE & BALDWIN..............................CLERKS

This new and elegant light draught steamer will make regular trips between Leavenworth and New Albany, leaving Leavenworth on Sundays, Tuesdays and Thursdays of each week; arriving Mondays, Wednesdays and Fridays. For freight or passage apply on board. jy13

The Splendid Steamer
MORNING STAR,

A. T. GILMORE..................................MASTER.
M. D. WARREN..................................CLERK.

Passes Leavenworth, going down, every Wednesday and Saturday evening; passes up every Tuesday morning and Friday evening. jy13

The Beautiful Steamer,
TARASCON.

JAMES MATHER.................................MASTER.
FRANK O. SMITH...............................CLERK

Passes Leavenworth, going down, every Wednesday and Saturday evening; passes up every Tuesday morning and Friday evening. jy13

Low Water Arrangement,
The Light Draught Steamer,
ROSE HITE.

E. P. CRIDER....................................MASTER
PHIL. BEVERLY................................CLERK,

Passes Leavenworth, going down, every Monday and Thursday evening; passes up every Saturday and Wednesday evening. jy13

FIFTEEN

The Action At The Cliffs

ON THIS NIGHT in June 1863, Lt. Sam Buchanan had just woke up from his two hour attempt at trying to rest. Though not generally known, it's not easy to rest just before approaching battle. Sam made his way over to Capt. Herndon's position and said, "Captain, I'll take over now. It's time for you to try to get some rest."

"Okay, Sam, I am getting drowsy. I probably won't be able to sleep, but I'll try. Don't let me sleep past 4:00 AM if I do drift off. We must be on full alert and ready for whatever comes from then on. Lord, I haven't stayed up this late in years!"

So, at 2:00 AM on this night in June 1863, Capt. Elam Herndon wrapped a blanket around himself and his rifle. With his coat as a pillow, he leaned back against a mound of dirt to try to rest.

The men's small campfires were burning low and the conversations were getting lower as well. The night sounds were good and the air was fragrant with the good smells of the wood smoke combined with the aroma of brewing coffee pots, also blended, of course, with the tobacco smoke from the soldiers' pipes, cigars and home rolled cigarettes. All the good smells of a men's camp in the woods, but this was no ordinary camping trip. Elam knew, only too well, that in just a few short hours these pleasant smells and sounds would be replaced by smells and sounds of battle, the unmistakable stench of gunpowder mixed with the sounds of men trying to send each other into the company of the devil.

Elam was very tired and soon he was starting to drift off. It all seemed like a vague, fast moving dream, but he knew that the recent events were real and far from a dream. As he teetered between the edge of full alertness and that of dreamland, he started recounting the past few weeks.

Years ago, Elam had resigned himself to the fact that he was a partially disabled army veteran and was no longer fit for military service. Even if he were not handicapped, his age would make him an unlikely candidate for anyone's army.

But the fact was that here he was at 57 years old, with a leg that didn't work all that well, a shoulder that never let him forget that war in Mexico, and a group of men looking to him for leadership in a fast approaching battle.

Here in Southern Indiana, on a rock strewn cliff near the Ohio River, was where it would happen and now Capt. Elam Herndon of the L.H.G.R. was trying to remember Leavenworth as it was. He was also still finding it hard to believe that his accepting command of a unit basically formed for the purpose of babysitting a town in the absence of the regular Home Guard could ever lead to this. Never in his wildest dreams would he have thought that his little unit of citizen soldiers would ever find themselves in a situation like this.

But yes, as Elam drifted off, he thought, "This is real. We are here and we will do what we have to do!"

At 4:00 AM, Capt. Herndon passed the word, "Men, don't add any more wood to the fires. We have got to let them die down. At 5:00 AM, we will snuff out the fires and cover them. Drink your coffee while you can; it will be cold later on."

Jim Running Deer said, "Boys, if you'll put some rocks in the fire now and let them be getting hot, when we put the fire out the hot rocks will keep the coffee pots hot for quite awhile."

Chet Hatfield said, "Now, let us guess, Jim, another old Indian trick?"

Came the reply, "What else?"

As the fires were getting lower, so were the tales coming slower. But, though slower, the conversations went on.

Helmer Schmitt said, "I can see that old Newt is fast asleep over there so I can say this without hurting his feelings. Does anyone here know how booze got such a terrible hold on Newt?? We all know he is a real nice guy and a good entertainer. It's a shame that this has happened to him."

Dan Lyon said, "Yes, I know about Newt's problem as do some of the rest of you. True, it is a shame and right now he's trying awfully hard to control it. I know it's rough for him. Back a few years ago, he didn't drink much more than the rest of us around here. We all seem to drink our fair share. When he started playing his guitar in the saloons to make a living, his appetite for booze increased, but he still wasn't too bad off.

What took him down was that three years when he left Leavenworth and played music on that showboat from New Orleans to Cincinnati. When he got let go from that job, he has never been sober for very long at a time. The captain and I just said privately that by now he must be like a tight rope about to snap. We all need to help him if we can and try to keep his spirits up. This is the longest dry spell Newt has had in years."

As the morning draws closer, the talk starts to get more serious.

Nineteen year old Lemuel Moore said, "I know you men think I am a little different. Well, that's because I am. The reason is that I accidentally got kicked in the head by one of Dad's old cows back when I was ten years old. At first, Dr. Bowman thought I'd die, but I slowly got better. Sometimes, I still have bad headaches and move a little slow. Once in a while, I get confused and forget things. I sure would feel bad if I ever was the cause of any of you getting hurt because of my condition. I do want to tell you all, while I have the chance, that I am real proud of being part of this outfit and thank Capt. Herndon for letting me serve."

"Well said, Lemuel, I want to thank you for being willing to serve. You are one of us and we are all glad you are. Now, don't fret and stew. We all get a little confused and forgetful at times. In the next few hours, it might get confusing for the lot of us. Now, about being cow-kicked in the head, I don't know if you know it or not, but our Commander-in-Chief has something in common with you. Yes, it's true, Pvt. Moore, President Abe Lincoln was also head-kicked by a cow when he was young. See how far he has gone?"

The men laughed and Sgt. Wildman said, "See there, Lemuel, you are in some high class company."

Educated Tad martin said, "Lt. Buchanan, I have been thinking about the three to one odds against us we were told about earlier."

"Yes, Private Martin?"

"Well, Lieutenant, I have been going over the numbers and odds are worse than that, I think. True, if you figure at the rate of 63 of them against the 21 of us, the odds are three of them against one of us. But when you take into account them all being armed with repeating weapons, extra magazines, cylinders and such, I calculate much worse odds."

"How much worse, Private?"

"I figure, considering their rapid fire capability, that the odds could be more like ten of them to one of us. That could figure out like 630 of them against our 21 men."

"Well now, if the figuring ended up right there, you could be right. However, we are going to tilt those odds so that they make things a little more even, a little more in our favor. The captain will explain in more detail; the army calls it strategy."

Capt. Herndon began, "Now, for openers, we have the high ground advantage, much better to shoot downward than them trying to aim up high. Next, we will have the element of total surprise. That is, if we get it right. By the way we have our extra weapons loaded and placed, we should be able to fire three rather quick volleys of fire. I figure that with some good shooting, the first volley will turn the Southern Storm into a much smaller unit. The second volley should even up the odds even more.

Another thing on our side is the fact that these cliffs will make the echoes of our gunfire sound like we are a much larger force than we actually are. I have no doubt this will play on their nerves. The next thing is that they will be mounted on moving horses, which we all know makes it damn difficult to take good aim to return our fire. Then, of course, this will happen only after they decide where our fire is coming from. It will at least take them a few seconds to figure out our positions. In that few seconds, we intend to have them surrender. Some of our best marksmen already know what will be their prime targets. The rest of you will be assigned to a particular field of fire when we start getting prepared a little later on. Are there any questions?

Yes, Private Schmitt, what is your question?"

"What should we do if our second or third volley doesn't stop them?"

"If that were to happen, then the best thing to do would be to get up and run if you were able. Unfortunately, too many of us are too crippled up and too old to run. So, I guess we'll stay and fight. Seriously, men, we are in the right. We are trying to protect our families, homes and our way of life. We stand as brothers. We will make it through this together!! Stand fast; stand your ground."

The firelight is starting to get low. Jacob Silverstein has to make two last minute minor gun repairs. One of the old 1816 smoothbores that Chet Hatfield had by him had a loose flint in the lock, which might cause a misfire. He had just noticed it and Jacob was working on it in the dim firelight. He had no sooner finished fixing the old flintlock when Hibachi Takaguchi brought one of his antique Springfield smoothbores over for Jacob to fix. The barrel bands were not holding the barrel firmly in place in the stock of the musket, i.e., a loose barrel.

Hibachi said, "Jacob, I not can be good shooter with loose barrel. Also, with extra powder in her, she might just jump apart when I shoot."

"You're right Hibachi. I'm glad you seen this in time. I see now that the barrel band springs have grown weak on all three bands. I'll have her fixed in a few minutes. Jacob then found his knife and quickly whittled out three small wooden shims or wedges from a piece of hickory and tapped them in place between the bottom of the stock and the three barrel bands, thus compensating for the weak springs. "There, Hibachi, not good as new, but close."

"Thank you much, Jacob. I bet I now shoot much better."

"Good shooting, Hibachi."

Soon Capt. Herndon ordered that the two now nearly dead fires be snuffed out with water and covered with dirt.

Sgt. Wildman was checking the men and their positions. He could hear faint sobbing coming from one soldier's place. He softly walked up and saw it was young Private James Corbin. James would be 15 in only two more months. In a low voice, the Sergeant said, "What's wrong, son?"

"Sgt. Wildman, I guess I'm scared!"

"It's okay, son. We are all scared. It's nothing to be ashamed of. I have been in lots of battles. It's always the same. Any man that says approaching battle does not scare him is a damn liar. Just remember this, when the shooting starts, it all changes. We'll do what we have to do. Now settle down and try to rest some. Remember, we are all in this together. We stand as brothers; you are not alone. Your buddy, Pvt. Lyon will be back in a few minutes and he will be at your left, about seven feet from you. Old Dan has felt the heat before; you can count on him. I will be to the right of you about seven feet. Don't worry."

As the rest of the men started back to their positions after covering the two campfires, Sgt. Bratton was overheard telling the others about some lines in an old English soldier's story he had once read. It went like this, "Cowards die a thousand deaths, but the brave, they die but once."

Someone retorted, "Damn, Sergeant, ain't you the cheerful one!"

It was now about 5:00 AM. A rope was tied around a big rock and the end of the rope was thrown downward in the path of the quick exit route. Jim Running Deer slung his Sharps rifle over his back and secured his revolver in its holster with a leather thong, so as not to lose it in the dark. With the aid of the rope, he silently made his way down the steep incline. In two minutes, he was down on the road.

The captain passed the word, "Everyone—full alert, get ready, take care. Above all, no accidental gunshots. We must have total surprise!!"

The captain, Lt. Buchanan and Sgt. Bratton were talking in a low breath among themselves. Capt. Herndon says, "You know, if the Confederate troops ever get a good look at our group, they might laugh themselves to death!"

Sgt. Bratton said, "I vote that we don't let 'em ever get close enough to see us period, no how, no way, okay?"

Sgt. Wildman whispered, "We have a problem over here. It's Newt. He is shaking so bad that he could shoot a whole crowd with one shotgun blast."

The captain and lieutenant made their way over to Newt's position. The captain said, "Newt, what's the problem? Are you sick or are you scared or what?"

"Captain, no I ain't afraid. It's just that, well, I haven't had even one little drink now for over twenty-two hours. Hell, Captain, my body is crying for a drink. I know I'd be better if I could just have even one small drink!!"

"No, Newt, no booze. There ain't none here. I'm sorry. Just try to hang in there and tough it through. This probably won't take too long. Newt, I promise you this. When we get this thing over, you and I will go up to the Dexter Saloon and get real refreshed. You know, my nerves are a little jangled too. Dig in now. Think of what we have to do and let's all try to do it right!"

"Yes, sir, Capt. Herndon. I wish them Rebs would quit dawdling around and get to hell on up this way!!"

"They will be here soon enough."

Meanwhile, about five miles away, near Fredonia, Indiana, the camp where the Southern Storm had stopped for the night was coming to life. The men and horses were both well-rested from the long ride and engagements of yesterday.

On this warm morning in June 1863, Major Renfro Miles woke up on his bedroll feeling as good as any successful soldier had ever felt. This whole operation had been his brainchild. On this mission, they had raided six towns and villages while meeting only light or token resistance from the Yankees. Those that had put up that resistance had paid dearly, but, after all, that was the fortunes of war. He and the men of the Southern Storm had already disrupted the tranquility of the region. While at the same time, they had acquired a rather large amount of help for the Confederate cause, this being in the form of U.S. currency as well as gold and silver. The bank in this next town of Leavenworth would surely want to give them more help. As an added bonus, he now had around twenty-four fine horses, recently liberated from the Yanks. Of course, they had been paid for with good C.S.A. money. He had planned to start acquiring horses later on, but most of these looked too good to pass up so they had started collecting horses just out of Rome, Indiana. These horses would be remounts for the Confederate cavalry. Good horses were vital to the cause.

After washing the trail dust from his face, Major Miles and

his staff had a fine breakfast of recently acquired Southern Indiana ham, fresh eggs, fried taters and biscuits which was washed down with good old Louisiana coffee.

The major said, "Capt. Lewis, today you had better put the third man on the horse herd detail. We don't want to lose even one of those fine horses."

"Yes, sir, I'll see to it."

Shortly, they broke camp and mounted up, ready to head upriver. All among them were eager to proceed. Major Miles had ordered them to ride in a column of threes, with the herd of remount horses bringing up the rear.

This extremely well-armed column of cavalry made a formidable sight as they galloped on. They also felt sure that their reputation had preceded them, and it had.

Back at the cliffs, Pvt. Jim Running Deer had just sat up after doing another ground listen. He hollered up to the positions, "Captain, something is wrong. I can't tell for sure, but I hear many more than 65 horses. I think several more. We could be in for worse!!"

"Okay, Jim, maybe they picked up some volunteers. We will know when they get here. About how soon do you think they will be here."

"Captain, I'd say that in about 30-35 minutes they will be here in all their glory!"

"Well then, we will see just how many of them we can send to glory! Come on up, Jim. Sling your rifle and tie a big loop at the end of the rope. We will help you come up."

With the help of three men pulling on the rope, Jim Running Deer was back up at the ledge and he wasn't even breathing hard. He said, "Now, Capt. Herndon, you know that I never was real good with numbers, but I am sure that there are many more than 65 horses coming, maybe as much as 25-30 more."

"Thanks, Jim, we can only get ready and do our best. You already know what your prime targets are, don't you?"

"Yes, sir."

"Everyone move back into your places, company is coming!"

The men noticed in the early light that Capt. Herndon seemed to either be talking to himself or praying or both.

Tad Martin says, "Lieutenant, I can't hear what the captain is saying. Do you know?"

"Yes, Private, I know. He is repeating a poem he wrote many years ago before a Mexican battle. I have heard him recite it many times, usually just before battle. He says the poem sort of helps him get his mind straight and prepares him. It's sort of like a cross between a poem and a prayer. Elam calls it, 'The Soldiers Dance' or 'Just Before the Battle,' one or the other.

"Excuse me, Captain. Some of the boys would like to hear your poem. Would you start it again and maybe just a bit louder?"

The captain begins:

> "Back once, when we were younger,
>> We done a dance with death.
> Yes, in the heat of battle,
>> You can smell the devil's breath.
> But, when the noise was over
>> And all the smoke had cleared,
> Though we were badly wounded,
>> It was better than we had feared.
> And now these long years later,
>> We have done our dance with life.
> Now comes time for protecting
>> Your home, your kids and wife.
> You know a thing worth having
>> Is well worth fighting for
> And it seems there's no escaping
>> The coming sounds of war.

The enemy is coming there,
    Off in the early light.
His line is long; he numbers strong;
    He's ready for the fight.
So let's prepare for battle,
    We will do our dance with death,
But be braced in the midst of battle
    For you can smell the devil's breath."

Buford Beasley said, "Thanks, Captain. That has a strong message."

Back on the road, Renfro Miles felt as though he were riding on a cloud instead of his fine bay horse. He had the world by the tail on a downhill slide and things were going his way. He was quite naturally filled with confidence as he had been nothing but successful so far.

The bravado rubbed off on his men. They were indeed proud to ride behind such a brave and bright young leader.

The brave but brash young major had no idea of the coming change in his fortunes.

Back on the cliff, Pvt. Albert LeCroix said, "Capt. Herndon, ain't what we are about to do sort of like murder?"

The reply was, "Son, if this doesn't go right, we will really see what murder is. Let's do it right. Now settle down, aim close and do your damnedest."

Major Miles had just ordered his column to slow down to a trot as the mounts were getting lathered. They had a short distance to go, then they would be at Leavenworth, Indiana, whereupon the Southern Storm planned to really "kick some ass!" These Yanks needed to be taught a lesson, and yes, they needed it to be taught to them by the Southern Storm!!

The men on the cliff could now hear the approaching storm and they didn't need an ear to the ground either.

Lt. Buchanan said, "Now, men, when we fire into 'em, it will be like we stirred up a nest of hornets. If we don't stop them by the third volley, we will be in a tight spot. Now, settle down. Aim close!"

Now Herndon's men could all very plainly hear the thunder of horses' hoofs. Even those with less than perfect hearing knew the Rebs were close, very close.

The tension built and there were many sweaty palms, but the men of "Herndon's Hope" maintained their discipline as best they could and worked hard at showing no outward fear.

Major Miles knew from his map that just past those limestone/sandstone cliffs was the town of Leavenworth. He was growing anxious and was looking forward to turning his troops loose on the town. The Southern Storm was ready to ride by the cliffs at their left.

Now, the men on the cliff have the Rebs in plain sight and are taking close aim at their assigned targets. It's now or never—it's now!! The captain gave, "Ready, Aim, Fire!!" The first volley went off in close to perfect unison sounding much like one giant shot. The cliffs and hills echo the report of the guns, much like the sound of a violent midsummer thunderstorm.

Major Miles and his men were totally surprised to hear what they at first thought was the loud rumbling of thunder. It was too nice a day for there to be thunder!! When the major looked to the rear, he could see many of his men falling from the saddle. An instant later, the young major felt a searing pain in his left leg as a .44 caliber bullet shattered it. He remembered starting to scream in agony as he fell from his saddle. He could hear more confusion, excited screaming, yelling and more thunderous gunfire.

With military precision, the men of Herndon's Hope had laid down a withering wall of fire against the Southern Storm with devastating effect. Major Miles didn't know yet that 18 of his men had dropped from the saddle from the first volley of fire.

Of those 18 men, 14 were dead and four men were badly wounded. The second volley had claimed eight more casualties, four of them dead and four more wounded. The once proud Southern Storm, 63 men strong, was now reduced to a force of only 37 able-bodied men and 8 men wounded, some severely.

The cliff area, which just a short while ago was thick with the fragrant smell of coffee and good smelling wood burning fires, now had a horrible stench as would the gates of hell! The once fragrant air was now filled with acrid gun smoke and the yells and screams of men in agony.

The Reb soldiers remaining managed to get off a few poorly aimed shots at Herndon's men, but not with much effect.

Another fierce volley of fire came from the cliffs and more Rebels fell. Now a huge voice was echoing from the heights saying, "Surrender now!! You are surrounded. Lay down your arms and surrender or no one will be left to surrender!!" The huge voice echoed on and on.

Major Miles ordered his men to surrender just before he passed out. He was bleeding badly.

The men did as their major had ordered. A loud command from the cliff told them to disarm and to pile all their weapons in two piles next to the road in plain view. They started to obey the order.

The Southern Storm had been quelled.

Capt. Herndon yelled down, "Disarm all the way! Anyone who tries anything will be put down!!"

Capt. Herndon ordered Buford, Milo, Tad and Dan to quickly reload, stay in position and cover everyone as they made their way down the steep incline. James Corbin, Chet Hatfield and Helmer Schmitt had all suffered minor wounds, but were still able to come on down. The men were scurrying downward on the two paths of access. Newt was in the lead, about 30 feet ahead of the rest, with the double-barreled eight gauge shotgun at the ready.

One last attempt to resist the captors is made by five Reb soldiers. Before they could take aim, Newt gave them both barrels from the eight gauge shotgun. Three of them went down. The other two threw down their rifles and surrendered. Newt hollered, "Come on, Captain. Let's get this damn thing done!! It's been a long dry spell!!"

Newt had just reloaded the double barrel when a badly wounded Reb aimed his Colt revolver at him and fired one last shot before collapsing. Newt felt the sting as the bullet made a deep crease wound in his left shoulder. Newt yelled, "Captain, I've been shot!"

From higher on the steep grade, Capt. Herndon yelled back, "Newt, are you shot bad?"

Newt answered, "Dammit, Elam, have you ever heard of anyone being shot good?" Wounded or not, Newt was quite anxious to get this whole thing over with. He was commanding the Rebs to finish disarming and put 'em all in a pile, all of 'em. They were staring down the barrels of Newt's "cannon" and quickly did as they were told.

Buford whistled and shouted for the nurses to come on over. They were ready with the horse and buggy and what medical supplies they had.

They came on the double!

Capt. Herndon shouted to the captured men, "Start trying to help your wounded among you! Get with it!"

The Rebs were now trying to do what they could for their own as best they could.

Lt. Buchanan said, "Sgt. Wildman, quickly pick ten of our men to try to help them with their wounded. The other seven of us will stand guard and we have the other four of our men covering us from the cliff!"

Sgt. Wildman was busily picking men to aid the wounded Rebels. Some were overheard to grumble about being told to help the captured enemy.

Capt. Herndon heard the grumbling and said, "Men, they are not animals; they are soldiers like us! Now, they need help. It's the right thing to do! Let's try to help the best we can."

The men quickly fanned out among the captured soldiers and offered their help.

A second lieutenant, the Southern Storm's former financial officer, inquired of Capt. Herndon, "Captain, where are the rest of your men?"

"Lieutenant, this is all of us, the seventeen of us down here and the four men still in place up on the cliff."

Lt. Clay is deeply humiliated when he realizes that the once powerful Southern Storm had been stopped by such a rag-tag group of old men and boys, armed mostly with antique weapons. The humiliation of it all.

Only minutes later, but seeming like hours, Renfro started to regain consciousness. As he looked through hazy eyes, he could see that two people were standing over him and they seemed to be trying to help him. The man had put a tourniquet on his wounded leg and was trying to bandage it. The woman was telling Renfro, "Drink some of this for the pain!" She gave him a drink of laudanum (whisky/opium mix).

As Major Miles drifted between reality and fantasy, he dreamily started to think that he knew these two people. They were both black people. Could they be...?? Or, was he dreaming?

"Moses and Tillie, is that you?? Are you who I think you are??"

"Yes, Renfro, you are right. It's us. Lie back, son, and we'll try to help you. Boy, you came close to buying the farm, but that old Miles' luck must still be riding with you. Lay back and calm down. You might live. We will stay with you for as long as we can."

The laudanum started to work and Renfro drifted off. He was badly wounded and defeated, but still alive.

Major Miles no longer felt like a "King of the Mountain," conquering warrior. He now felt more like a badly hurt little boy in intense throbbing pain. Good Lord, he still was afraid that he had been dreaming. Was it really Moses Jefferson and Tillie Mae??

Finally, he realized that it was real. They were here trying to help him, much like they had done so many times when he was a child. "Oh," he thought, "how could a man be so unlucky and yet so lucky at the same time?"

Moses said, "Tillie Darlin', it's almost like our little boy comes back to us. The Good Lord does work in mysterious ways, don't he?"

"Yes, Moses, but I do wish our little boy had came back to us in better circumstances."

"Well, Tillie, one thing for sure, this here young soldier ain't in no shape to do nobody no harm now, and maybe never. Tillie, give him another swig of the pain medicine. We got to move on and try to help some of the others. Capt. Herndon is calling for us over there."

The next wounded Reb was Renfro's first Sergeant, Zeke Calhoun, about 45 years old. He had a bad shoulder wound. In great pain, he still could not believe what had happened to the all powerful Southern Storm.

As Moses and Tillie approached him, Zeke Calhoun hollered, "Whoa there, ain't no damn niggers gonna touch me. Get away!!"

In an instant, Moses slapped Sgt. Calhoun hard across his face, adding to his pain, and said, "Watch your trashy mouth, boy! It ain't fitting to talk that way around a lady. Now, shut your mouth and layback and we'll try to help you. If you don't go along with us, I'll put a pistol to your damn arrogant head right now and you'll be out of your misery!!"

Tillie gave Sgt. Calhoun a drink of laudanum and he lay back.

They then started treating his wound.

Sgt. Calhoun's pain diminished some and he suddenly felt very ashamed of himself. Here were two of the type of people he thought he hated and they both were hurriedly trying to tend to his wound. He thought, "And they neither one owe me a thing!"

Confederate Capt. Lewis asks Capt. Herndon, "Is there a Catholic priest anywhere around here? Two of our men are Catholics. One is not likely to make it; the other one is hurt bad."

"No, Captain, there are no priests close by, but we will do what we can."

Capt. Herndon quickly called for Pvt. LeCroix. "LeCroix, you take two of their best-looking horses and ride up to Frenchtown, on the double! Go to St. Bernard's Catholic Church and bring back Father Schmitt! Tell him he is needed here and it is urgent!! There are two badly wounded Catholic soldiers here. One or possibly both may need the Last Rites!"

Young Pvt. LeCroix quickly started to do as ordered. He soon picked out two good-looking saddle horses. He put a lead rope on the second horse, mounted the first and left in a trail of dust, off on a mission of mercy.

Capt. Lewis saluted Capt. Herndon and said, "Thank you, sir. Your efforts are much appreciated."

Capt. Herndon returned the salute saying, "I feel you would do the same for us, were the tables turned."

Young Nurse Susan Bowman is working her way through the wounded Rebs when she first sees Major Miles. The bandage that Moses and Tillie Jefferson had put on his wounded leg was by now blood soaked and needed to be changed. The bleeding was slowing some, but the bad wound needed to be redressed.

Susan felt nothing but revulsion for these Southern soldiers, for she could not shut out the fact that it was men of this army who had recently killed her beloved father in battle. She could barely bring herself to touch a hated Rebel soldier, but she knew it was her duty to try to help them.

Major Renfro Miles is only half conscious when he realizes that someone is tending to his horribly wounded leg. He is in somewhat of a dreamlike state from the laudanum that Moses and Tillie had given him, but he is slowly coming out of it. Dreamlike state or not, there is nothing wrong with his eyes and he sees a very pretty sight. Renfro has no doubt that this young brown haired, brown eyed woman is one of the most beautiful young women he has ever seen. "God," he thinks to himself, "is she an angel? Lord, I hope I'm not dreaming."

Susan Bowman, on the other hand, was not blind either. Even in his present condition, covered with trail dust, lying there in his now tattered, blood-splattered gray officer's uniform, Susan recognized him as a very handsome young man. However, the fact remained that he was one of those damn Confederate soldiers.

Their eyes met briefly and Susan Bowman continued dressing his wound. She had to keep telling herself, over and over, what her doctor father had often told her, "It does not matter whether it's one of ours or one of theirs. War is not supposed to be personal. Doctors and nurses have the obligation and duty to give aid when and where it is needed.

SIXTEEN

After The Storm

THE BATTLE WAS now over and the smoke and dust had cleared away. The men of the L.H.G.R. were pleased that they had won this engagement, but were not gloating over their victory. Had the least little part of their plan gone awry, they knew full well that they would be the ones dead and dying, or, at least, perhaps wounded.

The pitiful moaning of the wounded was plain to be heard. Capt. Herndon had ordered the captured Rebs to try to tend to their own wounded as much as possible. As well, he had ordered some of his own men to help as much as they could. Though some were not too enthused about helping the enemy, they did as ordered.

Nurse Bowman, the acting doctor; Susan Bowman, amateur nurse; and Tillie Jefferson were working as fast as possible trying to tend to the wounded and giving laudanum to try to ease the pain of the suffering men.

The sounds of battle gone, things start to settle down.

Capt. Lewis, the second in command of the Southern Storm, was now the acting commander since Major Miles was severely wounded and unable to function. Even as prisoners of war, the senior officer or non-commissioned officer in the group of prisoners assumes command of his group of prisoners. This is standard military practice.

Capt. Herndon walked next to Capt. Lewis and said, "Sir, we

are doing our best to help your fallen men. Now, we could use some help."

"Anything we can reasonably do, Captain. What help do you need?"

"Well, sir, four of our men are still upon the cliff. They are all in rather poor physical condition. If you would, Capt. Lewis, pick four or five of your strongest men and order them to go up there and help my men come down."

"Very well. Men, I need five volunteers!" Five men agreed to the detail not yet fully knowing what they were expected to do.

Capt. Herndon guided the way up to the positions where Buford, Tad, Dan and Cpl. Kinnaman were still covering the scene below with loaded weapons.

The POW volunteers carried Pvt. Buford Beasley down in fine fashion, he sitting in the pole carry chair with his rifle on his lap. One of the prisoners helped Cpl. Kinnaman down because his wounded left arm was nearly useless in grabbing rocks and shrubs coming down. The carry chair was taken back up and Pvt. Tad Martin was carried down, due to his crippled foot. The others helped 81 year old Pvt. Dan Lyon come down, even though he kept insisting he could make it on his own. Capt. Herndon even carried Dan's rifle down.

Four of the L.H.G.R. men had been wounded in the action. Pvt.Newt Watson had a deep crease wound in his left shoulder. Pvt. Helmer Schmitt had a painful graze wound from a Reb bullet on his left forearm. Pvt. Chet Hatfield was now missing a major part of his right ear lobe, it having been shot away by a bullet coming all too close. It was a foregone conclusion that he would never be able to wear an earring on that ear, should he ever want to. And, last but not least, the youngest soldier in the L.H.G.R., not yet 15, James Corbin had a deep crease wound to the left side of his face. Again, very close.

James was now no longer a scared boy, but rather a "scarred

veteran." He would more than likely have the scar for life. No doubt, he was now a veteran combat soldier with the scar to prove it. Though a boy, he had stood his ground like a man and was proud that he had. Though some of his fellow soldiers were old enough to be his great-grandpa, they had all stood together. Now, they all had much respect for one another and needless to say, all were quite proud of their little group of riflemen!

Nurse Alice Bowman soon had the wounded L.H.G.R. soldiers' wounds tended to and they were all still able to function and use their weapons, if needed. For now, the storm was over!

The men had remembered their training well when they had been told that a soldier only needs a weapon good enough to get a better weapon. Most had picked up the excellent lever action Henry rifles from the stacks of captured Reb weapons at the first opportunity. As they acquired these new modern weapons, they were quick to discard their outdated obsolete weapons in a separate pile. Most of the men were quite glad to discard their old weapons in favor of newer and better ones. The old weapons had served their purpose. Now, it was time to move on. Luckily, none of the old muskets and rifles had blown up in the shooter's face or misfired, much thanks to Jacob Silverstein.

In about an hour and forty-five minutes, Pvt. Albert LeCroix came back, his mount at a fast trot. A saddle sore old priest was close behind and, of course, they were riding two very tired horses.

Father Schmitt was quickly taken to the two wounded Catholic soldiers. He had barely gotten to the battleground in time. Father Schmitt had just finished giving the Last Rites as the young soldier from Louisiana slipped away. The young soldier had fought his last fight.

Much to the surprise of Capt. Lewis and everyone else, the other wounded Catholic soldier started showing signs of recovery. His bleeding slowed, his pulse got stronger and Nurse Alice

Bowman predicted that he would very likely survive. It could have been due to the power of prayer or, perhaps, his strong determination to live, but in any case, he was getting better.

Capt. Herndon and Capt. Lewis both gave their sincere thanks to Father Schmitt for coming.

The Father replied, "Gentlemen, no thanks are necessary; this was my duty. I want to thank you both for seeing that this man was looked after. I will stay 'til after his burial."

"Very good, Father Schmitt. After the burial, we will see that you have a good horse to ride back up to your church."

When Father Schmitt had mentioned the burying of the dead it quickly brought back vivid memories of the aftermath of battles in Mexico so long ago. These too were not pleasant memories. The reality of it was that it was summer, the weather hot, and the grim task of burying the dead soldiers needed to be taken care of and very soon.

It was now nearing mid-day. The wounded from both sides had received attention and treatment. All the wounded of the L.H.G.R. were "walking wounded," but such was not the case for all of the wounded from the Reb unit. Some were severely wounded.

Capt. Herndon, Lt. Buchanan and Nurse Bowman had a hurried discussion and decided to turn the Leavenworth School House into a temporary hospital, since school was out for the summer. The walking wounded among the Rebs were marched under guard to the school house turned hospital. The badly wounded were hauled there on Buford's wagon.

Capt. Herndon said, "Men, we need a place to hold the prisoners for now. Any ideas?"

First Sgt. Wildman said, "Captain, I think there may be enough room for about six prisoners in Sheriff Cummins' jail. Maybe put the most war like of 'em in there?"

"Good thought, Sergeant. The only other place I can think of to hold the rest would be the big freight warehouse room at the river port.

So it was: School house turned hospital, jail house holding some prisoners of war, and others being confined at the river port warehouse. Yes, things changed very fast in Leavenworth.

Capt. Herndon stopped dwelling on the sordid memories of Mexican battles so long ago and quickly realized that there were some things that needed to be done, here and now! The burial detail was the next order of business, of course, after the wounded prisoners had been taken to the temporary hospital in the school house, the bulk of the POWs had been confined in the wharf house with a few being furnished accommodations in the jail house.

Elam turned to Lt. Buchanan and said, "Sam, here's what I think we need to do next. Go pick four men for a work detail. As soon as Buford's team and wagon are through transporting wounded prisoners, use the men, team and wagon to scour the town for picks and shovels. There are nineteen dead Rebel soldiers that have to be buried and soon. Borrow all the grave digging tools you can find. I doubt if we will collect more than we need.

Lt. Buchanan agreed with Capt. Herndon's plan and before leaving, he said, "Where are we going to bury the dead. Our local cemetery at Cedar Hill is already starting to get crowded?"

Herndon said, "I think it would be more fitting if the Southern soldiers were laid to rest close to the place where they fell, down by our rifle range between the base of the cliffs and the river bank. Sam, while you and the men are finding digging tools, I'll go over to the wharf house prison and talk it over with Capt. Lewis."

Capt. Herndon found Capt. Lewis and told him the plan.

Lewis realized the need for the burials so soon and said, "Captain, I have some requests about this, if I may? Very well, sir, I know that it's a bit unusual, but would it be possible for my men to form a seven man rifle squad with rifles borrowed from those taken from us and enough blank cartridges to give a 21 gun salute to my fallen men?"

"Yes, Capt. Lewis, I think it will be possible to arrange for that. I can understand that you want to honor your own. What are your other requests?"

"The second request is a small one, but nevertheless important to us. We would like for the graves to be facing south in token remembrance of our Southern homeland that we fought for."

"Yes, Capt. Lewis, that will be seen to. Was there anything else?"

"Capt. Herndon, there is one more thing and it may not be possible. I know there isn't a military band here to play the traditional 'funeral dirge,' but would there happen to be a bugler anywhere close?"

"Yes, one of my men, Cpl. Milo Weathers, is a bugler. He is a gifted musician, started in the Union Army being a bugler but soon ended up being a rifleman. He has a bugle and I'm sure he would be agreeable. What tune would you request that he play at the service?"

"Capt. Herndon, are you familiar with the fairly recent new tune called 'Taps'?"

"Yes, I understand it is becoming quite popular at military funerals on both sides. It was written by a Southern soldier who was killed back in 1862 in a battle near Harrison's Landing, Virginia. As I understand, he had written the piece and put the musical notation on paper, and 'Taps' was played on the bugle for him at his funeral."

"You are correct, sir, and the saddest part of this true story is that the fallen soldier's father was a Union Army captain and he was the one who found the music in his dead son's pocket. When he asked his superior officers for permission to let the Northern unit's band play the 'funeral dirge,' the request was denied. However, the Union officer did allow one instrument, a bugle, to be played for the fallen Confederate soldier. 'Taps' was the tune selection and even though this happened just about a year ago, I predict that 'Taps' at military funerals will be a longstanding tradition."

"You may well be right, Capt. Lewis. I'll ask Cpl. Weathers if he could do the honors. I feel sure he will."

"Thank you for your understanding. It is much appreciated. Sir, where are my men to be buried?"

"We think that a place close to where they fell would be proper, close to the river bank of the Ohio River, not far from the base of the cliffs and also close to a grove of Kentucky coffee trees. It is a peaceful spot."

"Very well, Capt. Herndon, I volunteer my men for the grave digging, under guard, of course."

"Of course, they will be under guard, but understand, this will not be forced labor by POWs, but rather a needed task performed by willing volunteers in respect for their fellow fallen soldiers."

"Agreed, sir. Shall we get started?"

"Yes, Capt. Lewis, if your men who are able-bodied and willing will form up in a column of twos, my men will escort your group to the site. My men should be there by now with whatever digging tools they could find."

The column of disarmed Confederate POWs, under the command of Capt. Lewis and escorted by men of the L.H.G.R., proceeded to the selected site. Herndon's men were now armed with recently acquired Henry repeating rifles as well as Colt revolvers. It would take a fool to try to escape. None did.

The column of Confederate prisoners reached the place where their fallen soldiers were to be laid to rest at about the same time that Buford and four men of the L.H.G.R. arrived with the team and wagon containing the borrowed tools required to dig the graves.

Capt. Herndon said, "Capt. Lewis, you can now take charge of the laying out of the graves and the rest. There should be enough tools on the wagon to do the job. I tried to find some wooden coffins for the burials, but I wasn't very successful. Squire Weathers, owner of the Leavenworth Furniture Mfg., agreed to donate ten of his lower priced pine coffins for the cause. I then talked him out of three wooden shipping cases used to ship furniture in. I'm sorry, but there will be six of the dead who will have no coffins."

"Thank you, sir, for your kind efforts and also, please thank Squire Weathers for me and my men. I promise that somehow after this war is over, he will be paid for his kind act."

Capt. Herndon then told the men to go get the coffins and boxes as soon as the tools were unloaded.

'Capt. Lewis then said, "Lt. Clay, you lay out the grave sites as we discussed with them all facing to the south and mark the places for our men to dig. Again, as we planned, you make an accurate map of where the graves are and the name, rank and unit of each man. There will be no time for markers now, but this will have to be done later."

Lt. Clay saluted smartly and replied, "Yes, sir, as you wish."

The prisoners started digging and after about two hours of hard work, the graves were ready.

Capt. Herndon passed the word among his men that this would be a Confederate military funeral and, as such, the proceedings would be under the Confederate flag. We were only there to observe. Since it was done under the Confederate flag, no Union men would salute.

The Men of Herndon's Hope understood that this was only a courtesy that was being extended to the Confederates, letting them conduct their own services.

Father Schmitt said the proper words for the Catholic soldier, then he tried, as best he could, to comfort the surviving soldiers for the loss of their friends. The elderly priest did his best, but it was awkward for him as he had never spoken at a Protestant funeral before. He did his best and it was appreciated.

Capt. Lewis then spoke, with tear filled eyes, some words of praise for his fallen soldiers. Then, he read their names from the roster. All present then repeated the Lord's Prayer in unison.

The honor guard, with borrowed rifles that once belonged to them, was called to attention! Ready, aim, fire. Seven rifles fired three times each on command then came the mournful sounds of "Taps" being played by Milo Weathers on the bugle. All the Confederates saluted as "Taps" was played. The men of the L.H.G.R. did not salute, since this ceremony was done under the Confederate flag. As ordered by Capt. Herndon, his men did take off their hats in a show of respect, but did not salute.

Most of the world thinks of the tune "Taps" as only an instrumental tune, but it does have words:

> "Day is done.
>> Gone the sun from the lakes,
> From the hills,
>> From the sky.
> All is well.
>> Safely rest.
> God is nigh.

> Fading light
>> Dims the sight
> And a star gems the sky
>> Gleaming bright.
> From afar, drawing nigh
>> Falls the night.

> Thanks and praise
> For our days
> Neath the sun
> Neath the stars
> Neath the sky.
> As we go,
> This we know—
> God is nigh."

Some of the men who knew the words had quietly whispered them as the mournful tune was played on the bugle. A military funeral is a very somber ceremony anytime, but this one was ever so sad. There were few dry eyes on either side when it was over.

Capt. Lewis then said, "Capt. Herndon, I respectfully ask permission to leave our flag here, flying at half staff."

"Yes, sir, for the time being, you may."

The Confederate honor guard turned their rifles back over to the Union men and then turned to the task of covering the graves.

It had been a long, fast moving day, but now it was nearing sundown. The POWs were formed in a column of twos and marched under escort back to their new temporary home.

Capt. Lewis asked Capt. Herndon if he might be taken over the school house/hospital to see Major Miles and tell him how the funeral had gone.

Capt. Herndon granted his request, but he had First Sgt. Wildman accompany Capt. Lewis to the temporary hospital.

At the hospital, Major Miles was in so much pain and dulled by the laudanum, he barely recognized Capt. Lewis. The captain gave him the details anyhow. After talking to the major, mostly a one sided conversation, he started to realize full well the extent of Major Miles' wound. Capt. Lewis talked with Nurse Alice

Bowman. She said that, in her opinion, if infection did not set in, Major Miles would be permanently crippled due to the bone in his leg being shattered so badly. He had already come close to bleeding to death at any rate.

"Nurse, what do you mean 'if infection does not set in' he would be crippled?"

"What I mean to say is that if infection should set in, we may very well have to take his left leg off in order to try to save his life. I can say for sure that this young soldier is out of the war for good."

Capt. Lewis checked on some of his other wounded men then asked the sergeant to take him back to the wharf house prison.

Capt. Herndon had left Lt. Buchanan in charge for a few hours, only saying that, "Newt and I are on a mission."

Meanwhile, up at the Dexter Saloon, Newt and Elam were getting "real refreshed" as promised. The last few days had been very tense for both men. Even though Newt couldn't use his left arm very well, due to his wounded shoulder, he soon realized that his right arm still worked perfectly well in tilting a glass of brandy.

Meanwhile, over at the school house turned military hospital, the oil lamps were lit and the three nurses were steadily working at tending to the wounded Confederate soldiers. Five men were seriously wounded and five had suffered lesser wounds. Two of the walking wounded had agreed to help the nurses care for their fellow soldiers, as best they could.

Susan Bowman had just checked on Major Miles again. Her mother, Alice said, "Girl, that's the third time you have been at his bedside in less than an hour. You know we have several more wounded here. They need attention too. What's so special about that one?"

"Oh, I don't know, Mother. There's just something different about him. He is a handsome man. I really wish he were one of our soldiers."

"Daughter, don't let yourself start getting too attached to him. He still may not live if infection sets in. Even if he does survive, he will very likely be crippled for life. That is a very badly wounded leg; the bone was shattered very badly." "Oh, I know, Mother, but I can't help how I feel."

Major Miles was just waking up from a laudanum induced sleep. As he opened his eyes, he was dreamily looking at Susan Bowman's pretty face and thought to himself, "That young woman is enough to make a dying man want to live, just to be near her. Oh Lord, this Southern Indiana hill country grows some pretty women!"

Susan then moved away to help another wounded man.

Renfro Miles thought to himself, "If this is a dream, I don't want it to end." He then drifted back into laudanum la-la land.

Tillie Jefferson was working next to Susan and quietly she began, "Girl, it's plain to me that you are starting to care for Renfro. Child, it shows. Everyone else can see it too."

"Yes, Tillie May, I guess you are right. I don't know why I am growing attached to him, but I am. I know I should hate him, but I just can't. Tillie, the rest of us couldn't help but notice, but it seems to us that this Confederate major acts like he knows you and your husband. Is this true? How can that be?"

"Yes, Susan, Moses and I both think of him as our little boy and he almost is. His mommy and daddy were our masters at Meadowland Plantation. Me and Moses tended to him as a baby and tried to guide, train and look after him. We also did the same for his little sister, Virginia. Their momma and daddy are both good people, but they were very busy people and that was the way things were done in high class rich families down there. When Moses and I escaped back some ten years ago, it nearly broke our hearts to leave them children. They were as much ours as any ones.

When we left back in '53, Renfro was ten years old and little pretty Virginia was eight. We missed them kids something awful, but we knew we had to try for a better life. So now, Miss Susan, I got to tell you one thing. That man over there is like my little boy, or, at least, me and Moses think of him that way. I know that this hateful old war does strange things to people, but I just know that whatever Renfro was doing was what he felt was the right thing to do. He is a good boy and we love him. Susan, I love you too and I wouldn't want to see either of you get hurt. In matters of the heart, sometimes it pays to move slowly."

"Okay, Tillie, now I understand. Lord, it's almost like God brought him back to you. No, Tillie, I promise you that I would never hurt your little boy, at least not on purpose."

"Now, Miss Susan, I'll tend to this other wounded soldier over here. I'm sure you need to check on Major Miles again, don't you?" A blushing Susan Bowman agreed that it must be time to check on her special patient again and headed in the direction of Major Miles.

Meanwhile, back at the saloon, Capt. Herndon and Newt were not only into some serious drinking, but the conversation was turning serious as well. Elam said, "Newt, we won that battle, but now we also have two or three other serious problems that come with the victory. Do you see them?"

"Not yet, Elam. You tell me. You're the man in charge."

"Well, Newt, the first problem is this—now that we have the prisoners, what the hell do we do with them? We can't just keep 'em cooped up in the wharf house, at least for not very long. Secondly, they ain't animals. They have got to be fed and that's one big item. Number three, it will take too many of us to guard and hold them twenty-four hours a day, seven days a week. Newt, they just can't stay here very long!"

"Okay, Captain, what are we gonna do?"

"Newt, I think that the quickest, best way to handle this is to take them back down to Derby to the little POW camp there. If we sent them back down there on a boat, someone, somewhere along the line would have to pay for their passage. If they go by land, it will be free."

"I agree with that, Captain, but I have a thought also. I know I've had a few brandies and I may not be the sharpest knife in the drawer and too, I sure ain't no leader, but one thing I know for sure, don't let 'em ride their horses back down there! They are all real good horsemen and most of us are not! If we try to escort them with all of us mounted on horses, they'll get away from us sure as hell!"

"Newt, I swear, I don't think brandy drinking hurts your thinking! You are so right. My thoughts exactly! The men of the Southern Storm need to be marched back down to Derby. Some of us will escort them on horseback. The walk will do them good. Also, it would give them time to reflect on their poor choice of army to join.

It's only about thirty miles from here to there, two fifteen mile marching days and they won't be so full of vim and vigor. Newt, let's have one more for the road. We need to get some rest. Tomorrow will be another busy day. I have another idea or two to think out by morning. Maybe I'll have them thought out by then.

See you in the morning, Newt. By the way, how's the wounded shoulder feeling?"

"Well, Captain, right now I ain't feeling no pain."

Leavenworth, Indiana Wharfboat, with the packet boat
Rees Lee alongside
Courtesy Stephenson General Store

C1

SEVENTEEN

Some Rebs Return To Derby

BRIGHT AND EARLY at 6:00 AM, Capt. Herndon ordered Confederate Capt. Lewis to have his men stand in formation. A head count showed that, counting all prisoners at the wharf house, there were thirty able-bodied prisoners. They were then served breakfast which consisted of biscuits and gravy and coffee. Poor fare perhaps, but this was wartime.

Next, Capt. Herndon and Lt. Buchanan checked on the prisoners at Sheriff Cummins' jail. Four of the most militant prisoners were being held there.

At the temporary school house/hospital, there were ten wounded prisoners. Four of these men were seriously wounded and six men would pass for walking wounded.

Promptly at 7:00 AM, another formation was held at the wharf house. After the prisoners were brought to attention, Capt. Herndon made the following announcement: "At ease men, but pay close attention to what I have to say!! You are all now officially prisoners of war until this war is over. In the absence of any higher authority, I, though only a captain, will have the final say on what is done with you men. We are not in a position to continue holding you all here at Leavenworth, which leads to my next statement. There is a Union Army POW camp at Derby, Indiana. Remember coming through there?"

There was an audible groan amongst the prisoners.

Herndon continued, "Yes, had you known it was there when

you came through you could have set the Rebs being held there free. At the time, you would have had plenty of weapons to arm them with as well. Oh well, it was not meant to be. In any case, here is the deal. Life in the little POW camps is not a bed of roses. The commander there will not be cruel, but he is firm. The POW camp has a four acre garden. A prisoner there will not be forced to work, but rather he will be allowed to work in the garden. All those that work in the garden will eat better and share in its bounty. Those that refuse to do garden work will still be fed, of course, but mainly on army issue hard tack and beans. The choice is yours.

"Also, I want to point out that the POW camp is not a great place for wounded men. They do have one medic there, but not a hospital. Also, as with any prison, anyone trying to escape will be shot or shot at. However, men tired from work aren't likely to try to escape.

"Now, I have a better offer for some of you to think about. Since I am the one in command here, I have the authority to offer a parole to any man that will agree to the terms. The parole agreement is an honorable thing and is legal in written form and enforceable. The people and businesses in this area are all short-handed due to the war, being badly in need of help of all kinds. The parolee would have to swear under oath that he was, in effect, dropping out of the war and would stop fighting. Then, instead of sitting out the war at a POW camp, a man could easily get a job and earn decent pay. Also, I will point out that a wounded man would be far better off to be paroled than be in prison.

You have all heard your choices. Any man who wants to be paroled, take the step now by raising your right hand."

Only four men agreed to the terms and were granted parole.

Capt. Herndon told Capt. Lewis that he was going to make the same offer at the jail house and also at the hospital.

There were no takers at the jail, holdouts 'til the last. It was probably a good guess that these four would live on beans and hard tack 'til war's end.

At the hospital, Major Miles was in much pain and barely coherent. Moses and Tillie Jefferson pleaded on his behalf and agreed to the parole terms for him. Also, they asked that he be placed in their care. As it was, he might not make it. In a POW camp, he most surely would not.

The wounded Catholic soldier who had survived was much better and opted for parole.

Much to the surprise of all concerned, Rebel First Sgt. Zeke Calhoun agreed to parole terms. His wounded shoulder would keep him down for some time, but he knew that he might not survive prison camp life.

In all, seven Confederate prisoners were paroled. Four of those were able-bodied and three were wounded, Major Renfro Miles being the most seriously wounded.

For the time being, all ten of the wounded would stay at the makeshift hospital even though three were paroled.

In a few minutes, Lt. Buchanan had the prisoners in formation that were to be taken to Derby POWCamp. He began, "Men, there are thirty-seven able-bodied prisoners here. Thirty-six of you will start for POW Camp soon. For now, Lt. Clay will stay here, but he will be coming along later. First Sgt. Wildman will now tell you men how to prepare for the trip and what you will be allowed to take. Sgt. Wildman, take over."

"Yes, sir."

"Okay, men, you all heard the lieutenant. Now, here is what you will be allowed and required to take with you. You will take your saddlebags containing only your clothing, personal items and your mess kit. Also, you will have your bedrolls and, last but not least, your canteens full of water, of course. I suppose by now that you are all wondering where your horses are. Well, don't worry about your horses. They are getting a much needed rest. This will be a walking tour of scenic Southern Indiana. You will be marching the approximately thirty miles to Derby, hopefully, in two days' time. Capt. Herndon has offered Capt. Lewis the privilege of riding a horse on this trip as a matter of courtesy, since he is your commanding officer. Do you want a mount, sir?"

In a huff, Capt. Lewis answered, "No, Sergeant. No horse for me. If my cavalry troopers walk then so shall I!!"

"Very well, Capt. Lewis, it's your choice. As you wish, sir."

Sgt. Wildman then gave the group of POWs "at ease" and said, "Go gather up the things you are to take with you and form up back here in thirty minutes. Dismissed."

Meanwhile, back at the hospital, Alice Bowman, Susan and Tillie were feeding the wounded prisoners and tending to them. Of course, Susan Bowman was more concerned about one patient in particular. Obviously, this was unprofessional conduct for a nurse, but budding love knows no bounds.

Major Miles was somewhat better this morning; his fever had eased some. However, when pretty Susan Bowman's dainty hand touched his brow, his temperature started climbing higher, no doubt about it. Nurse Alice Bowman saw that Major Miles was clearheaded enough now to more fully understand recent events, so Alice and Susan started to give him the details. They told him of his men, under Capt. Lewis, being sent to Derby POW Camp. Then, they explained to him that he and six other prisoners had been granted military parole. The County Clerk, James Lemonds, was to draw up the official parole papers this morning and to have them signed and witnessed by all concerned as soon as possible.

Major Miles then asked, "How can I be left out of things? I am in command of the Southern Storm!"

Alice Bowman came back, "No, you were in command, but now you are out of the war. The war is over for you. You are lucky to be alive and may very well be permanently crippled. You have been paroled and placed in the custody of Moses and Tillie Jefferson at their request. They wouldn't have it any other way."

"Moses and Tillie—it doesn't seem real. It's like a dream."

"No, Major, it's not a dream. It's very real. You are one lucky man."

"Nurse, has my family been told of my whereabouts yet?"

"Yes, Tillie is writing a letter to your mother. They will soon know."

"Thank you, Ma'am, I'm very grateful to you and your nurses for all you are doing for my men and myself."

"Susan, I think the Major needs another small dose of laudanum for the pain and change his bandages and bathe him as best you can."

"Yes, Mother, I'll see to it."

It was then that Renfro Miles understood that Alice was Susan's mother.

Meanwhile, back by the wharf house, the POWs had gathered up their belongings and were being formed up for the march. The once proud Southern Storm had arrived at the cliffs in regal style, wearing fine uniforms, riding the best horses to be had and armed with the latest and best weapons to be found anywhere in the world. Now, preparing for the long march, they were in sharp contrast to the striking impression they made before. Though still dressed in good uniforms, they carried no weapons or ammunition. Now, each man carried his saddlebags, containing clothes, personal items, mess kit and a canteen along with a bedroll.

One Reb corporal grumbled, "Damn, cavalry troopers ain't meant to carry all this gear. This is a horse's job!" Nevertheless, this time it would be a trooper's job.

The guard/escort made up of some of the men of the L.H.G.R. would not be walking, no, not even close. Now, they would be the ones riding in style. Capt. Herndon had picked eight of his men to take the prisoners to the POW Camp. The men were Sgt. Bratton, Newt Watson, Jim Running Deer, Moses Jefferson, Hibachi Takaguchi, James Corbin, Lemuel Moore and last, but not least, the old sharpshooter, Mike Baysinger. This would be part one of the plan. Today, it would only be the prisoners marching with their guards riding horseback at a slow walk.

It had been decided that it would have been too risky to try to return the ill-gotten money and horses back to their rightful owners all in the same operation. It would have been much too tempting for a POW to try to escape with horses and money as well so close at hand.

So, Capt. Herndon and Lt. Buchanan had devised the following plan. As already described, Capt. Herndon and eight men would march prisoners, starting today. Tomorrow, at 7:00 AM, Lt. Buchanan, First Sgt. Wildman, and Cpl. Weathers along with Jacob Silverstein, Helmer Schmitt, Chet Hatfield and Albert LeCroix would herd the horses, twenty-four in all, back downriver. They would also have the large amount of money and valuables that the Southern Storm had accumulated in their campaign for support of the Southern cause. Of course, they would have Confederate Lt. Clay, the Southern Storm's former Financial Affairs Officer, along to try, as much as possible, to see that the right items were returned to the right people.

By dividing the groups into two parts, one day apart, it was estimated that they would probably both arrive in the area of Rome and Derby at around the same time. In any case, the plan was for the L.H.G.R. men to meet at Derby and come back together.

For the rest of the plan, five men were to stay in Leavenworth and hold down the fort there. Cpl. Hiram Kinnaman would be in charge and Dan Lyon, Buford Beasley, Tad Martin and George Armstrong would be the town's defenders.

Now, it was time for the POW's march to start. Capt. Herndon said, "Men, you came here in a column of threes and so you shall be leaving here in a column of threes. Take notice that me and my men are all armed with very good lever action Henry rifles as well as Colt revolvers. Thanks very much. We appreciate it. Oh, I did forget to point out that one of my men is not carrying a Henry rifle. Pvt. Newt Watson prefers to carry that double-barreled eight gauge shotgun which we all refer to as 'Newt's cannon!' It is a very nasty weapon, as I'm sure some of you already know. Anyway, be forewarned that anyone attempting to escape will be making a bad choice. Do you all understand?"

The answer from the prisoners was a resounding, "Yes, Captain."

"Very well, Capt. Lewis, form your men in a column of threes. And, sir, if you will, count cadence to head 'em out at a march step!"

"Yes, sir."

"Men, attention, right face, forward march!" And so it went as the remnants of the Southern Storm headed toward their new home at the Derby POW Camp.

Capt. Herndon quietly remarked to Sgt. Bratton who was riding beside him, "You know, Sergeant, these Rebs rode into Crawford County in regal style, but now they are marching out in rather humble fashion."

"Yes, Captain, but they still have great looking uniforms, shiny boots and brass with all the trimmings."

"Right, Sergeant. You know, they came here in a column of threes which seems to be their formation of choice, so I thought it only fitting that they leave in a column of threes. Don't you agree?"

"Captain, I'm sure you're right."

And so it was, the well dressed men of the Southern Storm, still looking like the pride of the South, were being marched by their captors who, in all honesty, presented a very motley appearance, to say the least. Capt. Herndon was wearing his cap and partial uniform from the Mexican War, Sgt. Bratton wore an old Indiana Militia coat and hat from his Home Guard days. Only Pvt. Mike Baysinger was wearing a complete proper Union Army uniform from his service in the current war. As for Privates Watson, Running Deer, Jefferson, Takaguchi, Corbin and Moore, they were all wearing their every day work garb which ranged from old high-bib overalls to jeans and shirts of every description. As was common, they all wore slouch hats of one kind or another. The one common thread that told the world that they were all members of the same unit was their big bandanas worn around their necks, neckerchief style. They wore these neckerchiefs with pride as they had been adopted as the trademark of the Leavenworth Home Guard Reserve members, since no uniforms were available to them when they were organized. As said before, officers wore bright yellow bandanas and enlisted men wore bright red.

From the point of view of the prisoners, it tended to 'grind their grits' being herded by such a motley group of old men and boys. They further resented the fact that their captors were a widely racially mixed group. Oh well, the fortunes of war!

The people of once friendly Fredonia were no longer acting friendly toward the Rebs. In fact, they acted downright hostile. Oh what a change from their hospitable nature only two days ago. One or two other changes were very obvious to Capt. Lewis and his men. Yes, it seemed that there were plenty of fine looking horses in town now, when the other day, there were only a couple. Also, it was plain to see that the town's people were dressed in much better clothes today. Thought Capt. Lewis, "Oh, what a deceitful bunch. There seems to be no honor these days!"

Some of the citizens were hurling insults at the prisoners, but Capt. Herndon warned them against hurling anything else. Loudly he said, "Folks, they are in our safekeeping for now. Let us pass through peacefully. Don't worry. Some of my unit will be through here later and their mission will be to try to straighten out whatever was not straight the other day." The crowd calmed and parted and the march continued on…and on, and on!

They proceeded through Cape Sandy with no incident. However, today, the store owner refused to pump water for the horses of Herndon's men as he had for the Rebel mounts.

Some rations had been brought along. All stopped for a lunch break at the banks of the Little Blue River. After some salt pork and hardtack, they got the attention of the ferry boat operator who was on the other side by Fullenwider's Grist Mill.

Young James Riddell was quick to remember the Confederates using his boat to cross the river recently. And, by the way, he was still damn mad about it! By his calculations, the Rebs owed him at least five dollars for the last crossings which he hadn't helped with, but they used his ferry anyway without his permission. He made his living by commissions on the boat crossing fares. He demanded payment before he would do a damn thing!

Capt. Herndon soothed James down with a promise that, when the next group came to cross, they would settle the score. Capt. Herndon signed a voucher to be shown to Lt. Buchanan for the amount owed and to be paid when he and his men crossed.

James Riddell was still ticked off and said, "I ain't pulling on one single rope to get that damn Rebel rabble across. If they ride my boat, they will have to pull their own weight!!" And so it was.

In town in Alton, things did not go the least bit smooth. The people there were in a lynching mood. They had lost some good people in the raid and were furious. Capt. Herndon had to resort to ordering his men to cock their loaded guns to get the crowd to back off. It went against his grain, but as he explained, the Rebs were under his protection and they were headed to prison camp anyhow. Again, he promised the people of Alton that the next group of L.H.G.R. men would be there soon to settle accounts. This calmed them some, but not completely.

The march resumed. Capt. Herndon now wished that he had sent the horses and money back first, before trying to march the POWs through.

Capt. Herndon began thinking of the best place to bivouac for the night. From what he had seen at Fredonia and Alton, he decided not to risk stopping for the night in Rono for there had been trouble there as well. He and Sgt. Bratton checked the map together and both realized that they had found the best spot for tonight. It was near Buzzards' Roost, a place known as "Penitentiary Rock." It would be perfect. It was a rock walled canyon rumored to often be used by horse thieves and the like. Perfect!

It was late and nearly dark when the exhausted POWs marched into the canyon. After wolfing down some more salt pork and hardtack, they were anxious to spread their bedrolls, very anxious indeed. No doubt, too tired to run.

The L.H.G.R. men were in better shape after the trip, but they still were sore because they were not used to sitting a horse all day. In any case, all of Herndon's men agreed that it beat the hell out of marching.

Capt. Herndon ordered that the POWs would be guarded all night long by two men at a time in two hour shifts. The guards had ham and beans and cornbread for supper thanks to Buford Beasley putting this tasty fare in some saddlebags unbeknownst to his friends. Not only was old Buford a right decent soldier, he was also a real good cook.

Meanwhile, back at Leavenworth, three very tired nurses were still tending the wounded prisoners and doing their best. It now seemed that all the wounded would recover. The worst wound of the lot was to the left leg of Major Renfro Miles.

Anxiously, Susan Bowman had just asked her mother once more, "Mother, do you think we can save his leg?"

"Maybe, Susan, just maybe. He does seem to have better than usual luck most of the time. Now look, Tillie and I are going home for a few hours for some rest. We will leave you in charge. We will be back early tomorrow. Now, Susan, don't forget, you have more than one patient!"

A blushing Susan could only answer, "Oh, Mother!" But it was becoming very obvious that Renfro Miles was fast becoming her very special patient.

Promptly at 7:00 AM, Capt. Herndon, his men, and the POWs were ready to march. In just a few minutes, they came by the Prather place, but no one seemed to be at home.

Reb Capt. Lewis remarked that, "Perhaps these 'horse dealers' were away trying to find more horse deals."

A very short time later, they were in the village of Rono, Indiana. Again, as at Fredonia and Alton, the local citizens were in a foul mood as well as in an agitated state. Again, Capt. Herndon had to order his men to cock their weapons and hold them at the ready to hold the crowd at bay. The crowd kept talking of ropes and a big white oak tree.

Again, Capt. Herndon explained that these Reb prisoners were under his protection and he would not allow them to be harmed in any way. He assured the crowd that the POWs were headed for prison camp and would likely not leave there for some time. This tended to quell the crowd a little.

Capt. Herndon then explained that a second group of his men would be along later to set things straight as possible.

As the group was preparing to resume the march, Mr. Job Hatfield came out of the Post Office. He knew Elam Herndon from back when and he hollered loudly above the crowd, "Capt. Herndon, weren't there bout twice as many Rebs that came through here as what you got now?"

"Yes, sir, Job, I reckon there were."

"Well, Captain, where are the rest of them?"

"I guess I'd just have to say that they are up at Leavenworth."

"Well, I remember that bunch ate us out of business at the Hatfield Meat Packing Company. This many couldn't eat that much, not even close."

"You're probably right, Job. Well, some more of my men will be by soon to try to set things straight, as much as they can. Have a good day, Job. See you later." And the POWs marched on, and on.

Meanwhile back at Leavenworth, Lt. Buchanan had formed his men for the second part of the repatriation mission. It was 7:00 AM and all were anxious to start. This group consisted of Lt. Buchanan, First Sgt. Wildman, Cpl. Weathers along with Privates Jacob Silverstein, Helmer Schmitt, Chet Hatfield and Albert LeCroix. All were armed with their recently acquired Henry repeating rifles as well as a Colt revolver for each man. Lt. Buchanan was wearing what was left of his Mexican War uniform. Sgt. Wildman and Cpl. Weathers were both dressed in the proper Union Army uniform of the current time. The four privates were dressed as usual in a wild mix of old work clothes, jeans, high bibs and so on. All the privates were wearing old slouch hats as well. Again, the common thread that identified them as a group was their neckerchiefs which they wore with great pride.

From the pen full of captured horses, the men picked eight very fine mounts and soon had them saddled. One of the horses had been saddled for Reb Lt. Clay to ride. As the Southern Storm's former Financial Affairs Officer, it was very important that he be along to help in this redistribution of wealth.

Every saddled horse had a set of saddlebags, most of them fat, full of U.S. money and other valuables.

The herd of 24 horses that the Rebs had acquired was then rounded up. They would simply have to be herded or driven, cowboy style.

Lt. Buchanan explained to Lt. Clay that trying to escape could be hazardous to his health.

Lt. Clay took the advice to heart, saying that he had no intention of striking out on his own.

Shortly, this group of eight riders and 32 horses left Leavenworth raising a cloud of dust, men whooping, whistling, hollering, to drive the horse herd. The lucky ones rode at the front. Riding drag was a mess, but they would take turns.

Cpl. Kinnaman and Privates Dan Lyon, Buford Beasley, Tad Martin and George Armstrong were now the town's only security. Though only five of them, they were now very well-armed.

Nearly to Fredonia, about five miles traveled, the horses and men both needed a break and a drink of water. The river bank was much too high here to get down to the Ohio River to drink. Actually, it was more like a cliff here and you could see for many miles. They were in luck and found a very small stream with good cold water. All drank from it.

During the break, Lt. Buchanan and the men were talking. Cpl. Weathers said, "Lieutenant, I know we are almost to Fredonia and that we will start setting things straight, as for money and horses. But, there's something I don't understand."

"What's that Milo?"

"Well, how in the wide world are we gonna know who was the rightful owner of the horses and also who should get any money back?"

"Well, Corporal, I was wondering that very same thing last night until Jacob Silverstein came up with a foolproof solution. Sometimes Old Jacob absolutely amazes me. You know, when it comes to money, Jacob don't miss a trick."

"And what did Jacob come up with, Lt. Buchanan?"

"Well, Corporal, it was so damn smart and yet so simple that, at first, I couldn't believe my ears. Jacob, go ahead and tell the rest your plan about the money and such."

"Yes, sir. Look, we just have to think it out. We simply ask the people, "Who has Confederate money?? Whoever produces a dollar and a half in Confederate money, we simply give them back one dollar in U.S. currency. I figure that only the village idiot or a fool would have had any Confederate money before the Southern Storm came through. As for the horses, I figure their former owners will recognize their horses."

Young Chet Hatfield said, "Okay, Jacob, but then what are we gonna do with all the Confederate money we get back?"

At which Jacob replied, "No offense to Lt. Clay over there, but I say we don't want any Confederate money back. We might as well let 'em keep the Reb money. They might want to use it for wallpaper sometime. Don't know what else it would be good for."

Jacob's disparaging remark did not set well with Lt. Clay, but he was in no position to make any loud objections. After all, he was only along for the ride.

Meanwhile, back with Capt. Herndon's group, they had left out of Rono without further incident. The former Confederate cavalrymen were footsore and out of sorts, but they continued marching toward Derby. Of course, they were still carrying their saddlebags, bedroll, canteen and such. One might well imagine that by now these men had renewed respect for their horses which they no longer had. Now, instead of their mounts carrying the trooper plus all his gear, the trooper was carrying himself and his gear on his own two feet in cavalry boots. It is a well-known fact that cavalry boots ain't made for walking!

When he overheard some of the prisoners grumbling in the ranks, Sgt. Bratton remarked loudly, "Boys, after this hike, working in that big old garden is gonna seem like fun. Don't you think?"

Confederate Capt. Lewis was quick and said loudly to Capt. Herndon, "Captain, I ask you to tell your Sergeant to quit taunting my men. Sir, it ain't one damn bit funny!"

Capt. Herndon winked at the sergeant and with a grin said, "Okay, Harley, give it a rest."

The march was now in the tiny village of Dexter, Indiana. Things went peacefully, with the captain explaining as before about his other men coming to set things straighter. It would still be a long march, but it was looking like they would reach Derby in time to have the Rebs checked in by sundown. Oh, what a relief it would be to be rid of them!!

Meanwhile, back at Leavenworth, nurses Alice and Tillie were back at the makeshift hospital. Alice said, "How did it go last night, Susan?"

"It went okay, Mother. They all seem to be improving and Renfro's fever is down. He doesn't need the laudanum as much now."

"Daughter, you called him 'Renfro.' His proper title is Major Miles, isn't it?"

"Yes, Mother. He can be Major to you, but he'll be Renfro to me."

Jokingly, Alice said, "My, my, that does seem to be one extremely close nurse/patient relationship."

"Susan, why don't you go home and get some rest now. Tillie and I can handle things here."

"Oh, Mother, I just think I'll stay here a little longer."

"Now, Susan, we won't let your patient die if we can help it."

"Oh, I know, Mother, but I do worry about him so much."

Renfro could tell that every time he opened his eyes and saw this beautiful brown eyed girl, he felt more like living.

This morning Cpl. Kinnaman had a talk with the four able-bodied POWs that had been paroled. Within an hour, all four of them had jobs and there was no doubt the town needed help. Two of the men had past experience as carpenters and were quickly hired at a good wage by Squire Weathers at his furniture factory. One of the others had worked at a distillery in Tennessee before the war and he was quickly hired at "Tasty Brand Distillers." The fourth man was hired as dock hand at the river port. Instead of sitting out the war in a prison camp, these four were earning their salt!

Meanwhile, back at the edge of Fredonia, break was over and Lt. Buchanan headed his unit toward town.

When the group stopped in town, a crowd was quick to gather. Lt. Buchanan loudly announced, "We are here to straighten things out the best we can! It is my understanding that Confederate Lt. Clay had some business transactions with the people of this town a few days ago. In view of the fact that you dealt with him before, you can now deal with him again. You will find Lt. Clay over at the table with some saddlebags and two armed guards. Don't try to hurt the lieutenant. We need him and don't none of you get grabby. We are trying to see that this is done as fairly as we can do it!!"

In less than one half hour, the two horses were back with their former owners and cash and other valuables had been exchanged. Well, not exactly exchanged because Lt. Buchanan had proclaimed that after showing the amount of Confederate money to get U.S. currency back, he ordered the people to keep the Confederate money as well. This got a rise out of the townspeople as many exclaimed joyously, "You mean we get to keep it all? Oh, what a lucky day!!"

Some how, the crowd's exclamations seemed to lack sincerity, but what the heck. They were now in a much better humor.

The L.H.G.R. unit was quick to leave town. Thanks to Jacob Silverstein's masterful little plan, the transactions had gone rather well.

Three more horses were returned to their former owners between Fredonia and Cape Sandy. As before, the farmers were "oh so grateful" to get to keep all the Confederate money as well.

At Cape Sandy, the store owner politely asked Lt. Buchanan if he would, please, water his horses from a stream down the road as it was just too much pumping to water so many horses at his trough. The men were allowed to fill their canteens from the well, however. The good hearted store owner donated ham, cheese and crackers to the group for their lunch which they ate down the road about one half mile at the stream where the thirsty horses drank.

After a short lunch break, they were moving again creating one large cloud of dust. In about one hour, they were at the bank of the Little Blue River. James Riddell, the ferry boat operator, had seen the large cloud of dust off in the distance and could now hear the thundering horses' hoofs quite well. He pulled his ferry boat from the side by Fullenwider's Mill to the opposite shore and stood ready. When the lieutenant came down the ramp, James was again in an agitated state and sputtered, "Whoa now! No one comes aboard 'til I'm paid first. No more of this damn credit stuff. It looks like it will take three crossings to move you and all them horses across. Also, I have a paper all properly signed by a captain yesterday saying that you would pay up. Now, let's see the color of your money and no damn Confederate money neither!! I figure the whole total will come to about twenty-five U.S. dollars!"

Lt. Buchanan ordered Lt. Clay to pay Riddell and the crossing began.

Again, the townspeople of Alton were in a somber mood. One man pointed a pistol at Lt. Clay, but was warned by Lt. Buchanan to stop 'cause if he fired, he would also be shot! The man lowered his pistol and changed his mind.

Lt. Buchanan loudly ordered that the wrongs of before would now be righted. Some horses were reunited with happy owners and much U.S. currency was returned. As before, folks were delighted that they got to keep the Confederate money as well. The business done in Alton, the men and horses went on their way.

Lt. Buchanan and Sgt. Wildman checked the map and decided on Penitentiary Rock as the place to stop tonight. Perfect place to hold the horses, almost like one giant corral made of stone. It was getting late when they got to Penitentiary Rock, near Buzzard's Roost.

Both men and horses alike were tired. There was good water and grass for the horses. The men each had a small bag containing ham and cornbread compliments of Buford. Lord, the men were glad that Buford was part of their outfit. He was the ideal soldier. He could shoot well and he could cook as good as he could shoot.

After supper, the decision was made to only have one man on guard at a time in two hour shifts. The rock walled canyon would make it very easy to hold the horses. It was decided that tonight, the guards would be, in order, Silverstein, Schmitt, Hatfield and LeCroix.

Lt. Buchanan said, "Now, men, here's the plan for guarding the saddlebags full of money tonight. Me and Sgt. Wildman will be using them for pillows. Neither of us are very sound sleepers and will both be sleeping with our guns real handy. Lt. Clay will be bedding down between me and the sergeant so if he would get restless during the night, we will hear him. Understood, Lt. Clay?"

"Yes, sir, understood."

Sgt. Wildman asked of young Hatfield, "Chet, how bad is that shot away earlobe bothering you?"

"Not bad, Sergeant, not much pain, but me riding drag keeps the wound awful dirty from all the dust and such. It's healing slow."

"I'm sorry about that Chet. I didn't think. Okay, tomorrow, you'll be more toward the front. I'll have Schmitt and LeCroix ride drag."

"Thanks, Sergeant, I appreciate it."

Lt. Clay said, "Oh, by the way, the horse herd gets much smaller tomorrow morning. We won't have all that many left."

"How do you figure that, Lieutenant?" said Buchanan.

"Well, sir, it's because twelve of these horses came from right here in this canyon."

"Are you sure about that, Lieutenant?"

"I'm quite sure. I'm also quite sure that the people we obtained them from weren't their rightful owners. I'd bet on it. In any case, we paid for the twelve head in good faith."

Whereupon Jacob Silverstein said, "Yes, sure."

Buchanan said, "Well, no matter, we are not judge and jury. If twelve horses came from here, the same twelve come back here."

Answered Lt. Clay, "As you wish, sir."

"Where do the owners or whatever of those twelve head live, just for my information?"

"Well, sir, Mr. Prather and his four horse dealing sons live only about one half mile from here. Maybe we will catch them at home tomorrow if they're not away on business."

The night went without any problems and the "redemption crew" was up bright and early. Some coffee, bacon and eggs were quickly consumed. The horses were saddled and, in a very few minutes, the men and horses were at the Prather place.

The sergeant remarked, "We are in luck. They all seem to be at home."

Mr. Prather and his sons were quickly out on the porch. The old man said in a loud voice, "Listen, if this is about wanting more horses, well dammit, we ain't got any!"

Buchanan said, "No, sir, that's not why we are here. We are bringing your twelve horses back. Just come out here and identify them and we'll cut them out of the herd and you will have them back."

The horses were soon picked out and Mr. Prather said, "Praise be. There is something good and right in this old world of sin!! Just a minute and I'll go in the house and get that money that was give to me for them horses. You can have it all back!"

Buchanan said, "No, Mr. Prather, you keep that money for your troubles."

"Why, thank you ever so much, Lieutenant. You sure are a fine bunch. Just stop on by anytime. Have a good trip."

As the men of the L.H.G.R. rode out of hearing, the oldest Prather son said, "Pa, why did you act so gushy and grateful when they said we could keep that Confederate money?"

"Well, son, it's like this. It ain't all that fur to some Southern territories where that money could be used to actually pay for horses. Think about it, actually pay for them."

"Why, Pa, us boys would have to ride plumb to Tennessee to do a deal like that."

"I know, son, but nobody ever said that all the good deals were close to home. Sometimes, you just gotta go where the pickings are better. You boys might enjoy a ride down Tennessee way."

"Okay, Pa, but I still think we could maybe find some good horse deals closer to around here."

"Don't know, son. This here horse dealing business is getting stranger by the day."

Meanwhile, back on the road with Herndon's group and their disgruntled group of cavalry without horses, they were just out of Dexter, Indiana. Capt. Herndon could see that they would, no doubt, make it to Derby POW camp in time to check in before the evening meal. Elam then decided to send Pvt. James Corbin on ahead to the POW camp and let the commander know that he could expect thirty more guests and that they would be hungry and looking forward to supper. The captain said, "You know, James, with this many more people coming, they may have to add more water to the soup. And also, James, when you get to Derby, just go back downtown and wait for the rest of us. We may need some help if the citizens grow warlike. It might be a good idea to find their Home Guard officer and clue him in to help us keep order. I think that part of their Home Guard unit is still in town. Also, let everyone know that our second group with money and horses will be along later. That ought to ease the tension a bit. The way Lt. Buchanan and I figured it, his group will gain on us if they don't get bogged down repatriating stuff. Hard to tell. In any case, we will stay at Derby and rest up some. No use in us going on to Rome. Buchanan and the rest can handle that part. See you at Derby, James. Go for it!"

Pvt. James Corbin saluted smartly saying, "Yes, sir, I'm gone." He kicked his horse in the flanks and left at a fast trot, his bright red neckerchief billowing in the breeze and his old slouch hat held to his chin by a string. Added to this, he was wearing another bandana over his face as a mask to help hold the bandage to his cheek wound that he had received in the action at the cliff.

As he headed out, Capt. Herndon said to Sgt. Bratton with a smile, "Damn, I forgot about him wearing that mask over his face. I hope they don't think he's a bandit and shoot him. Maybe I should have sent someone in uniform."

"Oh, Captain, he'll be alright. His luck has been running pretty good."

About three and a half hours later, the column of tired footsore cavalry men and their mounted L.H.G.R. escort were at Derby, Indiana. As Capt. Herndon had guessed, the townspeople were in an ugly mood. Luckily, Pvt. Corbin had done as ordered and Home Guard Second Lt. Harris had rounded up four of his men to help keep order. The crowd hurled insults at the POWs, but nothing else.

Capt. Herndon shouted above the noise of the crowd that the rest would be along in a reasonable time to settle accounts. Tensions eased some and the column turned right and proceeded up the very steep hill past St. Mary's Catholic Church and on beyond to the little prison camp.

Pvt. Corbin had forewarned the first lieutenant who was the

camp commander and he was waiting with four armed guards to receive the prisoners. The lieutenant invited Herndon and his men to have supper with him and his men.

The L.H.G.R. men were quick to accept these soldiers' hospitality. The meal was mainly vegetable soup made from vegetables grown in the prison camp's large garden. It was very good, no doubt about it, but Elam had the feeling that the new prisoners would be eating lots and lots of vegetable soup this coming winter. Oh well, better than eating snowballs.

The horses were watered and fed some U.S. Army oats and were put in a pen with the rest of the camp's small bunch of horses.

Capt. Herndon and his men elected to sleep outside the prison fence. It just felt better out there somehow. They unrolled their bedrolls and camped close to the horse pen. They were all very relieved that they no longer had those prisoners to worry about.

As was their plan, Capt. Herndon and his men were to go down by the Derby River Port in the morning and wait for Lt. Buchanan and his men to meet up with them after the exchanges had been completed at Rome. They saw no point in Herndon's group riding those extra miles as everyone knew beforehand that all concerned would, for sure, be saddle sore. And, they were.

Back on the road with Buchanan's group, they had just arrived at Rono early in the day. Mr. Job Hatfield had succeeded in calming down the locals as Lt. Buchanan and men rode in with their, by now, small bunch of horses.

Lt. Buchanan announced the procedure for the exchanges in his loudest voice. As before, Lt. Clay verified the exchanges as being properly made. All went smooth until Buchanan announced that there was no need to return the Confederate money and that the folks could just keep it. At that announcement, the crowd booed loudly. Oh well.

Lt. Buchanan and group headed out with their few remaining horses.

They were almost to Dexter when some confusion arose. Pvt. Chet Hatfield had not seen an overhanging sassafras tree limb that was too low to ride under. The tree limb had whacked him soundly on his forehead and had knocked him from the saddle. From where Lt. Clay was, it looked like Chet was about to be trampled by some horses. In an instant, Lt. Clay made the very quick decision to go to Chet's aid. He was headed to him at full gallop!!

First Sgt. Wildman saw Lt. Clay galloping away and thought he was trying to escape! The sergeant quickly raised his Henry rifle and was muttering to himself, "Dammit, I told him what would happen to him if he tried to escape!!"

Just as the sergeant started to squeeze the trigger, which most surely would have been the death of the Reb lieutenant, Cpl. Weathers reached out with the barrel of his rifle. He poked it under the barrel of the sergeant's rifle and raised it, spoiling his aim, just as the rifle fired. At the same time, he was yelling, "No, Sarge, it ain't like it looks. He ain't running. One of our boys is down and he's going over to help him!!"

The bullet from the Henry rifle passed over Lt. Clay's head only by about one foot and he plainly heard it whiz by. No matter, he jumped to the ground then pulled Chet out of the way of some running horses. Lt. Clay saved Pvt. Chet Hatfield from being almost surely trampled. Now Chet not only had a very sore ear, but he had a huge lump on his forehead as well. Chet was hurting, but even so, he knew that Lt. Clay had most probably saved his life and was quick to thank him. Lt. Buchanan thanked Lt. Clay as well and an embarrassed Sgt. Wildman apologized profusely. The sergeant was truly sorry, but things can happen fast and sometimes things aren't what they seem. War and anything that goes with it can be dangerous business.

After things settled down and Chet recovered enough to ride, the group headed out once more. They returned two more horses near Dexter and also exchanged some money. The folks around here were insistent about returning the Confederate money. One irate farmer even stated that it was even too slick for outhouse use!

Soon, Buchanan's group, with their small bunch of horses, was at Derby. The captain of the mail boat, "Lady Pike" had seen them up by Dexter and had told the people at Derby that the group was on their way. Everything was under control at Derby and the returns went smoothly. Derby Home Guard Lt. Harris and men, as well as Capt. Herndon's group, had calmed the waters before Buchanan's arrival.

Capt. Herndon and Lt. Buchanan had a quick powwow. Buchanan said, "Captain, there's enough daylight left for my bunch to go ahead to Rome and finish with things yet today. What do you think?"

"Good idea, it's only about six more miles. But, you know, me and my boys are saddle sore. Why don't you go ahead and we will stay here and rest. We will meet here tomorrow and start back to Leavenworth. Is that okay with you, Sam?"

"Sounds good, Elam. We will be spending the night under the stars somewhere in Rome. See you tomorrow. Okay, men, we're heading out. Forward ho!"

As Buchanan's group headed out, sharp eyed Newt said, "Captain, have you noticed the same thing I've noticed?"

"What's that, Newt?"

"Captain, this town has not one but two taverns!"

"By George, Newt, you are one observant rascal. You're right. There are two taverns!"

"Captain, don't you think we ought to check them both out. You know, just to make sure they are selling high quality spirits?"

"Yes, Newt, I like the way you think."

Capt. Herndon said, "Men, listen up. Everyone is off duty tonight. Have fun. We will start back tomorrow when the other boys get back!"

The next morning, Capt. Herndon and his eight men had breakfast in the dining room at the hotel. The owner would not charge for breakfast as he was very grateful to these soldiers for seeing that his U.S. currency was returned to him. After breakfast, the men got ready for the long ride home. They were all saddle sore, not being experienced horsemen. To say the least, they were not looking forward to the long ride.

They were at the Derby, Indiana, river dock and waiting for Lt. Buchanan and his men to show up. Capt. Herndon remembered that there was one more piece of unfinished business here. When the other group came back from Rome, the Reb Lt. Clay still had to be taken up the hill to the POW camp since he had chosen that instead of parole.

It was about 9:30 AM and Capt. Herndon had just remarked to Sgt. Bratton that, "Buchanan's group could be showing up most anytime now." It was then that a very familiar sound came from downriver. Yes, that steamboat whistle had a very distinctive three chime whistle, no doubt about it!

The captain said, "What boat is that one coming up, Newt?"

Newt was quick to reply, "Ain't no doubt about it, Captain. That's got to be the "Concordia Queen" coming and I'll say she can't be but about one mile from here?"

Newt was right on target. Shortly, the "Concordia Queen" was in plain sight and headed to the Derby dock. As the big boat drew closer, all could see some familiar faces standing on the bow deck. It was Lt. Buchanan's group. These saddle sore soldiers had got lucky and found a better way to travel.

One of Capt. Eli Mattingly's deckhands threw a hawser and Moses Jefferson quickly tied it to the dock. The gangplank was let down and the conversation began.

Capt. Herndon hollered, "Eli, how did you happen to come

across this bunch of misfits?"

"Well, Elam, they were waiting at the dock at Rome and they looked so pitiful, I thought I'd let them and their horses ride. But, the catch is this, they have got to be freight handlers and help fire the boilers. They ain't riding for free!!"

"Capt. Mattingly, it sounds to me like you ain't lost your touch. Good deal."

Herndon then said, "Sam, how did it go at Rome? Were there any problems?"

"Nope, no problems, Captain. It went finer than frog hair. You remember old Jesse Esary, don't you?"

"Sure do. He was with us for awhile down in Mexico."

"Yes, right, well he wondered how you were doing here of late. I filled him in about everything. Jesse was a big help and we got the money back to the right folks as best we could tell. As you might guess, the bank got the most of it. Jesse seen that we had plenty to eat and the grateful merchants would not take any payment either. They are some good people in that little town. Well then, Jesse arranged for our horses to be fed, watered and to stay in the pens at the river port for the night. We slept under the stars on the lawn of the old Rome Court House.

Then this morning, we had breakfast and saddled up. We were just ready to pull out to head for Derby when Jacob Silverstein said, 'Boys, be quiet! Do you hear that?' By then, we could all hear it. It was the sweetest sound I've heard in years. It was the steam whistle on the "Concordia Queen." We were both surprised and glad to see old Eli and his boat.

"Not being dimwitted, we all pitched in and helped him unload and load freight. As we had hoped, the old River Rat had us all come aboard, horses and all, provided we would work for our passage. I bet this is the largest crew Capt. Mattingly has ever had. Also, Elam, some more good news. You know that the word was out up and down the river about the food onboard Eli's boat getting worse all the time. Well now the food is great. A new cook, Mrs. Liz Mattingly, is in charge in the galley now. She is one fine cook. Eli is one lucky old man." Capt. Herndon said, "Well, Eli, I remember you saying you were gonna start taking the 'comforts of home' along with you and I see you did. Good to see you, Liz. It's been awhile."

"Good to see you too, Elam. You know, now I don't give a hoot if he steams right on by Concordia without stopping. This way we are always at home."

Then Capt. Herndon remembered the unfinished business about Reb Lt. Clay. The captain said, "Lt. Clay, I'll offer you a parole one more time. What do you say?"

"Thanks, Capt. Herndon, but I think I had better go up on the hill. I know you mean well, but I had better stay with my comrades."

Jacob Silverstein said, "Lt. Clay, I just want to say that when this war is over, I think you could have a brilliant career as a banker or something of that nature. For sure, you have a way with money." Jacob was smiling and winked.

Lt. Clay saw the humor in it and smiled as well.

Capt. Herndon said, "Pvt. Hatfield, why don't you escort Lt. Clay up to the gate of the camp and see that he and his gear get checked in. Bring the horse and saddle back, please."

"Yes, sir, I'll be doing that."

On the way up the hill, Chet thanked Lt. Clay once more for risking his life to save him from being horse trampled. At the gate, they shook hands and parted. Chet had told the lieutenant that he hoped he might come to Leavenworth and visit someday.

Capt. Mattingly invited Elam and his men to get on board, horses and all. Packet boats like the "Concordia Queen" are specially designed to haul people on the upper deck or decks and general cargo or livestock, or any combination thereof, on the lower deck. Now, besides the five passengers and cargo the boat was carrying when the Rome stop was made, the boat now had an additional cargo of seventeen horses and gear plus sixteen more passengers. Herndon's Hope was now riding in style.

Capt. Herndon had almost forgotten what a pleasure it was to ride in comfort on a big boat like this while watching the naturally pretty scenery on both sides of the Ohio River.

Sam Buchanan thought aloud, "Boys, it shore is one beautiful old river. This is the right way to see it too!"

Capt. Mattingly said, "Boys, I feel that I've been blessed to be able to make my living this way. I love Liz, but I love this river and this old boat too."

Eli was at the pilot wheel of the "Concordia Queen" as he talked to Elam and Sam who were sitting on the bench that is a traditional fixture in all steamboat pilothouses. Though against the "rules of the river," all three men were sipping brandy.

Capt. Mattingly said, "You know, boys, here lately I've been letting my engineer, Josh Freedman, take his turn at piloting the boat and he learns fast. It was a lucky day for me when he came aboard this boat back then. You know, I really ain't supposed to drink and drive. I think I'll let Josh take the wheel." Capt. Mattingly then took the speaking tube and hollered down to Josh in the engine room, "Josh, are any of them part-time soldiers down there sober enough to keep the boilers fired if you come up here?"

"Yes, Captain, they are and I done been showing them how things are done down here?"

"Good, Josh, come on up and take over. I figure that anything worth doing is worth doing right. So, me and my friends are gonna have some refreshments in the hospitality lounge!"

Josh was quick to take the wheel and said, "It's okay, Capt. Eli. I know this part of the river real good."

In the lounge room, Sgt. Bratton was acting as bartender and the glasses were soon full again. Elam Herndon said, "Oh, Eli, I plumb near forgot. I have got some news for you that you might like. Well, one of those wounded Reb prisoners that I paroled is still at Leavenworth. He has a right bad shoulder wound, but I think it will heal pretty fast. He was the First Sergeant of that Southern Storm bunch. His name is Zeke Calhoun. Anyhow, he and I were talking and he said that he had been an engineer on a steamboat down on the Tennessee River for a few years. He said he liked life on the river and wanted to go back to it someday. I told him about you and the "Concordia Queen" and being short-handed and all. He is interested and I know he is bound to still be at the temporary hospital."

"Great, Elam! Real good! You know, this is some day. I want to talk to this Zeke Calhoun when we get to Leavenworth. You see, Josh Freedman is starting to be a real good river pilot. He is smart and learns fast. If I can hire this man to be my engineer, I will promote Josh up to the first mate position and pay him more money too. Elam, thanks. That's good news."

The "Concordia Queen" made a stop at her home port of Concordia, Kentucky, to unload some freight and take on some more. With all the extra deck help, it did not take long. Since Liz was on board, there was no need to check in at home and the big boat was soon churning water. The "Queen" made a quick stop at Rono, Indiana, one pickup at Wolf Creek, Kentucky, and soon they made a stop at Galey's Landing, on the Indiana side. Before sundown, the "Concordia Queen's" whistle signaled her arrival at Leavenworth.

Cpl. Kinnaman and his army of four were waiting at the dock to welcome everyone home. The men of the L.H.G.R. were soon leading the horses down the gang plank after which all the men pitched in at unloading and reloading freight.

Everyone thanked Capt. Mattingly for the "excursion trip" and all gave special thanks to Liz for her great cooking.

Capt. Mattingly decided to stay tied up at Leavenworth tonight. He was not looking forward to starting tomorrow shorthanded again.

Well, it had been a hassle, but now that most of the POWs were gone, things would be much less complicated.

Eighteen

The Home Guard Reserve Receives Honors

At Leavenworth at the temporary hospital, Nurse Susan Bowman arrives at 5:30 AM. Tillie says, "Susan, Renfro is very down and depressed. We have got to try to talk him out of it and some how get his spirits up. This is not like the Renfro I know!"

"Okay, Tillie. What has he been talking about? What has he been dwelling on?"

"Well, Susan, from what I gather, he is having big guilt feelings. He's starting to feel like he let his men down by being here in a bed being tended to while most of his men are prisoners of war. Also, he keeps rambling on about the bad judgment he used in not sending out a scouting party and being too over confident."

"Okay, Tillie, let's try something. Let's let his wounded sergeant, Zeke Calhoun, and the rest try to help things by talking him out of his depression. Let's talk to the other wounded men first." The two nurses had some very quiet conversations with the rest of Major Miles' men.

Soon, First Sgt. Calhoun went to the small room where the badly wounded major was.

Sgt. Calhoun said, "Major, we need to talk, not only you and me, but all the rest of us. We need to have some serious talk?"

The rest of the men crowded into the little room and gathered around the major's bed. Sgt. Calhoun said, "Major Miles, you just got to quit feeling guilty about being here. You ain't got much choice and neither do the rest of us. That old Yankee, Capt. Herndon, is a straight shooter in more ways than one. When he said that the POW camp was definitely not a good place for wounded men, he was right for sure. Most of us would very likely die in there. Now, as for your judgment, we all feel that your judgment was up to snuff. Who would ever have dreamed that some old men and boys could have set the trap that they set for us? Major, not one of the rest of us would have handled things different than you did. Now, Cpl. Valdez wants to say a few things."

Cpl. Miguel Valdez, the wounded surviving Catholic soldier spoke next. "Major, all the rest of us want you to know that we do not blame you for anything that happened. We are all full grown men and we all knew full well that this was war and that there were always risks. Every man here agrees that you are a good leader and we all would follow you again if we had the chance."

At this, the group of wounded men said as one, "Cpl. Valdez speaks for all of us."

As the men started to leave the room, Susan leaned over Renfro's bed to put a cold wet towel on his forehead. As she leaned over, Renfro reached for her dainty shoulders and gently, but quickly, pulled her close and gave her the most intimate passionate kiss she had ever imagined. As their kiss lingered, Renfro's men cheered and whistled as they left the room. They knew that their leader's outlook would soon be better and they were happy for him.

After the morning formation of the L.H.G.R., Cpl. Kinnaman starts to fill Capt. Herndon in on the details of the paroled prisoners, the one's who were not wounded and chose parole.

"Corporal, what were you able to work out with those four Rebs?"

"Well, Captain, they are now all four gainfully employed and are on their way to becoming decent and productive citizens of Leavenworth. Two of them had been carpenters before the war. Those two were hired by Squire Weathers at his Furniture Factory. One man said that he was an experienced whiskey maker and had worked down in Lynchburg, Tennessee, at a distillery. So, the owners of Best Brandy Distillers were quick to hire him. The fourth man went to work as a freight handler at the river port."

"You handled it quite well, Corporal. Good job. Cpl. Kinnaman, tell both Sergeants and Lt. Buchanan we need to decide some things."

"Yes, sir, I'll round 'em up!"

Soon Capt. Herndon, Lt. Buchanan, First Sgt. Wildman and Sgt. Bratton were talking things over.

Herndon said, "Now, men, it may look like this thing is over, but we still have lots to do and several decisions to make."

"Like what more is there that needs done, Captain?" said Sgt. Bratton.

"Well, for openers, we have ten wounded men still at the temporary hospital. Now, I have already granted parole to three of these men, namely their Major Miles, the Reb First Sgt. Zeke Calhoun and also the Catholic Mexican, Cpl. Miguel Valdez. These three should be but little more problem. The problem we still are faced with is the other seven wounded Rebs. They turned down my offer of parole, but we can't take care of them much longer. After all, the hospital is only a temporary, makeshift emergency thing and we can't keep it open much longer. Besides that, our three nurses are bound to be worn out. Does anyone have any ideas?"

Lt. Buchanan said, "Yes, Captain, I have a thought or two. Okay, I think you need to see those wounded Rebs again and make them another parole offer and this time sweeten up the offer a little. And also, I think you should point out to them that this will probably be your last offer because the regular Home Guard or the regular Army could show up no telling when. If a higher ranking officer showed up, he might well overrule your parole ideas and those wounded Rebs might well rot in a prison camp somewhere. Captain, do you see my point?"

"Yes, Sam, I see your point. Also, as you know, my authority to grant military paroles was kind of 'iffy' anyway. But I felt that we were in an emergency and it made sense. Now, what would be your idea of sweetening up the offer?"

"Captain, I was thinking like offering to give these seven men back their horses and maybe a small amount of cash to go back home with. Those that ain't able or willing to ride home on horseback might could sell their horses to buy steamboat passage back to the South. We do have some money left that the Rebs acquired from the passengers on those two boats, don't we?"

"Good idea, Sam. Yes, we have some cash left. Both steamboat companies will try to track down the money's rightful owners, but, probably, will never find near all of them. Yes, let's go up to the hospital and sweeten up the offer and make our pitch again. We need to see the nurses and plan out what to do anyway."

When the four men got to the hospital, Capt. Eli Mattingly was already there talking to Zeke Calhoun. Even though Zeke's arm would still be in a sling for awhile, Eli had been delighted to hire him. Experienced steamboat engineers don't grow on trees! Capt. Mattingly agreed to continue on upriver to Brandenburg and Tobacco Landing and stop to pick up Zeke on the way back downriver. This would give Zeke a couple more days of healing time. They shook hands on their deal and Eli started out the door as Elam was coming in.

Capt. Herndon said, "Did you make a deal with that river man?" "Sure did, Elam. I think it will work out. I've got to stop over on Big Bend at Crecelius Landing to pick up a shipment of brandy, then stop at Booth Landing and take on wood from their wood yard. After that, I need to pick up and deliver at Brandenburg and Tobacco Landing, then I'll start back down and get my new engineer. Now, don't let him get away! And I plumb near forgot, I've got to go to the Brandenburg Bank. It's payment time again."

Elam quipped, "You better remember to make that payment, Captain, 'cause you know they won't forget it! Thanks again for the boat ride. Me and my men really appreciated your hospitality."

"You and yours are welcome. It was the least I could do. See you on the return trip."

Capt. Herndon talked it over with the nurses and they were quick to agree that it was nearing closing time for the temporary hospital. No more than two or three more days was the time set.

Capt. Herndon made another parole offer to the seven wounded Rebs. They agreed to the sweetened up offer and realized that it might well be their last chance. They readily signed the agreements. They all opted to leave by boat so it was agreed that each man would receive twenty dollars, the equivalent of about two months army pay, plus fifty dollars each for selling their horses to the local livery stable. Capt. Herndon and men agreed to help the men get aboard the next available boat heading downriver. They would all have enough money to take them home.

Nurse Bowman said that the men should be well enough to travel, though most would not be completely healed for some time.

Reb Cpl. Miguel Valdez asked Capt. Herndon if he knew of any job possibilities around here for a saddle maker or harness maker.

Capt. Herndon replied, "Is that your trade?"

"Yes, before the war down in South Texas, I was an apprentice saddle/harness maker. I can do the work well enough if there is someone that needs my skill."

"Yes, Corporal, I know who you need to see. Just a minute and I'll get one of my men to guide you over to see someone in your kind of business."

In a few minutes, Jacob Silverstein had been detailed to take the wounded prisoner to see about a job. Miguel Valdez had a bullet wound that had barely missed his heart, but was healing fast. He was moving slow, but on the mend. Miguel asked Jacob, "Where are we going?"

"Well, there's a man, name of W. M. Ellsworth, who has a saddle making, harness making business and I think he will be glad to see you."

"You can see that I am different. Do you think that the people here would accept me."

"Yes, I do Miguel Valdez. The way it works in this little town is, you be good for this town and it will be good for you!"

After an introduction and a few questions, Mr. Ellsworth quickly hired Miguel with the understanding that he would not have to work full days until he healed a little more. Also, Mr. Ellsworth arranged for Miguel to live and eat at the Ourerbacker Hotel until, when and if he decided to live elsewhere.

Back at the hospital, the closing plans were proceeding. The hospital would return to being a school house in a day or two. It was arranged that Renfro Miles would be moved to Moses and Tillie Jefferson's house the next day. Their extra bedroom was to be Renfro's room for as long as he needed. Moses and Tillie were very happy to have Renfro with them once more. Even with his condition being what it was, they were glad.

Capt. Herndon and his men were making progress at sorting things out, but much still needed to be done. Herndon called for Sgt. Wildman.

"Yes, sir, what now?"

"Sgt. Wildman, take two or three of the men and go find a couple more straight backed chairs and rig 'em up to be pole carry chairs like the one we already have. We will probably have to carry some men tomorrow if a down bound boat comes in."

"Yes, Captain. I'll see to it!"

"Lt. Buchanan, we have to find a place to securely store a pretty big bunch of arms and ammunition. Buford's wagon is almost full of weaponry!"

"Okay, Captain. I think we need to go to John Bahr's Warehouse and see what we can work out."

Sgt. Bratton hollered, "Cpl. Weathers, get a detail of four men, then ask Buford to bring the team and wagon up to Bahr's Warehouse. We have to put some stuff in storage."

Soon, all were at Bahr's Warehouse. It was obvious that one room would not hold it all, so two rooms were rented.

Lt. Buchanan said, "Pvt. Martin, go get a ledger book of some kind so we can keep an accurate record of what we have accumulated here. This is gonna get confusing if we don't do it right."

Tad Martin limped across the street to a general store to find a proper ledger. Of course, being a school teacher as well as a freelance reporter for the local newspaper, he was never ever without a pencil or two. Soon Tad was back and the job began.

First, the nearly new modern revolvers were taken in. The L.H.G.R. had procured twenty-one for their own use, one revolver per man plus two extra cylinders per man. This meant that one hundred and five revolvers and extra cylinders for each were stored and recorded. Next item was the Colt revolving rifles, all with extra cylinders, then the captured lever action Spencer rifles along with their extra tube magazines. All of this with a large pile of ammunition for the various weapons. Pvt. Tad Martin carefully recorded all information, numbers and descriptions. In this time in history, this was a "treasure trove" of the latest and most modern weapons. After the weapons came fifty-three cavalry saddles, along with bridles and saddle blankets.

Capt. Herndon had decided to keep ten of the horses and saddles for L.H.G.R. use temporarily. When the windowless storage room was properly filled, it was secured by two of the best padlocks to be had and only Capt. Herndon and Lt. Buchanan were to have keys. Herndon had two keys to one lock and Buchanan two keys to the other, thus it took the two of them to get in the room.

The next order of business was that of recording and storing the mixed up mess of outdated weapons that they had won the battle with, and then, only by the grace of God. But then again, thank God they had the old weapons to use!!

They had moved the wagon to the next storage room and were ready to inventory and store their old weapons. Sgt. Wildman said, "Captain, has anyone checked around town to see if anyone who loaned any of these pieces to us wants them back?"

"Yes, Sergeant, we asked everyone except Major Woodbury, because he ain't back yet. It was plain to me that no one wanted any of these old guns back. I imagine that they all realized that they were close to the same as being junk."

Buford chimed in, "Well boys, junk or not, they served us well. Had it not been for those pore old guns, a bunch of us might be taking 'long dirt naps' by now."

All agreed that Buford Beasley was right.

Capt. Herndon said, "Men, you know, I've been thinking for some time that there should be a museum in Crawford County. It occurs to me that this bunch of antiques and relics would make one damn good start towards filling up a museum."

Buford said, "You're right, Captain. The next generations need to see some of the primitive weapons that our little band of soldiers used in battle."

Tad Martin quipped, "Boys, not only do most of these old guns qualify as antiques and relics, but I think that some of them would even qualify as heirlooms."

Good naturedly, Lt. Buchanan said, "Okay, Tad, you're the educated one among us. What is the correct definition of an heirloom?"

"Very well, Lieutenant, the Webster's Dictionary says, and I quote, 'An heirloom is any treasured possession handed down from generation to generation.' I contend that one of those old flintlock Springfields that Hibachi Takaguchi used would surely have been handed down for several generations."

At which Takaguchi said with a smile, "You mean to say that I, Hibachi Takaguchi, helped defend Leavenworth with an heirloom weapon? Oh, how nice. I must write home to Japan and tell my family?"

All of the men laughed, but it was a fact. For the most part, the Leavenworth Home Guard Reserve had been armed with antiques and relics.

The second storeroom was nearly two-thirds full and it was also double locked.

The captain said, "Okay, men, listen up? We still have more to do and more things to decide on. Now, we got so many horses that, so to speak, we are knee deep in horses. To start with, the Rebs had sixty-three saddle horses of their own plus one packhorse. This morning, I sent Cpl. Weathers along with the packhorse carrying the explosives, which never reached the Howard Boat Works, out to the stone quarry. The quarry people were generous enough to give us powder when we were in dire need. So, now it's payback time and they have some powder and explosives returned to them. Milo should be back shortly. I think that for now, we should keep no more than ten of the captured saddle horses and those only until we are taken off active duty. What do the rest of you think? Will ten horses be enough?" Everyone pretty well agreed that ten horses would be plenty and Sgt. Bratton answered for the group, "Yes, Captain, ten head ought to do it. After all, we are formed as infantry and we all know that taking care of horses takes time, work and money!"

"Agreed. We will keep ten of the best mounts, but they won't be permanent members. Now, that leaves forty-seven horses after the parolees sell their seven horses to the livery stable. This is still a bunch of horses to feed and water. As you all know, the horses are at Buford's place for now. Buford, how long will that many horses be able to stay with you?"

"Well, Captain, they are okay for now, but they need to go somewhere else by no more than two months from now. A dry August and September, which often happens, and that many horses would have my pasture nearly eaten bare."

"Okay, Buford, I think we need to send word to the Commander of Camp Noble up at New Albany and let him know that we have some fine remount horses for his army. Then, he could take care of the arrangements for moving them to Camp Noble. After all, the Confederate Army ain't the only ones in need of horses!"

The men gave their resounding approval to the captain's plan.

As is most always the case when citizen soldiers are put on active duty, their community will be short some key people. It was no different here. By rights, the parole agreements should have been drawn up by the County Judge. However, Major Woodbury, an attorney in everyday life, had been acting as "Judge Pro Tem" during a vacancy caused by an elder judge's death. This left the only county official at the court house, Mr. Lemond, to draw up the parole papers for the seven Rebs.

Capt. Herndon said, "Cpl. Kinnaman, I have a detail for you!"

'Yes, sir, what do you need?"

"Corporal, go up to the court house and see if Clerk Lemond is going to have those parole papers done today. If a down bound boat should stop tomorrow, those ex-POWs are gonna need those papers to go aboard. Also, stop by the stores where we got supplies on credit and see what we owe them!"

"Yes, sir," and Cpl. Kinnaman was on his way.

In about forty-five minutes, the corporal was back and said, "Captain, all the stores refuse to charge us anything. They said, 'No charge.' The County Clerk said that the parole papers would be ready in the morning."

"Thanks, Corporal, good news and that is real nice of the store-keepers." It was then that Capt. Herndon noticed that Hiram had several newspapers lying in his arm sling on top of his left arm.

The corporal then said, "And, Capt. Herndon, you just ain't gonna believe this!" Whereupon, he started passing out the newspapers to his fellow soldiers. The paper was the just printed edition of the town's weekly newspaper, "The Arena." The headlines were in bold triple size print and read as follows: "Herndon's Hope Quells the Southern Storm."

THE STORY

"A few days ago, a sixty-three man unit of Confederate cavalry crossed the Ohio River a short distance downriver from Rome, Indiana. They were armed to the teeth with the latest in rapid fire repeating weapons and comparison as to their rapid fire capabilities would be that one of their men, armed in such a manner, would be the approximate equal of ten of our men, using single shot muzzle loading weapons.

They claimed at every village and town that they were on a legitimate military mission as part of Gen. Braxton Bragg's Army of Tennessee. They further stated that no horses or property would be taken from our citizens without being properly paid for. They did, however, neglect to tell everyone that they would be paid with Confederate money.

These Confederate raiders overwhelmed everyone in their path at Rome, Dexter, Rono, Alton and Fredonia, Indiana resulting in loss of life at nearly every place.

By now, they knew that they were nearly unstoppable. When they learned that Leavenworth, Indiana, was rumored to be nearly defenseless as their well-armed Home Guard unit had been called away, they eagerly looked forward to having their way in Leavenworth.

What the Confederate raiders, who called themselves 'The Southern Storm,' did not know was that, in fact, Leavenworth was not defenseless. At the encouragement of Major Gen. John Love of the Indiana Dept. of Militia and also Indiana Gov. Oliver P. Morton, Leavenworth Home Guard Major Woodbury had been authorized to see that a Home Guard Reserve unit be organized. In simpler terms, a reserve for the reserves. Major Woodbury had the good fortune to find Capt. Elam Herndon, a much respected battle scarred veteran of the Mexican War, to lead the Leavenworth Home Guard Reserve.

To the shame of the State of Indiana, they were not provided with arms, ammunition or uniforms. But, being resourceful Hoosiers, Herndon and his men supplied themselves.

When the Leavenworth Home Guard Reserve was being organized, the men of the regular Home Guard were amused at the sight of the varied group of young boys, previously wounded veterans and old men drilling and training. Many were partially disabled in one way or another. As well, they were, for the most part, armed with antique, inferior, outdated weapons. One of the 'wags' in the regular Home Guard unit playfully dubbed the newly formed unit as 'Herndon's Hope,' and the name stuck. I have a feeling now, after their victory against overwhelming odds, that the nickname of 'Herndon's Hope' will remain as a matter of honor and not derision.

Though the L.H.G.R. only consisted of two officers and 19 men, they trained as much as possible and were as ready as they could be.

When notified by a riverboat captain named Eli Mattingly that the Southern Storm was soon to be at Leavenworth, Capt. Elam Herndon and his small band of citizen soldiers made ready to make a stand. The members of the little band of patriots ranged in age from 14 years 10 months to the oldest member, age 87. Very poorly armed with substandard, obsolete and outdated weapons, these courageous citizen soldiers made their stand at the cliffs of Leavenworth.

Capt. Herndon used some splendid battle tactics and his men did their duty as well disciplined soldiers while, at the same time, they were fearless in battle. This outstanding group of citizen soldiers was victorious.

One of the heroes of the day was Pvt. Newt Watson, jokingly dubbed as the 'Cannoneer' of the outfit because of his preference to be armed with his weapon of choice, a double-barreled eight gauge shotgun with beefed up ammunition. At a very critical point towards the last of the action, some Rebs tried to stage a comeback which was quickly put down by Cannoneer Pvt. Newt Watson running ahead in the face of great danger and ending the resistance.

So in summary, to repeat the headlines, 'Herndon's Hope Quells the Southern Storm.'

Out State and nation as well is very pleased to have men the caliber of Capt. Elam Herndon's men and we should never forget that they went that extra mile for us."

After reading the news article Capt. Herndon said, "Pvt. Tad Martin, this looks to me like some of your handiwork! Well written, son, but hell, if we were any better you would have said so, wouldn't you?"

"Now, Captain, you know that every word of that article is the pure unadulterated truth. As a reporter, I felt it my duty to let the world know the story. Actually, the world needs to know. It might prevent some others from making the fatal mistake of not being fully prepared by not taking advantage of all their resources. We have done a first here in having a backup reserve unit for the Home Guard!"

"Oh now, simmer down Tad, I was just kidding. I admit it is a little embarrassing to read about yourself, but as your article points out, it pays to have something or someone to fall back on. You know, kind of like wearing a belt and suspenders too."

"Absolutely right, Captain, I just hope others will prepare like we did. You know, this old war doesn't show any signs of ending anytime soon."

"Yes, I know and to my way of thinking, there's only one way to play it. Get prepared and stay prepared."

"Okay, men," said the captain, "we can't spend the rest of the day reading the newspaper. There is more to do! We still need to patrol the town to guard against looters and the like. Lt. Buchanan!"

"Yes, Captain."

"Line up a roster of men for guard duty. I think we need two men on duty at all times between sundown and 6:00 AM. As always, the guards will be under strict orders to shoot anyone caught looting. The guards can either patrol on horseback or they can walk, their choice. Also, we need to keep a close watch on that herd of captured horses at Buford's place. We already know that there are some 'horse dealers' not far away that could succumb to temptation."

Lt. Buchanan answered, "Yes, sir," and returned a sharp salute.

Meanwhile, back at the soon to be closed school house/hospital, Susan Bowman was doing her best to make her Renfro as comfortable as possible. She was now very deeply in love with Renfro Miles and was looking forward to the time when she could tend to all his needs everyday and, hopefully, forever. The feeling was mutual and he had already proposed marriage to Susan and she had accepted his proposal, almost before he had finished speaking.

Renfro was now in the process of getting up the nerve to tell Susan's mother, Alice, of their intentions. However, he had a feeling that his future mother-in-law already knew. He hoped very much that she would approve.

Alice Bowman came into the room and Susan started pleading her case, "Mother, you know that the plan is for Renfro to be moved over to Tillie and Moses' house tomorrow?"

"Yes, that's the plan, Daughter."

"Well, Mother, I don't see why we couldn't just move Renfro over to our house. You know that Tillie must go back to work at the hotel soon. That will mean that he will be by himself most all day long!"

"No, Susan, that wouldn't look right in the 'eyes of the town' and, honey, you know for sure that this town does have eyes!"

"Yes, Mother, and many wagging tongues as well!"

"So, Renfro needs to be at the Jefferson's house. I feel it won't matter much as I think you will soon have a worn path in the grass from our house to theirs."

"Now, Mother, don't poke fun. I do love him so!"

"Yes, Susan, I know. I'm not blind."

Meanwhile the men of the L.H.G.R. were standing their last formation of the day and Capt. Herndon spoke, "There are a couple of details before we fall out men! The captain of a down bound Union Navy gunboat just made a quick stop at our dock. He said that the steamboat 'Rees Lee' should be stopping here sometime in the morning tomorrow. That's the boat that the seven parolees need to take to start home because it goes on down the Ohio to the Mississippi. Lt. Buchanan!"

"Sir!"

"Lieutenant, arrange to have the money and the parole papers ready in the morning for our seven departing soldiers."

"Yes, Captain, I'll see to it."

"First Sergeant!!"

"Yes, Captain!"

"Sergeant, arrange to have Buford's team and wagon at the hospital right after our first formation in the morning. Also, have the three pole carry chairs with the wagon. Some of those men will have to be carried aboard the boat. We will let the departing Rebs have two of the pole carry chairs to take with them."

"Very well, sir."

The captain dismissed the men until morning except for those on guard duty. Elam was relaxing a little more each day as the problems seemed to be dwindling down. The captain and Newt headed toward the Dexter Saloon at a brisk pace, for it was very nearly "happy hour."

The next morning, promptly at 7:00 AM, the men of the L.H.G.R. stood in formation and answered roll call. All members were present and standing tall. Though the little band of citizen soldiers had come from a rather humble beginning, they had come far. Of course, they were still dressed in a mix of different uniforms and partial uniforms along with various everyday work clothes of the time. As was their custom now, they always proudly wore the distinctive neckerchiefs. One striking difference from before was the fact that all the men were now extremely well-armed. Thanks to the generosity of the Southern Storm, each man, except for Newt, was now armed with excellent lever action Henry .44 caliber rifles as well as one .44 caliber six shot revolver with extra cylinders. Also, there was no longer a shortage of ammunition. Newt carried his prized double-barreled eight gauge shotgun which kindhearted Buford had given to him, along with a nice .44 Colt revolver as well. To say the least, they were probably the best equipped unit of their kind, anywhere, anytime.

They could now hear the whistle on the "Rees Lee" signaling that it would soon be docking at Leavenworth. Capt. Herndon marched the men up to the temporary hospital and the evacuation proceeded. Moses Jefferson, along with Albert LeCroix, Helmer Schmitt and Chet Hatfield placed Renfro Miles in a pole carry chair and Renfro said some quick goodbyes to his men. With the four men carrying, they soon had Renfro at Moses and Tillie's house as planned. They then proceeded to the boat dock with the pole carry chair.

Meanwhile, the rest of the paroled POWs were helped up in Buford's wagon and with their belongings, papers and money, they were hauled down to the waiting boat. Capt. Herndon and Lt. Buchanan went aboard and talked with the Captain of the "Rees Lee" to arrange passage for the wounded men. Since the boat was a packet boat, the lower deck was only for cargo and livestock. The men of the L.H.G.R. pitched in and did four man carrys with the pole carry chair to get four of the wounded up to the passenger deck. Three of the wounded were able to walk up the steps with some help. Two of the carry chairs were given to the group as it was obvious they would be needed. There were some thank you words given by the Rebs. Herndon's men left the boat as it was in a hurry to leave. Much to everyone's surprise, as the boat moved away from the dock, the three walking wounded of the Rebs were standing at the rail. In unison, they gave and held a proper salute to Herndon's men. To a man, all returned the salute and the Rebs were started on their way home.

Things were winding down now and Capt. Herndon told his men that he felt sure that, very soon, they would be able to return to their regular occupations. He figured that the retired men of the group with maybe a volunteer or two could then handle the "night watch" until the regular Home Guard returned.

As Capt. Herndon walked up the street, he was confronted by an agitated middle-aged woman waving a newspaper at him. He had hoped to avoid this little encounter, but he hadn't seen her in time. If he had noticed her in time, he would have quickly crossed the street to avoid her. But, too late. This lady was a crusader to say the least. Elam privately referred to her as "Mrs. Temperance Hatchetmouth" (not her real name). She was firmly convinced that all forms of spirited beverages were a product of the devil, and all that partook of the spirits were disciples of the devil. Mrs. Temperance Hatchetmouth, still waving the newspaper in Capt. Herndon's face, began her assault! "Capt. Herndon, what's the meaning of this part of this front page article about Newt Watson??"

"What about it, ma'am?"

"Well, the way this is written up, everyone is trying to make him out to be some kind of a hero! Everyone in this town knows perfectly well that he is the town drunk. Why, it's common knowledge that Newt practically lives on brandy! Whoever wrote this should be ashamed of himself!!"

Elam was under attack and people were watching. He had to counterattack somehow and quickly. Thinking fast, he brazenly borrowed a line recently used by President Abe Lincoln when con-

fronted about Gen. U.S. Grant's drinking. Ever so calm and un-
ruffled, Capt. Herndon quickly retorted, "Why, thank you ma'am
for pointing this out! I guess that in view of that, perhaps I had
better find out what kind of brandy Newt drinks and buy a bottle
for each of my men! Thanks for your kind help. Good day."

The disgusted Mrs. Temperance Hatchetmouth stopped waving the newspaper in Elam's face and went on her way.

Herndon's men laughed and he said, "Damn, I'd as soon face
them Rebs out in the rocks with nothing but a slingshot as to
face that old biddy. She's downright dangerous!"

Over at Moses and Tillie's house, things were going just about
the way that Alice Bowman had predicted. Susan had already
made three trips over to see Renfro and a path was starting to
show in the grass. That evening Susan said, "Mother, when we
go over to dress Renfro's wound tonight, he wants to talk to you
about something."

Smiling, Alice said, "Oh dear, I wonder whatever he could want
to talk to me about?"

"Now, Mother, Renfro is rather shy. Try not to make it difficult
for him. You know, he believes in trying to be proper about everything."

"Okay, Susan, let's go tend to our patient."

When Susan and Alice arrived at Moses and Tillie's place, they
had Renfro propped up in bed and the three were in the midst of
talking of other days, years ago at Meadowland Plantation. Tillie
was saying, "Renfro, how is little sister Virginia? She was such a
cute little girl. I'll bet that she would be a grown woman now."

"Yes, Tillie, she is eighteen and grown up now. I guess I'm brag-
ging on my own sister, but I'd have to say she did turn out to be a
striking woman. I haven't heard any news from home for awhile.
I do miss them all."

Susan and Alice knocked at the front door and Moses greeted
them warmly. Soon the three nurses went about redressing Ren-

fro's leg wound. Renfro asked, "Nurse Bowman, in your opinion, how am I healing? I can tell I'm feeling some better, but I can't seem to move my left leg very much?"

"Well, Renfro, here is what I think. Unless you get infection really bad, I think you will be able to keep that leg. The downside of it is that the bullet shattered the bone quite badly. I really don't think you will ever be able to walk very well without an aid of some sort. I think that in another week or so we can get you some crutches and then you will be able to meander about some. Eventually, you may be able to get by with just a cane, but you will probably always have to use a cane. Also, the pain may come and go for years. Susan tells me that you wanted to talk to me about something. Whatever is it?"

Susan and Tillie slipped out of the room, hopefully to make this easier for Renfro.

"Well, Mrs. Bowman, I feel real awkward in view of the fact that I've just been told that I'll likely be a cripple for life. But, in any case, I still want to say something important. Now, Mrs. Bowman, I know about the loss of your husband in this war and I fully understand your feelings toward us Confederates. But, please try to understand that I have lost people that were important to me as well. Anyway, the thing I want to say to you is this —Mrs. Bowman, I love your daughter very much and I want to ask for her hand in marriage. I do hope you could see your way clear to approve, Ma'am."

"Now, Renfro, I know that Susan is deep in love with you and I know enough to not try to stand in the way of love. But, I do have one big concern."

"What is that, Mrs. Bowman?"

"I don't want to be crude or cruel, but the fact is that you are and probably always will be a cripple. Renfro, how do you intend to support yourself, my daughter and any children that the two of you might someday have?"

"Mrs. Bowman, that part of things should not be a problem. You see, I am from down in Warren County, Kentucky, not very far from Bowling Green. My home is at my family's plantation known as Meadowland Plantation. I can assure you, ma'am, that we are not the poorest family in Warren County. It is already set up that, since I am the only son, one day it will all be mine and my little sister's holdings. My plan would be, when I have recovered enough, to marry Susan and take my beautiful bride home with me to Meadowland."

"Very well, Renfro. Though I do have some misgivings about you moving my little girl so far away from me, I give my approval. Just promise me that you will be good to her."

"Mrs. Bowman, Susan is very precious to me and I promise I will always love and protect her."

"I'm sure you will, Renfro."

Of course, Susan and Tillie had been quietly listening at the bedroom door, but they never let on.

Alice then said, "Susan, we just had that important talk. He is one convincing speaker. Now, your patient needs some help with bathing. You had better go tend to him!"

A blushing Susan said, "Yes, Mother, and proceeded to get a pitcher, wash basin and towel. She then tenderly helped Renfro bathe, but only after a very intense kiss. Then he said, "Well, I mustered up the courage to have my talk with your mother."

"Well, how did it go?"

"Much better than expected, Future Mrs. Renfro Miles, much better."

This morning, the beautiful nearly new packet boat, "The Tarascon" was up bound and made a stop at Leavenworth to let off some passengers and deliver some mail and newspapers. There were newspapers from Owensboro, Kentucky; Evansville, Indiana; and Tell City, Indiana as well. They all had the same large print headline starting with "Herndon's Hope Quells the Southern Storm!!" The stories were all nearly the same as it had been when printed in the Leavenworth paper. The story of the action at the cliffs nearly filled the entire front page of each of the different papers.

Later in the day, the mail packet boat "The Lady Pike" was down bound and also delivered mail and newspapers. This delivery had newspapers from Indianapolis, Chicago, New York City, and Louisville. The front pages of all the papers carried the same bold headline, "Herndon's Hope Quells the Southern Storm!!" They also had nearly the same versions of the front page story. The town was buzzing about all the publicity. It was quite obvious that most people in the country knew the story by now. Part-time citizen soldier, school teacher and newspaper reporter Tad Martin had first reported the story and now it seemed to have a life of its own! Ah, the power of the press.

It was nearing the Fourth of July and things had returned to being a little closer to normal in Leavenworth. The war was still raging and was not showing signs of ending very soon. All too many of the community's men were away at war and, to add to that, eighty or so members of the Leavenworth Home Guard were still on active duty up at Jeffersonville, Indiana. The town fathers came close to canceling plans for the Fourth of July celebration due to so many people being gone, but at the last minute they decided to have the traditional celebration. Somehow, they would have a parade as usual, but just a smaller parade.

Capt. Herndon was asked to get the men of the L.H.G.R. prepared to be in the parade. Capt. Herndon pointed out the fact that his men would not look real good in a parade due to their lack of proper military uniforms for all members. They were assured that it was the men, not the clothes, that mattered most.

On the afternoon of July 3, the men set about decorating Buford's wagon with small flags and red, white and blue bunting. Patriotic decorations were also made ready for Buford's beautiful

Belgian horses. For sure, they had also done their part. For good measure, they made a second seat the width of the wagon just behind the regular wagon seat and about one foot higher.

To everyone's surprise, early in the morning on July the Fourth, the very large steamboat, "Grey Eagle," docked at Leavenworth. As the passengers disembarked, it looked like something big was in the works. First to come off was the army's 66th Regimental Band, also its honor guard, all in dashing army dress uniforms. Next off the boat was the Governor of the State of Indiana, Oliver P. Morton, along with his aides. The next dignitary was Major General John Love, Commanding Officer of the Indiana Legion of State Militia. The next surprise guest was Major Horatio Woodbury, Commander of the regular Leavenworth Home Guard. His men were still at Jeffersonville, but he was here for the day. It appeared that something very important was soon to take place.

Soon it was time to form up for the parade. At the head of the procession was the Army's 66th Regimental Band, then there were the ladies of the Temperance League led by Mrs., oh, you know. Then came the various floats sponsored by local churches, fraternal organizations and businesses. Then came the section of the parade that was the most famous, the members of the Leavenworth Home Guard Reserve. As was their custom, they had formed up with all men marching except for Buford, driving the team, and Tad Martin and Milo Weathers, riding, all on the front seat. For the parade, the three nurses, Tillie, Alice and Susan were riding on the second seat. All the men had decided that the three nurses should wear red neckerchiefs, the same as theirs, for they were very much a part of the L.H.G.R.

The rest of the men were marching in a column of twos, nine long with Capt. Herndon and Lt. Buchanan in the lead. They were all proudly marching with their Henry rifles, except for Newt's cannon, at right shoulder arms, all carrying Colt revolvers as well. They still were all wearing a mixed lot of uniforms, partial uniforms and nondescript work clothes. All were wearing their, by now, trademark neckerchiefs which told the world that they were proud members of the Leavenworth Home Guard Reserve. All were much surprised when, just as Capt. Herndon ordered, "Forward march," two more soldiers had decided to march with them. Gen. John Love was marching at Capt. Herndon's left and Major Woodbury was marching at the right of Lt. Buchanan.

The procession finally stopped at the reviewing stand, near the court house. The Leavenworth Home Guard Reserve was directly in front of the reviewing stand and were given, "Parade rest." Though not supposed to talk in the ranks, Sgt. Bratton quietly said to Lt. Buchanan, "Gosh, I hope they are not planning on more fireworks. The display we had at the cliffs was quite good and would be hard to beat!"

Smiling, the lieutenant said, "Sergeant, I quite agree. Now hush up!"

The 66th Regiment's chaplain gave the opening prayer. Then, the color guard put the American Flag on a large staff on the stand while those in the military stood at attention and saluted. The army band played a stirring rendition of the "Star Spangled Banner," then they played the "Battle Hymn of the Republic."

It was now time for the speakers and their speeches. County Clerk Lemonds acted as master of ceremonies and introduced the first speaker of the day. "Ladies and gentlemen, please allow me the pleasure of presenting the Governor of the Great State of Indiana, Governor Oliver P. Morton. Governor, I respectfully turn it over to you, sir."

"Thank you, sir. Ladies and gentlemen, I do consider it a great honor to be invited to be a part of this celebration in your beautiful little town. As Governor, I probably would have been giving a speech up at our State capital at Indianapolis, had it not been for the fact that I got invited to speak in the presence of some of the bravest and most gallant citizen soldiers our State or country has ever had. Of course, I refer to the officers and men of the newly conceived and formed Leavenworth Home Guard Reserve. I am doubly proud that the formation of a unit such as this, a reserve for the reserves, was a result of the collective thinking between myself and Major General John Love, Commanding Officer of the Indiana Legion of State Militia. Together, Gen. Love and myself developed this unusual concept. Gen. Love then contacted your local Home Guard Commander, Major Horatio Woodbury, and he proceeded in the formation of this Home Guard Reserve unit, the first of its kind in our State. It should further be said that Major Woodbury is an excellent judge of men due to the fact that he picked Capt. Elam Herndon to command this new unit of citizen soldiers.

Had it not been for Capt. Herndon and his men, the impending raid on Leavenworth would very likely have been very bad for your town. However, thanks to the captain's tactical skills and leadership of his brave men, disaster was averted.

It is now my and Gen. Love's joint goal to see that Home Guard Reserve units such as this one be formed in all parts of our great State, starting as soon as possible."

The Governor then said, "Capt. Herndon, would you, please, step up here?"

Capt. Herndon, with his usual limp, went up on the reviewing stand as requested.

Gov. Morton then said, "On behalf of myself and the people of the State of Indiana I want to present to you and your men this 'Certificate of Meritorious Service' from a grateful State. It reads as follows:

> *The people of the State of Indiana and its Governor, Oliver P. Morton, hereby commend the officers and men of the Leavenworth Home Guard*

Reserve for their brave and meritorious service to the State of Indiana in a time of dire need. They unselfishly gave their all to the defense of their fellow citizens and their possessions. Against seemingly overwhelming odds, these brave men stood their ground and were victorious.' Indiana is indeed truly proud to have men of their stature being part of our military forces.'"

Signed:

Gov. Oliver P. Morton

State of Indiana, U.S.A.

Capt. Herndon accepted the certificate from Gov. Morton. As they shook hands, the crowd applauded.

Gov. Morton then said, "Now I will turn over the podium to Maj. Gen. John Love, Commander of the Indiana Legion of State Militia."

"Thank you, Governor. People, I want to echo the Governor's words for I too feel very proud and honored to have been invited to be here on this special day. First of all, I want to proclaim that the Leavenworth Home Guard Reserve is a shining example of what patriots can achieve when banded together with proper leadership and training. The Governor and I intend to see that units like this will be formed statewide as soon as possible. We also hope that our entire nation will take notice and follow our lead as well. I also want to point out that this unit is living proof that age, certain disabilities and lack of previous military experience matter little when willing volunteers come together in the proper spirit. This serves as an inspiration to us all."

The general then said, "Now I want to present a very important document to Capt. Elam Herndon. It is an official charter issued by the State of Indiana authorizing the official existence of the Leavenworth Home Guard Reserve to be a part of our militia or reserve for as long as it feels the need to exist. Reading in part, this charter further states that no man shall ever be stricken from the rolls of a Home Guard Reserve unit due to age or health reasons, unless that member requests to be relieved from serving."

Capt. Herndon took the charter handed to him and saluted the general.

General Love continued, "There are a few more things that need to be said. The State of Indiana hereby officially apologizes for not supplying this unit with proper arms, ammunition and uniforms. I promise that henceforth reserve units such as yours will be furnished proper weapons along with an adequate supply of ammunition for ongoing practice to maintain your high level of marksmanship and readiness.

As I said, the Dept. of State Militia will see that proper uniforms of your choice will be made available to your group, as soon as possible. However, Gov. Morton and I agree that we hope that your unit would keep the distinctive neckerchiefs as part of your identification. We both think the neckerchiefs are a good touch."

Capt. Herndon smiled and said, "Thank you, General. The neckerchiefs stay."

Gen. Love continued, "It has always been my contention that when it comes to the Constitution of the United States, the second amendment could very well be one of the most important of all. It reads, and I quote, 'A well regulated militia being necessary to the security of a free state, the right of the people to keep and bear arms, shall not be infringed.' Arguably, these words are true, but I have always felt that 'the right of the people to keep and bear arms' should be changed to read, 'It shall be the obligation of the people to keep and bear arms.' Also, I think it should further read, 'It shall also be the obligation of the owner of arms to do marksmanship practice on a regular basis to ever be in a state of readiness.' At least, these are my opinions."

There was applause from the crowd and Gen. Love carried on, "Folks, I know it's hot, but there is another important piece of business. The men of the Leavenworth Home Guard Reserve will now be recognized on a more individual basis. I will read off the names from up here and Gov. Morton and Major Woodbury will present the proper honors to the men in the ranks. Every officer and enlisted man of the L.H.G.R. will be awarded the 'Indiana Meritorious Service Badge,' all twenty-one men and all three of the unit's nurses as well. These awards will be followed by the presenting of 'Purple Hearts' to the four men wounded in the action at the cliffs. They are as follows, Pvt. James Corbin, Pvt. Helmer Schmitt, Pvt. Chet Hatfield and Pvt. Newt Watson."

After the Purple Hearts were awarded to the wounded men, Gen. Love read the following: "Capt. Elam Herndon is hereby awarded a very high honor from the Indiana Legion of Militia, the 'Excellence in Leadership Medal.' One last award, being the 'Army Certificate of Merit' to the L.H.G.R.'s cannoneer, Pvt. Newt Watson. It reads, 'For fearless action in the fact of great danger to save his fellow soldiers from certain harm.'"

As Newt was receiving his awards, most of the men noticed that Mrs. Temperance Hatchetmouth's lips showed unmistakable disapproval and, indeed, her face was as red as Newt's neckerchief.

Gen. Love then said, "Now Gov. Morton has a message from the Commander in Chief, President Abraham Lincoln that he would like to read for all to hear."

Gov. Morton began, "This message was sent directly to me from President Lincoln and he asked that I read it on this occasion. It reads as follows:

'Governor Morton, in the face of bad news coming my way all too often, you cannot image my delight in reading the account of the men of Herndon's

Hope being victorious against such overwhelm-
ing odds. It made my day and did my heart good.
Please relay my heartfelt thanks to Capt. Herndon
and his brave men for a job well done. Let's hope
that your plan of Reserves for Reserves can and will
be copied and duplicated across our land. Also, I
want to point out, lest the world forget, that I spent
the greater part of my youth in Indiana and patri-
ots such as Herndon and his men make me very
proud of my time living there. On a more personal
note, I understand that one of the men, a Pvt. Le-
muel Moore, and I have something in common. To
Pvt. Moore I would just like to say that it takes
more than being head kicked by a cow to keep a
good man down! Good luck, Pvt. Moore!'

And that is the message from our President. I know it's hot and you all are tired, but we have just a little more to go on these proceedings. The next and last speaker of the day is Major Horatio Woodbury of the Leavenworth Home Guard."

The Major began, "I just want to say that I felt I had picked the right man for the job when I picked Capt. Elam Herndon and he in turn picked the right men for his troops. You have all done yourselves and our county and State proud. Your fellow citizens of Crawford County, along with many of the Town Fathers here have tried to come up with a token of their gratitude. Here it is in a nutshell; Squire Weathers has donated the approximate five acres where the Leavenworth Home Guard Reserve has their rifle range, down by the cliffs, to the group as chartered. The next show of gratitude is from the many generous people hereabouts. They have collected enough money to pay for having a building built by the rifle range to serve as an armory and meeting place for the L.H.G.R. Last but not least, it has been decided that the unit's land and building shall for now and all time be exempt from being taxable property."

Capt. Herndon thanked all concerned for their kindness. This was truly a good bunch of people and he was so glad he lived here.

The 66th Regimental Army Band started playing a lively march and soon the picnic was underway. And so it was on July 4th, 1863.

Tillie said, "Come on, girls. Let's eat. That barbeque smells so good and just look at all the pies and cakes!"

Alice quickly agreed, "Let's go girls!"

Susan replied, "Oh, Renfro is all alone. I'll take lunch to him. He has been there by himself most all day."

To which Alice quipped, "Yes, girl, I'm sure he needs you. Tillie and I won't be back real soon."

A blushing Susan said, "Yes, Mother."

Ind. Gov. Oliver P. Morton

Picture courtesy of:
Governor's Portraits Collection
Indiana Historical Bureau
State of Indiana

Maj. Gen. John Love, Indiana Legion of Militia
Picture courtesy of Craig Dunn/CivilWarIndiana.com

• NINETEEN •

Some Improving Relations With North

AS THE SUN was setting low, the Fourth of July festivities were well underway. The speeches had all been made and the army band kept on playing soul stirring patriotic music and military marches. Finally, it was time for the fireworks display. The rockets, aerial flares, and bombs made a very beautiful reflection in the Ohio River. It was quite spectacular. However, as Sgt. Bratton had pointed out, the fireworks at the cliffs a few days earlier were nothing to be sneezed at.

The steamboat "Rees Lee" was waiting to take the visiting dignitaries and guests back upriver. About 10:00 PM, everyone went aboard and soon the "Rees Lee" blew a farewell whistle and her large stern wheel churned the water in beautiful rhythm. The reflections made by the big boat's lights and the sparks from her smokestacks painted a majestic picture in the water of the Ohio. The crowd was melting away as most people headed home.

Moses Jefferson was going to stay a while longer and visit some more with his fellow soldiers and friends. Alice Bowman and Tillie Jefferson were ready to call it a day. It was late. Alice remembered that daughter Susan would, no doubt, still be at Tillie's house with Renfro. The two women quietly entered the Jefferson's home and were not very surprised to find Susan, clothing in disarray, fast asleep in Renfro's arms. Quite flustered, the young lovers woke up. A blushing, embarrassed Susan stammered quietly, "Now, Mother, it's not like it seems!"

Smiling a gentle smile, Alice said, "Of course, honey, I'm sure it isn't."

Renfro sheepishly said, "Mrs. Bowman, I guess we must have drifted off listening to the fireworks."

Tillie coyly said, "Yes, children, it's a fact that fireworks can make people relaxed and drowsy."

Alice said, "Come on, Susan. Let's go home."

"Yes, Mother, as soon as I tell Renfro goodnight."

Though he didn't know it yet, July 5th was going to be a red letter day in the life of Cpl. Hiram Kinnaman. Everyone had heard the distinctive whistle signaling the approach of the "Concordia Queen" coming upriver. Cpl. Hiram Kinnaman happened to be the first person at the wharf when Capt. Mattingly maneuvered the big boat up to the proper place. The first thing that caught Hiram's attention was two ladies standing close to the ramp, waiting to leave the "Concordia Queen." Obviously, they were very well-dressed. The second thing that Hiram noticed was the fact that the younger of the two ladies was a stunning black haired beauty and she filled her dress very well and in all the right places. If Cpl. Kinnaman had been in battle at this particular moment, he most surely would have been killed for he was not in full control of himself.

Quickly gathering his wits, Hiram slipped his left arm out of its sling and discreetly dropped the sling in the river. He did not want this beautiful creature to see him as partially disabled, even if he was. He met the two ladies at the ramp. Very politely, he doffed his hat and said, "Ladies, please allow me to introduce myself. I am Cpl. Hiram Kinnaman. How may I be of service to you ladies?"

"Yes, Corporal, we possibly could use your help. I am Mrs. Melissa Miles and this is my daughter, Virginia. We got word that my son, Major Renfro Miles, was wounded in a military action here and is in the care of two black people, Moses and Tillie Jefferson. Could you help us find their home?"

"Yes, ladies, I'll be delighted to be of assistance. Please wait here by your luggage while I get a horse and buggy. Too far for ladies to walk!" Wanting to make a good first impression, Hiram was thinking quick. Yes, there, only about a block away, was Nurse Alice Bowman's horse and buggy tied up at the hitching rack close to her office. At the risk of being accused of being a horse thief, he took Alice's rig without her permission. Surely she would understand. After all, this was a mission of mercy. He trotted to the horse and buggy and at a trot was soon back at the wharf. He soon had Mrs. Miles and Virginia seated in the buggy. He avoided using his still nearly useless left arm and put the ladies' things aboard.

Soon, he had the ladies at the Jefferson's home. There, he gallantly helped them from the buggy and knocked on the door. Tillie answered the door knock and was soon standing at the door with her ever present, pretty smile. She greeted everyone warmly and said, "Oh, Mrs. Miles, it's so good to see you! My pretty little Virginia, oh honey, how you have grown! Ladies, please come in, you too Hiram." All entered the Jefferson home. Tillie showed the way to the bedroom where Renfro was sitting on the edge of the bed. Mother and sister embarrassed Renfro with all their hugs and kisses. They were just so glad to see him still alive, even if he was crippled.

Cpl. Kinnaman saw that they all needed to talk privately. He was also mindful of the need to get Nurse Alice Bowman's horse and buggy back, hopefully before she missed it. Hiram leaned close to Virginia Miles and whispered softly, "Ma'am, I should be going now, but I would like to see you again. Perhaps we could become better acquainted?"

Much to Hiram's pleasure, Virginia softly answered, "Why yes, Corporal, I would like that very much."

Cpl. Kinnaman more or less floated out to the horse and buggy and quickly had it back to the Bowman's hitching rack. The rig had not been missed. "Lord," he thought to himself, "lucky twice in the same day!"

Back at Tillie's place, Melissa Miles was having a heart to heart talk with Tillie Jefferson. Melissa began, "Now, Tillie, you know I will always be grateful for what you have done for my son. I don't know how I could ever even begin to repay you enough for all the kindness you and Moses have shown. I thank you from the bottom of my heart. However, to be honest about it, Tillie, I still harbor some resentment about the way you and Moses left us back at Owensboro back in '53! You and Moses were well thought of at Meadowland. You two belonged there and it hurt us all very deeply the way you left."

"Very well, Melissa, let's talk openly and honestly about this. Moses and I both thought very highly of you and Col. Miles. Even more, we simply loved little Renfro and Virginia. We had grown to thinking of them as being our children. It nearly tore our hearts out to leave Renfro and Virginia. And while we are saying it like it is, the fact is that Moses and I had as much to do with raising those children as you and your husband did. It is no wonder that we thought of them as ours.

Now, as for leaving you all and Meadowland, the fact was that we knew we had to reach for a better life and to be free. We left and never looked back. Moses and I have built a good life here in Leavenworth and we are very much a part of this community. These are good people here, for the most part. The good Lord done right guiding us here. There is no more 'master and servant' here. That way of life is over for us. Hopefully, it will soon be gone across the whole country. When Renfro ended up here a while back, me and Moses thanked the Lord for sending him our way. We still love our 'little boy' and Virginia. We feel the same for you."

"I can understand the way you feel, Tillie, but we all hated to see you leave just the same. I just want you and Moses to know that you would both be welcome to move back to Meadowland and be a part of things again."

"I know you mean well, Melissa, but those days and that way of life are gone for us. This is home and this is where we will stay. Thank you very much, just the same. Now, I'm going to move some things into the room we use as a study and make a place for Moses and me to sleep. Then Melissa, you and Virginia can share the bed we usually sleep in."

Melissa Miles' pride would not allow her to accept Tillie's offer of the bedroom. Her long standing feelings of superiority stood in the way. She felt it just would not be proper to sleep in the bed of former slaves. In any case, she very politely declined the offer and said, "Oh now, Tillie, we just couldn't impose on you and Moses. Virginia and I will get a room at that hotel up the street after we visit with Renfro for a while longer. However, we thank you for the offer."

"Very well, Melissa, if that's the way you want it. I'll let you all visit now. It's near time for me to go to work. I run the dining room at the hotel up the street. Its name is the Ourerbacker Hotel."

Melissa asked, "Renfro, are you all alone while Tillie works?"

"No, Mother, I'm seldom alone for very long. I have a very special friend who helps look after me."

"Well now, Renfro, you seem to make new friends rather quickly."

"Yes, Mother, in this case I did. I am a very lucky man to have found her. She is very special and I love her so much. Her name is Susan Bowman. She is a very pretty young lady and she and I are going to be married in the near future. For my part, the sooner the better."

"Renfro, are you quite sure about this? Your father and I had hoped you would find a Southern girl, one who would be more likely to share our values and standards! Son, this is rather sudden."

"Mother, I am quite sure. Susan is the love of my life and I am quite sure that she is the right woman for me. I know you will like her too."

Susan let herself in and was surprised to find the two women visiting Renfro.

From his bed, Renfro said, "Mother and Virginia, please allow me to introduce my future bride, Susan Bowman, soon to be Mrs. Renfro Miles. Susan, this is my Mother, Melissa, and my sister, Virginia." Renfro then pulled Susan close and kissed her tenderly.

The two Miles women quickly saw that they had best be getting ready to welcome Susan into the Miles family.

While Renfro and his mother were talking, Susan and Virginia were becoming acquainted and were quickly finding much to talk about. Softly, so her mother would not hear, Virginia said, "Susan, do you know a young soldier named Hiram Kinnaman?"

"Why, yes. I know him well. We grew up close together. He is sort of a handsome rascal, isn't he? He is one nice man, Virginia. I presume that you two have met already. How well do you know him?"

"Not nearly as well as I'd like to know him."

"How long are you and Mrs. Miles going to be able to stay in Leavenworth?"

"Mother says that eight or ten days will be our limit. Then, we must get back to Meadowland."

"Well, Virginia, I'll put a bug in Cpl. Hiram Kinnaman's ear as soon as possible. I'm betting that his first look at you sort of left him off balance. I do know for a fact that Hiram has always had a fondness for pretty dark haired women and you, no doubt, fall into that category. I'll see what I can do."

"Thank you, Susan. You are going to be a great sister-in-law. I do believe that my brother is one lucky man."

"Thanks for the kind words, Virginia. I know that I am a very lucky woman. I'm sure you'll be a very fine sister-in-law as well."

Cpl. Kinnaman asked Capt. Herndon, "What are our plans for tomorrow, sir?"

"Well, Hiram, since the town has been so generous in their offer for us to be able to build our own meeting place, I thought that maybe we should all sit down, make plans and get started building. Why do you ask?"

"Well, Captain, something pretty important has come up and I need to be excused from duty tomorrow if at all possible."

Smiling, Capt. Herndon said, "Well, Hiram, if that 'something pretty important' happens to be that fine looking black haired beauty I seen you with yesterday, I'd definitely agree that you need a day off. Boy, I'd say you just had a stroke of luck!"

"Thanks, Captain. It's good to see that your pore old eyes ain't failed you yet."

Hiram then went by Nurse Bowman's office and asked permission to borrow her horse and buggy for awhile tomorrow. Note: this time he asked.

As he expected, good-natured Alice said that he could borrow her rig, but just don't go too far, in case she had to make a house call on short notice.

Much to the surprise of everyone, the Leavenworth Home Guard arrived back in town early in the morning on July 6th. Major Woodbury and his men had been relieved from active duty at Jeffersonville. Very anxious to get home, they had ridden all night with only a few breaks. The eighty man group was very tired and dust covered, but were glad to be back.

Capt. Herndon and the men of the L.H.G.R. were also very relieved to see Major Woodbury and his men back. Now, Herndon and his men could turn their attention to starting on their new building. Capt. Herndon explained to the rest that Cpl. Kinnaman would be off duty today, that he had important business to take care of.

Capt. Herndon and Major Woodbury talked things over. The major told Herndon that his group would now be back to "reserve status" and would drill and train as such. He then asked Capt. Herndon how the paroled Reb prisoners were doing. The major was pleased to learn that it looked like the parolees who had stayed would probably end up as permanent residents.

At about 8:00 AM on the 6th, Melissa and Virginia Miles were back at Moses and Tillie's house to see Renfro. Melissa had done some soul searching and had a change of heart. For one thing, one night at the Ourerbacker Hotel was quite enough for Melissa Miles. She was now ready to come down from her "high horse" and meet Tillie on equal terms. Tillie had let the ladies in and after greeting them warmly, things started to change.

Melissa said, "Tillie Mae, if it's not too late, we would like to reconsider your offer to let us stay here while we are in Leavenworth."

"Melissa Miles, my home is your home. You and Virginia are welcome to stay here for as long as you like. Moses and I will both be delighted to have you all stay with us and share our home."

"Thank you very much, Tillie. You are a very kind lady."

This was to be the start of a long lasting genuine friendship between Melissa and Tillie. No more as "master or mistress and servant" but rather as equals. The old days were gone and they both would adjust accordingly.

About 9:00 AM, there was a knock at the front door. When Tillie answered the knock, she was not at all surprised to see Cpl. Hiram Kinnaman standing there—shiny boots, clean uniform and clean shaven. "And what can we do for you, Hiram?" At the same time, Tillie gave Hiram a sly wink.

"I'd like to speak with Miss Virginia, please, ma'am."

Virginia came to the door and Hiram made his suggestion, "Miss Miles, with your mother's permission, of course, I would like to give you a guided tour of our town and show you some of the sights. I have a horse and buggy and also a picnic basket."

"Okay, Corporal, I'll check with Mother."

Tillie Mae served as a character reference for Hiram and Mother Miles grudgingly gave her permission for Hiram to escort her daughter. Privately, Melissa wished that Hiram had been an officer and not a corporal and, better yet, a Confederate officer and Southern gentleman. "Oh well, she thought, we won't be staying here all that long."

The corporal helped Virginia up to the buggy seat and soon the tour began. Virginia was sitting very close to Hiram's left side, as horse drawn vehicles are customarily driven from the right. (The driver sits at the right side.) She was leaning close so as to hear his every word as the narrated, guided tour began. As Virginia leaned so close to Hiram, he could smell the beautiful fragrance of the lilac perfume she wore. Hiram thought to himself, "Good Lord, this girl drives me out of my mind!" Virginia coyly rested her right hand on Hiram's arm, letting him know that she did not find him unattractive either.

He thought about driving her down to the cliffs, but thought better of that idea. It might not be a good idea to see the place where her brother had been shot. Even more, not good to see the fresh graves there. Besides that, Capt. Herndon and the rest would probably be down there staking off the site for the new building. He was very proud of this beautiful lady, but today, he didn't want an audience. He just wanted to get to know her better.

Then, Hiram thought of the perfect place. Yes, perfect. He turned the horse out toward Buford Beasley's farm and home then on past Jim Running Deer's land and on past Jim's cabin to the bank of the Big Blue River, where it flows into the Ohio River. Yes, a very pretty place among the rocks and sycamore trees, perfect for a picnic.

Hiram found a good spot to tie the horse and proceeded to help dark eyed Virginia down from the buggy. As she was getting out of the buggy, she lost her balance, or so she would have him think, and Hiram caught her as she fell into his arms. His left arm hurt, but he tried not to let on. With this sweet smelling beauty so close, he could restrain himself no more. Their lips met in a deep prolonged kiss. It may have been sudden, but Hiram knew then that somehow, some way, he would want to be with Virginia Miles for the rest of his life. He only hoped the feeling was mutual.

Hiram's mother had packed a delicious picnic basket and eventually Virginia and Hiram ate most all of it. Virginia said, "Hiram, your mother is a very good cook. I'd like to meet her one day."

"Yes, Virginia, I want you to meet her. I want her to see that her son can pick a really fine woman."

"Corporal, you really know how to charm a girl. You are one silver-tongued rascal, no doubt about it. Hiram, I promised Mother that you would have me back before dark. Don't you think we had better start back?"

"Yes, Virginia, I guess we had better start back. I have never seen a day go so fast."

"Uh huh, or more perfectly," as she was being helped back in the buggy.

Hiram drove Virginia back to the Jefferson's place and saw her up to the porch. Mrs. Miles was watching so Hiram and Virginia did not embrace in front of her. Hiram softly whispered, "I hope we can do this again, pretty lady?"

And just as softly, Virginia whispered back, "So do I. So do I. The sooner the better."

Hiram was more or less in a dreamlike state as he took Alice Bowman's horse and buggy back. "Lord, what a day!" he thought. He thanked Alice very much for her generosity. After which, he unhitched the buggy, un-harnessed the horse; brushed, fed and watered it; and took it to the small pen and barn out back.

As Hiram was walking up Nelson Street, he met Capt. Herndon. The captain said, "Well, Hiram, did you get your important business attended to?"

"Yes, Capt. Herndon, I did. It was a very good day."

"Well good. Come on. Let's go up to the Dexter Saloon and have a brandy on me."

"You are one slick talker, Elam. Let's go!"

"Hiram, we need you tomorrow. We want your input and opinion on some things concerning our new building."

When they reached the Dexter, Newt and Harley were there waiting. Happy hour was about to start. Before they had time to order the first round, Dan Lyon came in followed by Sgt. Wildman and Buford.

Capt. Herndon jokingly said, "Damn, I hope the Home Guard doesn't have to leave right now or the town will be left nearly undefended! Cheers boys to a good town, a good bunch of men and our cause—the right cause. Salute!"

The bartender proclaimed, "Boys, the next round is on the house."

They all thanked Charlie for his generosity. The fact of the matter was that most of the boys were only "social drinkers," but some were very sociable!

Meanwhile, back at the Jefferson home, Susan was beginning to feel a little closed in with Renfro's mother watching their every move. Being an innovative girl, Susan had thoughtfully arranged for her mother, Tillie, Moses, Melissa and Virginia to have an evening meal together at the Ourerbacker Hotel's dining room. Susan hoped that they would all have a delicious, leisurely meal and take their time visiting and getting better acquainted after the meal. Of course, Susan Bowman had volunteered to stay with Renfro while the others were gone. She knew full well that the evening would go all too fast for her and Renfro. For lovers, time seems to race by.

Early on July 8th came another unexpected event. The mail packet, "Lady Pike" was down bound approaching Leavenworth. Her steam whistle was loudly signaling her approach! There was an urgent message for Major Woodbury of the Home Guard from Camp Noble, New Albany, Indiana. This was an emergency!! Confederate Gen. John Hunt Morgan with approximately 2000 men had raided Brandenburg, Kentucky. With ease, he had captured two boats, the "Alice Dean" and the "McCombs" and was crossing the Ohio River to the Indiana side. The crossing would take a total of around seventeen hours. The town of Corydon, Indiana, was next to be victimized. The orders were for Major Woodbury to put as many of his Leavenworth Home Guard troops, horses and weapons on board the "Lady Pike" as was practical and proceed immediately to Mauckport, Indiana, on the double. Those of the unit not able to board the "Lady Pike" due to space limitations were to wait no more than two hours, in case another boat came by. If none came, they were to proceed overland and meet the rest of the unit somewhere around Corydon. Major Woodbury was also ordered to reactivate the Leavenworth Home Guard Reserve to take over during the absence of his unit.

Capt. Herndon and Lt. Buchanan were called aside and Major Woodbury filled them in and relayed the orders. Tongue in cheek, the major said, "Dammit, Elam, your men are better armed than mine. Maybe we should stay here and you and your boys should go chase after Gen. Morgan and his raiders?"

With a smile, Capt. Herndon replied, "Well, Major, we might be better armed, but we move too damn slow. You and yours had better go ahead. Good luck! At least this time, we have some honest to God good weapons, thanks to the Southern Storm!"

"Ain't that some coincidence, Elam. Gen. John Hunt Morgan's bunch have been given the nickname the 'Thunderbolt of the Confederacy,' and the bunch you just locked horns with were known as the 'Southern Storm.' Imagine that, two bad weather disturbances from the South, all in the same summer."

"Well, Major, this storm belongs to you and, I hope, a bunch more. This sounds like one hell of a big thunderbolt."

"It is. We will need a bunch of help. The message says that Union Gen. Edward Hobson is in hot pursuit of Morgan and Gen. Hobson has around 4000 men. The problem is that Hobson might not get to Brandenburg in time to battle Morgan before he finishes his crossing."

As they would later learn, Morgan completed the crossing before Gen. Hobson and his men caught up with his group. Morgan forced the captain of the "McCombs" to proceed upriver and stay away. The "McCombs'" captain was an old friend of Morgan's. When the last crossing was made, Morgan had ordered the packet boat "Alice Dean" set on fire and set adrift. It was still smoking, burning and sinking as Gen. Hobson watched helplessly, stranded on the Kentucky shore. This was not one of Gen. Hobson's brightest moments.

Back at Leavenworth, the men of the Home Guard Reserve were on the alert and standing by. Capt. Herndon divided the L.H.G.R. into three groups of seven men each. They started patrolling the area in eight hour shifts, eight hours on duty and sixteen hours off. With some of the men now on horseback, they patrolled a wider area than they had before the Southern Storm had arrived. Now, they kept watch from up at Big Blue River, near Blue River Island, all through Leavenworth and down to the cliffs area. No enemy appeared nor did anything suspicious happen. As Capt. Herndon had originally thought, the main mission of the L.H.G.R. would be, they were basically babysitting the town. They were maintaining law and order, preventing looting and doing fire watch.

Two days later, the boat "Lady Pike" was down bound and docked at Leavenworth. They had a shipment of several boxes and crates addressed to Capt. Elam Herndon of the Leavenworth Home Guard Reserve. The shipment was from the U.S. Army Quartermaster Supply Depot at Jeffersonville, Indiana. Capt. Herndon got his men together and loaded the things in Buford's wagon.

Everyone was delighted. Gen. Love and Gov. Morton had made good on their promise of ammunition and uniforms. The papers with the ammunition stated that there would be monthly shipments of ammunition adequate for ongoing firing practice or for combat use, whichever came first! The uniforms were new but were leftovers from the Mexican War, very sharp uniforms indeed. They had been in the depot as surplus from the Mexican War, 1846-47. The Army was delighted that Herndon's group had chosen these old uniforms since they had been bought and paid for ages ago. Included was a package containing an assortment of the appropriate chevrons, rank designation patches and so on.

The men of the L.H.G.R. now looked like an honest to God military outfit, complete with their distinctive neckerchiefs which would be their trademark from now on. There was some discussion about Cpl. Kinnaman and Cpl. Weathers wearing different uniforms since they were only temporary members on convalescence leave from the army. But, for now, they would wear their usual Civil War style uniforms. In any case, Capt. Herndon issued both corporals new uniforms and expressed the hope that in the future they would both become permanent members.

Back over at the Jefferson house, relations between the North and South were improving with each passing day. Mrs. Melissa Miles was starting to really like Susan Bowman, her future daughter-in-law, and likewise Susan now considered Mother Miles a friend.

Tillie and Moses were, as far as they were concerned, on equal footing with Melissa Miles and interacted with her at that level. Their whole relationship was rapidly changing, no more master/servant or big me/little you. They were now genuinely friends, as they should well be. After all, these three had known each other most of their lives.

One "sticky wicket" though, Melissa Miles could not help but notice the attraction between her daughter and Cpl. Kinnaman. Yes, she could see why Virginia was attracted to Hiram. He was a handsome young man, but he was only a corporal and a Yankee corporal at that. If only he were an officer and a Southern gentleman. Oh well, perhaps they would return to Meadowland Plantation before things got out of hand.

Little did Melissa Miles know that Virginia and Hiram would be closely entwined once more this afternoon at the beautiful place by Big Blue River. When they were together, they were in a world all their own and a wonderful world it was!!

When Cpl. Kinnaman was on duty the next day, he had to take some ribbing from the boys over his semi-dreamlike state nowadays. Sgt. Bratton remarked, "Boys, when Hiram is around that pretty woman, he acts just like a blind dog in a smokehouse!" Everyone laughed. But, Hiram knew it was true. It was hard to keep his mind straight when he was around Virginia Miles. Life was good and getting better.

Mother Melissa Miles made an effort to talk Virginia out of seeing Hiram Kinnaman any more. She began, "Honey, don't you realize that this corporal you have been seeing may well be the one who shot your brother? Think about it!"

"Yes, Mother, I have thought about it a lot, but there is something else. Moses Jefferson was there in the battle, same as the rest. You know perfectly well that he would never ever hurt Renfro knowingly. As you well know, Moses was doing his level best to help Renfro and it is very good that he did. You see, Mother, war is not a personal thing, at least it's not meant to be. So you see, Mother, any one of the Yankees may well have shot Renfro, Moses or any of them. It really does not matter. Also, lest we forget, Susan Bowman's father was killed by Confederate soldiers and she has learned to live with it. War is very ugly, but not personal. We must also remember that this Yankee girl, Susan, will soon be very much a part of our family. You and I already like her and Renfro deeply loves her." "Yes, Virginia, I'm starting to accept things for what they are. You know, just as I do, that Col. Miles will not be quick to welcome a Yankee into the family with open arms!"

"Oh, I know, Mother, but the world is changing every day and Daddy will just have to change with it, whatever the outcome."

"Virginia, I know you are right, but it won't be easy for Col. Rafe Miles to accept."

Back with the L.H.G.R. building and planning crew, Capt. Herndon had another meeting with his men. He began, "Boys, according to the newspaper accounts, Gen. Morgan and his raiders are heading up through Indiana toward Ohio. A bunch of Union troops are chasing close behind and that includes Major Woodbury and his Leavenworth Home Guard. It looks to me like we can come off the twenty-four hour guard and cut down to just two men on duty, dusk 'til dawn."

First Sgt. Wildman agreed with the new plan as did the rest.

"Now," said the captain, "I think there is something else we need to turn our attention to."

"What's that, Captain?" asked Sgt. Bratton.

"Well, men, you well know that we now have these new Henry repeating rifles and Colt revolvers, but we have had very little chance to practice shooting either weapon and, of course, have not had to use the Henry's in combat. I want all of us to learn our new weapons intimately, inside and out and front to rear. I want us all to learn them well enough to load, shoot or take them apart and put them back together in pitch dark. In short, I want us to be as ready as we can be and try to turn into a band of sharpshooters. I know we can do it and now we have the ammunition and time to do it. I want us to train and practice all day on Saturdays and Sundays and from after work until dark every day. Is this understood?"

From the men came a loud, "Yes, sir" in unison.

The next evening around 6:00 PM, the men met at the rifle range with loaded weapons as ordered.

Capt. Herndon had Lt. Buchanan read a front page article from an Indianapolis newspaper to the assembled men. In general, it gave a glowing report of the new Home Guard Reserve units being formed far and wide. Further, it said that the new program was a grand success and gave full credit to the men from Leavenworth for being a first of their kind.

Capt. Herndon then said, "See, men, the rest of the world is watching us so let's don't make a bad impression. Let's show 'em what a unit like ours can do when armed and equipped properly. Let's give it our best. Train hard and shoot straight!!"

The men were divided into groups of five men each with one in each group being a shooting coach. Rope pulled moving targets and swinging targets were used again and soon the cliffs and hills echoed the reports from the firing much like the sounds of a thunderstorm. Very much like the day the Southern Storm arrived. Though the sounds were much the same, there was no unpleasantness and no loss of life this time. Soon the marksmanship of the group was greatly improved. It is easier to do better with good equipment.

Young Lemuel Moore was becoming an expert shot with both pistol and rifle. Tad Martin, though not quite an expert yet, was no slouch when it came to shooting straight. In general, they were becoming a credible group of marksmen and Capt. Herndon and Lt. Buchanan were quite proud.

After calling "cease fire," the captain said, "Now, men, we are going to learn the art of working in the dark."

"But, Captain, it is not dark. How can we do this thing?" said Pvt. Takaguchi.

"It's easy, Hibachi. The man working in the dark will be blindfolded. Now, men, pair off in twos. One man takes his neckerchief off, folds it and blindfolds himself. No peeking. The partner will coach and help train the one working in the dark. The idea is to learn to load and/or disassemble or assemble your rifle or revolver by touch and feel. You will soon learn your weapons very well by doing this." Soon the men were training as they had been ordered.

Always quick of wit and glib of tongue, Sgt. Wildman said, "You know, Captain, when we were learning military hand signals, it looked like a scene at the School for the Deaf at Louisville. Now, it looks like we are at the Blind School."

Smiling, the captain said, "I know, Sergeant. It may look that way, but most of our boys are as sharp-eyed as a hawk. Damned if I don't think they're turning in to a pretty well oiled military machine."

"Yep, Captain, I think you're right."

Back at the Jefferson Home, Renfro Miles was now getting around on crutches, but still moving very slowly and with difficulty. Susan had been waiting for this day and the wheels were turning in her pretty head. Susan wasted no time. The next morning, she fixed a picnic basket and borrowed her mother's horse and buggy. Moses Jefferson helped Renfro up into the buggy and soon the young lovers were gone. This would be their turn to enjoy the pleasant surroundings 'neath the sycamores near Big Blue River. The beauty of the place, combined with the beauty of their love, made for a wonderful day. Getting Renfro back up in the buggy was not easy, but finally they headed back to town.

When they arrived back at Moses' and Tillie's, they saw that Mother Melissa and Virginia were starting to pack for their trip back home to Meadowland. They planned to leave on the next down bound boat tomorrow.

That evening when Hiram came over to see Virginia, he was crushed to learn that his lover would be leaving tomorrow. When they were alone, Hiram said, "Virginia, I do love you so much. I can't do without you, darling. Please wait for me. I will come for you. Promise me you will wait??"

"Yes, Hiram, I am yours and I will wait for you, honey. But Lord, I hope we don't have to wait too long!" They were soon in each other's arms and their kiss was very long and very sweet. Their embrace was interrupted by the sounds of Melissa Mile's approaching footsteps.

Mother Miles was hoping that she was taking Virginia home before it was too late. Little did she know that it was already much too late. Hiram and Virginia were destined to be as one and for all their days. Love knows no bounds.

The next morning, the packet boat, "Lady Pike," was down bound and Moses, Tillie, Renfro, Alice and Susan, along with Cpl. Hiram Kinnaman saw Melissa Miles and Virginia leave after an emotional, tearful farewell.

At the time Hiram did not realize it, but the same boat that had carried away his sweetheart had also brought official U.S. Army mail for him and also for Cpl. Milo Weathers. They had both received orders. The army was well aware that Leavenworth no longer had a real certified medical doctor. Hiram and Milo were ordered to go to Alton, Indiana, and be examined by Dr. Hawn to see if they were physically fit enough to be put back on some sort of active army service. The orders further stated that if the doctor passed them for return to service, the doctor was to sign in the appropriate place and they would then have three days to report at Union Army Camp Noble, New Albany, Indiana, and await further orders.

The next morning, Capt. Mattingly and the "Concordia Queen" happened to be down bound and were at the dock. Capt. Herndon and Capt. Mattingly were having a lively conversation as usual. Capt. Eli was running behind schedule this trip and the usual happy hour would have to wait 'til another time. Capt. Herndon suspected that wife Liz being on board was digging into some of Capt. Mattingly's happy hours and he was right.

Renfro Miles got word that the "Concordia Queen" was in port and asked Susan to take him down to the boat.

Susan asked, "Renfro, you're not wanting to leave are you?"

"No, darling, I'll never leave without you. I just want to see my old First Sergeant, Zeke Calhoun. You know, he now is working on the steamboat called the 'Concordia Queen'."

"Yes, Renfro, now I remember. I suppose that he is nearly recovered from his wound by now."

"I hope so. Zeke is a hard man to keep down in any case."

Zeke saw his former commanding officer, Major Miles, at the dock and made his way down the gangway to visit with him. They were close friends and had served together in many sticky situations. Out of force of habit, Zeke snapped to attention and saluted smartly.

For an instant, Renfro forgot himself and returned the salute from his former First Sergeant. In a low breath, Renfro said, "Zeke, maybe we had better dispense with the salutes. That was in another life, my friend."

"Yes, Major, I know. That was a slip. How is your leg healing, Renfro?"

"Not very good, Zeke. I'll probably always be a cripple to some degree, but at least I'm still kicking, even if only one leg can kick. Say, how is that wounded shoulder doing?"

"Oh, it's about healed up. It's okay as long as the first mate don't make me work too hard. Just kidding, Renfro. You know, when I came aboard, a black man, Josh Freedman, was the engineer. Well, old Capt. Mattingly promoted Josh up to being first mate then he made me the boat's engineer."

"Zeke, you actually mean a black man is your boss? Isn't that hard to take?"

"No, Renfro, Josh Freedman is a real good man. We get along great. I'd have never dreamed it, but we work together real good. Hey, Josh, come on down here. I want you to meet a friend of mine!"

Soon the three of them were talking and getting acquainted. Renfro Miles was beginning, just beginning, to see the way things were bound to be in the future. A man would be judged not by what he looked like, but by what he was. In his heart, he knew it was right. The boat was about to leave and they said their goodbyes.

Cpl. Kinnaman and Cpl. Miles had come aboard to ride the "Concordia Queen" down to Alton to see Dr. Hawn.

Josh Freedman was at the helm. He pulled on the whistle chain and the distinctive three chime whistle signaled their departure. Capt. Mattingly was still talking to Elam Herndon over the rail as the "Queen" churned up a frothy foam as it backed out into the main channel and headed downriver. Josh was starting to notice that more and more he was at the helm while old Capt. Eli Mattingly spent more and more time socializing with passengers and customers. Only recently, Josh had said, "Capt. Eli, sometimes I think you just came along for the ride!"

"You may well be right, Josh. You learn fast. There may come a day when I make you captain of this old lady."

"Lord have mercy, Capt. Eli. Me be the captain?"

"Yep, Josh, it just could happen." Then Capt. Mattingly headed for the boat's lounge room, remembering some extra good

Meadowland bourbon that had been brought aboard at Owensboro. After all, nothing says that the captain can't have a taste while off duty. On parting, he hollered back, "Josh, keep a close watch out for snags!"

"Yes, sir, Capt. Eli!"

It was only a short ride down to Alton, Indiana. Cpl. Kinnaman and Cpl. Weathers made their way to Dr. Hawn's office. No more than two hours later, they had both been examined by the doctor. He had passed Cpl. Weathers as fit for full duty. He had passed Cpl. Kinnaman for only light duty as his arm was not fully healed, but nevertheless recommended that he return to duty. It was as they had known way down deep. They were going back to being fulltime soldiers.

They had to wait 'til about 10:00 PM and the big boat, "Rees Lee," came in up bound. The two young corporals made it back to Leavenworth in time to have a nightcap or two at the Dexter Saloon before closing time. In fact, Capt. Herndon and Lt. Buchanan were still there and they told of their soon coming return to the Army.

Capt. Herndon was disappointed, but he had known that this day was coming. He said, "Well, Sam, now we only are an army of nineteen. We are losing two of our best men."

"Well, Captain, our loss is definitely the army's gain."

"There ain't no doubt about that. Boys, this damn war ain't gonna last forever. When you come back, we want you both to rejoin us. Would you consider it?"

Both corporals readily agreed that they wanted to stay as members when they came back.

"Very good," said the captain, "Now, since we are going to have to pick a couple of men to be corporals now that you two are leaving, who would you recommend for the promotions?"

Cpl. Kinnaman said, "Captain, I think that in view of the way that Pvt. James Corbin stood his ground like a full grown man out at the cliffs, I think he should be made a corporal. After all, he will be fifteen years old any day now."

The captain and lieutenant both agreed. It would now be Cpl. James Corbin.

Cpl. Weathers said, "I think that Pvt. Lemuel Moore should be a corporal as well. He came from having never shot a gun to being among our best marksmen. It would be good for him and the outfit both."

It was agreed. It would now be Cpl. Lemuel Moore.

Capt. Herndon said, "How long are you boys gonna wait before you head up to Camp Noble?"

Hiram said, "Me and Milo are going on the next up bound boat after tonight. If one comes tomorrow, we are going. We don't think putting it off is gonna help none. The sooner we get this war over, the better."

Milo agreed, "That's how we both feel about it."

"Well, boys, Charlie is wanting to close, but me and Sam are setting up one more farewell toast on us. Good luck, boys. Come home in one piece. Salute!"

As luck would have it, at 10:00 AM the next day, the packet boat "Tarascon" was up bound and Cpl. Kinnaman and Cpl. Weathers were ready to go aboard. Both had their bags and Cpl. Kinnaman was also carrying his Sharps carbine. Capt. Herndon had promised to keep their Henry rifles safe 'til they came back. They were both carrying their Colt revolvers. As the "Tarascon" pulled away, the remaining nineteen men of the Leavenworth Home Guard Reserve, in full uniform, neckerchiefs and all, stood at attention and presented arms.

Hiram and Milo stood at the rail and returned the salute. They were both very proud to have served with this little group of soldiers. They only hoped that the next unit they would have to serve with would have men of this caliber, probably not.

Cpl. Kinnaman and Cpl. Weathers got off the "Tarascon" at

New Albany, Indiana, and walked up to Union Army Camp Noble. They underwent further medical examinations. Cpl. Weathers was declared fit for full military service. Cpl. Kinnaman was declared to be not fit for combat duty yet, due to the limited movement of his left arm. However, he was cleared for lighter duty until fully healed.

Two days later, Hiram and Milo, along with about two hundred other soldiers, were placed on a train at Louisville, Kentucky. They were headed for Nashville, Tennessee. At Nashville, they were separated. Cpl. Weathers was attached to an infantry regiment that was headed farther south to where the action was. Cpl. Kinnaman was ordered to duty at a Union Army Supply Depot at Nashville. He was given a desk job so his only danger was that of dying of boredom. This was a distinct possibility.

When Hiram noticed the large map on the wall which showed all roads, railroads, rivers and supply routes, his mind suddenly came back to life. Cpl. Kinnaman studied the map as if he were a general planning some great military campaign, but such was not the case. He was plotting the route and estimated travel time from his position at Nashville to Bowling Green, Kentucky, and from there, the short distance up to Meadowland Plantation.

There were regular passenger train connections up to Bowling Green. From there, he could rent a saddle horse from the livery stable and then only a ride of a few miles to Meadowland.

The next item of business was to get a three day pass or even a two day pass would do. He could just go, but that would be risky as it was wartime and the army sometimes shot deserters. When he thought of that beautiful dark eyed girl, it even crossed Hiram's mind that she would almost be worth dying for.

In any case, Cpl. Kinnaman did it right. He asked for a three day pass and got it. He then wrote a quick letter to Virginia giving her his mailing address and also wrote many words of endearment. He did not dare to mention his planned trip to Meadowland for fear her family might snarl his plans somehow. He would just surprise Virginia. Only six more days and he would have that pass, six very long days!

Back at Leavenworth, Capt. Herndon and the rest were taking full advantage of every chance to sharpen their shooting skills. The cliffs and hills echoed the reports from their weapons every evening and most all day on weekends. They were all doing some real accurate shooting and, of course, some of the younger boys were getting smug and cocky about their shooting skills.

The next evening before they started firing at the range, Pvt. Mike Baysinger said, "Captain, I want to say a few things if it's okay with you?"

"You have the floor, Mike. Go ahead."

"Okay now, you men are all pretty good shots, but it won't hurt none to get better. Now, we have been shooting at some swinging targets like the pendulum on a clock. Let's change that to a way that will separate the men from the boys. Okay? Now, let's not shoot at the pendulum, but shoot the string that holds the pendulum. Also, here is another shooting skill thing that was done many years before my time but it still works. The old-timers say it was first done with old Flintlock Kentucky rifles. See here. I've rigged a target up like none you have ever seen. See, it is a box holding the sharp edge of a hunting knife toward the shooter, then there is a candle about an inch or two on each side of the knife. Now, here's how it works. The two candles are lit. You shoot at the sharp knife blade trying to split the lead bullet. If done right, the split lead will put out the flame on both candles with one shot. Who wants to try first?"

Sgt. Wildman lit the candles and started the pendulum swinging and moved clear.

There were no volunteers to be the first to try, so Pvt. Baysinger let go of some tobacco juice, wet the front sight of his Henry rifle with a wet thumb, smiled a crafty smile and said, "Okay, boys, here's how it's done."

Mike squeezed off one round from the Henry and cut the string holding the pendulum target. As he levered the next round into the chamber, he paused only slightly, spat a dab more tobacco juice and squeezed off another round from the Henry which split the lead on the knife blade and put out the flame on both candles.

Mike laughed as the rest cheered and hollered then said, "Now, boys, you know it can be done. Now do it!"

As was said in ancient times, "Let the games begin!" Shooting practice had started to be a little boring, but now, thanks to old Mike, it became very competitive and exciting. It was not long before candle targets were in use. More and more every day, more of the men were hitting the difficult targets. Capt. Herndon and Lt. Buchanan hit their fair share and were very proud of this group.

Cpl. James Corbin said, "Captain, I say that when the Home Guard gets back from chasing Gen. Morgan's Raiders, we should invite them to a shooting match. How about it, sir?"

Pvt. Dan Lyon chuckled, "I second that motion, Elam. Let's have a match with them!"

"Okay, boys, but let's let 'em rest a little when they get back so 'tired' won't be their alibi."

That very evening, both George Armstrong and Hibachi Takaguchi had started bullet cutting the pendulum strings. Neither had put out both candles yet, but they were getting close. Practice does make perfect and Hibachi was quick to point out that a good gun helps. He was no longer shooting with an heirloom weapon. All agreed that the Henry rifles were very good weapons indeed.

The next innovative shooting practice suggestion came from old Pvt. Buford Beasley. He said, "Now, boys, we all have good Colt revolvers and some of you are getting pretty good with them. Now, here's an old sharp shooting trick that makes for good practice."

Buford had an old pack of playing cards in his shirt pocket. He had cut some thin slots in a piece of wood so that a playing card could be set in the slot showing the face of the card as a target. He also had cut slots in a second piece of wood so that playing cards would only present their thin edge as a target. He asked Sgt. Wildman to set them both up at 50 feet from the firing line. He then asked, "Who wants to get laughed at first?" No one volunteered.

Buford calmly shot six times at the faces of six playing cards and hit near the center of the cards each time. Buford's revolver was now empty so Newt Watson quickly handed Buford his loaded Colt. Buford smiled, held his breath, took steady aim and fired six times. He hit the thin edge of four of the playing cards.

"Well, boys, old Father Time is taking his toll. There was a day—oh well!"

The rest of the men were thrilled to see what a great marksman old Buford really was. Now, they had a better understanding of who had done some of the best shooting that morning at the cliffs. These things were all just little showoff games of shooting skill, but they made all the rest try all the more. Of course, they thought, "If old Mike and Buford could shoot that well, as old as they were, then surely we could too!" The competition got keen!

At breakfast at the Bowman home, Susan and Mother Alice were in serious discussion.

"Susan, you know I have been treating lots of people lately for their aches and pain and other ailments. More and more I find that I'm working by myself. Does Renfro really need all of your time? I thought you were supposed to be my nursing assistant!"

"Now, Mother, I'm sorry, but I just can't stay away from Renfro. I want to be with him all day every day. Mother, Renfro and I want to get married, the sooner the better. I think in about a week or so."

"Very well, Susan, if you're absolutely sure about this. You have my permission, for whatever it's worth. Now, what are you and Renfro's immediate plans? Oh, I know he wants to take you home to Meadowland, but he is not in shape to travel that far yet. One slip or one fall on his bad leg and he might never walk again, even on crutches. You know, honey, all those trips out to the sycamores at Big Blue River are not good for him from the standpoint of healing. If he should fall getting out of the buggy, it would be bad!"

"Mother, how did you know about those trips to Big Blue River?"

"Now, girl, you go right past Buford's place and also Jim Running Deer's place to get there. How would you guess I know?"

"Well, I guess there's no secrets in Leavenworth, is there?"

"No, Susan, if there are any secrets, they are few and far between."

"Okay, Mother, Renfro and I want to get married nine days from now, the Saturday after next. Now, when we are married, could Renfro move in here with us 'til he's well enough to travel?"

"Of course, honey, that would be all legal and proper. I will welcome my new son-in-law to our home. Just remember, you two should wait a while longer before trying to go back to his home."

"Thanks for your understanding, Mother. I can't wait to tell Renfro!"

The next day, a very tired and dusty Leavenworth Home Guard was back home. Most were saddle sore, but none were wounded. Major Woodbury's men along with hundreds of others had pursued Gen. John Hunt Morgan's raiders all the way to Harrison, Ohio, just west of Cincinnati. They had engaged in a few firefights and skirmishes with some of Morgan's rearguard troops, but had suffered no ill effects from the actions other than thirst, lack of sleep and fatigue. The eighty man Leavenworth Home

Guard had been gone for a total of eleven days this time and were very glad to be home.

Capt. Elam Herndon and his men were very glad to see Woodbury's men back. Now, the L.H.G.R. could once again turn their attention to building their new meeting place.

Herndon's men pitched in to help the Home Guard troops feed and water their mounts and unload tack and gear. However, some things can't wait and before the horses had finished drinking, Capt. Herndon had challenged the Home Guard to a shooting match two days hence.

A smiling Major Woodbury said, "Okay, Capt. Herndon, what are the contest rules going to be? You know, there are eighty of us. How many men do you have?"

"Well, Major, we are now down to nineteen including myself. While you were gone Cpl. Kinnaman and Cpl. Weathers had to go back to active army duty. I propose that you pick nineteen of your best marksmen out of your eighty men and they will shoot against the nineteen of us. The rest can be onlookers and pull targets and the like. Remember, just to make it fair, we are giving you two days to rest up. Okay?"

"Very well, Capt. Herndon, agreed. By the way, your group looks very sharp in their new uniforms. Gen. Love and Gov. Morton came through in good time it looks like."

"Thanks, Major. Oh, by the way, there is going to be a wedding Saturday after next."

"Who is the couple?"

"Well, our Susan Bowman will be marrying the ex-leader of the Southern Storm, Confederate Major Renfro Miles. I should say 'paroled leader' I suppose."

"Well, Captain, all I can say about that is that this Major Miles may have suffered a defeat on the battlefield, but marrying Susan Bowman makes him a winner, no doubt about it. She is one pretty girl."

"I agree. We will miss Susan when she leaves. And by the way, my Cpl. Kinnaman is hot in pursuit of Renfro Mile's sister, Virginia. She is one fine looking lady. If Hiram gets her, I'll also declare him a winner. He will need lady luck on his side though. No telling where the army will send him. I'll have to say though, so far in this war, Hiram has been lucky, everything considered."

Two days later it was time for the games to begin. Major Woodbury had picked eighteen of his best marksmen besides himself. He was widely known as a good shot. He was smugly confident that this would not be much of a contest. After all, the men of Herndon's Hope had a lot against them.

Buford, Moses and Tillie had made lots of cornbread and three huge pots of stew which were simmering, hung by tripods over the fires. The shooting match would take some time. Many of the townspeople gathered to observe and many had brought their own chairs and benches.

As there was now a wide range of rifles and revolvers that could be used, Capt. Herndon graciously offered to let anyone shoot with whatever weapon they preferred.

Major Woodbury's men chose to shoot with their regular weapons, Sharps breech load carbines and Colt revolvers, since they were more familiar with these.

Herndon's men chose to shoot with their lever action Henry rifles and their Colt revolvers. Since there were to be nineteen men on each side in the shooting match, it was decided that they would shoot in four teams of four men each and one team of three men, the three firing last.

There would be rifle targets, both moving and still, at fifty yards, one hundred yards and one hundred and fifty yards. Each man would shoot ten rounds each at each target beginning with closest to the farthest. For revolvers, the shooting distances would be ten yards, twenty-five yards and fifty yards.

With revolvers, each man would shoot six rounds at each target, closest to farthest. A coin toss decided which side would shoot first. The regular Home Guard won the toss and their first team of four commenced firing. They did some very good shooting indeed. The Home Guard Team of three consisted of Major Horatio Woodbury, Capt. G. W. Lyon (Pvt. Dan Lyon's son) and their First Sgt. J.C. Smith. They hit a combined total of eighty percent of the total possible targets, team wide. Major Lyon was smiling broadly. At eighty percent hits, he was very sure his team had this thing won.

Then it was time for the L.H.G.R. to shoot. Capt. Herndon, Lt. Sam Buchanan and First Sgt. Wildman shot last. When the shooting score was tallied, Herndon's men had hit an amazing ninety-two percent of their targets. Capt. Herndon was ever so proud of his men. Not very long ago, they had been nothing more than a roughhewn group of old men, boys and people with handicaps of one kind or another. Some had never even shot a gun before joining the Leavenworth Home Guard Reserve. Now, they were a formidable group of much better than average marksmen. Everyone else was proud of these men as well.

Major Woodbury was a gracious loser and smilingly congratulated Capt. Herndon and men. He was not a sore loser for he felt that he had won. You see, he had picked a winner in picking Capt. Herndon to lead and, in turn, Capt. Herndon had assembled a group of winners. As the major saw it, it was a win/win situation.

After the large gathering had scarfed down three huge pots of stew and ample helpings of cornbread, a close order drill competition was next. Tad Martin excused himself from this event due to his bad foot. He did take notes for the newspaper article he was working on.

The Home Guard team easily won the close order drill competition, as expected.

Now, it was time for some fun, skill, showoff shooting. First

Sgt. Wildman suggested, "Since we have a father and son here, I think they ought to have a shooting match. Pvt. Dan Lyon, 81, was the father of Home Guard Capt. G. W. Lyon, 49. It was agreed to have a match with Henry rifles. Son Gene owned a Henry and was familiar with one. Dan said, "Son, er, Captain, why don't we do this? Let's each load fifteen rounds in a Henry and the first shooter 'calls his targets' and shoots fifteen times. Then, the second shooter has to fire at the same targets. Who has the most hits wins. Son, you go first!"

Capt. Lyon kept calling his targets and shooting. His total was eleven hits out of fifteen shots.

Pvt. Lyon shot next and he had fourteen hits out of fifteen. There were cheers, whoops and hollers from all around!

Next came the pendulum targets for rifles at fifty yards. Capt. Herndon challenged Major Woodbury to a match. They each got three hits out of three shots. The revolvers were used next at the same distance. Major Woodbury hit three out of three. Capt. Herndon hit two out of three.

Next came the hunting knife/two candle targets. Mike Baysinger had made up three targets. Mike explained the contest in case anyone didn't know the object. He said, "Are there any takers? Who wants to try first?" No one answered, so Mike said, "Okay, I'll go first."

One split bullet puts out two candles. As usual, he unloaded some tobacco juice, levered a round into the chamber, sucked in his breath, and squeezed the trigger. The first two candles went. He shot twice more and he had put out six candle flames with three shots. Again, more whoops and cheers. Now, everyone wanted to try. There were several very accurate shooters in the crowd and soon, now and then, one round would hit the mark.

Buford brought out his slotted pieces of wood and his deck of playing cards and soon started things rolling in that department. Buford was having an off day today and with six shots from his revolver, he hit six cards facing him. Newt handed him his Colt and this time, Buford only managed to hit three of the six playing cards edgewise.

It did make a fun-filled day and the shooting went on 'til dusk. The shooting match was considered a great success and was to be only the first of many such gatherings. It was agreed that these two groups would have a shooting day every month, weather permitting. It became a regular event for many years and several became excellent marksmen because of regular practice. They all agreed that it was best to be prepared and as ready as they could be.

Back at the Army Supply Depot, Nashville, Cpl. Hiram was ready to head out, three day pass in hand. He was clean-shaven, hair slicked down, boots shined and, for a change, wearing a uniform that had been pressed. He made it to the train station, bought a round trip ticket to Bowling Green, Kentucky, and soon was headed north.

At Bowling Green, he found a livery stable only about one block from the train station. He rented a saddle mare and tied his satchel onto the back of the saddle. He asked directions to Meadowland Plantation. The livery man obligingly gave Hiram directions. Hiram's head was more filled with thoughts of sweet Virginia than anything else. Due to this, he wrote down the directions just in case. He was off at a trot, headed toward Meadowland. It was about a seven mile ride, but it went quickly. The countryside hereabouts was pretty and appeared fertile and lush. He passed many very prosperous looking farms, but none as prosperous looking as Meadowland Plantation. As he rode up the winding lane bordered by cedars and magnolia trees, he observed many fat cattle and fine looking horses in the pastures. There were tobacco fields as well as some fields in corn. Now, the aroma of a whiskey distillery filled the air. Then he remembered that Virginia had told him about whiskey, cigars and tobacco products being the main source of income for her family's place.

Now the main mansion was in full view, tall porch columns and all. Everything looked so perfect. Yes, and they had a perfect looking daughter and that was why he was here!

Old James had seen Hiram riding up the long lane and was standing at the hitching rack. "Good morning, sir, how may I be of help to you?"

"I have come to visit Miss Virginia Miles. I'm surprising her. She doesn't know I'm coming!"

Old James smiled and thought to himself, "Yes, sir, and I'll bet old Col. Miles will be damn surprised for shore to see a Yankee soldier calling on his daughter. Oh well, times were a changing."

"What is your name, Corporal, and I'll tell Miss Virginia that you are here. Never mind your horse, sir. I'll tend to it in a short while."

"Thank you, uh, sir."

"No, I'm not 'sir.' My name is James. Blacks are not called 'sir' hereabouts. I'll be right back. You just wait here at the front door."

Soon the massive front door opened and Virginia was face to face with the man of her life.

Hiram could not control himself and held her close and they kissed passionately, again and again.

Old James tried to act like he wasn't seeing this and was leading Hiram's horse toward the watering trough and the stable. Again James thought to himself, "I'll bet this will make old Massa Miles froth at the mouth!"

When Virginia and Hiram regained control, as she knew they had better, she asked, "Darling, where did you come from? It's so very, very good to see you!"

"Well, pretty lady, the army called me back to duty and sent me to their Supply Depot at Nashville. The doctors say I'm not well enough for combat duty yet, so they put me in a desk job for now. In front of that desk there is a huge map that starts me to thinking of you again every time I see the short distance from Nashville to Bowling Green. Anyway, I'm here and very glad of it too."

"Have you seen Renfro? How is my brother?"

"I understand that he is better and that he and Susan Bowman will marry very soon. I guess I've only been gone from Leavenworth about ten days or so."

"Come, Hiram, I'll take you in to greet Mother. I think she will be okay. However, it's my Daddy that will probably be a problem. He is Confederate to the core and I do mean to the core. Hiram, your Union Army uniform is likely to set him off. Oh well, Daddy will have to learn to adjust, I think."

Melissa Miles treated Hiram politely, but was not overly warm. "It's good to see you, Hiram. I'll not ask the purpose of your visit.

How long will you be staying at Meadowland?"

"Well, ma'am, I only have a three day pass. I am stationed at Nashville so I must catch the evening train at Bowling Green on Sunday to go back."

"Very well, you'll be staying in one of our guest rooms. Mandy Mae, please show our guest to his room so he can settle in."

Virginia said, "Hiram, put your things in your room and meet me out front. I'll give you a guided tour of Meadowland."

"Yes, Miss Virginia, I'll be right back."

While Hiram was putting his things away, Virginia had old James go to the stable, harness up a horse, hitch it to a one seat buggy and bring it around.

When Hiram came out he was surprised to see Virginia by the buggy. She said, "Come on soldier. I'll show you around!"

As Hiram and Virginia drove away, Col. Rafe Miles saw the young lovers leaving. Hiram's uniform had caught Rafe's eye and he gave it full attention. Col. Miles was livid. He damn near had a seizure right then and there. A damn Yankee courting his beautiful daughter. The shame of it all. And to think, a Yankee had grievously wounded his son!!

Rafe quickly went into the house and found Melissa in the drawing room. He shouted, "Woman, what do you know about this?"

"About what, Rafe? You don't need to shout. I'm not deaf! What time did you start drinking today anyhow?"

"Melissa, don't answer my question with a question. What the hell is going on? I just seen a damn Yankee soldier in a buggy with Virginia and the way they were sitting was way too close in my judgment! What is going on?"

"Now simmer down, Rafe. His name is Hiram Kinnaman. He is a good friend of Virginia's. They met while we were up at Leavenworth."

"I'll wager that he is a 'good friend.' Melissa, how could you let this happen? You know how I feel about Yanks."

"Well, husband, times are changing and I think we will just have to change with the times. Anyway, Hiram showed up unexpectedly. He will only be here tonight and tomorrow night. He has to catch a train back to Nashville on Sunday evening. I took the liberty of giving him one of the guest bedrooms."

"You done what? You welcomed him into our home? Melissa, what were you thinking?"

"Rafe, I was thinking that you would act like a gracious host and be a gentleman about this. After all, our Renfro is living with Moses and Tillie Jefferson up in Indiana. Just today, I got a letter from Renfro saying he and Susan would be getting married very soon. Now, as I said, times are changing so try to change with the times!"

"Melissa, you go ahead and change with the times. But for me, I never will!!"

"Okay, Rafe, but if you keep on ranting and raving like you've been sampling too much Meadowland Bourbon, I'll see if Mr. Carter can find a place for you to sleep out in the distillery. That seems to be where you spend most of your time these days!"

Col. Rafe Miles saw that he best hold his tongue or he would be sleeping in another bed. In disgust, he shuffled out to the game room to find another bottle of bourbon and sulk. Damn the changing world anyhow!

Virginia and Hiram had a most enjoyable tour of Meadowland Plantation and were gone nearly three hours. Two hours of this most pleasant time had been spent by the babbling brook out back of the grassy meadow full of wildflowers. Horses can't talk and that is just as well.

Old James was waiting when they came back. As he started to take the horse and buggy toward the carriage house, he said, "Miss Virginia, your momma said for y'all to get ready for a social hour on the south veranda before dinner. You have about one hour 'til then."

"Thank you, James."

"Hiram honey, we need to go freshen up some. I do want you to make a good impression on Daddy. I just hope he's sober enough to act decent and carry on a conversation. It seems that the worse the war news is for the South, the more he drinks."

Hiram said, "Yes, darling, I'm really looking forward to meeting your daddy." Then to himself, under his breath, he mumbled, "Like the first time I got shot at in a battle!"

During the social hour on the south veranda, Col. Miles surprised everyone. He stayed off of the subject of the current war and contained the conversation mostly to small talk. He tried to be as polite as it was possible for him to be toward a Yank. He was mildly surprised to see that Hiram held his whiskey fairly well.

After the social hour, Mandy Mae announced that it was time to dine. Mandy and the kitchen staff had prepared an excellent meal and everyone soon turned their attention to the food. Well, not everyone, for Hiram could not keep his eyes off of Virginia and she was little better acting like he was just another houseguest. Secretly, Virginia had plans for later and Hiram was part of the plans.

As was the custom after the meal, the men retired to the drawing room for after dinner drinks and cigars. Mr. Carter, the head distiller, was there as well as a couple of other men who were tobacco buyers from Owensboro. Melissa played piano as Virginia accompanied her on violin. As usual, George Carter joined in with his guitar.

The evening went quickly. It was enjoyable. Good music, good Meadowland Bourbon and excellent plantation made cigars. Col. Miles over imbibed as was his custom here of late. About 9:30 PM, he excused himself and went up the winding staircase to the master bedroom. Melissa Miles soon followed. George Carter put his guitar away and went to his little house back by the distillery. Everyone else soon made their way to their respective rooms. It seemed the evening was over.

As Virginia well knew, her daddy would be sleeping like a log after such a long day of taste testing and quality control. She also knew that Mother Melissa would not be able to hear much because of Rafe Mile's snoring. About 10:30 PM, Virginia quietly made her way to the south veranda by the bubbling spring fed fountain. There, next to the sweet smelling roses, she waited for Hiram.

Hiram, as noiselessly as possible, made his way to this charmed spot. Soon, he found sweet Virginia Mile's lips and it was magic once more. The soft moonlight cast its gentle beams on her beautiful features and they explored each other as lovers do, ever so tenderly, ever so gently. The fragrance of the roses, the rhythm of the bubbling fountain, combined with the beautiful stars and moonlight. After a time, the bubbling of the water barely muffled the faint moans of ecstasy and squeals of pleasure. The night was perfect for the two lovers. Afterward, in each other's arms, they planned their future together.

The weekend went by in a flash for the two lovers. All too soon, Hiram Kinnaman was riding back toward Bowling Green to catch the evening train to Nashville. He now knew one thing for sure, he would have to take Virginia home to Leavenworth with him when the time was right. He knew that he and Virginia were the right combination. He also knew that he and Col. Rafe Miles were like oil and water.

As Hiram and Virginia saw it, there were "improving relations between the North and South."

TWENTY

New Master At Meadowland

THIS SATURDAY WAS very special. Today, Susan Bowman would become the bride of Renfro Miles. At 2:00 PM, Rev. Jasper Harrison would perform the ceremony. The little Baptist church was small, too small in fact. Most of the townspeople attended and most had to stand outside. Susan Bowman was a very well-liked girl and had many friends. Some people were not so happy that she had chosen to marry a Confederate soldier, but they also felt that if Susan was happy, that was what really mattered.

The men of the Leavenworth Home Guard Reserve attended in full uniform. They did this not in respect for Renfro Miles, but rather for Susan as they considered her one of their own.

Jacob Silverstein, soldier/jeweler/gunsmith had made a beautiful pair of gold wedding bands for Susan and Renfro as a wedding gift.

Newt Watson had healed enough to resume playing the guitar and sang an old country wedding song "A Sweet Bunch of Daisies" as the bride and groom walked down the aisle of the church.

Mother Alice Bowman gave the bride away. Tillie Jefferson was Susan's matron of honor and Moses Jefferson was Renfro's best man.

Preacher Harrison performed the ceremony as Renfro Miles stood on crutches with Moses steadying him. The couple lovingly slipped the beautiful wedding rings on each other's finger.

They were ever so grateful to Jacob for the rings. The words were said and the groom kissed the bride.

A wedding reception was held at the Ourerbacker Hotel. They received many nice gifts, but one of the nicest gifts was from the officers and men of the L.H.G.R. All of them had chipped in and bought the largest Ohio River mussel pearl Hibachi Takaguchi had found thus far. It was a treasure, but Hibachi had almost given it away for the occasion. Again, Jacob Silverstein had made a fine gold chain necklace with a mounting for the huge pearl. The note in the gift package said, "To Susan Bowman on her wedding day from her fellow members of the Leavenworth Home Guard Reserve. May this Ohio River pearl always serve to remind you of your home along the beautiful Ohio."

Since Renfro was in no condition to travel just yet, there would be no honeymoon trip for the newlyweds, not even to the sycamores at Big Blue River. Alice had made it plain to Renfro, one fall and he might not ever walk. He took the advice seriously and decided to listen to the nurse/doctor who was now his mother-in-law.

Alice then said, "Children, I'll be moving in with the Jeffersons for a week or so. Now that Renfro's bed is empty, I'll use it. You two just use my home as if it were yours. Welcome to the family, Renfro. If you two need me, which I seriously doubt, you know where I will be."

Susan answered sweetly, "Yes, Mother," as she and Renfro left for their temporary home.

Most of the men of the L.H.G.R. who had regular occupations were now back at work. However, in the evenings and on weekends, they helped the others in the construction of their new building. It was more or less a labor of love and was going together quickly.

Of course, they always found time to work in a little target practice. Capt. Herndon kept repeating one of his favorite lines,

"It is not enough just to attain a level of skill. One must always try to maintain that level of skill!" Everyone took their training "as serious as a heart attack" for Capt. Elam Herndon had drummed it deep into their minds to always be as ready as you can be!

Things were getting back to normal, as much as possible, at Leavenworth. In any case, the war was showing no signs of ending very soon. The town was busy and there was lots of Ohio River traffic as well.

Back at Meadowland, the Miles family had just received a letter from Renfro. He proudly told his family of his new bride and how things were going. He also told them that, as of now, he was in no condition to come home but planned on coming when he was well enough.

Nothing much was right in Col. Rafe Miles' world these days. He was suffering wide mood swings and lots of the time, he was depressed. Further, he was spending more time at the Meadowland Distillery than anywhere else. The world was changing and he did not like it!

More and more, it seemed that the South was not going to be able to win this war. But, then again, they fought on. When Col. Miles heard of a Union victory somewhere, he became more depressed and tried to blot it all out with a bottle. It became especially hard for Rafe when, from time to time, news would come regarding his close friend Gen. Braxton Bragg. When Gen. Bragg had a victory, Rafe Miles was elated. When Gen. Bragg suffered a defeat, Rafe was also defeated.

Among Col. Miles' other problems was that he was now starting to have financial problems. This was due, in part, from his continued support of the Southern Cause. Early in the war, he had started supplying Gen. Braxton Bragg and most of his higher ranking officers with Meadowland Bourbon Whiskey along with large quantities of Meadowland Cigars. He had even had a special cigar band and box label printed for the cigars going to the South. They were labeled as "The Confederate."

The cigars sold to the North bore the label "Commander." In any case, the Meadowland Whiskey and tobacco products sold to the North were bringing in genuine U.S. currency. The ever increasing orders being shipped to the Confederate Army were being paid for with nearly worthless Confederate money. Col. Rafe Miles' pride would not allow him to really believe that Confederate money was in such dire straights. He kept on accepting the Confederate money and was now beginning to suffer financially because of it.

The direction the war was going and Meadowland's financial problems were not nearly all of Col. Miles' problems. That Yankee corporal had just spent another weekend at Meadowland courting Virginia and Rafe Miles had become so agitated over this that he nearly had a stroke.

As Col. Miles sat in his chair on the veranda during his not so "happy hour," he talked to himself about his problem. "Dammit, my son who was living with blacks up in Indiana is now married to a Yankee girl. My beautiful daughter is being courted by another damn Yankee and an enlisted man at that. Gen. Robert E. Lee lost the battle at Gettysburg and now Gen. Bragg is having problems over at Chattanooga. Damn, why me??" As was becoming more common lately, Col. Rafe Miles either fell asleep or passed out in his chair.

Soon old James came out to the veranda to let old Massa know that dinner would soon be served. Once more, James had to splash cold water on Rafe Miles' face to revive him. Needless to say, Melissa Miles was not happy with the way things were going, but didn't seem to be able to make the needed changes.

The next morning, just after breakfast, old James came in and said, "Col. Miles, Rufus Dowell is at the backdoor and he says he needs to talk to you, sir."

"Very well, James, tell him I'll be right out."

Col. Miles met his overseer on the back porch and said, "What's the problem, Rufus?"

"Well, sir, in case you haven't noticed, we have one hell of a big problem and it's getting worse. Another family of blacks moved out of the quarters yesterday. That means we are short four more field hands this morning. There ain't enough of them left to do the field work!"

"What is their problem? What could they find to complain about? You know we feed and clothe 'em good and they have a good place to live back in the quarters. What more could they ask for?"

"Col. Miles, they say that Meadowland Plantation has got to start paying them wages, and decent wages at that, or they are all gonna start packing up and leaving and we can just do the work, their words, 'our own damn self!'" Personally, Colonel, I think it's damn ungrateful of them. If you would let me do it, I think a few well placed lashes would change some of their stubborn minds!"

Col. Miles was cold sober now and the reality of the situation sunk in quickly. "No, Rufus, those days are over. Damn Yanks set 'em free long ago. I guess it's a wonder that they haven't started leaving before now. Tell them that soon we will have a talk and work this out."

"It had better be soon. They are dead serious!"

"Rufus, how come I haven't heard any complaints from George Carter about his distillery crew being unhappy?"

"Colonel, you know why. You couldn't run that bunch away if you tried."

"Okay, Rufus, for now I'll get some of the house servants and kitchen help to work in the fields part-time 'til we can get things worked out. Also, maybe you could start working and help out a little too?"

Overseer Rufus Dowell became quite upset and said loudly, "No, sir, I flatly refuse to do field work. It ain't fitting for a white man to do slave work!! Overseers don't work. They oversee workers!! Damn, what's this world coming to?" End of conversation. Rufus left to find a bottle and a cigar.

The next day, Col. Miles had the rest of Meadowland's people meet with him to talk things over. It did not go very smoothly, but Col. Miles agreed that Meadowland would start paying its people wages. The wages were very low and he knew this would not pacify them for very long. The world and the times were closing in on Col. Rafe Miles and Meadowland Plantation. He kept on thinking to himself, "If the South could just win this damn war, things would be better right away!" This was his hope and dream and what kept him going.

At Nashville at the Union Army Supply Depot, Cpl. Hiram Kinnaman had just learned some bad news and some good news, all in the same day. Hiram's commanding officer had noticed that Hiram's left arm wasn't getting much better, from the standpoint of having full use of that arm. The major had arranged with the army hospital to have Cpl. Kinnaman reexamined and his physical condition reevaluated.

The bad news was that the army doctors agreed that Hiram's arm would probably never be much better. The good news was that in five days he would be processed out of the army and would be given a small disability pension along with an honorable discharge.

When Hiram heard this news, he wrote a letter to Virginia Miles at Meadowland. In part, the letter said, "Darling, Virginia, the army surprised me. Very soon I will be discharged and then I will come for you as we planned. It is very plain that your father will never accept me so I will take you home with me. As I see it, there is no other way. Virginia, I don't know the exact day yet, but just pack your things and be ready. This time, I will come with a horse and buggy. Do not tell anyone you are leaving with me. They will all find out in due time. See you soon, darling. With Love, Hiram."

As with any good distillery, there are most always different types of products, some of higher quality than others. All Kentucky bourbon whiskey produced at the Meadowland Distillery was of high quality, but the very best of all produced there carried the label, "Meadowland Mist." It was aged two years longer than the rest and was truly a sipping whiskey. Of course, Meadowland Mist was very expensive and was sold only to VIPs or reserved to be served to special guests. Here of late, Col. Rafe Miles was sipping more and more Meadowland Mist. To his thinking, if he was going down the tube, he would go in style.

Things settled down a bit and the plantation's former slaves, now turned low paid employees, kept working and trying to do what needed to be done. This was much, for most everything had to be done the hard way. Old James and wife, Mandy Mae, along with some of the other house help, were now working half days in the fields doing the best they could.

The following weekend, Cpl. Hiram Kinnaman, recently discharged from the army, showed up at Meadowland Plantation once more. This time, he had rented a horse and buggy from the livery stable at Bowling Green.

Col. Miles was curious why Hiram showed up with a horse and buggy rather than a saddle horse, but he said nothing about it. In fact, Rafe Miles would only talk to Hiram as a last resort. They mixed like water and oil. Such was not the case with Hiram and Virginia. The two of them were the perfect blend.

The next morning while Col. Miles was diligently doing quality control and taste testing at his distillery, Virginia Miles had old James take her luggage to the buggy and put it in the luggage boot, out of sight.

Virginia said to her mother, "Momma, please try to understand. I'm going to Leavenworth with Hiram. I love him very much and we will marry very soon. I will write soon and you already have Moses and Tillie's address so you know how to reach me. Don't tell Daddy 'til later. Someday, I'll try to explain to him. For now, just tell Daddy that we will be late."

Melissa and Virginia hugged and said their goodbyes. Shortly, Hiram and Virginia were riding down the beautiful drive from Meadowland Mansion and headed for Bowling Green.

At Bowling Green, Hiram took the horse and buggy back to the livery stable. From there, they went to the railroad station and bought two one way tickets to Louisville. About two hours later, the train was rolling north and the two young lovers were headed for a new life together.

That night, they got a room at the Bluegrass Hotel near the river. The Bluegrass was a very nice place and they got a room with a great river view. However, they spent very little time viewing the river. After breakfast, they were ready for the next leg of their journey.

As luck would have it, the large Lee Line packet boat, the "Reese Lee," was getting ready to start downriver. It was close, but Hiram and Virginia boarded just before the boat pulled away. Hiram bought two one way tickets to Leavenworth, Indiana, and later that day the familiar sight of the cliffs and the beautiful little town of Leavenworth came into view. Hiram then told Virginia about his new job that would be starting in a few days. "I'm a very lucky man to have a guy like Elam Herndon for a friend, Virginia. Mr. Smith, the manager of the Leavenworth River Port, is going to retire very soon. I have been hired to replace him. I'll have to start learning the job next week. The next step is to find a place for us to live, my plantation princess."

"No, Hiram, the next step is not a place to live. The next step is for us to get married first, then a house. Do you understand?"

"Yes, Darling, I understand. I'll see Preacher Harrison tonight."

"Hiram, in the meantime, I'll stay with Moses and Tillie Jefferson. You know how this town is about being proper."

"Yes, Mrs. Kinnaman, very soon we will be proper."

When Hiram and Virginia arrived at Leavenworth, Mr. Smith and Elam Herndon were the first to welcome them home. Mr. Smith was so glad to see his soon to be replacement that he could hardly contain himself. He was quite ready to retire from being the river port manager.

Elam Herndon also greeted the young couple warmly. He was so glad to see Hiram back in town. However, he did realize that when Hiram and Virginia married, it would likely put a crimp on some of their social time up at the Dexter Saloon.

Hiram borrowed Alice Bowman's horse and buggy and soon had his future bride and her luggage at Moses and Tillie's house. Moses and Tillie were so glad to have their "little girl" back. The feeling was mutual for Virginia was also very fond of Moses and Tillie. They were both so much a part of her pleasant childhood years at Meadowland Plantation. In a way, it seemed so long ago and then again, it seemed like only yesterday. Hiram kissed Virginia and said, "Honey, I'm going straight up to Preacher Harrison's house and see when he can say the words. After that, I'll take my things over to Mother's house and I'll see you tonight."

"Okay, Hiram, until tonight. Honey, don't be late."

Hiram was in luck. He caught Preacher Jasper Harrison at home and the Reverend said that he would be delighted to perform the wedding ceremony this coming Saturday.

The next stop was at Jacob Silverstein's Jewelry Shop. Jacob was busy at making jewelry, but was glad to stop to welcome Hiram Kinnaman home. Jacob grinned and winked as he shook Hiram's hand and said, "Soldier, are you legal? You didn't cut and run, did you?"

"Hell no, Jacob, the army didn't give me much of a chance to cut and run. All they let me do was sit at a desk because of my arm. Then, to top that off, they gave me a discharge and sent me home. How about that?"

"Well again, Hiram, the army's loss is Leavenworth's gain. What are your plans?"

"Lots of plans, Jacob. Lots of plans. First off, I brought Virginia Miles back with me and we are going to get married this Saturday. I not only stopped by to see you, Jacob, but I need to buy a pair of wedding rings."

"Of course, friend, I will have two rings made up by Saturday. I'll get your ring size now and you tie a string in a loop for Virginia's ring size and bring it back to me. Okay?"

"Jacob, what was that you were working on as I came in?"

"Well now, it's something new for around here and I think it's going to sell real well. Hibachi Takaguchi and I have formed a little partnership business in making pearl necklaces and jewelry using Ohio River mussel pearls and Hibachi's private sideline mussel beds. Look at this string of pearls, Hiram. Wouldn't they look beautiful on your new bride? Come on. Let's deal."

"Okay, Jacob, you slick talking old rascal. Of course, I want the pearls for Virginia. I'll be starting to work at the river port soon and I have my army pay and mustering out pay. I'll be able to pay you, but you may have to wait for part of it."

"No problem, Hiram. You have a beautiful woman and I believe these beautiful pearls will even enhance her beauty. Soldier, in my opinion, you certainly did not come out a loser in this war."

"Thanks for the kind words, Jacob. I also feel like I won, at least for now. I only hope her dad doesn't hunt me down and shoot me when he figures out that I took her for keeps. Thanks, Jacob, I'll be back tomorrow with her ring size."

Hiram Kinnaman's mother was so glad to have her son back home. He wasted no time in filling his mother in on all the details and said that he would only be living back at home but a few days. He said, "Mother, would you pass the word around that I am getting married and am looking for a small house to rent or buy. I will need to find a place soon."

Mother Kinnaman agreed to help house search for her son and started searching right away.

The next Saturday, it was time for wedding bells to ring again at the little Baptist Church.

For the wedding, at first the plan was to have Virginia's brother, Renfro, be the one who gives the bride away. However, Renfro on second thought said, "You know, after thinking it over, I had better not be the one who gives Virginia to a Yank. If Col. Miles ever found out he would likely disinherit me. Instead, I think it more appropriate for Moses Jefferson to be the one who gives the bride away. This would still "grind the Colonel's grits" when he finds out, but I don't think he was planning on leaving Moses anything in the first place."

Elam Herndon was Hiram's best man; Susan Bowman Miles was Virginia's matron of honor. Newt Watson played and sang "Sweet Bunch of Daisies" as he did for Renfro and Susan's wedding. Preacher Jasper Harrison performed the wedding ceremony with an overflow crowd at the church. Since Hiram Kinnaman was one of their own, all members of the Leavenworth Home Guard Reserve attended in full uniform. It was a colorful wedding indeed.

After a wedding reception at the Ourerbacker Hotel, the newlyweds went to their new home. Hiram had been lucky enough to find a rather nice little cottage up on Cedar Hill. A small down payment and a large mortgage, the usual combination for newlyweds, and one day it would be theirs free and clear. The couple had managed to round up a few pieces of furniture. As Virginia pointed out, Hiram had seemed more concerned about finding a good bed than any of the other furnishings.

The small cottage in Leavenworth was a far cry from living in Meadowland Mansion, but Virginia Miles Kinnaman was as happy as if she were a queen. And as far as Hiram was concerned, she was his queen. Every time he cast his eyes on this pretty girl, he had trouble believing he had been so lucky. All their friends and neighbors let the newlyweds have their privacy for a few days. Then, they would become part of everyday life in Leavenworth.

One week later, the strength of the L.H.G.R. was back up to twenty men for Hiram Kinnaman had rejoined the group. The difference now was that he was also the river port manager. Besides that, he now had a wife to support, a house to pay for, as well as being an L.H.G.R. member. It was a good life though and Hiram was happy to be home.

Back at Meadowland Plantation, things were not going all that well. Col. Rafe Miles had been in a foul mood ever since Virginia had run away with Hiram three weeks ago. To add to that, he could see that his former slaves, now low paid employees, would not continue working under these conditions for very much longer. Rufus Dowell gave Rafe daily reports on the way things were going in the fields and the cigar factory and it was not good news.

Col. Rafe Miles was further depressed by current war news. Things were not going all that well for the South. He was spending more and more time on the veranda in his favorite chair engaged in sipping Meadowland Mist. At times, he gulped it rather than sipped it. He felt betrayed by Virginia for leaving. He did not feel kindly towards Renfro for marrying a Yankee girl. He felt wronged by the Union for setting the slaves free and grew more sullen and withdrawn by the day. He was living in the past and spent much time mumbling to himself about the "good old days" and how things used to be before the damn Yankees invaded. At times, he would softly whistle "Dixie" to himself between frequent drinks of Meadowland Mist and puffing on a primo Confederate label cigar.

Here lately, both old James and Mandy Mae came out to revive the colonel to come to dinner. As usual, they brought cold water and a towel to revive him from his usual state of semi-consciousness. Most of the time, it took both of them to help the colonel to the house.

This day was different. From several feet away, they could tell that something was terribly wrong! Col. Rafe Miles was no longer master of Meadowland. He was slumped in his chair in an awkward position. His last and final glass of Meadowland Mist Kentucky Bourbon had spilled down his shirtfront and a half smoked Confederate label cigar had fallen from his left hand and was still lying on the veranda giving off its fragrant smoke. Col. Rafe Miles was now out of the picture for good, for he was dead. Old James went to the dining room and broke the bad news to Melissa Miles.

It had always been Col. Rafe Miles' contention that good Kentucky bourbon whiskey never hurt anyone. He firmly believed this to be true, as did many others. However, at times, the colonel would tend to overdo and overdo he did on a regular basis.

Some observers maintained that it was not the quality of the Kentucky bourbon that ended Rafe Miles' days as master of Meadowland, but rather it was the quantity of Kentucky bourbon that led to the untimely demise of Col. Rafe Miles.

It was a sad time at Meadowland. Mrs. Melissa Miles quickly sent a letter to Renfro and one to Virginia relating their father's death. The letter said, in part, "Renfro, I know that by the time this letter reaches you, we will already have had your father's funeral and he will be laid to rest here at Meadowland in the family graveyard. Son, I know you are really not able to travel yet, but you are urgently needed here. Please come home soon as possible. You will have to take over here. I see no other way that we and Meadowland can survive. If Virginia can come, she will be most welcome too, but if she can't come right away, I'll understand. Your Loving Mother, Melissa Miles."

It took five days for the letters to reach Leavenworth and, of course, the news was a shock for Renfro and Virginia. Renfro and wife Susan quickly packed and made plans to go to Meadowland. Virginia would go along as well, but would only stay a few days to comfort her mother. Hiram could not leave because of his job and would stay in Leavenworth.

The next morning Renfro, Susan and Virginia got aboard the packet boat the "Tarascon" headed upriver to Louisville. They spent the night in Louisville and caught the morning train to Bowling Green. At Bowling Green, they hired a livery taxi to take them out to Meadowland.

Susan Bowman Miles had only heard descriptions of the lush beauty of Meadowland Plantation told to her by Renfro. When the carriage started up the long winding lane to the main house, she saw for herself and was quite impressed. She could not yet imagine living here, but that was soon to be the case. She was the wife of the new master of Meadowland, Major Renfro Miles. It would take some getting used to.

At the same time, Susan was being awestruck at the beauty of Meadowland, Virginia was already starting to miss her loving husband and their cute little cottage on the hill at Leavenworth. She loved Hiram so much that she would live in a tent with him if need be.

The livery man unloaded the luggage at the front of the main house. Renfro thanked the driver, paid him and he was gone.

Old James was so glad to see everyone. James had his son Lonnie standing by to help with the luggage and soon they were in the parlor with the recently widowed Melissa Miles.

Melissa hugged her new daughter-in-law and warmly welcomed her into the Miles family. After a short talk, they all walked very slowly to the family graveyard to pay their respects at the grave of Col. Rafe Miles. Renfro was worn out walking that far on crutches so James sent Lonnie to the stable to bring back a buggy to take Renfro back to the house.

Mandy Mae had fixed a delicious dinner as usual and it was enjoyed by all. After dinner, Melissa Miles said, "Now, all of you please listen. I know it's not proper to talk of business matters so soon after Rafe Miles has passed away, but we simply must. I didn't realize how bad things were 'til a few days ago. Meadowland Plantation and its businesses are in trouble in several ways and we all must talk. First of all, there will have to be many changes made if we are to survive. The first two changes I will make here and now are, number one, from now on the women of this family will be expected to know the details of what is going on. Not like me being kept in the dark about financial matters 'til almost too late, maybe too late. Is that clearly understood?"

Renfro, Virginia and Susan answered, "Yes, we understand."

Melissa continued, "The second change I am making here and now is very necessary. I am a woman and getting older. I am not capable of running this place efficiently and I know it. So, as of now, I will take a backseat, so to speak, and Renfro Miles will be the new master of Meadowland. Renfro, you will have my blessing and the full authority to make needed changes and manage as you wish. We are in trouble and we are looking to you to see us through it. Is this agreeable with you?"

"Yes, Mother, you already know that I'm somewhat disabled, but I'll do my best."

Melissa then proceeded to fill Renfro in on Meadowland's mounting problems.

Renfro was shocked to hear of some of the problems. As far as he had ever known, things had always been rosy for Meadowland. Renfro then said, "James, please pass the word to everyone, all of our people, white and black, that there will be an important meeting on the south lawn at 8:00 tomorrow morning. This means men and women as well."

"Yes, sir, Mr. Renfro, I'll pass the word."

"Thank you, James."

When everyone assembled on the south lawn, it was a sizable crowd of people. Besides the Miles family, Rufus Dowell (the overseer), George Carter (the Distillery manager), the main house and kitchen staff along with those that worked the farming operations as well as those that made cigars and other tobacco products. Meadowland Plantation was quite an operation.

Chairs and benches had been brought out for some of the older people, both white and black. Renfro sat in a chair with his crutches close by. Renfro began, "Folks, this meeting is very important! I'd like to talk first then everyone will have their turn to speak. It does not matter if you are a man or a woman, black or white, old or young. Before we are through here, you will have your chance to speak your mind. I promise!

Now, I know most of you people. Some of you have been here since before I was born. In a way, we are a family here at Meadowland in that we all count on this place to sustain us and we all live here. This is the only home most of you have ever known and I am hoping that Meadowland Plantation will continue to be your home.

I want you all to know that I am the one who will be in charge now since Col. Rafe Miles passed on and I will be the one who makes the decisions that affect the most of us."

Old James answered for the crowd, "Yes, Massa Miles, we all understand that you will be the new massa."

"Well, folks, here is the first change I am making here and now. I do not want anyone to call me 'Massa or Master Miles.' My name is Renfro and that will do just fine. If anyone chooses to call me Mr. Miles, that will be okay. I understand, but no more calling me master. Those days are over and in the past. Also, I know most of you by your name and those that I don't know, I soon will know.

The second change is this. You people are no longer slaves. Those days are over as well. You are all free to come and go as you please. No one owns you! What I want to do is to make you all fairly paid employees of Meadowland Plantation and have you all contented enough to want to stay here and be a part of things. We all need each other to survive as I see it. We all have a part to play in this to make things good for everyone. I hear that some of your people have already moved away and more are thinking of leaving us. What is the problem? Let's talk about this. Who wants to speak first?"

James and Mandy Mae's son, Lonnie, held up his hand to speak first.

"Okay, Lonnie, let's be open and honest and say it like it is. It's your turn to talk and I will listen."

"Thank you, Renfro. Now, here is the first thing. We hear that even black folks can go to town, get a job and make one dollar a day. In these times, that's pretty good money. You may not know it, but your daddy was only paying us twenty-five cents a day. We all work hard and that just ain't enough. Besides that, he only started paying us that small amount just a short while ago!"

"Okay, Lonnie, I just found about the low wages yesterday. You are right—that is not enough money. However, there is something else that you have not thought about. Here at Meadowland, we provide the food, clothing, and housing for all of you. Now, if you leave here and move to town, you will have to pay for everything yourself."

"Yes, Renfro, we all have thought of that, but a quarter a day still ain't enough wages."

"Very well, now hear me out, I have a plan and an offer that I think will please most of you. I know that it may look like the Miles have lots of money. Well, the fact is that the Miles used to have lots of money. There were some bad business decisions made by the colonel. On top of that, the war hasn't helped things one little bit. The cold hard fact is this: Meadowland is just on the brink of being in real trouble. The only answer, as I see it, is for us to work out our differences, stay on here and pitch in to do our part to make it all work."

Old James said, "And how can we make it work as you say, Mr. Miles?"

"Very well, now listen close. I have a four part plan so hear me out, please. First off, I feel that the most we can pay in wages in fifty cents per day and this includes all family members who work. How would that be?"

One of the oldest field hands, Azro, spoke next, "Well, Renfro, a half dollar surely beats the dickens out of a quarter, but what else do you have in mind?"

"Okay, Azro, the next part of the plan is this. The plantation owns a very good tract of land containing one hundred fifty acres, just about one half mile from where we are now. It is good fertile ground and a creek runs across the back part. I have figured that among you people there would need to be fifteen different places for you all to live should you decide to move out of the quarters. Here is my plan. The land will be plotted off into fifteen ten acre plots of land. These parcels of land will be picked or chosen by seniority. In other words, the oldest person who has been with us the longest gets first pick of the parcels and this includes the two widow ladies among you all. The way I figure it, old James and Mandy Mae would have their choice first, then Azro and Pearl the next pick, and so on down the line. Do you all understand?"

Lonnie said, "Yes, I think we all understand, but I don't see the big benefit of the parcels of land. It's starting to sound like a company town in the making to me!"

Renfro replied, "No, not a company town. The land will eventually be deeded to the one who qualifies to own it. The benefit to Meadowland is this. To own this land, you do not have to pay for it, but you do have to agree to work at Meadowland Plantation for five years. Of course, you will be drawing wages all the while. At the end of five years, each parcel of land will be deeded to the qualifying person, free and clear."

Azro said, "Would this here all be done all legal and proper, Mr. Renfro?"

"Yes, I promise it will all be done legal and proper. Also, after the land is deeded to you, you can do with it as you please. You could sell it, keep it or pass it on to your kin."

Lloyd, one of the middle-aged field hands asked, "Mr. Renfro, what could we do with the land before the day it is deeded over to us?"

"The answer to that is this. You can do anything you want with your chosen parcel, except to sell it, before the five years is up. The next benefit in my plan is this. You will be encouraged to grow a garden to help feed yourself if you so desire. If not, you can still share in the bounty of Meadowland's gardens provided you work in the gardens.

If anyone should want to raise a patch of tobacco on their parcel, Meadowland will agree to buy the tobacco at the fair market price at the time. The same deal would apply to grains used in whiskey making at our distillery. This way, some of you should be able to make some extra money from these cash crops. Does this deal sound fair enough? Let's see a show of hands from those that like my proposal!"

Everyone raised their hand in approval except, of course, for George Carter and Rufus Dowell. The deal did not apply to them as they were already being paid quite well.

Lloyd raised his hand again and said, "Mr. Renfro, you said it was a four part plan. Sir, what's the fourth part?"

"You're right, Lloyd, there is another part. I hear that some of you would like to move out of your old quarters and I understand this. If you want to start building a house on your parcel, that is okay. But, we do not have adequate funds to build houses for you. The best we can do is this. There is a large stand of timber near the proposed land parcels. There are literally millions of stones in and along the creek bed and there is a sawmill just two miles down the road. I would let you borrow tools and a team of mules to use in the building of houses but, of course, only on days off or evenings. Meadowland would donate the timber and pay the bill for custom sawing at the sawmill, but that's as far as we can promise."

All agreed and all liked the plan.

Renfro said, "Does anyone have anything else they want to talk about? If so, feel free to speak your minds."

Old Azro held up his hand and said, "Mr. Renfro, there is another thing we need to talk about."

"Okay, Azro, let's hear it."

"Well, sir, your overseer, Rufus Dowell, has been making noises here lately and saying as how he would jump at the chance to start using his old blacksnake whip on some of us again like he used to do. Now, we all want you and him both to hear this. If he ever tries to use that damn whip on anyone around here ever again, you will probably find him hung up by his heels with it somewhere high in the barn."

"Understood, Azro, there will be none of that ever again. While Rufus Dowell is being mentioned, I have some words for him."

Rufus was standing only about four feet from Renfro and his face was already red as a beet from the threatening remark that Azro had made. Rufus said, "What do you need to tell me, Mr. Miles?"

"Just this, Rufus, the position of 'overseer' is being done away with. We are very shorthanded, as you well know, and we can no longer afford the luxury of having someone standing around.

From now on, there will be no overseer but instead, you will be a 'working foreman.' This means that you will work the same as the rest after you assign work for the others to do."

At that, Rufus flew into a rage and lost control. He hollered, "Miles, I flat refuse to do work meant for slaves. I've said it before and I'll say it again, overseers don't work; they oversee workers. If that's how you want it, I'll be riding out and be damn soon about it."

"Okay, Rufus, if that's the way you want it to be. This meeting is 'bout over. I can have your final pay for you by the time you get your belongings packed."

Rufus stomped away muttering to himself.

One of the teenage boys taunted Rufus with, "Rufus, don't forget your whip!"

Renfro said, "Now, I know we have spent considerable time talking all this over, but there are a few more things. As you all know, we are really shorthanded and we have got to do all we can to make up for it. The house and kitchen help will need to do other work on the place for at least half of each day. Production is way down in the distillery bottling operation. And, as well, we are way behind in the cigar operation. If we don't get production up and running soon, there will be no money to pay anyone for anything. I'm counting on all of you to give it your best. Oh, there is one more thing. Now that Rufus Dowell is leaving, we need to pick a man from among you to be the working foreman. I want you people to pick one of your own for the job. Whoever gets the job will be paid an extra twenty-five cents a day."

As this job did not apply to the distillery, the others picked the next foreman. After a quick discussion, James and Mandy Mae's son, Lonnie, age twenty-five, was picked for the job.

Lonnie beamed with pride and told the rest that he would be a fair man and that he didn't even own a whip.

Rufus Dowell was quickly paid off and he rode out in disgust.

He would soon be forgotten and Meadowland would be the better for his leaving.

The next morning, Renfro was quite surprised and pleased when all of the employees of Meadowland voluntarily started work one-half hour early and passed the word that they would work one-half hour later in the day 'til things got better. The mood and outlook of all concerned was now much better for everyone realized that they all had a stake in Meadowland.

A further surprise came when some new help showed up at the cigar factory. Melissa and Renfro Miles, along with Susan and Virginia, came out to help and learn the skills involved in rolling and making cigars. Azro's wife, Pearl, was the master cigar maker and she was a good teacher. The meticulous work of making cigars was done sitting at a worktable which worked well for Renfro. The ladies could chat as they worked, much like a quilting bee, and soon started to rather enjoy the work. The cigar operation was soon humming with activity.

Things were soon looking up for Meadowland Plantation. Renfro Miles could not pull it off by himself, but with many good people on his side, he now felt sure that Meadowland Plantation would survive.

Mother Melissa Miles insisted on moving into a guest bedroom on the first floor and Renfro and Susan now slept in the huge master bedroom on the second floor. Thus, the new "Master of Meadowland" who would not allow himself to be called "Master" was now the man in charge.

Renfro and Susan were quite happy and deeply in love. Their time together was always very special.

Melissa Miles was happy seeing that her children were happy. She tried to think less of Meadowland's problems and turned her thoughts more in the direction of the cute grandchildren which she hoped for. She did love little children so.

Meanwhile, Renfro and Susan were doing their best to make

Melissa's dreams come true.

Virginia Miles Kinnaman stayed at Meadowland for one month. She missed Hiram so much and was hatching a plan to get back to Leavenworth.

Renfro said, "Sister, I know you want to go home. Tomorrow, we are sending two wagons to Owensboro loaded mostly with whiskey and some cigars. You could catch a boat headed upriver at Owensboro, if you wanted to."

"Yes, Renfro, I need to go. I can see you have things under control here. Mother has been dropping hints about wanting grandchildren. Well, I'm headed home to make her dreams come true."

The next morning Virginia was packed and ready early. Azro was driving the heaviest loaded wagon pulled by four horses. Lloyd was driving two horses which were pulling the much lighter load which consisted of about one-half of a full load of whiskey, rounded out by cases of cigars and some twist chewing tobacco. Both Azro and Lloyd had double-barreled shotguns aboard for protection because their cargoes were quite valuable. The trip would take two and one-half days to travel the approximate sixty-five miles to Owensboro. Virginia felt safe and secure traveling with Azro and Lloyd for she had known them both since she was a child.

When they arrived in Owensboro, the merchants were quite happy to be getting more high quality whiskey and cigars from Meadowland Plantation. Their products were in great demand. Soon the two wagons were empty and they proceeded up to the riverfront area to load some farm equipment and empty glass bottles to take back home.

As luck would have it, a familiar packet boat was at the dock on loading some farming equipment. The "Concordia Queen" would be up bound very soon. Azro and Lloyd carried Virginia's things on board. They both gave her a farewell hug and they left her with old Captain Eli Mattingly.

Eli said, "Lady, we are sure glad to see you headed home. That husband of yours is not the same since you've been gone. Every boat that stops at Leavenworth is the one he hopes is bringing you home. Virginia, Hiram acts like his grandma just passed away ever since you had to leave. He is one pitiful person these days, but I know that will soon change for the better. My Liz is aboard with me most of the time nowadays. She will be glad to see you and there will be plenty of time for you ladies to visit. We have lots of stops to make on the way up."

First Mate Josh Freedman and Capt. Mattingly carried Virginia's things up to the passenger deck and showed her to her cabin.

Capt. Mattingly said, "Virginia, I don't know if you know it or not, but you are retracing the same route that Moses Jefferson and Tillie took to Leavenworth back in '53 when they left your family at Owensboro. In fact, the cabin we just put you in is the same one they used going up back then."

"Remember now, I was only eight years old, almost nine, when they left. I did remember the trip from Meadowland to Owensboro though. Isn't it strange how things have worked out over the years?"

"Yes, Virginia, very strange, but also very good I think."

"Liz, guess who we have on board?"

The ladies found much to talk about so the two days passed quickly.

When the "Concordia Queen" docked at Leavenworth, Hiram was waiting for his wife with open arms. They were both wildly happy to be in each other's arms again. Hiram knew for sure that without Virginia, his life was not complete. Virginia was so happy to go back to their little cottage on Cedar Hill. True, it was not Meadowland Mansion, but she had Hiram Kinnaman and that was what mattered the most.

• TWENTY-ONE •

War Finally Ends

IT IS NOW June 1864, and the War between the States keeps grinding on and taking its toll in loss of life and the country's resources. Thus far, other than the invasion by the Southern Storm back in '63, there have been no more Confederate raids or anything of the kind. When Morgan's Raiders crossed the Ohio at Brandenburg in '63, that would have been the closest any Rebs came to Leavenworth, Indiana, anytime since.

Although there was currently no fighting in Leavenworth, many men from Leavenworth and the surrounding area were in the thick of things fighting in the war. Just because there was no fighting in Leavenworth at this particular time, did not mean that there never would be any trouble here. Keeping this ever in mind, the Home Guard and the Home Guard Reserve kept on training regularly. They intended to stay on the alert and be as ready as possible for whatever might come.

The monthly shooting matches between the Home Guard and the Home Guard Reserve were becoming a huge event for the people in the area. The State of Indiana continued to live up to its promise of adequate ammunition for training and target practice or combat, whichever came first. During these shooting matches, there was lots of friendly rivalry and many good marksmen developed into excellent marksmen. Of course, maintaining and improving military skills was part of the whole plan and it worked. Along with the shooting competition, there were always contests involving Manual of Arms, close order drill and marching. Also in conjunction with these monthly events, there was always a cookout or picnic of some sort blended in, weather permitting of course.

Now, more wounded or disabled soldiers started coming home. The men of the Leavenworth Home Guard and the Reserve as well had to make frequent use of the pole carry chairs to help some of these soldiers from the boats. Every man clearly understood the phrase that Capt. Elam Herndon had used back in '63, "It's a damn poor bunch of soldiers that can't carry their wounded home!"

Most remembered what the captain said and never forgot. A few flag draped coffins had to be carried from the river port from time to time. This was the saddest duty of all. Most would agree. Of course, military honors were always given up at the cemetery on Cedar Hill. When the gun salute was given, it always made thundering echoes in the hills which served as a haunting reminder of that morning at the cliffs. The men of the L.H.G.R. would never forget. For the most part, fallen soldiers in this war were laid to rest close to where they fell and were never taken home.

Hiram Kinnaman was now a proud father. Virginia had given birth to a very healthy baby boy. The boy was named Elam in honor of Hiram's good friend, Capt. Herndon. The captain was quite pleased at the boy being named after him as he and Ruth had never had any children.

Shortly after this, word came from Meadowland that Susan and Renfro Miles were the proud parents of a little boy. Renfro Miles did not name his firstborn Rafe as some had expected. Instead, the boy was named Moses in honor of Moses Jefferson. As well, Moses and Tillie were named as little Moses Miles' godparents.

The Fourth of July celebration was a bigger event in 1864 than it had been in 1863, mainly because this time the Leavenworth

Home Guard was at home. This time, five wounded veterans from the town sat in the honored place on the reviewing stand as the parade passed. The Leavenworth Home Guard marched behind the army band sent down from Camp Noble. The L.H.G.R. in their new uniforms complete with neckerchiefs were next in the procession, with Buford Beasley's decorated team and wagon behind the marchers. Buford, Tad Martin and nurses Alice and Tillie rode in the wagon. Cpl. Milo Weathers was absent as he was back on active duty serving with the 80th Indiana Regiment somewhere in the South. Also, Susan Bowman, former nurse, was not there for she now lived at Meadowland.

Late in 1864, things were not going well for the Confederate Armies. Union Gen. Sherman had started his infamous "March to the Sea" in mid-November around Atlanta, Georgia, and ended the gruesome campaign on December 21, 1864. He relented in his original plan of destruction and spared the beautiful city of Savannah, Georgia.

In early April, 1865, the war was very close to being over and the South was losing. Part of President Abe Lincoln's original plan was to "not harbor hatred over the conflict, and let the nation heal." He planned on "being charitable to all," and even planned to let most Southern soldiers that had horses take them home to till the land to plant crops. He believed in "turning swords into plowshares" and, in general, he had no major objections to the Southern soldiers taking their weapons home with them.

These noble and generous ideas were not all implemented however. On April 14, 1865, assassin John Wilkes Booth shot President Lincoln and the President died on April 15th.

Vice-President Andrew Johnson was quickly sworn in as President and the country had a new leader.

On May 26, 1865, Gen. Simon Boliver Buckner surrendered the last Confederate Army at New Orleans, Louisiana.

On May 29th, 1865, President Johnson granted "general amnesty to all in the existing rebellion."

Renfro Miles had kept abreast of the war news and had made some special arrangements for his former soldiers. He was still only getting around with difficulty and pain, but progressing some. Renfro was keeping in touch with his men who were still prisoners of war at the little camp in Derby, Indiana. He had started a bank account in the Bank of Derby. He then mailed a bank draft to Capt. Lewis with instructions on how to use it when the ex-members of the Southern Storm were released. Renfro had asked Capt. Lewis, upon his release from prison camp, to go to the bank and get money from the account to give each of the men one hundred dollars to enable them to return home and perhaps have some left. He then requested that Capt. Lewis and Lt. Clay go back up to Leavenworth and arrange for proper grave markers to be placed on the graves of the men lost at the cliffs.

On May 30th, 1865, all prisoners were released at Derby and Capt. Lewis took care of the traveling money for his men. All the men were grateful for Renfro's consideration. Had it not been for his thoughtfulness, they would have been thrown on the mercy of the world.

Most all the released POWs caught boats headed downriver, but Capt. Lewis and Lt. Clay caught the "Tarascon" headed up bound and rode to Leavenworth, Indiana. They contacted Hiram and Virginia Kinnaman as Renfro had suggested.

Hiram and Virginia helped Capt. Lewis and Lt. Clay with the grave marking project. Soon, the two ex-Southern Storm officers were on their way home also. For them, the war was now over.

When Cpl. Hiram Kinnaman and Cpl. Milo Weathers had been ordered back to active duty in mid-eighteen sixty-three, they had been separated from each other at the Nashville Army Replacement Depot. Hiram had been put on light duty at a quartermaster supply desk job and was later discharged and sent home.

Cpl. Milo Weathers' records showed him to be a skilled bugler, which had been his first job back when he had enlisted. The 80th Regiment, Indiana Volunteers was in need of a bugler so Milo was made part of this unit. He soon became fast friends with Private James Watson from Vincennes, Indiana, who was a drummer and they served together in some of the bloodiest battles of the war. The 80th Indiana was in so many battles and so many places that it would take an entire book to do a proper job of telling the unit's story. Of particular note was the fact that this unit had the dubious distinction of having lost more men and marched more miles than any other Indiana regiment in the war.

One of this unit's proudest moments, however, was not a battle, but it happened at war's end. The 80th Indiana was at Salisbury, North Carolina, when the war ended. They were discharged at Salisbury, but instead of starting back to Indiana right away, they volunteered to stay for a few weeks to help the local farmers save their crops. Officers and men alike turned their hand to farm work. Milo Weathers and drummer friend James Watson did their share in the fields before heading home. Needless to say, the soldiers all worked free gratis! It was just their way of trying to apologize for their share of the damage the war had caused. It was appreciated.

At Leavenworth, many returning soldiers were bringing the town's population back up. Sadly though, some had to be helped off the boats. The pole carry chairs were indeed coming in handy.

War over or not, Capt. Elam Herndon was keeping a close eye out for likely recruits. He was now confident that he knew how to pick the better men. He had proved that.

Sgt. Bratton, being ever in jest, had made up a little rhyme poking fun at Capt. Herndon. It went like this, "14 to 87; walk, run or ride; with just a little training; we will be the winning side."

The captain took this in good humor, but the sergeant had more or less hit the nail on the head. As for the lower age mentioned in the rhyme, there were more of the very young involved in the war than most people realized. The fact was that the minimum legal age for soldiers in the Union Army was age 16. Those allowed to serve under the age of 16 were supposed to be musicians only. After the war, it came to light that there had been at least 100,000 boys, age 15 and younger, fighting as combat soldiers in the Union Army. In any case, most made a good accounting of themselves.

River traffic was extremely heavy for many weeks after the war had ended. Nearly every boat was overloaded with soldiers and military units headed for home. Many of these men did not travel in comfort, but at least they were headed homeward. The packet boats were designed to only haul cargo on the lower deck. The upper deck or decks, whichever the case might be, was for passengers to travel in comfort. These days, the cargo decks of most of the packet boats were crowded with homeward bound soldiers. Most all agreed that even traveling like this was far better than the muddy trenches and the battlefields they had been accustomed to.

Nowadays, with Hiram Kinnaman in charge of the Leavenworth River Port and Elam Herndon working there part-time, they more or less had the pleasant duty of being the official greeters to those coming back home.

A few days later, the "Rees Lee" was up bound and stopped at Leavenworth. Hiram and Elam were as delighted to see Milo Weathers come home as Milo was to be there. As they were helping Milo carry his things down the ramp, they were in for another pleasant surprise. Right behind them was a man wearing the uniform of a U.S. Navy Captain. Capt. Nathan Collins, hero of several Mississippi River battles, was back home.

Hiram sent a message to Tad Martin, by way of a boy playing marbles, and asked Tad if he could please come down to the river port and tend to business for a while.

In a few minutes, Tad was there as requested. He was very

glad to see that Milo was back and said, "Now, Corporal, the Leavenworth Home Guard Reserve will be back to full strength, twenty-one. Right?"

Milo answered quickly and said, "Tad, you are right, back to twenty-one. Well, provided of course if Capt. Herndon will let me rejoin."

Capt. Herndon said, "Well, boys, let's head up to the Dexter Saloon. We need to have a business meeting!"

Hiram, Elam, Milo and Nathan Collins started toward the Dexter and very soon happy hour began. It was beginning to be more like old times. Soon Sam Buchanan, Harley and Dan drifted in for their usual. Newt had arrived early with his guitar and already had a head start.

Around the large table and around the room, the storytelling began. Most of the stories were true life adventures and needed no embellishment of any kind. Milo told of his nearly two year tour of duty with the 80th Indiana and how he and his drummer buddy, James Watson, had to try to dodge bullets while playing their respective instruments.

Elam said, "Milo, we thought that you would have been back before now. What took so long?"

Milo then told of his outfit volunteering to help the farmers at Salisbury, North Carolina, in trying to save their crops. Then Milo said, "So I stayed with my outfit and my friend James Watson all the way back to Vincennes, Indiana. I stayed with James and his family for two days and caught a train to Evansville, Indiana. At Evansville, I went to the river port and caught the "Rees Lee" headed up bound. And, to my surprise, Capt. Nathan Collins was waiting to shake my hand as I went aboard. Nathan, we have all heard and read about some of your close calls. Are you glad it's over?"

Nathan sat down his brandy glass and said, "Boys, from here on out, I don't aim to fight anything any rougher than the current on the rivers. I have already been in contact with the owners of the Lee Steamboat Line and they said they would give me a boat pretty soon. That "Rees Lee" that me and Milo came up on is one damn fine boat. I hope I get it or another one just as good. Some of them old tubs the navy had me on take a lot of the joy out of being a river man."

More and more of Leavenworth's soldiers came home. Now the population was nearly back to what it had been before the war. It was down some though due to some men being killed in action, or worse yet, from complications of wounds. One thing was quite apparent, Leavenworth had more than its fair share of disabled veterans.

As is usually common, industry and business slow down after a war. It was no different for Leavenworth. The first to notice the slowdown was Horatio Sharp's Woolen Mill. There were no more large orders for woolen yarn for use in military uniforms. There were some orders, but no large orders as before. Squire Weathers' Furniture Factory not only made furniture, but they made caskets and coffins as well. The furniture side of the business remained steady. Soon, there were no more orders for military coffins. The army canceled orders for bridge pontoons and flatboats at both C.G. Paxton and Co. and D. Lyon's Boat Works. All the business owners agreed that they would gladly accept the downturn in business and profits due to the war's end. No one in Leavenworth wanted to profit from such horror and misery as this war had brought to so many.

The L.H.G.R. had completed construction on their new armory/meeting place and had worked out a share agreement with the regular Home Guard. Both units kept on training on a regular basis and tried to always be in a state of readiness.

One meeting day, Jacob Silverstein said, "Capt. Herndon, I have a question!"

"Okay, Jacob, let's hear it!"

"Captain, is there anything in our rules that says that an ex-Confederate soldier could not join up with us?"

"No, Jacob, not that I know of. Tell me about it. Who is it?"

"Well, sir, you remember that Mexican corporal, Miguel Valdez, that you paroled—you know, the saddle maker? Well, he says that he misses being around the military. He says he will never be one hundred percent physically fit due to his battle wound, but he says that he would like to join us if we would have him."

"Jacob, we would love to have him. We wouldn't care if he was colored purple; we'd still like to have him. Why don't you go try to find him right now. Maybe we could swear him in at this meeting!"

Jacob said, "Well, Captain, I won't have to look far. He's waiting just outside. Come on in Miguel 'er Corporal Valdez."

Miguel Valdez took the oath of allegiance then and there and became the twenty-second member of the L.H.G.R.

Capt. Herndon, as a matter of courtesy, let Miguel retain his rank of corporal. This did make the little unit long on corporals as Miguel Valdez made the fifth one. However, as First Sgt. Wildman said, "We will just have to recruit more privates to even things up."

The fact was that Capt. Herndon never stopped looking for recruits or likely candidates. To his way of thinking, "the more, the merrier."

The Fourth of July celebration in 1865 was to be one of the biggest and best ever. Everyone's spirits were up and the future was looking bright. The terrible War between the States was over and the nation was trying to heal itself. It was arranged for an army band from Camp Noble to follow right behind the army color guard from there. The various fraternal organizations would be followed by the marching veterans just returned from the war. Then would come the Leavenworth Home Guard followed by the L.H.G.R. with Buford Beasley's team and wagon carrying a few, as usual. In addition to the usual fireworks, hog roast and picnic, there were other activities as well. There would be a huge day long shooting match at the rifle range and it would be open to all. There would, of course, be some nice prizes for the winners. Besides that, Capt. Eli Mattingly had agreed to have the "Concordia Queen" take people on one hour excursions throughout the day. On the reviewing stand for the parade were eight wounded or partially disabled veterans.

The Grand Marshall of the parade and also the main speaker was hometown hero Capt. Nathan Collins, recently of the U.S. Navy. Nathan was one of the best known and most shot at figures on the Mississippi River during the war and especially around Vicksburg.

Tad Martin was still a school teacher and part-time newspaper man. Ever since his submitted story back in '63 about the action at the cliffs had been printed nationwide, he was looking forward to the day when he could be more of a news reporter and less of a teacher.

Tad had learned that Maj. Gen. John Love of the Indiana Dept. of Legion of Militia would be at Camp Noble, New Albany, Indiana, and arranged to interview Gen. Love in depth about his views regarding Home Guard units and the like.

The following are Maj. Gen. John Love's comments and views:

"The history of minutemen, militia and Home Guard units is long and honorable. This type of military unit has been, and still is, the backbone of our nation's defenses. They have come through and performed well in our country's time of need many times in the past.

One problem in the past was that these military units slowly but surely became more ceremonial, fraternal and social in nature rather than being serious military combat capable units. Part of the reason for this was the fact that our government did not provide them with proper up to date weapons, ammunition and equipment. Neither did we pursue the matter of adequate ongoing training.

When Gov. Morton and I conceived the idea of the Home Guard Reserve system back in 1863, we made a major mistake in not seeing that these units were properly armed and supplied right from the start. Once again, we apologize for this blunder. Had it not been for some good leadership and innovative thinking, the Leavenworth Home Guard Reserve would not have won at the cliffs.

There is nothing wrong, as I see it, in the Home Guards or their Reserve units having a fraternal, social, ceremonial side to them. These are the things that will help bind them and hold them together over the long run. However, the State will expect and even demand that there be ongoing meaningful training which will be taken seriously.

Now, so much for what the State expects from you men and your units. Here is what you can expect from the State. You will all, even the Reserves, be provided with up-to-date weapons and ammunition for whatever may come. As well, we will keep supplying enough ammunition for proper firing practice or combat, whichever. No one knows when or if any Home Guard or Home Guard Reserve might be called on for active service. It is possible that the need for your service might never arise. However, if that need would arise, it should not be considered a surprise or an emergency. It is only an emergency when you are not properly trained or equipped."

Tad Martin's article on Gen. Love's comments and views was printed in papers over most of the country. He was starting to feel more like a real news reporter all the time.

Not long after this, on August 14, 1865, Tad Martin had the sad experience of reporting another important story. A steamboat, the "U.S.S. Argosy III," was coming upriver with a large group of soldiers. Lots of the men were Ohio soldiers and all were headed home from the war. Approximately three hundred of the men on board the Argosy III were the surviving members of the 70th Ohio Regiment and had suffered terribly in the war. They had boarded the boat at Vicksburg, Mississippi, and were headed for Cincinnati, Ohio.

A sudden storm came up and drove the boat into the Indiana bank of the Ohio River about one mile or so downstream from Rono (present day "Magnet"), Indiana. When the wreck happened, the mud drum (part of the steam system near the bow of the boat) blew up spraying steam and boiling water over approximately 40 soldiers who jumped overboard trying to escape the scalding steam. Nine men drowned and two of those scalded died. Ten men were buried on the Indiana bank next to the river. One of the grave markers is for an "unknown" soldier of the 39th Indiana Infantry. (Note: These graves are well marked and maintained to the present day.) The next up bound boat was the "Argosy I" and it carried the survivors to Louisville, Kentucky.

Although for all practical purposes the Civil War had been over for around four months, the war was not officially over. It was April 2, 1866, when President Andrew Johnson officially declared a final end of the war.

◆ Twenty-Two ◆

Leavenworth In Later Years

IT IS NOW 1873. Lots of things have changed in Leavenworth and yet, lots of things are about the same. Of course, no one escapes the wrath of old Father Time and this should come as a surprise to no one.

After the war, the town of Leavenworth seemed to stop growing and there were signs of the town becoming less of a hub of activity than it had been in earlier years. Although no railroad was ever built to Leavenworth, there was one just a few miles north. Of course, this took away some of the town's importance. As well, river traffic was in a state of decline. The mighty Ohio River, once the town's highway to the world, was used less as more passengers and freight went on the railroads. Also, slowly but surely, more and better roads were being built in this part of Indiana.

Leavenworth now had a full-fledged doctor again. Alice Bowman had gone back to medical school at Louisville shortly after the war. Now, she was officially "Alice Bowman, M.D.". Another change in her life was that she was the grandmother of three. Renfro and Susan were the parents of Moses, age 9; Tillie, age 8; and Rafe, age 7. The Miles family always came up to Leavenworth from the Meadowland at least twice a year, usually in early June and again at Thanksgiving.

Hiram and Virginia Kinnaman were still living in their home on Cedar Hill and were the parents of two children, Elam, age

9 and Melissa, age 8. Hiram was still manager of the river port and, of course, still a member of Herndon's Hope or the Leavenworth Home Guard Reserve. Virginia was as happy as any woman could ever be and for her and Hiram, the honeymoon still was not over.

The war had been over now long enough for most wounds and hatreds to heal. There had been four men in town who had left to fight on the Southern side at the start of the Civil War. Three of these men had eventually come back. They were tolerated by the town, but obviously would never be the most popular people around.

The distinctive sound of the "Concordia Queen's" whistle signaled her approach from upriver. It was later in the day and Elam Herndon was glad for this meant that it was very likely the "Queen" would tie up for the night. He was right.

As was the case most of the time, First Mate Josh Freedman was at the helm and expertly docked the boat. More and more these days, old Capt. Eli Mattingly was just along for the ride. Josh Freedman and Engineer Zeke Calhoun were more or less running things. Josh often jokingly referred to old Capt. Mattingly as the boat's Social Director.

The Captain's wife, Liz, was back to staying at home in Concordia, Kentucky, these days as old Father Time was catching her as well.

Now that Liz was staying at home, Capt. Mattingly had more time for visiting old friends and for "happy hours," even some happy evenings.

Elam said, "Good to see you, Captain. Come on. I've built up a thirst today. How about you?"

"You know, Elam, that sounds like one damn good idea."

When the two reached the Dexter Saloon, they were not surprised to see that the usual evening crowd was, for the most part, a group of longtime friends. As usual, it was not long before the reminiscing and retelling of old tales began. In a way, lots of them were living in the past, but this was no disgrace for the past had been quite interesting for most of them. Dan Lyon still occasionally told a tale about the War of 1812. Elam, Sam and Levi Wildman often recalled their days in the Mexican War. And, for sure, those above mentioned and most of the rest always talked of the most recent war, which now was starting to seem farther back in time. When old river Capt. Eli Mattingly sat down his glass and told a river story from his vast collection, there was never a dull moment.

Eli began, "Boys, I think that pretty soon, the "Concordia Queen" will have some new owners!"

Elam said, "Who are you selling it to?"

"Well, we have talked it over and it looks for sure like Josh Freedman and Zeke Calhoun are going to be co-owners and equal partners. Josh will be captain and Zeke will be first mate. They get along right well and I think it will work. The next trip upriver we three are going to the Brandenburg Bank and work out the details."

Sam said, "Well, Eli, we kind of hate to hear this. Does this mean you won't be coming to see us anymore?"

"No, Sam, nothing of the kind. I have a deal with Josh and Zeke that I will have a free pass to ride, sleep, eat and drink on the "Concordia Queen" anytime I choose."

Harley laughed and said, "Sounds like a good deal for you, Eli, but I'm afraid that free drink part will put the boys in the red for sure!"

Capt. Mattingly smiled and said, "A deal is a deal."

Elam quipped, "Well anyway, word was out sometime ago that Josh was saying that these days you just came along for the ride."

"Yes, boys, and it's been a good ride."

Meanwhile, back down in Kentucky at Meadowland, everything seemed to be getting better except Renfro Miles' leg. Things had settled down since the war was over. The people who had chosen to stay and work were all doing well. There were now modest, but decent homes on all of the fifteen parcels of land. As Renfro Miles had promised, all the parcels had been deeded to the rightful owners. As well, Meadowland was buying and paying fair market price for the grain and tobacco bought from their employees' private land. There was no talk, nor would there be, of "former slaves." Instead, they were valued employees of Meadowland Plantation.

The distilling operation was still producing very high quality Kentucky bourbon which was still in demand in all directions, thanks to the head distiller, George Carter. His expertise at making Meadowland Mist was becoming legendary. George was still a crucial part of Meadowland's operations and Renfro saw that George was rewarded very well.

The Meadowland cigar making operation was also a continuing success, again, thanks to skilled dedicated employees.

As said before, everything seemed to be getting better except Renfro's leg. Renfro and Susan now had three children, Moses (9), Tillie (8), and Rafe just barely 7 years old. The kids were at the age where they were always asking questions about most anything and everything. This morning Renfro's cane slipped and he nearly fell down. This prompted little Rafe to say, "Daddy, tell me the story again about how you were in the war and why your leg doesn't work right."

Before Renfro could tell that story again, little Tillie jumped in with, "And, Daddy also tell us why Uncle Hiram, Aunt Virginia and Grandma Alice live so far away up in Indiana?"

"Okay, kids, it's storytelling time. Let's sit here by the fountain and I'll tell it all over again."

Renfro retold the stories once again and his children listened closely to every word. He was glad that the kids had hungry minds and they were good listeners.

Renfro had barely finished when his oldest son, Moses, said, "Dad, I'm still having trouble understanding why you call those people up in Indiana 'Uncle Moses and Aunt Tillie?' We are white and they are black. How can that be?"

"Okay, Moses, that's a fair question. Now, here's how it is. When I was a little boy, Moses and Tillie Jefferson lived here at Meadowland. They looked after me and your Aunt Virginia and helped raise us. They were with sister and me more than Grandma Melissa or Grandpa Rafe was. Moses and Tillie never had any children of their own and they thought of us as if we were their very own.

When I was about ten years old, Moses and Tillie went away. Virginia and I missed them so very much. We thought we would never see them, ever again.

When I was grown up, I became a soldier. Well, up in Indiana, we got in a terrible battle where my leg got shot up real bad. I didn't know it yet, but this was the place where Moses and Tillie had moved to when they left Meadowland. Anyway, your mother's mother, your mother, Moses and Tillie all helped me because I was badly wounded. Moses and Tillie took me in and took care of me.

So, here I was, a full grown man and they were taking care of me again. Now you are right, Moses. They are black and we are white, but I call them Uncle Moses and Aunt Tillie out of respect for they are two of the most caring people I have ever known. Also, I want you children to call them Uncle Moses and Aunt Tillie, the same as I do. They mean more to me than you might think and I want you to respect my wishes. Do you children understand?"

"Yes, Daddy, I think we all understand."

"You know, kids, it's about time for us to take another trip up to Leavenworth. Your mother and I will start working on that plan now."

That evening Renfro made Susan a happier woman. He said, "Honey, don't you think it's time for us to take a little fun trip up to Leavenworth? You know, early June is a very pretty time up there."

"Okay, Renfro, you are the best husband a woman could have. Darling, you are so considerate. Do you think Meadowland could operate without us for awhile?"

"Yes, I sure do. Lonnie does a fine job as foreman and I have no doubt that George Carter can get along without me in the distillery. Which way would you like to go? Railroad to Owensboro and take a boat upriver or railroad to Louisville and catch a boat going downriver?"

"So the kids can see more country, let's go up through Louisville and come back through Owensboro. Would that work?"

"Yes, sweet woman, that will work. We will leave tomorrow!"

Azro drove the Miles family, including Mrs. Melissa Miles, to the train station at Bowling Green early. They caught the northbound train at 8:00 AM. At noon, they boarded the Lee Line steamboat Rees Lee. That evening, they were at Leavenworth with many happy people who were all glad to see them. There were hugs and kisses all around. Moses and Tillie Jefferson were always happy to see Little Moses, Tillie and Rafe and showed it.

Melissa Miles and the three Miles children would stay with the Jeffersons during their stay in town. Renfro and Susan would stay with Alice, now Dr. Bowman.

These visits were always a happy family reunion, Hiram and Virginia Kinnaman's children playing with Renfro and Susan's children. Tomorrow would be a very special day because "Uncle Moses" Jefferson and "Uncle Elam" Herndon promised to take the kids fishing on the Ohio River. And, what's more, Uncle Elam had promised that they would have a real Indian guide to help them.

Good natured Jim Running Deer had agreed to do the Indian guide part. When Elam had asked Jim, Jim had said, "Elam, do you think I should put an eagle feather in my hatband to look the part?"

"Jim, that would be great. You know those kids will talk about this for years."

Tad Martin had quit teaching school about three years ago and was now a newspaper reporter up in Indianapolis. Tad was becoming quite well-known as a good reporter and his stories often were in newspapers far and wide. His reported story of "Herndon's Hope Quells the Southern Storm," back in '63, had been the story that really gave him a start. That was a tough story to cover though because Tad had been required to play an active part in the true story.

When Tad left Leavenworth, his leaving had brought the membership of the Leavenworth Home Guard Reserve down from twenty-two men to twenty-one, which was the unit's original strength. When Miguel Valdez had joined, he had made a total of twenty-two men.

Just two years ago, the men of Herndon's Hope, as they were better known these days, had just completed another community project. They had finally built the museum that Elam had dreamed of. It was now filled to the brim with items of historical interest. A large part of the display was the large collection of obsolete weapons that the men of Herndon's Hope had used back in '63 at the cliffs. As Hibachi Takaguchi had said, "Some of these old pieces were relics, and yes, even heirlooms!"

The monthly shooting matches had become a long lasting ongoing tradition in this area. For some time now, other Home Guard and Reserve units from other towns, even some from the Kentucky side, had been invited to attend and compete. Competition was very stiff.

Of the Leavenworth marksmen, old Mike Baysinger was still

the best shot by far and he was now around eighty-one years old. Dan Lyon could still outshoot his son, which always amused the onlookers.

Dan, a veteran of the War of 1812 was now very close to being ninety-one. Dan did use a "shooting stick" these days to steady his aim as the Henry rifle seemed to be getting heavier. He would steady his revolver aim by resting it on his crossed left arm. In any case, whatever aids he used seemed to work. Buford Beasley was now ninety-seven, but he still liked to participate in the matches. Years back, Buford had found it necessary to rest whatever weapon he was shooting to steady his aim, but he could still hit a fair amount of targets. He still was no slouch, but as said before, old Father Time must take his toll.

The Home Guard and the Home Guard Reserve still met on a regular basis and would seriously train and drill. All would agree that target practice was the best part of the meetings.

The members of the Home Guard Reserve, Herndon's Hope, have kept their organization going and all have a tight bond, more or less like brothers. With the exception of Cpl. Miguel Valdez, they had all stood as brothers in the face of great danger and impossible odds. It was a feeling that they never would forget. Though they never reminded Cpl. Valdez, he was there too, shooting back. But, oh, that was so long ago. Now Miguel was one of them.

All members of Herndon's Hope realized that increasingly their group was becoming more of a social, ceremonial, fraternal thing than a strictly military unit. However, they still took their training "serious as a heart attack" and remained "armed and dangerous."

Not only was old Father Time taking his toll on Herndon's men, or rather Herndon and his men, their equipment was starting to become victims of time as well. The Reserves' prized Henry rifles and Colt revolvers had been real state of the art, up-to-date weapons when they had captured them from the Southern Storm. However, that was ten years ago. The weapons had some use before they had been captured. There had been very many rounds of ammunition fired through these pistols and rifles. They were not worn out by any means for they had been well-maintained by Capt. Herndon's men.

That was not the whole story though. Although these Henry rifles had been the best in the world, now there was the new Winchester '73, an advanced type of lever action rifle with more modern features and an easier loading method. As for the Colt revolvers the unit still used, they were cap and ball type and difficult and tedious to load. Of course, carrying extra preloaded cylinders made reloading somewhat easier, but still a rather slow process. The new Colt army model '73 was now a cartridge type revolver and was much better, simpler and faster to reload.

Herndon and his men had discussed the possibility of buying some of these more modern weapons on their own. Some of the men already owned them. The problem was that the State was not eager or willing to furnish the modern, more expensive ammunition to the Reserve units. Since there was no longer a war or the immediate threat of a war, the powers that be were becoming less enthused about keeping the Home Guard or the Reserves properly armed with up-to-date arms. They also explained about a current budget crunch. Now everyone was starting to see how the defense system had been in the sorry state it was, years back.

In any case, the State kept on furnishing ammunition for the now outdated weapons. They had lots of surplus from the Civil War and it had been bought and paid for ages ago. The ammunition kept coming and the Reserves kept using it, but only on various targets. Sgt. Bratton made the shrewd observation that, "Boys, if we are ever invaded by targets, they won't stand a chance!"

It was the Fourth of July, 1873. Once again, celebration parade time and all that goes with it. As usual, the Leavenworth Home Guard Reserves were in the parade. The major change was that now more of the men have to ride on Buford's wagon and fewer men march. This year, Tad Martin was back for the event and, of course, he rode. Also, George Armstrong, Dan Lyon, Mike Baysinger and Buford Beasley rode as did Dr. Alice Bowman and Tillie Jefferson. Miguel Valdez had to drive Buford's team because Buford was not feeling well.

That morning, Hiram's son, Elam had seen him putting on his uniform and getting ready for the parade. Nine year old Elam Kinnaman had said, "Dad, why do you put on that strange old uniform with the neckerchief and march with these people every Fourth of July? Lots of them look like old people to me and I think those red neckerchiefs look odd?"

Hiram answered very simply, "Well, son, I stay with those people because they are a pretty special group of men and I am very proud to have served with the likes of them. Yes, very proud."

This was to be Buford Beasley's last parade. Jim Running Deer's place was about one-fourth of a mile from Buford's house. Jim stopped by Buford's house and checked on him every day and sometimes twice a day. Jim and all the rest of the boys could see that time was starting to run out for their friend Buford. Just ten days after the parade, July 14th, 1873, Jim Running Deer found Buford slumped over, dead in his favorite chair. On Buford's lap were some old newspaper clippings he had been reading. The articles were about that day back in 1863 at the cliffs. Buford had been eighty-seven when the Southern Storm came. He was ninety-seven when he passed away. It was Running Deer's sad duty to go to town and tell the rest of the boys.

Buford had requested a military funeral and wanted to be laid to rest up on Cedar Hill. Since Buford's wife had passed on many years before, his friends took care of the arrangements. He was dressed in his military uniform, neckerchief and all, and placed in a flag draped coffin. His prized team of Belgian horses and his Owensboro wagon were used instead of a horse drawn hearse.

The funeral procession was long. It might have looked strange to some, but four of his friends rode on the wagon with the coffin. They were Tad, George, Mike and Dan. These men weren't able to walk the distance and everyone agreed that Buford would have wanted it this way. Tad drove the team. Everyone was in full uniform, neckerchiefs and all. The rest of the Leavenworth Home Guard Reserve marched somberly behind Buford's wagon. In full strength, the Home Guard, also in full uniform, marched next in the procession.

At the cemetery came the hardest part of all. Capt. Elam Herndon was going to give part of the eulogy, but was not able to get through it. Preacher Harrison said his part of the funeral ceremony and then it was time for military honors. A twenty-one gun salute was given in Buford's honor and the reports from the rifles echoed through the hills like a haunting reminder of that morning at the cliffs. Milo Weathers played the ever mournful song, "Taps" on his bugle and it was over. It was a fitting sendoff for a man who even in his twilight years had bravely stood with his fellow men to help defend his homeland.

It had been known for years that Buford was a kind and generous man, but he would prove to be even more generous than previously thought.

Soon came time for the reading of Buford's will in which he made some very special gifts to several people. He was a longtime gun fancier and collector. He owned many very desirable guns. He had arranged for his guns to be divided between Jim Running Deer, Elam Herndon, Sam Buchanan and Dan Lyon. He had previously tagged each gun with the recipient's name. As for his special shotguns, he had written, "I give all my shotguns to my good friend and cannoneer of our outfit, Newt Watson. He is the right man for a shotgun. Newt, use them well!"

The most special part of Buford Beasley's will was as follows: "It is a well known fact that governments, leaders, states and countries are often very grateful to the soldiers who defend them and fight their battles for them, but so many times their gratitude is short-lived. Those who fought these battles and served are all too soon forgotten in their time of need. In view of this, I am leaving my entire remaining estate to the Leavenworth Home Guard Reserve for them to use my home and farm as an 'Old Soldiers' Home' so that those that went the extra length to save the homes of others would be sure to have a place for themselves in their time of need. I am naming Capt. Elam Herndon to be the Treasurer of this 'Old Soldiers' Home' and I further name Newt Watson to be the home's first Resident Administrator."

Tad Martin wrote a very good and lengthy account of Buford's life and his unselfish concern for others. Tad figured that the more papers this article ran in, the more chance there would be that it could start some people in other places to thinking of the welfare of its old soldiers.

Back when Gov. Oliver Morton and Gen. John Love had conceived of the Home Guard Reserve plan, they hadn't fully realized the difficulty of finding enough able-bodied men of the right age to provide the manpower for such units, especially during wartime.

When the Governor and the General finally saw what could be accomplished by people who had before been thought of as "unfit for military service," they changed their way of thinking and wrote these rules in the Charter and Guidelines for the Home Guard Reserve System. It stated in part, "No man wanting to be of service to his country by joining a Home Guard Reserve unit should ever be rejected for reasons of age or disability. Surely anyone willing to serve can contribute something and should be allowed to serve." Then this was also written, "No man is ever to be stricken from the membership rolls due to age, infirmities or disabilities unless that member asks to be stricken from the rolls of his own free will and accord."

✦ ETUDE ✦

IT HAS BEEN a few days since Buford Beasley's funeral and things are settling down. Elam and Sam are down by Blue River Island fishing and thinking back on things over the past ten years.

Elam said, "Sam, do you remember back in '63 when Gen. Love made that moving speech on the Fourth of July?"

"Yes, Elam, I right near remember it word for word. I for sure remember the part about the Constitutional Second Amendment where it says about a well-regulated militia being necessary and about the right to bear arms."

"You're right, Sam, but Gen. Love said that his personal feeling was that 'the right to bear arms' should be changed to read, 'the obligation to bear arms.' And, Sam, if you remember, he said that if you were a citizen with arms, in his opinion, it should be your obligation and responsibility, and even your duty to practice and be proficient with that weapon. Do you remember that?"

"Yes, Elam, I remember and I also agree with Gen. Love's views. I think what he was talking about is that if your neighbors or countrymen need your help, you owe it to them to at least be familiar with whatever weapon you might own and be able to be a help in a time of need, rather than be a hindrance."

"Sam, you are right as far as I am concerned. It's plain and simple. In my mind, Gen. John Love has it right!"

"Elam, another thing, you know as well as I do that since the war is over we have been drifting into more of a ceremonial, fraternal, social type thing in the Home Guard Reserve. Do you think, even with so many of us being old, that we could make much of a difference militarily if we had to?"

"Yes, Sam, if needed we could prove our worth. Now remember, it's not nearly all socializing at our meetings and drills. We still train and drill and I'd bet that, as a group, we are about as good at accurate firing as they come. The way I see it, the fun and social part is necessary to hold the group together. The problem is that no one can look into a crystal ball and tell when we will be needed, if ever, or what would be expected of us if we were needed. If you will remember, it's like Gen. Love said, 'Nothing wrong with the social, fraternal, fun part of things just so long as you maintain your skills and be as ready as you can be.'"

"Elam, one thing that concerns me lately is the state government's attitude about not wanting to keep on supplying us with more expensive modern ammunition if we do buy new, more up-to-date weapons on our own. Do you think their memory is all that short? Why, only ten years ago, they would have damn near gave us the moon if we had asked for it. They were so grateful for what we had done back then."

"Yes, I know, Sam, but now there are no wars close enough to see them coming. Besides that, all they want to talk about is their budget crunch."

"Elam, do you think that the powers that be would ever let our State and country be caught off guard and unprepared, like back in '62 and '63??"

"Yes, Sam, I do think that it could happen and most likely will happen. You know, history does have a way of repeating itself. I believe a very famous man once said, 'Those that don't know their history are doomed to repeat it!'"

• THE END •

✦ ABOUT THE AUTHOR ✦

WILLIAM JAMES (JIM) Hubler, Jr. is a new author. He has been writing songs and stories for many years. *The Cliffs of Leavenworth* is Jim Hubler's first published novel. There are more to come. Jim and wife Shirley live on a high bluff overlooking the beautiful Ohio River, not far from Wolf Creek, Kentucky, population 15 or so. Jim jokingly refers to the place where he and Shirley live as Rainbow Ranch, since it is their retirement home. They are located in a truly beautiful part of the world and are quite happy to be living there. Surroundings such as this tend to make it easier for a person to concentrate on story and song writing and storytelling. At least, Jim claims this to be the case.

The novel,

The Cliffs Of Leavenworth,

is available at Trafford Publishing Company's online bookstore at www.trafford.com.

This novel can also be ordered through
- www.amazon.com
- Barnes and Noble
- Borders
- Chapters-Indigo (in Canada)
- as well as from an ever growing number of international online resellers.

Readers, please ask your library to order copies of this novel.

The Cliffs Of Leavenworth is Jim Hubler's first novel. More of his stories will soon be in print, also by Trafford Publishing Company.

Please be watching for: *Some Trucking Tales*, a collection of humorous short anecdotes about trucks and truck drivers.

Also in the works, *The Ranger Woodsie Stories*, children's stories written by Jim Hubler and beautifully illustrated by Nanci Williams. This is a collection of teacher friendly, librarian friendly, entertaining stories. Each one has a moral.

Jim Hubler also writes songs. In the not too distant future, some of his songs will be available on CD, through CD Baby Record Store, 5925 NE 80th Avenue, Portland, Oregon 97218-2891, or at www.cdbaby.com. This telephone is 1-800-448-6369.

The preferred way to order the novel *The Cliffs Of Leavenworth* is to order online through Trafford Publishing at their online bookstore, www.trafford.com or by phone, toll-free 1-888-232-4444 or 250-383-6804.

However, if you want to order an autographed copy of this novel, it may be ordered as follows:

ORDER FROM

Hubler Enterprises
P. O. Box 41
Battletown, Kentucky 40104

- The price is $25.00 (U.S.) per copy (check or money order).
- Kentucky residents: please add 6% state sales tax.
- There will be no shipping or handling charges.
- If you would like the book autographed, please denote the name.

ORDER FORM

Name:_____

Address:_____

City:_____State:_____Zip_____

Autograph to:_____

ISBN 1412074908